Devil House

John Darnielle

Devil House

MCD ⊛ FARRAR, STRAUS AND GIROUX NEW YORK

MCD

Farrar, Straus and Giroux

120 Broadway, New York 10271

Library of Congress Cataloging-in-Publication Data

Names: Darnielle, John, author.

Title: Devil house / John Darnielle.

Description: First Edition. | New York : MCD / Farrar, Straus and
  Giroux, 2022.

Identifiers: LCCN 2021040920 | ISBN 9780374212230 (hardcover)

Classification: LCC PS3604.A748 D48 2022 | DDC 813/.6—dc23

LC record available at https://lccn.loc.gov/2021040920

Canadian/International Edition ISBN: 978-0-374-60712-8

Designed by Abby Kagan

www.mcdbooks.com • www.fsgbooks.com

Follow us on Twitter, Facebook, and Instagram at @mcdbooks

1   3   5   7   9   10   8   6   4   2

To that most gentle of shepherds,

Mr. Barry Sanders,

at whose feet I cribbed the cant

"Dulcia," said Sibyl in a low, half weeping tone, as Grant and Beatrice moved away, "people always say strange things, when something happens, don't they?"

—Ivy COMPTON-BURNETT, *A House and Its Head*

1

Chandler

1.

MOM CALLED YESTERDAY to ask if I was ready to come home yet; I went directly to San Francisco from college, and I've been in Milpitas for five years now, but she holds fast to her theory that eventually I'm coming back to San Luis Obispo. "When you get done with your little experiment up there," she says. There are competing wrinkles in the mythical future she imagines for me; in one variant, she retires and finds a quaint little house in San Francisco, where I was living until I came here. Then we'd only be an hour apart from one another instead of three; we might see more of each other on weekends.

"Mom," I tell her, "nobody can afford to live in San Francisco anymore."

"Oh, but that can't be true," she says.

"You're right," I say, "there are still rich people there. There are also people who spend all their money every month on rent and food, and have nothing left over."

"It's like that everywhere," Mom says.

"It's a little less like that here, Mom," I tell her. She doesn't believe me. My mother is a prophet of ruin. The last time I went home, she kept pointing out places that would be, she said, the next to fall—old brick buildings, crumbling strip malls, grocery stores.

"Everywhere," she says again. "You'll see." She's probably right. A surveyor walked through the neighborhood last week; I watched from my window, and I saw several familiar faces doing the same from theirs. But it's hard for me to imagine anyone wanting to *do* anything to a block like mine. Around the corner and down the street, somebody did get a big idea at some point in the 1960s, and put up the identical duplexes that stand there now in facing rows, one after the other, driveway distances between each of them soothingly uniform, unit after unit. My block's the odd man out; there's not enough of it to make it worth anybody's while, though that didn't stop somebody from trying, once.

We kick the ball back and forth for a while, comfortable and familiar. "You'd like it if you saw it in the flesh," I say at one point, defending my house against the impression of it she gets from the pictures I share on Facebook: my porch with its flaking paint, the nasty seventies chain-link that marks the boundary between my backyard and my neighbor's, the freeway visible in the background.

"But Gage, you're descended from *kings*," she says, for the hundredth time in my life, or the five hundredth, or the five thousandth; and I smile, because it's true, it's all true.

†††

THE CHANDLER FAMILY'S CLAIM to royal blood traces back for generations; the only reason my last name is Chandler and not Davidson is that my mother spelled out the terms of engagement for my father long before she got pregnant. "I'm giving the family name to my children," she'd said. "Take it or leave it." It was the sixties; my dad didn't care.

It's hard to say how seriously Mom took any of it; she remembered challenging her own mother, my grandmother, regarding the bloodline, who, without a moment's hesitation, began rattling off a now-lost genealogy that took fifteen minutes to recite. "It was like she'd been saving all these names up to admonish me with," Mom told me, wonder in her voice. I was twelve; crawling through the library stacks that summer, I scouted out dusty, shelf-worn books that listed ancient names and estates. There were no Chandlers. Chandler was a workingman's name, I learned from a reference book—a maker of candles, a city trade. Any and all Chandlers in the genealogies were a long way from the castle—even if, as Mom had a habit of pointing out whenever the occasion arose, we owned the house we lived in free and clear: her pride in the matter so evident, whenever it came up, that it made imagining kings further back in the bracket a little harder still.

I wondered, but I didn't want to press her on the question. At some point we'd stopped being royal, I guessed. It can happen to the best of families.

But the story traveled with me as I grew up, learning along the way to let my mind wander: to tales of kings and princes wrongly deposed, sent from the great countryside to London, where they learned to live by the work of their hands, pouring wax into iron molds they'd spirited out of the castle's workshops as the barbarians sacked the great hall. Carrying their meager but vital plunder in packs on backs by night to the outskirts of the city, learning their way. The Chandlers, great lights made small. I was good at telling stories when I was a kid. It became a habit.

I wrote my first book while finishing my undergraduate degree in journalism at Cal Poly. It didn't hit the bestseller list, but in paperback it found its range. *The White Witch of Morro Bay* is the kind of true crime book around which small cults form; I knew about the White Witch from childhood. Her reign was my time, broadly speaking: I was three when she went to trial. From playground to playground and in every after-school haunt, her myth was still intoned with reverence and fear. She'd been a teacher at the high school; her legend told of how for years she lured young men to her many-windowed house overlooking the bay. There, having plied them with drink and sapped them of their strength, she would drain their blood while they slept; she rendered their bodies with flensing tools and then fed them, piece by piece, to the fish. It was this detail, the fable ran, that attracted enough attention from the authorities to force her into hiding, from which she'd never emerged: the tide turned red one morning while summer vacationers bathed in the surf.

The real-life White Witch, Diana Crane, had actually only killed two people, both students: high school seniors who, having arrived at her apartment unannounced, caught her in a headlock before attempting to drag her to her bedroom. She was shucking oysters when they showed up; in the struggle, she got her knife into the first boy's eye, and then, looking up to find the coconspirator immobilized by the sight of his friend's blood spraying out in jets, launched herself toward him and stabbed him in the neck three times. She continued stabbing until she felt sure that the present threat to her safety had been contained, which is to say, until both boys were dead; later, she dragged the bodies, in pieces, to the shore.

It was an ugly scene, and the jury sent her to the gas chamber; the prosecutors convinced them her tale of self-defense was a fabrication, something she'd made up to conceal her true nature: a crone-in-training who lived by herself in a seaside den, a place whose shelves and countertops boasted all manner of obscure arcana whose deeper meaning, they said, indicated that the downfall of young men had always been her goal.

Diana Crane's story was that of a blameless schoolteacher who paid a terrible price for defending herself. Nobody involved in her prosecution, conviction, and execution had anything to be proud about. I still get mad thinking about it. One of the boys she'd killed had a track record with women; old classmates, now nearing retirement, told me stories as I sat listening in vinyl-upholstered recliners under fluorescent lights. They'd carried these burdens with them almost their whole lives. Diana Crane had done a service to society by ridding it of Jesse Jenkins and Gene Cupp; for her trouble, she'd been strapped to a chair and made to breathe poison until she died.

But the popular account omitted everything prior to the oyster knife, and from the resultant open question of what happened next, schoolchildren and bored night-shift workers crafted the White Witch, the one all schoolchildren knew and feared: a Bluebeard in reverse, her crime hidden by apartment walls and the moon above the bay. In the legend, she'd never even been arrested; Diana Crane fled the scene by night, carnage in her wake, and, for all anyone knew, was still living somewhere by the bay, lying in wait.

The movie they made out of my book later didn't set any box office records, but I got paid up front. I've been writing about crimes ever since: the crimes people tell stories about, and the secret ones our stories seek to conceal.

†††

I WAS THIRTY-SEVEN when I came down to Milpitas. I had five books out under my own name and, under a pen name that I still keep secret, three paperback serial killer mysteries that sold well enough to get stocked in airport bookstores. My life was comfortable, if lonely. Ashton, my editor—he has three names instead of the usual two, all of which he uses in correspondence: Ashton Williston Clark—emailed me a news clipping about some especially lurid murders. The little town where they'd happened was a familiar name to me, not only because of the much more widely known case that had briefly thrust Milpitas onto the national stage—*River's Edge*—but because a childhood friend of mine had lived there once. Back in those days, we'd even kept up a halting correspondence for a while, some of the first letters I ever sent or received. "A proofreader was doing some fact-checking on a nonfiction book and she saw this," Ashton wrote. "I knew you'd love it."

I did love it, with a few reservations. It was a very small clipping and there weren't a lot of details. The few choice bits were tantalizing enough—dead bodies atop a pyre of pornography, cryptograms in graffiti, the specter of teenage Satanic rites jolting a sleepy old town awake—but the story seemed to have fizzled quickly somehow, which suggested to me that there was perhaps less than met the eye of a *Mercury News* reader in the mid-eighties, when catchy copy still meant real advertising dollars. I'd been having ideas about something more baroque and gothic than another California suburb.

"I hear you, but I feel like you're the guy," he said when I called him up to see if he was serious, mentioning my misgivings up front. "You move down there, you do your thing, you meet all the people now that they're grown up, you make your first really big book. You're ready."

"I'm tired of California," I said. "It's practically all I ever write about. I was thinking of trying to find something in the South. Louisiana, maybe."

"The house is on the market," he said. "These are your people, right? An actual self-made cult, grotto of the porno demons, teen devil worshippers in the Santa Clara Valley. You move in. Devil House. You move into Devil House. That's the angle here."

It felt like a joke. "I don't want to buy a house just to write a book about it," I said.

"It's kind of a natural extension of your method, don't you think?" Ashton has this way of talking about things as if they don't have any consequences. It's contagious. I try to be on my guard about it.

"Knocking on doors and buying houses are two pretty different things."

"That's what makes this a different book," he said. "That's how it gets bigger. You own the place. It's yours. Past history suggests it takes you about eighteen months to get it together. You can turn right around and sell it when you're done, it'll be like a short-term lease with return on your deposit."

"Did something happen I don't know about? My advances don't really cover down payments on houses."

"Chandler," he said. "This isn't the city. There's not even fifty thousand people there. You've got to have a decent enough credit history after your last few years. Besides, we get a cut of your movie rights. I know you're not exactly starving out there."

There was quiet for a few seconds.

"Even if you prorate for the down payment you'll be paying less on the mortgage than you pay now on rent in the big city," he said. "Come on. This has your name all over it."

That call was five years ago, all the way back in December

of 2001. This was a different place then; the cracks in the tech bubble were still fresh and raw, though property values would start to climb again soon enough. I've been hard at work ever since, but I haven't turned the book in yet, in part because, while this is that book, it's not the one that my contract obligates me to eventually write: *DEVIL HOUSE, a work of nonfiction, between 80,000–120,000 words, about the multiple murders committed in the ADDRESS TK block of Main Street in Milpitas, California, on or about the night of November 1, 1986.*

It is instead a book about restoring ancient temples to their proper estates. I got the idea from my grandfather, I like to say. I tried counting up the great-greats it would take to really get all the way back, but after a while you lose track and get lost. It happens every time. My grandfather, anyway. He lived in a castle but never forgot the grassy glades and wooded byways of his youth.

2.

THE OLD-FASHIONED GENERIC ANSWERING MACHINE was still holding its own against voice mail back in spring of 2002, even in burgeoning tech enclaves. I listened, with real pleasure, to the sound of moving parts forced into labor far beyond their intended life spans. On the outgoing message, a voice burbled through the warp and wobble of aging tape, managing to sound both bubbly and professional, a hard combination to hit: "Thank you for calling New Visions Properties. This is Whitney Burnett. None of our associates can take your call at this time."

It was a woman's voice, maybe someone in her twenties. I

start categorizing people from the moment I first meet them; it's a good habit to pick up if you're going to try to put stories together from the messy loose ends of people's actual lives. I imagined a young woman who, at some unfixed point down the line, intended to own her own business; a person whose ambitions were modest, and who had more drive than she really needed to meet them. "Please leave us a brief message telling us how we may be of assistance to you, and we will return your call. If you require immediate assistance, you may reach me on my mobile phone"—here she sounded out the number twice, area code included, in a cool, forceful voice that made me feel obligated to follow through.

"Thank you, and have a pleasant day."

I left a clumsy message, talking for longer than I needed to and interrupting myself frequently, but when Whitney called back an hour later she cut directly to the chase.

"I would love to show you the property," she said. "It's actually a really nice old building. I should warn you, it's kind of a mess right now, though. But it's nice, you'll see it. It's had a lot of lives. In the fifties it was even a soda shop for a while."

About the soda shop I already knew. I hadn't been able to find many stories about it online, but small scraps I'd managed to dig up—postings in local listservs, scanned pictures on people's still-standing Angelfire sites—all mentioned what a nice place it had been, once upon a time. It was called the Sunliner Grill back then. The building itself had origins dating a full century back, but there are no records of its function prior to the Ford Motor Company's announcement, in 1954, of intentions to open their Central California plant in Milpitas the following year. Few locals remember the soda shop now; the population wasn't yet young enough to support one, and there were two well-liked restaurants just down the road on Main Street, one of which had a license to serve alcohol. The Sunliner Grill did not survive the decade.

The building's timeline gets murky after that. I've been told once or twice that someone ran a hardware store out of it, but I haven't found any proof. Briefly, in the early seventies, someone seems to have had the bright idea to turn it into some kind of theater: a clipping from *The Mercury News* about regional growth makes note of an anomalous little cinder-block building near the freeway, referring to "the short-lived, unlamented Nite People Cinema," but the article offers no further details. A single-screen movie house in a building so small in the shadow of the freeway feels almost unfathomably optimistic.

Sometime after 1974, when completion of Interstate 680 seemed to guarantee future traffic through town, somebody took out a lease on the building and began operating a newsstand out of it. The newsstand became a porn store, and then a sort of house in which a crime took place, about which I knew mainly what Ashton had told me over the phone—some teenagers holed up in a dark porn store, the specter of devil worship and arcane private ceremonies culminating in at least two deaths. Few details, plenty of innuendo: this was how I had come to be talking to Whitney Burnett about making the drive south despite a nagging hunch that, if there were really more to know, I was a person who'd already know about it.

"I'd love to see it," I said. I felt a little weird putting on the mask of the reluctant client, since I meant to buy it no matter what condition it was in. If it looked uninhabitable, I would still make a way. There was even a sort of grim appeal in the possibility of finding the place a total wreck. "I'm in San Francisco, but I can be there next week, or even earlier, if you think there's any hurry."

I imagined I could hear her smiling patiently as she answered. "I wouldn't say there's a rush," she said. "It's actually really nice, as I said, but this is still a developing neighborhood."

†††

THERE ARE PLENTY OF TOWNS everywhere, I guess, whose reputations beyond their borders, if they have any at all, reside in single instances of popular misrepresentation or outright caricature. I try to be sensitive to this dynamic—*The Music Man* is all that millions of people will ever know about Iowa. Each instance of this effect further distorts our overall field of view, our sense of who we really are. Still, I couldn't help but feel some weirdly mystical twinge in the moment when I pulled in off the freeway, knowing that the town just over there on the other side of the windshield would be my home for the next year or two: a place that would be a totally blank slate if not for a single murder case that had made the national news some years back, and another that had managed to evade the radar.

Everything about the spot looked temporary, dreamlike. I could safely attribute some of this to finding myself a little off my bearings; I'd been at the wheel for forty-five minutes just getting out of the city, and the hour it ought to have taken after that had been stretched by traffic. It was a small freestanding building, a relic of a transitional age; there was a placard reading NEW VISIONS, LLC on the near side of some Persian blinds in its windows. The shadow of the freeway in which it stood was permanent; had it been even a quarter mile down the street, the bulldozer would have come for it ages ago. The town had been growing up and outward all around it, consigning it to a disappearing past. It was waiting for its turn.

I stood before it and took a few measured breaths. My mother always taught me to take stock of the moment you're in, to not miss the big transitions. "If you miss one, you don't get the chance to see it again," she said. When I was a kid, I thought this was just her way of trying to pry me away from the little Mattel handheld football game to which I'd become addicted like everybody else in my class. But after I started writing about murder investigations, I realized Mom was right: any given moment is loaded. You have to look hard at all the details of a scene before it changes on you. There may come a day when all you've got left are the notes you took: maybe a photograph or two, if you're lucky.

It was a sunny day, out beyond the reach of the interstate's shadow. The sidewalk in front of New Visions Properties was badly cracked; it looked like a bunch of giant jigsaw puzzle pieces turned image-side down and thrown into a pile. A couple of trees were doing their straggly best to outgrow the dirt squares in which they'd been planted, years ago, probably before the highway made it harder for them to find light. I looked around from the spot where I stood to find signs of anything else nearby, but in California there's often an agreed-upon solitude to the places where people join in with or depart from the flow of freeway traffic. Gas stations fit into such corners sometimes; neighborhoods don't, or didn't, anyway, before people began running out of room.

"You're Gage, do I have that right?" said Whitney Burnett, opening the door while I was still standing outside looking around. I felt like she was probably sizing me up, but she didn't let on; she took my hand and shook it with a firm, authoritative grip, her eyes meeting mine. Any aspiring salesman can learn about the importance of making eye contact, but it takes a natural to find the sweet spot like she did. It knocked me off balance. "Welcome to Milpitas!"

We walked into her odd, doomed little office building, a white cinder-block single-story number that had to've been at least fifty years old, and she motioned me toward her desk, which was new, spotless, meticulously ordered in its pencil cups and picture frames, and had almost certainly been shipped to the U.S. from Malaysia by way of Taipei.

†††

IDEALLY, YOU LEAVE AS LITTLE FOOTPRINT AS POSSIBLE when you're telling a true crime story: your job is to gather the facts of a case and arrange them as vividly as possible. Somebody else has already done all the dirty work for you. Arm yourself with some steady work habits and a well-lit work space, and there's really nothing to it—just the simple pleasures of research, footwork, and presentation. It's like being a florist. You ask a few questions about the occasion you're being asked to mark, and then you hide your own signature somewhere in the arrangement.

I wrote *The White Witch* without a blueprint, green behind the ears and itching to make an impression. When I started it, I held fast to a rule I'd heard repeated so often by creative writing teachers that I couldn't imagine a world outside it: *Write what you know.* Keep it local. Start in your own backyard and spread out from there.

But I didn't know of any other cases in San Luis Obispo like Diana Crane's. People get murdered everywhere, but not every murder blooms into myth; and few of the myths that do find enough oxygen to live on from generation to generation can be followed—by means of supplementary materials: clippings, transcripts, photographs—all the way back down to the flesh and blood at their roots. So I burrowed down in library basements north of Carpinteria but still well south of San Francisco, and I scrutinized old newspapers in the harsh light of the microfiche reader, practically throwing darts in the dark: *Does this victim seem like someone the neighbors might have gossiped about? Did this killer use some method gruesome enough to fire the local imagination? Does this story sound like kids might have spread rumors about it in their do-nothing towns?*

It takes a few weeks, but you need only the patience of those weeks and a little driving distance between neighboring towns to find what you're looking for. I always found plenty, more than I needed, and, after emerging from the library, I'd drive around with a Thomas Guide hunting down any places reporters might have mentioned in passing: Restaurant parking lots where somebody got shot. Liquor stores where a robbery'd gone wrong. Public schools where something awful had happened one weekend, left undiscovered until Monday.

It's voyeur work. There's no way it doesn't leave some kind of mark on you. The case I picked for my second book involved a home health nurse intentionally blinding a millionaire on her caseload in order to effect a miracle cure and maybe get rewarded: the patient died, and the family hired a private detective to look into it, who, after a little legwork, scouted out the families of a few other former patients. They'd all been surprised to find themselves burying their parents and grandparents, who'd all seemed quite healthy for their age right up until their sudden and precipitous declines.

I called the book *Spent Light*. I remember parking my car in front of the house where the nurse had once lived, gazing up at its porch, and trying to imagine her walking out, handbag stocked with the wood alcohol she'd be administering daily to some ailing old man until he died of evidently natural causes. I remember sitting in that car for half an hour, watching the sun sink behind the low hills, and then thinking: *This isn't enough.*

That was the night when, for the first time, I knocked on a stranger's door to ask if they'd let me inside, and the night I stumbled across my method, which, like anything else in the world, I guess, has both good points and bad.

†††

IN AN IDEAL WORLD, Whitney would have let me go into the property by myself for just a few minutes. I generally get great mileage out of first impressions. But I didn't want to seem any weirder than I already did, and it wasn't her job to safeguard my initial visions. So we walked in together: she with her practiced realtor's monologue, pointing out unique fixtures and shiny improvements; me with my eyes on the ceilings, the walls, and the corners, looking firsthand at places I'd read about in clippings and seen on archival tape. I was trying to get a feel for how the scene might have splashed when the shock of entry was still raw. I smelled something—cherry-vanilla; an air freshener somewhere, or residue from the cleaning crew, I couldn't tell which. The scent was dense, big-elbowed. You couldn't ignore it once you'd isolated it from the other smells in the house: fresh paint, wax, oven cleaner.

"This kitchen's all new," she said as we rounded a counter that divided what looked to have once been a single room. She gestured gracefully from point to point as she continued: "Gas oven, all new tile above the counters. But they've kept the look that houses in this neighborhood often have." She pronounced the *t* in "often" when she said it: *off-ten.*

"Vinyl floors?" I said.

"Linoleum, actually," she said, cocking her head. "People are using it again."

"Wow, really? Back when I was a kid—I don't know. It feels like you weren't supposed to like linoleum."

"Yes, that's right," she said. "It was out of fashion for a while. But it's actually organic. All natural materials. Plus you can really do a lot with linoleum, actually. The color goes all the way through."

They were nice floors, checkered in a brick-red-and-white pattern. I wanted to get down on my hands and knees and take a closer look at them, to compare them to what I'd seen in my initial research, but all that was going to have to wait.

"What were they before?" I said.

"This is an older place," she said. "They were wood."

"Did they tear out the wood, do you know?" I was trying hard to sound casual, but the more we talked, the further down in the zone I found myself: picturing the place as it once was, trying to see it with my mind's eye.

"Well, a total refurb costs a lot," she said. "I think the original floorboards are still under there, probably. But I know we hired a great firm to put down the new floors. They should be solid."

I felt bad; she had the wrong idea—that she might miss the sale if something wasn't right, that the house might not be nice enough for me. But it *was* nice; they'd prettied it up; the idea was to help it rise from its beginnings. What I represented, standing there, was a countervailing force to the current mood of the neighborhood. My interests lay underneath a surface in whose anticipated permanence people were investing time, and money.

"Oh, it's great," I said, "I'm always just curious about what houses looked like when they were new."

She laughed then with an openness you don't usually expect from people in her line of work. It was a small laugh, but genuine, coming from somewhere lower in the gut than you usually hear from strangers.

"It's been a long time since this house was new," she said.

†††

I FELT GIDDY, almost light-headed, as we walked back out through the front door to the sidewalk; she gestured me toward her car, a light blue Chevy Blazer, meticulously clean, either new or driven to the office straight from the wash-and-wax. I've done first visits that involved lock-breaking and climbing through windows. Those properties were abandoned, but the field trips I took to them helped set the tone for the way I work: learn a lot about a site, then physically enter it, breaching the barrier from the conjectural to actual while they're all still rich and vivid in my mind. To take this step with another person standing by the whole time, brightly outlining all the upgrades recently made to the place while leaving out all the details that accounted entirely for my presence there: it was disorienting.

Driving, she asked me a little about myself: my work, where I'd gone to school, if I had any children. But at lunch, seated in the outside patio of a Panera by a strip mall, she began to dig a little deeper. "Are you looking at any other houses while you're here?"

"Actually, no," I said. I looked up from my food; I didn't want to seem evasive. "Just the one."

"We have a number of really nice properties," she said.

"There's neighborhoods in town that are quieter but not really much pricier. Two of them I could show you after lunch, if you wanted."

"I leave later this afternoon," I said. This wasn't true; my reservation at the La Quinta was good until eleven the following day. Still.

"That's fast!" she said. "Do you mind if I ask . . ."

She waited for me to make eye contact.

"Many of our clients are first-time buyers, and a house like that is often perfect for them. But I have several places in newer neighborhoods, places with a little more elbow room."

Elbow room: she was young, and worked in a small market, but she was as good as or better than any high-end agent selling converted condos in Pacific Heights.

"It's specifically this house I'm interested in," I said.

"I know how that is," she said, brilliantly, I thought: There was no way she wasn't wondering what was wrong with me, why I'd want to get a place almost visibly destined for demolition. I suspected, faintly, that she was sounding me out for motives. People here had reason to be suspicious of outsiders. "But if you can find the time, at least look at this one other one. It's less than a mile from here. It just went on the market. *Super*-cute. Newer, and a little nicer."

I looked at my watch, which was strictly a performative gesture: my time was my own. "I can be a little flexible, I think," I said. There wasn't any need for me to seem busier than I was. I'm not sure what impression I was trying to make by tacitly suggesting I had a to-do list for the rest of the afternoon, but I did it anyway. You get used to this kind of talk in my line of work.

† † †

BACK AT THE MOTEL, I sketched in my tiny notebook: the entry-way, the home-improvement-store ceiling fan in the living room, the fresh tile above the counters. I also thought about the other house, the one we'd walked through after lunch: how it was nicer, just as she'd said. It was maybe forty years old, built in the hacienda style, with a freestanding garage original to the property: blue ARCO oil cans on its wooden shelves indicated that it held more history than much of the town that had long since outgrown its quaint modesty. According to market wisdom, the chief present virtue of the former porn store under the freeway was that it had been completely refurbished, inside and out; past that, there wasn't much to say about it. The nicer house was the sort of space people like me usually imagine themselves living in.

I told her I'd call her by the end of the week, another needless feint. I could as easily have stated my business and asked her to draw up a contract. But it would have been cheating, I thought. The proper procedure involves several needless steps.

So I waited two days after I got home, and then I wrote her at the email on her business card. She still had an AOL address. I hadn't thought we were that far outside the city. Most of my friends wouldn't have been caught dead.

But you couldn't have gotten a closet in San Francisco for what New Visions wanted for the whole of the Main Street house, anyway. From ceiling to floor, front yard to sidewalk, and including the modest backyard that ended at an ugly, awkward stretch of cyclone fencing, over which you could see some overgrown asphalt that had once been a parking lot. Had I been able to get to it before they put in all that new tile, it would have been even cheaper; I haggled anyway. You never know if you don't ask.

As I discovered going over the paperwork in subsequent

months, I'd probably still bid high. Prior to the renovation, it had been officially standing empty since 1986. Nobody had lived inside Devil House since forever.

3.

IT'S GOOD TO BE TIDY—not good like virtuous; I don't hold any medieval ideas about our outer selves reflecting the inner ones. I've lived with slobs, they were fine people, and I don't really mind other people's clutter. Messy people are like astronauts or long-distance truckers to me: I'm curious about how their lives feel. Not curious enough to try out their habits and live like they do—when I inhabit a place, the extent of my immersion usually ends at my skin—but curious enough to spend a little time in their lairs if the opportunity presents itself.

But I've always kept my own surroundings clean. I throw things away when I'm done with them; if I think there might still be some use left in them, I take them to the Goodwill. My mother used to tease me about this: "Hide the antiques, Chandler's home"—but keepsakes are just memory-prompts, and you don't really need them if you have a good memory. Mine is excellent.

So leaving San Francisco was, for me, an opportunity to set aside the few things I couldn't be without for longer than a day or two, and to dispose of whatever else was left. From a single bookshelf in my bedroom, I kept the essentials: a dictionary, some anatomy textbooks, a few outdated but still useful forensic reference manuals. The rest I bagged up and took over to Moe's in Berkeley, who had a books-to-prisoners program. From the kitchen cabinets, I selected a couple of wineglasses and coffee cups, stuffing them with leaves from the same newspapers I'd used to double-wrap my plates; I boxed the cookware and the silverware separately, and that was that, except for the furniture.

My friend André, who, like me, had moved to San Francisco after graduating from Cal Poly, helped load up the U-Haul. There was nothing really wrong with my futon, so I folded that and tied it with a bungee cord; I'd had my writing desk, a real antique, since college, so it had to go on the truck, too. Its exact vintage was a mystery; but it had to've belonged to a newspaperman back in the forties or fifties—an editor, maybe. Great blotches of India ink Rorschached its surface, and several deep grooves scarred its grain, probably inflicted in haste or anger by some unknown hand wielding a letter opener.

It weighed a ton. "Do they not have Office Depot in Milpitas?" André asked me, grimacing as we maneuvered it down the narrow stairway that led from my old apartment to the street.

"Sentimental value," I grunted.

"You're a cheap bastard," he said, followed by, "Fuck!" as the desk mashed his finger against the banister.

"Well, that's true, too," I said. "Flip it up onto the side?"

"Might as well," he said. There wasn't really enough room in the entryway for maneuvering; it was an irritating game of inches, and it seemed to take forever. But when we finally emerged on the sidewalk to find the smallest available vehicle in the whole U-Haul fleet parked and waiting for us at the curb, it felt momentous. The place I'd lived in for an age was no one's place now. What traces there were of me still in it would never be parsed by anyone: Twin half-moon grooves in the floor because I'd thought I could drag the futon in its frame over to a less sunny spot without anybody's help. A deep chip in the porcelain of the kitchen sink from when I dropped an antique champagne bucket into it after signing away the movie rights for *Omens*. A smudge on the bedroom wall that an ex-girlfriend put there on purpose late one Saturday night, applying lipstick to the heel of her hand and dragging it across the paint: "In case you need something to remember me by," she'd said. After the cleaning crew came, there'd be no trace of that memory left in the world.

††††

THERE WAS SO MUCH PAPERWORK. I was a first-time home buyer; everybody working billable hours was very happy to see me. We walked through the property with an assessor, we sat on facing sides of cheap tables in banking offices, we read through reams of fine print on legal-sized paper. I got preapproved. It seemed like a lot of work for a small brick building whose ultimate fate was clear to everybody involved; maybe it would change hands another time or two before somebody knocked it down and opened up a Mattress Firm, but such exchanges were stalling tactics. The writing was on the wall.

We were scheduled to close Monday, but I drove down early Friday afternoon. All my things were in shrink-wrap on pallets or secured to the floor of the truck; even my pillow was in there. For an idle moment I considered getting a cheap sleeping bag and pitching camp in the grassy side yard of the house; I wouldn't be the first to seek shade in the shadow of the freeway, I knew. There were some narrative possibilities in the idea, I thought: but I wasn't in my twenties anymore. So I booked myself into the La Quinta, fifteen minutes by car from the place I'd move into as soon as I collected the keys.

The motel room had two double beds; I used one as a combination work desk and dinner table, eating pizza as I went over my notes and printouts. The idea was to immerse myself deep enough in the facts of the case to make my arrival the next day feel like a return. You can do this to yourself, if you try hard enough: obsess over blueprints of houses whose original incarnations you never saw, memorize meaningless details of rooms you know only from pictures, sneak through hidden doors into imaginary spaces. Eventually it burrows into your skin, the place you're attempting, remotely, to haunt. You fabricate empty memories of walking from room to room, testing out light switches, knocking on walls. If you stay up too late doing it, it starts to feel a little risky, but that's the point of the exercise. It's like staring at an optical illusion for longer than the seconds needed to make it work. When you close your eyes, it's still there.

I stayed up later than I needed to, probably later than I should have. I had an appointment with Whitney scheduled for nine the next day. But it's exciting, setting off into the vast continent of the big new story. I get all caught up in the moment of departure. The future feels dramatic when you think you see a little of it cresting the horizon, the more so if the present feels routine.

I remember, before I finally fell asleep, feeling like there wasn't all that much to say about my life. I'd had several satisfying relationships; they hadn't amounted to much. I'd gotten better at my work, and been rewarded for it, but I sometimes felt like life had run out of surprises for me. I did what I did, and got the results I expected. I kept up my practice and it paid my way. My wheels made an agreeable noise when they spun.

The move to Milpitas didn't feel all that different. I'd done things like it before. It was a bigger play than parking down the block from somebody's house to watch them as they came and went, but that difference was a matter of scale. The stories I sought out weren't exactly interchangeable, but they shared a space where the distribution of light and shadow was governed by similar latitudes. I'd be moving into a new building, yes, but beneath the foundation, there wouldn't be much I hadn't written about before.

That was how I thought of things at one in the morning at a La Quinta in Fremont, anyway. As it turned out, I was almost entirely wrong. There's unexplored terrain lurking in known shapes, unmapped quadrants waiting to be located by means of simple shifts in perspective. "Unknown" and "unseen" aren't synonyms, but they're linked by more than their prefixes.

I'm sure of this now. Live and learn.

†††

THE ORIGINAL FOUNDATION of Devil House dates to sometime in the 1880s, a hopeful plot atop which several structures would perch during the decades to come. Then, it stood unremarkably among several buildings like it on an oddly shaped strip of land jutting out from Main Street at an angle, near the recently laid tracks of the San Francisco and San Jose Railroad; where the railroad ran, jobs and opportunities followed, and Milpitas, already an occasional harbor stop for prospectors, was growing. If you acted fast enough and set up a lunch counter near where the workers were still laying track, you might make your fortune, or enough to pass for one on what was still clearly the frontier. That was Devil House's original form: a diner on Main Street, six tables and a long wooden counter.

The bricks and beams belonged to the railroad, but the café from the walls in belonged to a guy named Lonnie Roberts. Lonnie was young and optimistic; he'd grown up in San Francisco, where restaurant cash registers great and small rang out from noon to midnight. It seemed like an easy way to make a dollar if a man could make it work. But competition had been stiff in town; San Francisco's boom cycles ebbed once in a while, and if you wanted to make any waves in its already-crowded chophouse-and-lunch-counter scene, you had to hustle. It seemed to Lonnie that there were other possibilities.

There are several extant photographs of the exterior of Lonnie's in Milpitas, at the time a leisurely Sunday drive from San Francisco. Block letters hand-painted directly on the brick storefront above the doorway advertise hopefully to the street: LONNIE'S OPEN DAILY 11–3. HOT SANDWICHES TO ORDER 15¢. I remember spreading three printouts across the bedspread at the motel: they were grainy, hard to tell apart. The price of the sandwich goes up in one of them, and the hours expand to breakfast in another. In one, there's a man in the frame; he has no hat or coat, which sets him apart from most photographs of the day, but he's very clean-cut, and he's wearing suspenders. A cook? A friend of the photographer's? Lonnie himself? The past is charming and safe when you're skittering around on its surface. It's a nice place to linger a moment before seeking the lower depths.

Roberts enlisted during the Second World War, and died in the Pacific Theater; you have to do a lot of digging to find his name in government records of the war dead, but it's there, KIA beside it. It's unclear whether Lonnie's remained open awaiting his return, but by 1945 it's closed. For the next few years it seems to have been used for storage.

Sometime in the mid-fifties it got rented out again, this time as a soda shop. In a contemporaneous *Mercury News* article about teenage lifestyles, you can see how its new owners had retained the grill, but traded out the counters for something more modern. A picture, probably staged for the newspaper photographer, accompanies the article: there's a waitress, a cook, and a few customers, all smiling a little too brightly. This one feels more alien to the eye than the older pictures in my file. I call this the proximity effect: the closer you get to the past, the less believable its particulars seem.

The Sunliner Grill has become a hub for young men and women in Milpitas on Friday nights, the story reports. *The latest hot rods can be seen parked along Main Street beginning from early afternoon, in contrast to the quieter hours of the workday in this growing suburban enclave.* Old pictures of Milpitas don't look far removed from the days when people came west in covered wagons; the line about the *growing suburban enclave* sets the stage for the approaching future.

Things get blurry for the Sunliner Grill after that. It would take a team of dedicated gumshoes going door-to-door to piece together any kind of consensus. In the online comments sections of news stories mentioning it, I found a few older people volunteering their memories; one recalled that he used to buy comic books there as a child, which was probably a superimposition of later memories onto earlier, fonder ones.

By 1974 at the latest, anyway, a place called Valley News is doing business from the same address. The proprietors of the Sunliner Grill may have owned the building outright by then, hoping to steer it into a different line of business; but there are several other possibilities, none of which can be determined without access to the deeds of sale, whose final resting places in dusty filing cabinets can only be conjectured. Often the holdings of large interests are sold at auction, but just as often they change hands with little or no public notice. Usually they leave traces: in the classified ads, in local interest stories. I haven't been able to find either such source here.

All I can say with certainty is that, at some point, the railroad sold the short strip of land on Main to a private owner, and that, while the railroad had been meticulous about keeping records, landlords are lone wolves. They enter and exit the scene without notice. At some point, a San Jose man named Vernon Gates shows up and buys out a few of the railroad's former holdings: their declining states made them perfect additions to his portfolio. His was a well-known name among many people in San Jose who hoped one day to forget it.

The people who lived in properties owned and managed by Vernon Gates couldn't afford to rent from anybody else. They were at his mercy. He owned at least half a dozen multi-tenant buildings; if you were to walk past any of them, you'd usually see several window units jutting out, condensation dripping to the ground below. Changes in local economies are the trade winds on which men like Vernon Gates drift; they try to land in spots where they won't be noticed, and they keep their eyes open for new opportunities, since doors begin closing after word gets around. To rent out rooms like the ones Gates had on offer is to be forever in need of new clientele.

But anyone who owns property in California knows it's a winning proposition, whatever your motivations; and however he chanced across the Milpitas listing, Gates knew a bargain when he saw one.

††††

NO ONE KNOWS HOW LONG Valley News sold books and newspapers and comic books; no one remembers who ran the place, or what the inside of it looked like before it settled on a winning business plan; no one's sure when it changed hands and began stocking *Playboy* and *Penthouse* behind the counter, or when it introduced harder fare to the racks.

But by the late 1970s it's not really a newsstand anymore. It's a porn store. *The Mercury News* didn't run an article about its opening, but on Flickr you can find a few scanned pictures of a picket line some locals formed shortly afterward. Comments on the pictures remember the scandal of it; by the time anybody noticed it had changed, people say, it had already been plying its new trade for a month or two. Comparing the exteriors to the ones in old stories about the Sunliner Grill, you can see that not everything's changed; the bricks are the same, the old awning's still there and wants replacing. But the front windows, through which you could once see the bustling lunch counter, have been blacked out, and now there's an OVER 21 ONLY sign nailed to the front door. A VALLEY NEWS sandwich board, in oddly cheery mock-Gothic lettering, still stands out front, but it strikes a discordant note within the scene that surrounds. The initial v and the terminal s are faded almost to invisibility, leaving only faint traces of themselves in the accumulating grime.

In a town so small, a place like Valley News operates on borrowed time. The picket line would eventually have gotten its way if other considerations hadn't gone out ahead of it. It's hard to believe, thinking about Valley News in Milpitas, that it ever existed at all, but photographs don't lie.

†††

ANTHONY HAWLEY WAS FROM OREGON; he had family all around the Pacific Northwest, and his childhood home on the northeast side of Portland looks, today, just like it did when he lived there. When the sailors came home in 1945, Anthony, then a child, would have seen firsthand inklings of the rapid growth that lay just ahead—new car lots, new factories, and new people moving west. Daniel, his brother, remembers Anthony in his teenage years as preferring late working hours to local nightlife. In town, there were ample supplies of both.

He'd taken a few adult education classes after high school; a few friends who were doing it had told him it was a good place to meet girls. They'd been right. You could work a day shift, get dinner, go take a class in business machines, and be out in time to make the rounds downtown with any friends you'd made in class. It seemed like an easy life, with plenty of prospects down the line.

But Anthony Hawley was twenty-two when the draft was conducted for the Vietnam War, and those same friends who'd told him to take night classes now pointed out that British Columbia wasn't even a half day's drive away. He didn't have to be told twice. Returning to Portland from Vancouver a few years later, he found himself adrift: either the time away had unmoored him, or the move north had made him restless. Whatever the case, he didn't stay in Portland long after returning. He went to Eugene for a summer, and he tried Colorado in the winter once; he worked easy jobs, keeping his expenses low.

At some point in his early thirties, after a few seasons in San Francisco, he found work on the second shift at the new Ford factory in Milpitas. The pay was decent enough, and he supplemented it with occasional afternoon shifts at Valley News, whose red HELP WANTED sign in a blacked-out window had faded to sun-washed pink. He saved money; it's easy to save money in a small town. By 1981, he had enough of it in the bank to ask his boss, one David Hodge, who never used his first name except in correspondence, if he'd be interested in selling the place outright.

"Shit," said Hodge when Anthony made the proposition shortly after the store's noon opening one slow weekday. "I'll absolutely take your money, but I can only sell you what you see from the walls in. Miss Evelyn Gates owns this building. You'll have to get on the lease with her."

It had been Vernon's before it was Evelyn's. She'd inherited it from her father after his house caught fire one night in 1978 with him still in it. Most people assumed the fire was no accident; he had few friends. Half his holdings were shuttered buildings, pitiable relics of their earlier selves in San Jose and Fremont drawing reliable monthly tithes from the people who lived in them and couldn't afford to move. There was a sense, among his former tenants, that justice, however extreme, had been served. (This feeling was short-lived; Evelyn Gates didn't overlook a payment on her father's former holdings, and the same bill collectors he'd engaged to knock on doors no later than the fifth of the month, every month, continued their errands without interruption.)

And so Anthony Hawley, a nomadic bachelor with few ambitions beyond his immediate needs, became the nominal owner of Valley News: of the stock inside, and the furniture, and the machines. To his budding entrepreneurial ear, the name lacked bite; the prospective customer needed a better idea of which way the business was headed. By this point, there was only one rack of comics left; pornography and inhalants were what kept the store afloat. So he hired a neighborhood kid named Derrick Hall and asked him to paint a new sign, something truck drivers would be able to see from the highway at night; and he gave the store a new name, something big and gaudy and mildly menacing: MONSTER ADULT X. He dug through business how-to books at the library, setting everything up to the letter of the law, incorporating MAB Enterprises as a limited liability corporation and writing out monthly payments to Evelyn Gates on legal-sized checks that came three to a page in a black binder. He retained the canceled checks in his records, which he kept in a safe, and they show his elegant handwriting, large looping letters suggesting pride of ownership. He hoped to try to buy the building at some point, not knowing, as longer denizens of the region did, that Evelyn Gates seldom sold an inch of land for a penny below list. But the store was his.

Subsequent developments within the walls that once housed Lonnie Roberts's luncheonette make up the story that has occupied my days since I left San Francisco, the story I came here to tell. California has a way of erasing its own history; I'm told that the place where Walt Disney first drew Mickey Mouse is a law office now. But among possessions retrieved from Devil House after the killings were some Polaroids of the edifice and interior of Valley News. In them, you can still make out the walls that once belonged to the Sunliner Grill, and the front counter where the cash register once stood. It's the same counter; the eye immediately classified it as an antique, even if its surroundings are now decidedly modern: the oversized VHS boxes, the lurid magazines, the enormous glass display case filled with dildos and inhalants. There's a rack of comic books near the door, certainly Derrick's doing, completely out of place. His hand is also evident in exterior shots: the stylized horror-poster lettering of the sign jutting out from atop the flat-roofed building shows great care and attention to detail, red rounded block letters with clean, brush-free black outlines. It sits at an awkward angle, trying to split the difference between facing the freeway and the street.

Yellow tape went up around the property in 1986. The crime scene stayed largely undisturbed until the final disposition of the case became known; the former Valley News building stayed empty for some time after that, as the right to the deed was in question. Once the contents of the building were no longer in dispute—the tapes and the magazines, the old 8mm projectors and the multicade video machines, the bags of spray-gold tokens and the boxes of off-brand condoms—it was all sent to the landfill. That was in 1990; all that's deep under several dozen strata of recent history now.

Twelve years later, I moved in. I entered the fully remodeled interior to find the smell of fresh paint still competing with a Coronado Cherry–scented air freshener on the kitchen counter, the visions I'd been hunting for in histories and blueprints and printouts difficult to reconcile with new ergonomic angles and muted hues: the hopeful face of this affordable, cheerful house I'd be getting at a price that wouldn't have fetched me a closet just a short drive and a bridge away in San Francisco.

4.

PEOPLE BRING EXPECTATIONS to the site of a massacre. It can't be helped. Often, they've formed these expectations in secret—not the small sort of secret you keep because it's a little unflattering or because it's nobody's business, but the deep cover of secrecy afforded by the infinite unlit corners and corridors squirreled away inside the human brain, where wishes and biases and preemptive guesses can be activated and established without the host ever knowing that the process has even taken place. This is a necessary dynamic for us to function in the world: we can't always be referring back to a table of which opinions we already know we have, which questions we consider already answered. But few things, at any rate, are more powerful than expectations. Blunt force, maybe. Firepower, certainly. Sword and steel. But even those have their limits. The imagination has none.

†††

THE MURDERS at Devil House were not, of course, the first time Milpitas had been in the news for murder. They weren't even the first time in its recent history. In 1981, a teenager named Anthony Broussard murdered fourteen-year-old Marcy Conrad without any apparent motive; he showed the body to several friends, who'd all been too afraid to call the police. There was a movie about it a few years later, *River's Edge*: it was popular, because people love to tell themselves stories about the grave dangers posed by wayward youth. They always arrive at the same questions—why don't these young people care? how did they get like this? where were their parents?—but the asking of these questions is an exercise in self-portraiture. They're not good questions; they're not even questions. They're ghost stories masquerading as concern.

I suspected that people in Milpitas had learned this the hard way, and I imagined they wouldn't be thrilled that a writer was moving to town to write a book about an even grislier local case: one which had somehow managed, for the most part, to duck the radar of the national news media. This was part of what made the case attractive to me: Why hadn't they swarmed? There are several ready-made narratives to be spun from any local crime story whose details call to mind some earlier communal shock; you just have to plug in a few particulars. *The Problem with Milpitas. The Soul of the Suburbs. A Small-Town Boy.*

If you live where catastrophe strikes, you're right to be suspicious of the people who come to gawk. They may dress up their motives—"telling the *real* story"; "getting it right"—but they'd say anything if they thought it would make you talk. Reporters are like the police. It's in their interest to tell you whatever you need to hear as long as it makes you cooperate. The same is true, too, of writers with bigger plans, greater ambitions. I had a detective once tell me, by way of declining to answer any further questions from me after a few facts-of-the-case softballs: "Everybody has a motive." He didn't elaborate. No elaboration was needed.

By the time I arrived in Milpitas you could track how locals felt about *River's Edge* without even having to play gumshoe about it. There were message boards, archived listservs, op-eds in *The Mercury News* about parole hearings. With very few exceptions, Milpitans felt like their town and its people had been misrepresented—by writers, by actors, by a whole host of moneyed people from the other end of the state who didn't know the first thing about what it was like to live an hour or more from the big city. It was a raw deal: stay invisible until somebody wants to spotlight your defects. Small communities whose murder cases are just lurid enough to attract the attention of outsiders learn and relearn this again and again; it's one of the unignorable facts of crime. The less you have to lose, the more it will end up taking from you.

So it seemed there'd been a collective effort to start forgetting about Devil House almost from the moment the story broke. This effort, by and large, had been successful. They hadn't been able to keep the camera crews away—nobody's strong or clever enough to drive off the camera crews—but somehow they'd weathered the onslaught quietly. It was a dark miracle of forgetfulness, a gift of near-erasure. There are few such gifts in a world like ours.

I mulled this over in my new house by the freeway—my new house! I loved saying these words, sometimes aloud, thinking about how most houses contain more stories than their present-day owners can really fathom; my work, and the way it worked, had bought me two houses for the price of one. It was a deeper level of engagement than my previous stakeouts, than the simple trespassing of my greener days, I considered; gazing all the while deeply—ridiculously—into its beige walls: trying to imagine them as they'd once been, and coming up empty-handed every time.

†††

I WISH I COULD SAY I got my box full of primary texts from a retired cop who requested that his name be withheld until five years after his death. I wish I could claim they came bundled like an enormous manuscript, tidily tucked into a box, and that atop the sheaf there'd been a typewritten note in which the anonymous officer who'd had access to this material all along details his anguish over having withheld it from people who, he knew, had need of it—even if, as he says in an aside, he can't imagine what actual use any of it might be. I wish I could tell you that I then drew up a comprehensive study of the department as it had been during the investigation, eliminating all serving officers still living, so that I might, from among the already narrow possibilities on the list of the dead, draw forth a name or two who might be likely suspects for putting such invaluable sources into my hands. Failing all that, I'd like to say I used social engineering to get into the evidence room at the precinct: bluffing my way past security, lying outright to the clerk, and finally luxuriating in the archives, avoiding curious glances as I pocketed several bagged and numbered exhibits, one-of-a-kind artifacts which I then spirited out of the police station inside the false lining of an overcoat. See me, waiting until I get home to examine my contraband, triumphant but unsurprised: I get away with stuff like this all the time. It's who I am and how I work, in this version of me.

But that version only exists in movies. I don't even own an overcoat. I made my first local inroads into the story of Devil House by doing what anybody else does these days: I went on eBay.

Buying source material from strangers on the Internet always makes me a little queasy. The hospital charts that arrived one day from Redding while I was working on *Spent Light*: nobody's even supposed to see medical records without a court order. They're confidential. But nothing's truly private anymore. There are people out there who will sell you anything.

In San Francisco they make you sign for a package; anything left outside your door will be gone in minutes. I remember the sound of the buzzer in my apartment the day the *Spent Light* charts arrived; as I signed the FedEx guy's clipboard I couldn't shake the feeling that he knew something was fishy. He stayed quiet, but I felt him watching me, I thought, while I scribbled on the signature line. What did he imagine might be in the box: Weapons, maybe? Drugs? What kind of drugs would you need shipped to San Francisco?

But probably he was thinking about how many more stops he needed to make before lunch, or whether he was meeting his hourly quota. I've repeated the process enough times now to know that it wasn't his expression telegraphing guilt or suspicion: it was my guilt. It's a feverish feeling, preparing to flip through a sheaf of paperwork to which you have no legitimate claim, making ready to glean information from it for the purposes of telling a story whose darker details ought to have remained hidden.

Shortly after I moved to Milpitas I learned that the FedEx guy here just leaves your package on the porch.

It was right there waiting for me when I got back from my shopping. I'd scoped out an enormous Goodwill down the highway, and it didn't disappoint: shelves were full of dusty plates and cracked cups, abandoned electric popcorn makers and can openers, pens and stationery and knickknacks. I meant to stock the kitchen cabinets with old things, things that might conceivably have passed through the hands of its former inhabitants. Not antiques: cast-offs. Things of no known vintage, the invisible bits of the past that form its greater part. When I immerse myself in the search long enough, I get a precise feel for what works.

I stood on my porch looking down at the package for a minute. Cars on the freeway above me buzzed by in the irregular rhythm of midday. Then I sat on my step, box in hand, and split the seam on the packing tape with a house key. I eased the bubble-wrapped bundle gently out from its housing. It's a grim sort of Christmas, the arrival of the primary texts: a time when the imaginary world of things I haven't seen collides with, and is always at least partially annihilated by, the world of the real.

But I'd been deep in secondary research for several months now, ever since Ashton's initial email. I was glad I'd kept notes from our call, because the contrasts between what I'd heard then and what seemed to be forming a truer picture had begun to sharpen:

> *Cult of teenagers*
> *Ritual murder*
> *Obscene staged crime scene*
> *No arrests*

I was ready to get down to work.

† † †

FIRST THERE WERE THE POLAROIDS: twenty of them, held together in bunches of five with skinny rubber bands. It was a decent haul for my first venture into the world of what might be out there. Getting lucky is at least fifty percent of good research; I've had whole projects go down the drain when I couldn't make a good connection in the early going.

These pictures, and the clipped newspaper stories that accompanied them, made for a promising beginning. They came from an eBay user in New Jersey called "tru_crimebuff973." She had all the usual entry-level stuff—local police bulletins with sketches of now nationally remembered suspects; inkjet reproductions of paintings by serial killers on death row: puppies, flowers, clowns; black Zodiac rifle sights against white backgrounds on one-inch badges, a dollar apiece. But among these run-of-the-mill finds, she also boasted several collections of photographs, which she claimed came from estate auctions. I didn't believe her; but my responsibility is to my story, not to whether the stuff I dig up might be admissible in court.

My guess was they were actually what I call outtakes: crime scene photographs discarded in favor of better, clearer shots, later fished from the trash behind the police station and subsequently passed from hand to hand over the years. Prices decline as the public's memory of the case fades, and these, in particular, were lowball items as far as the market was concerned—they had no bodies in them, no handwritten annotations, no context beyond the claims attached to them in the listing. *Scenes from the investigation of the crimes at Devil House.* Even so, they seemed quite inexpensive, given the usual rates of the actual-artifacts market. Some cold cases grow legs of their own. Mine hadn't.

But verifying the scene was easy, because the renovation, while thorough, hadn't been a complete do-over—in 1986, the building having until recently been a business, there'd been no porch at all—but the shot on the top of the bundle was a view from the street, and you could see where the addition of the porch had been a pretty hurried surgery. Even with all the smoke long since cleared, the scene remained. The bricks, the awning, the distances between the windows: they were all the same. They were just cleaner now, their details shinier but their general station unchanged. This was my house. This was how it had looked back then.

But the first thing that catches the eye in the shot is the sign, of course. Derrick's gift for lettering, had things gone differently for him, might have landed him a job on Madison Avenue. It's not fancy; the clientele it sought to attract didn't want fancy. They wanted to know that what waited for them inside was wild, and forbidden, and possibly dangerous. Accordingly, Derrick had chosen a style recalling the horror comics of the 1940s and '50s. The edges of the letters seem to ooze or bleed; only black outlines around each letter, neat and seamless, constrain the runoff. One word hermetically facing the street: MONSTER.

Its lure feels more violent than sexual, but this could be a function of phantom presentiment, and of the secondary work Derrick did after the building changed hands. By the time you see this picture, you probably already know that it used to say ADULT X in the space to the right of MONSTER, a space afterward occupied by the cartoonishly grotesque hairy tongue seen in many of the news stories. The hand that painted this tongue might as easily have extended it farther to the left, blotting out the rest of the original sign: but Derrick left MONSTER intact, either because a tongue all by itself might have seemed too much, or because he was proud of his lettering and wanted to leave it up long enough for more people to see it than the ones who used to come here seeking skin mags and video booths.

First looks mean a lot; I stayed with this frame a moment more. I could see, from my window, a telephone pole, also present in the photograph—but it was clean now; in the photo it had several layers of paper stapled to it, though I couldn't make out the text. The edges of another house on the lot a little to the north crept into the frame: that house was gone now, though I didn't know what had become of it. I wondered briefly whether it had been a business or a home. It made a difference: both to my story and to the people who'd either lived or done business there. For now it was just a blank.

Finally, there was a dog who'd just happened to be walking past when the picture was taken. It was of no particular breed: just a dog with dirty golden fur, its mouth open and its tongue hanging out. I was happy to see this dog. A dog brings something cheery to even the grisliest of scenes, or so it's always seemed to me, and the presence of a second tongue mirroring the painted one on the sign overhead seemed almost like an artist's choice, an Easter egg for the keen onlooker.

The other shots were all interiors. From them, it's clear that the Devil House of legend was really only a store into which some people moved their belongings for a short space of time. They'd made it their own, but most of the wares and fixtures remained. There was the old countertop, still boasting a cash register that must have been too heavy for kids to move it; several mattresses on the floor elude the eye, drawn instead to the magazine and video racks amid which they rest. In tighter shots, the squalor of the mattresses is clearer, and the magazines' titles are legible: *DIAMOND COLLECTION. EIGHTEEN AND SHAVED. GIRLS WHO EAT CUM.*

This was Anthony Hawley's store. Hawley is gone by the time this picture gets taken, and Derrick and his friends have been busy redecorating. Their rough work has brought a note of chaos to the already lurid feel of the scene: In the racks, on the tier nearest to the floor, you can see a few copies of *Daredevil*, the comic book about the blind-lawyer-turned-superhero, and also an issue of *Epic*, a science fiction magazine from the seventies. On the back wall, in spray paint, you can see all the blind-alley symbols and slogans that would successfully drive the investigation for months: A GENERATION OF VAMPIRES; SORCERER CULT; SET 4 SACRIFICE.

But it's the shot of the ceiling that got me. A silver pentagram in spray paint, familiar to me from the issue of the Fremont *Argus* in which a nearly identical shot ran after the press got access to the premises. The accompanying story, reported on by others and amended for their own purposes, fixed the narrative for the outside world. Different symbols occupied each recessed angle in the star, five in all; these were said to be letters from a Satanic alphabet, each corresponding to an occupant of the house, the stylized H at the center of Derrick's own sigil, a sixth hidden in plain sight.

I could see how the detectives had been unable to resist the bait. They took the back booths as a clear sign that there'd been six people living in the building. Their theory of the crime assigned a lot of weight to this number six; ideas about numerology in occult thinking, and the specific weights of given numbers, were the crumb trail they'd chosen to follow. These ideas were malleable, even plastic: there was no working code that stayed in play longer than a day or two. All of it was rooted in superstition, and all of it allowed almost total authority to the gut reaction, assigning, to the hard case of the creeps an onlooker might get if confronted with the scene, a primary role.

But the full-timers and the weekend wraiths envisioned by the investigators were phantoms of the imagination, fuel for the always-hungry furnaces of public outrage. Any collective names later assigned to people said to have lived in Devil House came from captions under pictures like this one: captions placed by people who hadn't actually known what they were talking about, but who, in their haste to avoid getting scooped, weren't afraid of a little conjecture. And the nicknames assigned to imagined residents after somebody noticed that some of the spray-painted symbols looked like astrological signs: these, too, were inventions, dots connected for the sake of the story.

In truth, Derrick had painted the symbols in the star because they looked cool. The star was supposed to suggest exactly what people took from it—but its detailing had been strictly an aesthetic exercise for him. That the number of symbols corresponded exactly to the numbers of people involved in their creation was a function of expectations.

People do all kinds of things with their expectations. I would be reminded of this much later, having spent my own long season in the valley of early assumptions.

5.

IT TOOK ME UNTIL SUMMER to get an outline together I could actually rely on: it's easy to draw up a plan with a bunch of Roman numerals and subheaders, but plans aren't outlines. An outline shows you the shape of something. Once the shape comes into view, you can follow it wherever it goes. It's magic.

I'd spent a week letting the Polaroids soak in. I wanted to see if I could correlate the terrain delineated by each one with the house as it lay now—this was rough going; the remodeling crew had been given license to rebuild from the ground up. But they'd left the basics intact. There's no point building a wall where a window used to be if you're only going to put a new window in a few feet over. So I made grease pencil marks on the floor, old Polaroids in hand, reckoning the proximity of objects in the frame to walls and doorways. Seeing how the light fell, imagining the place in the absence of the front porch and the windows that now let so much sunlight in: in Anthony Hawley's day, this place had been much darker by design. These were only initial explorations, I knew: they'd have to be recalculated several times during the next year or two. But they were a beginning.

Once I'd marked up the floor I began walking in circles around the room, tracing ghost objects whose shapes were suggested by the hash marks on the floor. It's a childish exercise, which is its value: kids have no problem believing absolutely anything. Tell a two-year-old you're going to feed a make-believe candy bar to his teddy bear. Half an hour later you'll still both be there, feeding a bear whose appetite never diminishes, and who demands, over and above his candy rations, ever-increasing supplies: of apples from imaginary orchards, of oats from bottomless feed bags, of carrots pulled fresh from the living room carpet. Spend an afternoon at this kind of play and you'll remember the carrots at the day's end. You may even smell them when you close your eyes. There is ample space in the brain for several worlds to occupy at once.

I walked up to the rim of one of my fresh greasepaint *x*-rings and I looked down into its center. Then I looked back at the dry Polaroid in my hand, its once-white frame aged nicotine-yellow. In it, I could see a pile of clothing on a floor, a rumpled denim jacket atop it obscuring any clear details of what lay beneath. T-shirts, right? It had to be mainly T-shirts. Socks, some puffy shirts, maybe. I thought I could see some loose ends poking out, possibly. But Polaroids fade as they age; I could only be sure about the jacket.

I closed my eyes and bent down, and I began to inhale deeply through my nose. Any reasonable person, looking through the window at that moment, would have come away thinking they'd seen an idiot. I felt like one, standing there bent at the waist, sniffing at the bare floor of my own house, trying to see if I could pick up the ancient scent of some teen-agers' unwashed clothes: to regenerate, in my mind's eye, a place whose subsequent buyers had spared little expense erasing all traces of who had lived there and what had happened to them. But I'm a professional. I don't care if I feel like an idiot. It's kind of an item of faith with me that my feelings aren't important when I'm working.

And so, venturing down interior pathways that have grown familiar to me, I smelled stale sweat, and cigarette smoke. I smelled cheap used paperback books and the baked-earth smell marijuana had before it became big business. I smelled bleach: they'd never wash that scent out of this place. And then something new and unwelcome got in the way. Berries. There was another air freshener in here, one I hadn't noticed, some-thing New Visions had hidden in a closet someplace.

I opened my eyes. Between the smell I'd been trying to conjure from the ghost of some clothes on the floor and the air freshener making itself inconspicuous somewhere, I had the beginnings of something, a way in.

I begin with rituals like this in part because the more distant a crime is historically, the harder it becomes to know just where to start. Some people focus on what makes their killer tick; others like to render the historical scene as vividly as possible. You see this latter a lot with people who cover the Son of Sam: they want the reader to feel the heat of New York City in the summer, to see the lakes of riotous color dripping down the sides of subway cars and taste the parched pavement on the air during a four-week stretch when it never rains once.

I always end up at the actual scene of the crime, no matter where I begin: that's my method. A feeling for the coordinates. A sense of place. To arrive on the premises, facts in hand. It helps, when it's possible, to begin in the same spot where you'll end up: you get both views this way, the bird's-eye and the worm's. But no matter what, I have to get my hands dirty. It matters whose air I'm breathing.

†††

VICTIMS FEEL HARMLESS, at first: they can't raise objections, they're finite objects at rest in a stable field. But in the wake of each victim come waves of hurt: the rooms in which they lived have to be cleaned up; their larger possessions have to be parceled out; the people with whom they had outstanding accounts, material or otherwise, must learn to swallow their complaints. Sooner or later, I'd have to locate any such creditors still among the living, I knew. I hoped to forestall the search as long as I could. Just thinking about it made me tense. Cold calling is a bad look in almost every profession.

But by June I'd made a friend, and he knew more than I did about the neighborhood. It was Ken from the apartments across the street. We'd exchanged several head nods while leaving our houses at around the same hour of the morning a few times, but nothing past that; I was out early one day when he called out to me, his voice gravelly, a lit cigarette in hand. "Hey, the new guy," he said, waving with the other.

"Gage," I said.

"All right, Gage," he said. We shook hands. "Ken."

"My mother's idea," I said preemptively; most people say something about how they haven't ever met anybody named Gage. Ken cocked his head a little.

"Well, all right," he said: he had a light tone to his voice, in which I thought I heard a note of correction. "Mom knows best, right?"

"Right, right," I said.

"Mine still calls me 'Kenny.' Makes me feel like a little kid."

"Whatever they call you for the first few years after you're born probably sticks with them forever," I said.

"Maybe that's it," he said. "Anyway, where were you before you got to Milpitas?"

"Oh, just up in San Francisco. You?"

Ken laughed; he looked down a little, toward the sidewalk. I wasn't sure what was wrong with my question. "I'm from here," he said when he found my face again. "Until pretty recently not a lot of people moved here."

"Real estate agent says it's coming up," I said.

"Well, that's true," he said. "It's growing. New people. Right here next to the freeway, though—don't take this the wrong way, but most of the people moving here . . . they don't move *here*."

"Oh, I know," I said, remembering my first visit to town.

"Whitney tried to show me a place in—what was it called? The neighborhood had a name."

"There's a lot of that now," said Ken. I was trying to guess his age without staring too hard: maybe thirty-seven, I figured. His clothes looked freshly laundered and his hair was neatly shaped. "Wolf Trail Crossing or whatever. I think they get to mark up the price if they give a block a name like that."

"Well, anyway," I said, "they were a good deal more expensive than this one."

He looked at me a little sideways; he'd noticed I wasn't volunteering much. "Yeah, I bet they were," he said after a second. "Listen, I'm on my way to work, I better get going. You want to get a beer later?"

"Sure," I said, a little surprised.

"Cool," he said, with a friendly smile; I thought I heard a note of suspicion in it, but I'd hardly had any company at all since getting to town, and solitude can do strange things to your hearing. "I'm home after five. You'll be around?"

"Haven't really figured out many other places to go," I said.

He laughed again. "I imagine you haven't," he said.

†††

AT ABOUT FIVE-THIRTY that evening, my doorbell rang; it was a cheery two-note chime, and it had to be new—who puts a doorbell on the front of a porn store?—but it sounded, to my ears, like a relic of the 1970s: there was something aspirationally optimistic about it, as if it were trying to climb above its actual station.

Ken produced a six-pack of Tecate and set it down on the coffee table by the couch in the living room. I don't think I'd seen a Tecate since college. We cracked our cans open simultaneously; the sound caromed off the walls with a weirdly metallic echo. Whoever'd done the refurb on the place hadn't given much thought to the acoustics.

What's your life like, where's your family: we took care of the basics first. He'd been born at the hospital in San Jose; his parents still lived in the house he'd grown up in. He said the place had seemed palatial to him as a kid, but that he could see, now, with all the new construction, that it had been incredibly modest. I thought about how every town this near San Francisco must have experienced some measure of seismic change almost the minute the information economy cranked into high gear, and how this was still going on, my own lodgings being just a single example.

He had a sister at Mills, and both his parents were college graduates: but they cared more about their children's happiness than about status, and he'd been good with tools since he was young, so he worked at an auto shop.

"I wouldn't have guessed," I said: leaving in the mornings, he looked like he was heading for a desk job.

"I only wear my uniform at the shop. Old habit. Leave my work at work, you know?" I cracked open a second beer; it was dark outside, but inside it felt hotter than it had in the daytime. "How about you?"

"I'm a writer," I said. "Mainly books."

"There you go," he said, raising his can like a champagne glass. We toasted my profession. Then we sat quietly for several minutes, each of us sort of staring into space at the end of the day, beers in hand.

It's pretty rare to meet someone who's comfortable just sitting quietly with you before you get to know each other better. Sometimes quiet people are trying to let you know they don't actually want to talk to you, but this wasn't that. It was easy. I'd meant to start asking questions—you never know if you're getting an opportunity you won't get again, or won't get again for a while—but I chose to wait. There was a gentle, blurry quality to the scene. I relaxed into it. You get susceptible to environments when you don't keep much company.

"So you came here to write?" he said eventually; the stillness resolved. I wasn't sure what to say in response: how much of the truth to tell him, I mean. He was an adult who'd lived here all his life. There was no way he didn't remember the murders at Devil House. That he hadn't already commented on the former life of the house in which we were sitting together drinking beers was, by itself, a clue of some kind—a sign of something delicate to be navigated, like a prison record or a death in the family.

"I came here to write," I said. "That's sort of what I do, I go places and write."

"About what?"

There was a beat. "Crime. I write true crime."

"I figured," he said. "I don't know if you know this, but when people saw somebody was moving in, the first thing everybody wondered was if it'd be somebody who knew."

"That was all a long time ago," I said.

"Here in town . . ." he said, looking for the right words. "Here in town it doesn't feel like a long time to a lot of people."

I didn't know what to say to that, so I tried to let the quiet open up again. It didn't work. Ken was looking at the beer in his hand, trying to think of how to say something.

"I don't know if you know this, too, but everybody mainly feels like they dodged a bullet when nobody wrote a giant story about it like with the other thing that happened here."

"Sure," I said. I decided to go ahead and hit the ice with a hammer. "*River's Edge* didn't go over real well around here?"

"Man, *no*," he said. "People are still mad about it. Almost none of it was actually true, the way they wrote it up. None of those kids were really like that, they were from families people knew. Normal moms and dads, you know. They didn't like feeling like everybody from the outside was going to be looking at them funny forever."

"I always try to be fair to the people I write about," I volunteered, "but it's always going to be different for the people who lived through it." I was a little surprised; among the crowd I ran with, *River's Edge* had always been seen as a good example of how to get a story right.

"I guess," he said. "You saw the movie?"

"Yeah," I said. "Yeah. But that's a movie. Writers have a little more headroom to work with."

It was quiet for a minute, and maybe for two minutes; an easy quiet, but not, I thought, without some meaning to it.

"But if you write a book, maybe somebody makes a movie."

"That's true," I said.

"Yeah," he said. There was another moment, a break—not enough for too much discomfort to gather, enough to let him ask directly if I was going to write about that *other* case, the one that had happened in my house before it became my house: the one hardly anybody remembered as of yet.

"Probably, yeah," I said.

He raised his can; I joined him in his toast before he delivered it.

"Well, good luck," he said, and then he told me a story about a guy who'd brought in a 1951 Mercedes for repair that looked like it came fresh off the production line, original paint and everything, and I took this as an indication that he'd said what he came to say and was winding things down; but he stuck around for another twenty minutes, which seemed very gracious to me, if I'd understood the point of our earlier conversation.

We shook hands when we said good night; I tried not to think too hard about it, but found later that I couldn't help myself, as I considered the increasingly colorful spread of butcher-block paper atop my desk, where, nightly, I was mapping out my list of the dead and their local connections. I reflected on how I'd seen *River's Edge* as a pretty good movie about a small town south of San Francisco: it felt true-to-life. Sure, the actors were mainly gorgeous Hollywood types; that can't be helped. But they'd taken pains to avoid shading things in black-and-white, hadn't they?

I couldn't say with any authority, I thought as I sketched my morbid family tree: red Sharpie for victims, green for suspects. And I thought back to the movie they'd made, out of *The White Witch of Morro Bay*, a film I only watched once, on opening night, in a theater where I felt embarrassed by what I saw: because I'd met most of the people who were being portrayed on the screen, people who, under the editing hand of the screenwriter, were now, at best, misrepresented, and were, in several cases, so wholly reimagined as to be entirely false to the reality I knew.

Certainly *River's Edge* was truer than that, I thought, but I had Ken's voice in my head, and several questions I intended to ask him if we found the time to have some beers again.

6.

IT'S A LUXURY TO WORK SLOWLY; I know it. But I don't dwell on it. That's the nature of luxury. You become accustomed to its presence. Even with its decor spruced up, no one could call the former Devil House extravagant, but my work allowed me to spend as much time as I needed on the most granular of details. Crawling around on the floor to see if any doorframes still bore nicks or scuffs. Staring at an imagined coordinate on a wall with my chin resting on my fists, narrowing my focus to these ridiculously specific parameters. Taking the time. Languishing in obscure details until they reveal their deeper secrets may not be wealth, but you're fooling yourself if you think it isn't luxury.

I thought about this when I drew up the list of the dead. It wasn't a long list; there had been no serial killer here, no extended crime spree to reconstruct. The story of Devil House, at first blush, was the story of a moment, and of how that moment came to pass. At first I wrote the names in red Sharpie, on a leaf torn from butcher-block, which I taped to the wall in the living room. I lived with that for a few days, but every time I looked at it, it felt like an imposition. It belonged to the present. The names on it could have been anyone's, and the glare of the shiny new paper kept reminding me that old photographs and clippings were the only view I had of the place as it once had been.

So I tore the sheet down and threw it away: and then, on all fours, I wrote out all the names again, but in chalk this time, directly on the floor. I was trying to summon the dead: as physical objects in space, as former presences—people who once stood where I was standing, who fell down where I was crouching, and who slowed to stillness in places from which I would get back up unharmed. Absent some feeling for the spaces through which they moved, I wouldn't be able to pick up the thread.

But these floors were new: gleaming replacements, skin-tight masks. The victims at Devil House had bled out onto filthy carpet laid over old pine. I looked around at the walls;

beneath new paint, they were the same as they'd been sixteen years ago. I thought about carving the names into them with a knife, but remembered the interior shots: spray paint and collage. A different aesthetic entirely. Details are important to me. And then, impulsively, using the heel of my hand, I began erasing what I'd written. It left a giant cloudy smudge on the floor that still suggested the shapes of names: perfect. This is how my process works, when it works.

I took pictures next—Polaroids; it was getting harder to find film since the bankruptcy, but there's no substitute. Digital's dry. Snapshots feel weird. Around here it was easier to find fresh packs than back home—in the city, people are hawks for the secondary market. They'll buy up anything just on rumors of scarcity. Elsewhere, you might still run across three or four fresh packs dangling from a spindle in the aisles of a former Rexall, waiting for an enterprising manager to come along and notice that their packaging has gone yellow. I'd cleared out two inventories since my arrival. I kept my hoard in a shipping box in the closet.

I retained photographs of all the preparatory work. Over the course of a few weeks, I incorporated them into my shoebox full of eBay finds. The new pictures and the old ones began to blur together after a while: as if, in secluded company for too long, they'd become confused about who'd gotten there first. This is a practice of self-deception; pressed, I'd have no trouble telling foraged finds from my original work. But in here, by myself, I can believe whatever I like if I just work at it hard enough.

By this point I'd been in the house about four months. I'd eased in gently, taking my time, getting my bearings before settling down to business. The profound indulgence of my work; the security it represents; the decadent spaces into which I insin-

uate myself, both external—ruins, remnants, reconstructions—
and interior: long hours of consideration and contemplation,
solitary reflections that touch total immersion on one side and
utter detachment on the other. Almost nobody I write about
knew days like these. The ones who were gone had largely
lived from day to day; those who'd survived the ordeals that
drew me to them would likely never again number "time to
think" among life's pleasures.

†††

EVELYN GATES YOU KNOW A LITTLE. She was forty-one on the
night she died; no deaths are painless, but hers, at least, had
been swift. A sword, in the hand of a capable assailant, accom-
plishes its work with almost surgical precision: the killer had
lanced her first in the neck, and then, gripping the hilt of his
sword with both hands at about the level of his midline, thrust
awkwardly but decisively upward. The point of the blade had
entered about an inch below her sternum. Her spine temporarily stayed its force; feeling it stick, her killer had tugged forcefully at the hilt, doubling the blade's damage on the way back
out of its victim's body. Most notably, it nicked the lung a second time. Her injuries were several, causing massive blood loss;
but it was that twice-punctured lung that made the blows fatal.
Struck, she'd fallen face-first onto the floor; her assailant had
pressed the heel of his shoe down against the back of her head
to muffle the sound of her screams before seeing his quest
through to its end. You can't breathe when your lungs can't
inflate. She suffocated to death.

Her life, up to this point, had been one of petty privilege.
Prior to her father's death, she'd owned a couple of Shakey's
franchises bought with family money; franchise owners usu-

ally hire people with management experience to man the house, but Evelyn had insisted on personally overseeing everything. She'd never worked in a restaurant a day in her life; she was incompetent at best, and a genuine menace when things were busy. She'd stand on the line advising the cooks on how to increase their work rate, or head out into the restaurant to patrol the tables, slowing down the needed flow of traffic and generally getting in the way. She seldom fired anybody; she preferred to dock pay on questionable grounds, and to keep doing it just enough to keep morale low—for showing up late, for long lunch breaks, for using the toilet during the work shift. Her employees were unlikely to file any complaints. Most of them were high school students, or needy retirees, or single moms returning to the workplace.

She was pretty, but had never married. Managing her father's properties had kept her busy. Had anyone known her intimately, they'd been discreet. It was hard for me to get a read on her beyond these immediately available details, which felt like a caricature: but I did manage to unearth a profile piece from about a year after her father's death.

In the picture that accompanies it, she stands beside an antique bookcase. Her smile seeks approval almost to the point of insisting upon it; her teeth gleam. The books on their shelves are protected by glass doors that swivel upward onto a track above them; I saw something like them in my grandmother's house when I was a child. The caption reads: *Evelyn Gates stands with her collection of rare books, which includes some of the oldest volumes to be found in California,* which may well be true. But the authors whose names I was able to make out from the spines of the books had all been popular at the turn of the century: H. Rider Haggard, Annie Fellows Johnston, Wilkie Collins. Johnston didn't even publish at all until 1893.

Among Californians whose ancestors came west early, a nostalgic mood sometimes takes hold: a feeling of having been born too late to enjoy the spoils that are rightly theirs, of finding themselves on the wrong end of always having to always ask for things. I wonder if Evelyn Gates was one of these, though her clothes, in the picture, don't suggest anything of the sort: a smart skirt and a crisp blouse, a modest pair of earrings in modern geometric shapes. She's in partial profile, with her hair cut just above the shoulder; I can see, if I set my imagination to it, how she might have looked with a braid hanging down to the middle of her back, her attire in the more severe and decorous fashions of an earlier age—a crinoline skirt rippling past her ankles, the sleeves of her blouse billowing until they cinched at the wrists. In this vision, her eyes don't change: they still demand respect, because the person who opens them in the morning and closes them at night has been raised to believe she deserves it.

Evelyn Gates's corpse had been found splayed atop the remains of Marc Buckler, thirty-one years old on the night he came to inspect the property, which he intended to purchase from Gates at a discount. She'd agreed to the markdown on the condition that Buckler buy two other of her properties, it didn't much matter which. At the time of the proposed sale, she had her eye on new ground then being broken in the same neighborhoods Whitney Burnett would try to steer me toward years later. In Gates's day, these lots still lay undeveloped; new arrivals, their wallets fat with new money, were the target buyers for the properties to be built atop them, in which Evelyn Gates saw an opportunity to improve her station.

She died before she was able to get in on the action. An investigator from the forensics crew, when her body had been turned face-up, cried out in shock: he'd grown up in a Gates house, and his parents still made out their rent checks to Gates Homes, Ltd., every month. As a child, he'd been present during some of Evelyn's surprise visits to her properties—humiliating, embarrassing exercises of power that left deep impressions on children made to see their parents showing deference to an overdressed, unexpected visitor. "Miss Gates," he said, standing over the pit, trying to think of something else to say, wondering who the body beneath hers had belonged to in life.

Marc Buckler was from Charter Oak, but he told most of his business associates he came from Hollywood: he hoped to cultivate an air of success. On the day he died, his plane out of Ontario was delayed several times; it finally took to the air bound for San Francisco almost three hours late. He was angry, and sweating through his business clothes. He'd wanted to fly up again, quickly view a property he already knew he intended to buy, and catch a red-eye home; the whole prospect made him feel metropolitan.

He rented a car from Budget. It was a white Ford Taurus, the economy option. At home, he drove a red 1968 Pontiac GTO with cream leather interior, which he pampered by hand every weekend; by the time he got to the offices of Gates Homes, Ltd., he was out of sorts. Evelyn's receptionist, a high school student working off the books, remembered him later: "He was mad," she told the detectives. "The way he came in, I thought he was going to hit somebody. I don't mean to be disrespectful, because now he's dead, all right? But he was all red and sweaty. Like, *hot*. He pushed open that door like, *I'm going to cause trouble*. I kept one hand on the phone just in case."

Gates took him out for a pick-me-up, presumably to improve his mood; he drank a Manhattan, which records show she paid for with her business Visa. Over drinks, beneath cut-out Halloween pumpkins and cartoon spiders, she showed him printouts of the several other listings he hadn't inquired about on his previous visit, just in case: Buckler talked fast and interrupted a lot, and she thought maybe she had a live one on the line. She was right. He harbored dreams of a big windfall. His friends kept saying the Silicon Valley boom was just now entering its actual growth spurt. Houses outside the city were still cheap. He wanted in.

They didn't arrive at the property until after dark. Most realtors will try to get you inside during daylight hours: everything looks more appealing in the sunlight. But Buckler didn't care that much, and it showed; his only concern was how much it would cost him to make any improvements needed to resell the place at a profit. Minus that motive, he wouldn't have even gotten out of the car to inspect this property: it was one of the unasked-for listings Evelyn Gates had brought along. She hadn't intended to show it tonight. It was a semi-distressed property in a nothing neighborhood, the sort of place you might point out to a client when you drove past it. But with a client all wet behind the ears like this, you never knew.

Inside, when the figure emerged from the shadows, Buckler froze right where he stood: he wanted to run, but his fear of the unknown wouldn't let him pick a direction. Evelyn Gates was standing flash-frozen in genuine horror at the sights that surrounded her, the thousand loving touches that illuminated the magnitude of her miscalculation, the innumerable things she didn't know or care enough to learn about the people who lived or did business in the properties she'd inherited from her father. Buckler watched her die, the whole sudden scene; when, as she fell, his survival instinct finally kicked in, someone was waiting to block his escape route. It could have been anybody; I have my suspicions, but, for several reasons which I hope to eventually make clear, I'm not inclined to put them down on paper.

I try to honor the dead in my books. It's one of the things, I hope, that sets me apart a little from my partners in true crime. When I read what others write about places where the unthinkable became real, the focus always seems off to me. Victims spend their entire time in the spotlight just waiting for the fatal blow, on a conveyor belt that leads to the guillotine: I pity their fates, but it's hard to grieve for them, because the treadmill on which they ran feels specifically designed to kill them. I brought this up at a convention once; I wasn't exactly shouted down, but a luminary I'll decline to name told me, on a live mic: "There aren't any villains in a true crime book. There's the hero, and there's his victims." Everybody in the room laughed. It left a bad taste in my mouth.

I swim against the tide on this when I can, within the limitations of my word count and the known parameters of my readership's attention span. At the same time, you don't want to make saints out of everybody: there are plenty of murder victims who, while they certainly didn't deserve to die any more than anybody else does, weren't exactly blameless in their lives. Everybody's complicated. I try to cleave to this precept. It usually pays off, and it hasn't been a particularly hard habit to keep, because it seems self-evident to me.

Once, in *Savage Coast*, I wrote about a rich family. I remember telling an interviewer after it came out that I'd had "fun" writing it, which I immediately regretted. The book detailed grisly crimes with real human cost; people who have more to lose often make bigger messes. They've never had to clean up after themselves.

It was my third book. The title came from a Randall Jarrell poem, a modern retelling of one of the Greek tragedies— brothers and sisters are always locked in battle to the death when it comes to the old masters, who invariably rise to their theme once the killing starts. I'd read the poem in college: I was up late one night trying to cram as much of the required reading as I could into the twenty-four hours before the final exam, but there'd been no way to understand the action without slowing my pace. To extract anything worth using from the poem, I'd had to read it out loud. It became a sort of self-hypnosis.

I was all by myself in the dorm, late spring in my sleepy Central California town, somewhere between midnight and dawn, caught up in a vision so vast that its import seemed to outstrip the drier themes of the class (Revenge Among the Ancients: it was an elective). A brother was sailing to an island to kill his sister, I still wasn't clear why; she'd become a priestess since they'd last laid eyes on one another, and her acolytes were now laying hold to her brother to bring him to the altar, where she would dispatch him with great and brutal ceremony.

> How strange to stand like a child, and tremble
> At a headless body—one more head
> To stuff and smoke and set on an empty stake;
> And if in the long nights of the long winter
> It still stares at you with its aching smile,
> And when you name it, and lean to it longingly,
> Its eyes seem to cloud in the firelight
> And it turns from you, slowly, in the stinging smoke—
> What is it but one more head?

In *Savage Coast* I tried to let Alan Halprin speak for himself. Son and presumptive heir to wealthy parents, he'd anticipated a windfall when his parents died; but his sister, Jessica, suffered from delusions, and couldn't take care of herself. So they'd left her the estate, a sprawling neo-baroque complex overlooking the Pacific; it had been their opinion that hospitals were beneath her. The will further stipulated that a nurse stay on the property with her, although whether she genuinely required acute care became an important question at her trial.

To Alan, they'd bequeathed any cash left over; to them, this seemed like a fair division of the estate, but he decamped immediately to Hollywood, quickly squandering half his inheritance on cars and dead-end investments. The remaining half ought to have been plenty, and he might have done well for himself, but he could also see the more likely end awaiting him: dwindling assets, work for hire.

So he drove back to his childhood home in a Spider Veloce he'd paid for in cash, and there he lay in wait, hidden by the riotous coastal overgrowth. He'd brought along a pickax in his JanSport backpack. He crushed the nurse's head when she came out one morning to water the zinnias; the first blow knocked her down, and the second one finished the job. But he hadn't counted on his sister's increasingly paranoid state; all the knives in the kitchen had been transferred to her dresser drawers, and she made short work of Alan when he came in through the back door: quietly, she thought, but not quietly enough.

The court was more sympathetic to Jessica than to Alan. The prosecution brought out huge blowups of the nurse's shattered skull: hers had been a senseless death. It was an easy case to take sides in. A sick woman stalked by a jealous brother, an act of self-defense.

This had been enough to keep the jury from dwelling too long on the hideous list of indignities she'd visited upon her brother's body over the next several weeks: the police don't sniff around the mansions of the wealthy, so she'd had plenty of time alone with the body before anyone's suspicions had been aroused. The long days she'd spent in the estate, enacting further mutilations upon the pliant cadaver at leisure until, an artist completing her work, she finally dismembered it, were awful to contemplate. To understand the particulars, I felt, was to feel pity for the person who had borne the brunt of them.

So I wrote *Savage Coast* in part to speak up for Alan, who was no prize, but whose death meant that one person's story had never been told. It's how my mother raised me: I think of the candle maker who wants to be king. I try to let him at least hold the keys to the castle in his hand, even if he never gains entry.

But as my time atop the foundations of Devil House grew longer, my long-cultivated stances toward victim and perp, as they call them at the conventions, began to pull at their moorings. It was an uneasy feeling for me. I resisted it, but I followed the facts where they led: to the other bodies, to the neighborhoods in which they'd lived and died, to the streets beyond them and the highway above. Measure, measure again, then cut. It's what you're supposed to do, if you're honest.

7.

FOUR BLACK-AND-WHITES PULL UP in front of the building at exactly 4:30 a.m. It's November 2, 1986: in bigger towns, Halloween parties probably are still going strong, but here it's quiet. An onlooker, in the dark, might take the garish graffiti all down the door that faces the street as seasonal decoration, an invitation to trick-or-treaters who might otherwise skip the house by the freeway. But as the arriving officers begin to ascend the porch steps, they take note of the devastation around them, which is general.

Broken bottles are planted out front, jagged sides up. It's like something out of an old cartoon but for the stench, which you can't miss: these are Thunderbird and Ripple empties, their cheery upside-down labels like distress flags, raised foil highlights glistening in the dark. Mingling with their winey sweetness is a smell of fresh soot: vaguely runic shapes have been burned onto the concrete walkway. Off to one corner, atop a broomstick jutting up from a patch of grass at an angle, there's a mannequin's head, its hair scorched to the roots, its eyes painted matte-purple. If this particular detail is meant to scare people away, it's strangely positioned: only one officer sees it going in, but the later inventory confirms his impression.

Across the steps that lead to the front door, someone's scattered dozens of small animal bones—chicken, fish—and these, as boots advance across them, break the carefully observed quiet with a chorus of loud snaps. Everyone freezes, on the lookout for traps; but no lights go on inside the building, and no sounds come from within. The team leader waves two officers around to the back of the house, where there's a door that used to be an employee entrance; it's padlocked, but the wood is warped and splintered. Anybody could easily kick it open from either side.

The remaining two officers stand guard near the patrol car—it's only paces from the scene; the lot is small—their guns drawn in case anyone tries to run. From their position, these two have the best view of the proceedings. They get only seconds to take it all in: the element of surprise is indispensable in a raid. In the glint of the streetlight, they note that the planks of the porch have been painted in alternating colors—red, black, two reds, another black, recurring voids in a crimson field. On the front door, silver paint: a pentagram inside a circle that heralds a riot of words in red that bleed over into the door-frame and onto the outer siding both right and left:

SICK SATAN SENTRAL FAITHFUL 4EVER! BY THIS

SIGHN CONQUER BY THESE LIGHTS COME TO

SEE

Beneath the door, where a welcome mat might be, two great bloodshot lidded eyes, painted by a hurried hand, pupils misty purple: two coats of paint, color over primer, to make them pop. The eyes look to their right, toward the vacant lot below the freeway, away from the overgrown side yard.

When, seconds from now, the battering ram breaks down the front door and floodlight fills the room, the scene that greets the team claims its intended effect: believers and nonbe-lievers alike are temporarily frozen in their tracks. Half-melted action figures, hulking blobs of plastic or rubber, hang from light fixtures, their heads shapeless or snapped off at the neck. Mirrors and jagged pieces of mirror, some painted with slogans like the ones from the front door, dot racks that once held only porn: many of the old VHS housings and magazines are still there, defaced, and joined now by comic books or scarecrow-like figures hand-twisted from old newspaper, their feet jammed between spindles to hold them steady.

Where the racks give way to a clearing, in the middle of the room, yellow DO NOT CROSS tape has been affixed to the floor around what seems at first to be the outline of a body. Trained eyes catch as much as they can from the information overload confronting them. Through their protective visors, each member of the team begins screaming, in his own rhythm and pitch: *POLICE! GET ON THE GROUND!*

Someone thinks they see something move; shots, a riot of fireworks, sound out loud enough to cause immediate ringing in the whole team's ears. Later, having recovered evidence, detectives will claim in their report that several officers saw a figure in the shadows hoisting a sword with both hands.

I see this figure clearly in my mind's eye, but, in truth, none of the bullets fired that night find purchase: they ricochet off the walls and blow through cardboard VHS cases, but they don't hurt anybody who wasn't already past hurt.

†††

MY NAME IS GAGE CHANDLER. I've been here for almost a year. I moved into this house to tell a story: to employ my usual and usually successful methods to the task. To inhabit the carapace of the crime scene, to retrace the steps of the killer in order to better know his path. I have spoken with my neighbors, and with police, and with any surviving relatives willing to speak with me. I went to the high school and talked with the teachers; I talked with a caseworker, Marsha Gaines, who worked with Seth. Anyone who knew Derrick and could still be located, I have found, making contact and never once taking no for an answer: I've charmed people when I could, playing up Hollywood friends when I had to, always finding a way to get them to talk. I did this with everybody. I gained access to police files and court records. I reenacted scenes I wasn't present for. I've unrolled butcherblock for days, drawing maps and diagrams and flowcharts to show me how things looked before I came here, and to light a path toward my rebuilding of the fortress that stood here for a brief time before it was made new, and then made new again, cloaked in fresh paint by people who'd like to erase 1986 from this neighborhood's memory. I have surrounded myself with artifacts to keep the earlier days of this place vivid before me, to push back against the advancing crust of renovation. I have conjured the past in order to know more of the present. I know what happened here, and how what happened here differs in several important ways from the fragment Ashton unearthed for me, and what will happen if those differences are brought back out into the light. What I've learned contradicts the account I first read, which I understand to have sprung from the need for a certain sort of telling, a hunger for known quantities. I have combed every inch of the ground where something dreadful happened some years back, and it is time now for me to tell the story I was sent here to tell.

I don't want to do this, and I'm not going to do this.

2

The White Witch

1.

YOU BUY *EVERYDAY WITCHCRAFT* at Jordano's on impulse one day: a Sunday, your shopping day. You plan to cook for yourself tonight and every night this week until Friday, when you'll treat yourself to some restaurant with a view of the bay—maybe you'll invite a friend out, unwinding at the end of a long week, or maybe not. From here, Friday is a world away.

Idling happily through the busy supermarket, you pick out small yellow potatoes and bagged carrots from the produce section, then find some canned tuna you'll fix with noodles and sauce during the week. You get a loaf of bread, and some plum jam; at the deli counter, you ask the high school student in the smudged white smock to slice you a quarter pound of pastrami. He does a slapstick pantomime routine with the slicer as he works, pretending it's harder to operate than it really is, grimacing once as though hurt, watching your face over his shoulder to see how you'll react. You play along, opening your eyes wide and raising a free hand in mock-panic. He cracks up. When students see their teachers walking around in the real world, it always seems funny to them.

"Didn't figure you for the pastrami type!" he says when he hands you the package in white butcher paper, wrapped and taped on the seal with its price written in red grease pencil.

"No?" you say. "What type am I?" He scrutinizes you theatrically, squinting with one eye, pretending to inspect your face from several angles. You place his name: Scott. Scott from composition class last year. He'll be a senior now.

"Turkey on whole wheat," he says. You laugh together, on equal ground or something like it. It's amazing how they grow up right in front of you: kids when you meet them, little men when they leave. From the freezer case, you get fish sticks and a quart of strawberry ice cream; and then, waiting in line, you begin your weekly dance of resistance with the pocket-sized booklets nested in the rack above the chewing gum: *Prophecies and Predictions*; *50 Different Casseroles!*; *Strange Tragedies of the Silver Screen*. And then, next to these, *Everyday Witchcraft*, the one that's caught your eye today because its front cover seems so weird: a picture of a white cat sitting next to a crystal ball on a table draped in black velvet cloth—felt, most likely. The scene clearly staged in a photographer's studio somewhere. It's funny, in an out-of-place way. You drop it casually into the basket, as if it had been the last thing on your shopping list: fish sticks, ice cream, book of spells. It looks pretty hilarious among the vegetables and cold cuts. You smile, not too big, waiting your turn in line.

In your life, the rhythm of these little routines is like the gentle path of a ditch creek: predictable movement through unremarkable straits most days, but with enough small surprises in it to make it feel worthy of the space it takes up. For the creek, a surprising chorus of frogs on a summer night, or the sudden appearance of an improvised waterfall built with rocks by local kids; for you, an unexpected conversation, or a small purchase on impulse, a little byway brought to you by chance and peripheral vision. You learned these rhythms from your mother: where to hear them, how to spot the signs of their presence, how to honor the code by declining to name it. She'd always been like that, keeping to-do lists in her head rather than writing them down, never talking up the usefulness of her habits or trying to impose them on her daughter, speaking few rules aloud but making the ones she valued manifest in her manner. She left room in the routine for variation. The practice spoke for itself. It made home a place worth returning to every day.

This recipe made of you a person who could do as she wished, but whose wishes were usually modest; because even small wishes, once gained, seemed to make such lovely ripples in the life you've assembled for yourself. No fate but the one chosen lightly; no destiny but the present moment. In 1972, you were an early bloom in a hedge about to run riot, a deep red bloom with pastel accents at the edges of the petals. Not many in your own life noticed what you were; the first signs of dawn are reserved for those who keep watch. But the practice was enough for you. "I've always wanted just to be myself," you might have said during the self-help craze of the 1970s, at some encounter group, say. "That's always seemed like a pretty high calling, just the challenge of it, really," you might have said to this imagined gathering, which came to be plentiful near where you had lived: in houses with wooden back decks and garden torches, some even with swimming pools and bars for four or five at poolside. "I feel like what I'm always doing is just learning what it means to be who I am," you might have said as the evening wore on, the hum of conversation at poolside and tangy pink wine in a glass, good friends in the warm dusk, Central California on a summer evening like few places on earth: they say that the Greek islands feel like this. Or parts of Italy. Crete. Magic places whose names call out from deep in the imagination. Places everybody hopes to see someday.

People who're lucky enough to be from such places sometimes lose sight of the blessing. You never did. You kept it at your fingertips, right there where you'd be able to call it up at any moment, in the slightest of circumstances. You held it right there near the surface all your life, right up to the end. And when the end came, they called you the White Witch: because of the beaded macramé plant holders hanging from hooks in your apartment, and the God's-eye in the window, and the leaded crystal prism on the sill; and because of the bracelets you were known to wear to work, for example at the ends of the loose, long sleeves of your beige turtleneck, sometimes as many as six or seven bracelets all together on one wrist, jangling or rattling depending on the material: silver, or Bakelite, or amber, or jade, or plain plastic; and because of those small booklets you'd been unable to resist at the checkout counter, Fawcett publications that retailed for forty-nine cents apiece. There were always four small racks of them at eye level, just above the bigger tabloids, which you found gauche—*who buys this stuff?*—but the booklets were cute: *Predictions 1973*; *Hollywood After Dark*; *Everyday Witchcraft*. They found these three in the junk drawer of your kitchen during the preliminary investigation, on a chaotic afternoon when a reporter from the *Telegram-Tribune*, who had a friend inside the department, stopped by to see what he could see.

You weren't there at the time. You were down at the station, answering questions patiently. They would hold it against you later, how patient you were with their questions, how forth-coming you'd been with the details when pressed. But you hadn't been there to playact: to perform some ridiculous act of penance for what you'd done, to begin laying ground for exten-uating circumstances. You weren't there because you were tor-mented by your conscience and wanted to come clean, and you weren't there to offer excuses or alibis.

You were there because of the tides.

2.

YOU'RE AT WORK. There are only three weeks left in the school year; there's no single word in the English language precise enough to describe the atmosphere on campus when it gets this close to summer break. There's electricity in the air, but it's tempered by languor, the promise of lazy days ahead, of long warm mornings with no to-do lists attached; there's excite-ment, but it's checked by an impending sense of loss among the seniors; there's hope, but there's also suspicion.

It's different for the teachers. You feel friendly today, even toward the ones you don't usually get along with; you say good morning to them, and they say good morning right back, their voices light, ready for the long-promised unburdening. This promise is visible in the steadily accumulating big red Xs on May calendars all around the halls of the social sciences build-ing; your time together in these cramped quarters is running out, for this year, anyway.

Someone's made the coffee; there's no set rotation for the task, and some days the pot sits clean and empty until after Advisory, almost certainly a symbol of unvoiced petty resent-ments: *I made it yesterday, it's somebody else's job today.* But this morning, you catch the rich, bright scent as soon as you enter the building; it feels part of that early-summer charm today, a general enchantment in the air. You take down a cup—one of many hanging from hooks on a fiberboard rack; these are the unclaimed cups, left behind, possibly, at this very time of year by teachers whose contracts weren't renewed, or who moved elsewhere, or who retired—and, filling it, flash briefly on your station.

You are young: you're older than your students, but not so much older as they seem to think you are. You're certainly not older than anybody else in Humanities; the two other history teachers are from different generations, their hair short and greying, their shirts starched. But they're not stuffy: you've been here four years now, and you've come to see your trio as the intellectual wing of the department. Mr. Leavitt teaches both the general and advanced placement sections of U.S. government. His students reflexively defer to him; his presence in the classroom demands it without requiring any extra effort on his part. Soon he'll retire, and his replacement will almost surely come from the new breed of teachers, the ones who want to be their students' friend.

Mr. Grenning, who teaches the non-elective economics class every college-bound student is automatically enrolled in at the beginning of senior year, seems like a man from a different age. Whether that age has passed or is off somewhere in the hazy future is difficult to say. His dress is stern, his glasses stark and horn-rimmed, and he parts his hair to the left with a careful comb and a little oil: it's Vitalis, you can't miss it. But his manner is gentle, and his eyes have a dreamy cast to them that's lost on the kids, but not on you. Sometimes you find yourselves lunching together, both brown-bagging it: there's a general-use table for lunch and breaks in the lounge, an ash-tray in the middle of it, almost always half-full.

Today, you sit together briefly before heading off to your morning sections; he reads the paper. He looks up to ask if you're going to the year-end potluck next week, always held ahead of finals to boost attendance—when the grading of exams has begun and the specter of commencement exercises looms, people tend to start making excuses.

"Yes, but I can't think of what to bring," you say.

"Dibs on the deviled eggs," he says. "Wouldn't want to break with tradition."

"'Tradition!'" you sing, not too loud but clenching your fist dramatically: the drama department has just closed out their year with *Fiddler on the Roof*, and the teachers all attended opening night.

"Your predecessor used to bring a Crock-Pot full of Swedish meatballs every year," he says, smiling warmly, his eyes on yours: he's old enough to be your dad, there's nothing untoward in his look unless affection between colleagues is strictly off-limits, which it isn't. These are changing times. The hippies still talk as though older people had nothing to say worth hearing; but when you're talking to Peter Grenning, you feel glad about your place between extremes. You're not too square, but you're skipping the protest. You're casual, but you're certainly not a slob.

"You've mentioned it!" you say, laughing. Last June, around the same time and certainly at this same table, he'd pined aloud for the days of Mollie Brunhardt's Swedish meatballs until you'd taken the hint. Finding a recipe in an old cookbook from the library, you gave it a test run a few days ahead of time; on the morning of the potluck, you made a few final adjustments to make the dish your own. It came out light, and tangy, and delicious; everyone came back for seconds.

"Well, they'd certainly go well with my deviled eggs," he'd said, rising; it was time for class. "I'll see you later!" You nod, following him out: the hallways are humming with young bodies, bustling at their lockers, chattering like squirrels. At the end of the school year, you take stock of how much youthful energy you've absorbed, and it feels like a real accomplishment. You wonder how you made it all the way to the end. Everything ought to be as free and easy as planning potlucks with Peter Grenning, you think, idly. Maybe someday.

†††

THERE'S NO NEED TO CALL roll this close to the end of the semester—you can do it just by looking around the classroom and seeing which desks are empty. But classroom routines resist variation, rightly, you think; you consider them valuable in and of themselves. They're known rhythms. As you stand at the head of the class, reciting names whose order is a mystery known only to the massive computer that prints them out in a room it gets all to itself over in the administration building, you note that variances the students introduce to break the monotony are, themselves, now part of the score:

"Michael Adams?"

"Here."

"Jason Fenton?"

"Present." Two stray giggles, pebbles down an empty well.

"Anne Higgs?"

"Here."

"Gene Cupp?" Nothing. "Gene Cupp?"

You know he isn't here; you look over to his friend Jesse,

who raises his eyes from their focus on a threadbare spot in the knee of his jeans just long enough to shrug.

Gene hasn't been here in over a week. No one answers at his house when the secretary calls to report his truancy. No one seems to care about Gene enough to say what's become of him, not even his friend, who must know, but who sits with his eyes averted, patiently waiting for the moment to pass.

You know how Jesse feels, you think. You remember. You became a high school teacher because you hoped always to keep the days of your youth close at hand: days when your desire to help others pricked at you like a thorn. From an early age, you'd been in love with the world: there was so much in it, a life so full of surprises if you only stayed open to them, ready to receive the transmissions when they came. A devotee of the chance encounter, the found pleasure, the happy accident, your eyes always open, trying to spread some of your inner light around: that was you, the you everyone knew. You cheered up every room you entered when you were a child; your mother, in her plea for clemency, said you had always been "the best part of anybody's day."

How the press ran away with that one! In those days before cable TV, it was harder for a local killing to get national traction, but your mother's letter proved so easy to contrast with the details of your crime that columnists from as far east as Baltimore found it impossible to resist. "She was not the best part of Jesse Jenkins's day, however dire a piece of work he may have been," read an unsigned editorial that ran in the *Sun* while the world waited out your sentencing phase; its headline was "The Good Person Fallacy." "She wasn't the best part of Gene Cupp's, either."

They were wrong about that. It's in the nature of the news cycle to untangle knots and to cast the duller threads aside: to simplify a narrative so that readers can take in a few details, confirm opinions they probably already held, and move on at minimal cost to themselves. But the weight of the evidence about you shows that you'd often been not only the best thing about Jesse Jenkins's day, but possibly the only good thing in it. Today, for example, Jesse's been riding the nostalgic waves that seem to float down the halls this time of year, but for him nostalgia is the portal into horror. When you wait hopefully for his friend Gene to reply, "Here," it gives him a good feeling. A good feeling is sometimes enough.

Jesse's childhood had been awful: he was five years old the first time he told a teacher about the "whippings" his father doled out whenever he got angry. That teacher reported it to the police, who then visited the Jenkins house in a black-and-white car. The officers came away half an hour later with a noncommittal report that they wrote up dutifully, filed, and forgot: *no bruises noted on upper or lower extremities, child denies c/o*, runs a piece of it, this abbreviation at the end borrowed from medical charts and misunderstood to mean "complaints" rather than "complains of." This misuse, quite common, points toward the actual purpose of reports like these: they're mainly marks on paper, things to have on file in case somebody gets called to account for something later.

But no one did get called to account for leaving five-year-old Jesse Jenkins at the home of his father. Hardly anybody knew until later. Most of what we learned later about Jesse's life at home came from his mother, Jana; her testimony against you during the trial's sentencing phase, delivered in a wandering, looping monologue, seemed, at times, more likely to win you clemency than condemnation. It wasn't Jesse's fault that he was the way he was, she said. His father made him that way. He was a good boy once, but I could never handle him after he turned twelve, she said. But he didn't deserve to die like a dog, she said finally, in audible pain, and then she said it again. My son did not deserve to die like a dog.

The blow landed in your gut; by then you'd had plenty of time to think about the kid who'd known nothing but violence his whole short life, the kid shrugging gently this morning and possibly sharing a gentle moment of concern with you, but possibly not. Need; warmth; the suggestion of a secret. Later, you would wonder.

You wonder a little now, too, here in the present moment, but there are also twenty other kids to worry about. You mean to try to ask Jesse privately after class about Gene. Someone should ask someone about Gene.

But Jesse is gone when the bell rings: the stampede for the door has lost the urgency it maintained for most of the year, but it's still a stampede. Tomorrow. You will ask him tomorrow.

3.

DESPITE THE NAME by which you'll come to be known in the press, you don't actually live in Morro Bay. The high school where you teach is there, but rents are cheaper over here in Los Osos. It's a beautiful place now: it will remain one, though the accelerating world devours what it catches up with, and the Los Osos of the future will be built in large part atop the foundations of places still standing during your time on the outside. It's California. Nothing lasts.

The housetops are mainly flat around here—a Mediterranean architectural instinct, the feeling that there's no need to overdecorate—and there's landscaping on the sides of all the driveways, big bottlebrush bushes and night-blooming jasmine. Your building, which will be an anachronism on the distant day when the renovation crew arrives, is modern. Round windows dot its oversized cedar shingles, the hint of a dream in which houses can float. At the far end of the parking lot, there's a gymnasium-sized building; it houses an Olympic-sized swimming pool, and a hot tub, too—the sort of amenity that makes visitors from the east feel in the presence of some new decadence, one whose excesses derive not from wealth or status, but from the brute opulence of the landscape. The shore, the dunes; the sunlight on the ocean; the unvanquishable oleander up and down the highway, the coast live oak with its twisting branches like segments of brain cortex wriggling up from the ground. They set a scene, these views, pulling into the parking lot of Oakside Court, the apartment complex you call home, such as it is: modest on the inside but almost regal on the outside. In the right light, toward the end of the day with its windows glinting in the sun, it can resemble a Spanish medieval fortress set against the ocean, the stories of ages safely tucked away inside.

Its name sounds like a vague promise of luxury living, but it's still cheap in 1972. However grand the visions of its landscapers, nobody local sees it and thinks, *That's where the rich people live*. They know better. Your near neighbors down the hallway, in fact, are graduate students and new divorcées, people trying to live in as nice a place as they can afford while looking forward to something better. You know each other—from the parking lot, from the hallway, from the pool. Next door, in Apartment 9, there's Thomas, a dairy tech student cutting corners until he can finish his master's degree; across the hall, in 8, there's Don, whose wife served him with divorce papers last fall. He's seldom here on weekends anymore. It's a good time to be a bachelor in America.

The others, around the corner, you know by name and face only: Gladys, who looks too young to have her own apartment and also too young to be named Gladys; Milt, who looks to be your age; and an older man you call "Mr. Adler" even though he always corrects you: "Call me Max."

"Right! Max," you say. He smiles.

"Good to see you, Miss Crane," he says with a genuinely harmless wink as you turn the key in your door, opening onto the small world you've made of the interior of your apartment.

There will be much talk, in days to come, about the interior of your apartment.

††††

SOME PEOPLE ARE COLLECTORS. They seek outstanding examples of things tailored to specific interests: a bust of the Frankenstein monster, production run unknown, sold through the mail in the early sixties and now seldom seen except at yard sales; issue #9 of *Vampirella*, with the cover story and art by Wally Wood; Japanese swords from specific dynasties. These are destined for display cases, most often, or for boxes in the garage should things get out of hand. Collectors are curators: they arrange their finds with a specific purpose in mind, even if it's only, *Look how much of this stuff I have all to myself.*

You're not a collector. Like anybody else, you decorate your home with personal touches, things that might give a guest an idea or two about who you are; but here, as in all things, you've tried to embrace chance a little, to let your whims speak for themselves. Decorations are as likely to have entered your house by accident as by design, and few of them last longer than a season or two. They get donated to church bazaars when you're done with them; you like to imagine the former things of your daily routine going on to new lives about which you'll never know a thing. Should thieves besiege your apartment tomorrow, there isn't much you'd miss.

Take, for example, this gnarled chunk of driftwood later marked *Exhibit 3-B* by the prosecution. It caught your eye one morning at the shoreline: you were looking down, and you thought you saw a miniature canoe, possibly an abandoned child's toy. It was an elongated arc of wood about a third the length of your arm, twisting a little midway through; but something had eaten dozens of holes in it: Insects? Tiny sea worms? Some pattern of accelerated decay brought on by long immersion in water?

Whatever the cause, the surface of the wood had been so thoroughly riddled that its composition was now more air than solid substance. What remained of the wood was a memory of its former condition, a reminder of its own past. You held it in your hand for the rest of your morning walk, and then it sat on your coffee table for a month, until you burned a steak one night and, needing something to mask the smell, remembered those tiny holes and thought of a use for them.

In a drawer, you located sticks of incense, also chance accumulations, fished from a glass case near the cash register of a San Luis Obispo record store by a clerk who cracked a smile when he asked: "Anything else?" The incense sat alongside pot pipes and hippie jewelry. The smile was because you didn't look like the type.

But it appealed to your taste for hidden things. Its packaging was musty paper lettered from top to bottom in tiny clusters of italic text, devotional outpourings you sometimes skimmed but never really *read*: quotations from the *Bhagavad Gita* and the Upanishads, something called the Ten Virtues of Koh that delineated the specific benefits of burning incense; and, from Second Chronicles, this passage:

> Every morning and evening they burn to the LORD burnt offerings and fragrant incense, and the showbread is set on the clean table, and the golden lampstand with its lamps is ready to light every evening; for we keep the charge of the LORD our God, but you have forsaken Him.

Two packages, Celestial Sandalwood and Dragon's Blood, sit open on the kitchen counter behind your ad hoc censer. The sandalwood is a disappointment: it smells like men's deodorant. But the other one's sweet. You think you might buy another package of it when it's time to replenish the supply, unless you feel like trying out another one with a fancy name: Vrindavan Flowers, or Night Phoenix. Possibly—probably—you will have moved on from incense by then. But, for now, there's the drift-wood and the Dragon's Blood, a sweetly spicy smell that also reminds you a little of vanilla ice cream, just the thing for a lazy Tuesday afternoon.

Beneath the counter, the drawers: this one holds the cut-lery, that one the spatulas and slotted spoons. Across the small space of the kitchen, there's an extra bit of countertop next to the refrigerator—it looks like a space-filling afterthought. The single drawer underneath it stores dishrags and dry sponges; on the wall above it, there's an antique knife rack, another of your serendipitous finds. Who knows how old this knife rack is? You found it at a yard sale for seventy-five cents; it was quite dirty, and probably long past its proper days of usage. But it was hand-painted, and you can never resist old hand-painted things, though it feels like the rest of the world is running out of patience with their kind.

The rack is painted matte-white with a little insignia of an iris in the center. It always takes your eye a minute to resolve on the stylized design of the iris: the three lines making up the stem look like licking flames until you find the four purple brushstrokes ingeniously placed atop, which might also be a dog, or a fox, or some flying creature carrying something dead in its mouth. But they're a flower. Once you see it, finding it becomes a known route, a path to a familiar place. It cost you less than a dollar, and hardly anyone will ever comment on it, which is exactly the sort of thing you like. The knives it holds come from all over: estate sales, hand-me-downs; only two were bought new, the oyster shucker and the butcher knife. There's a store with kitchen gadgets in a galleria over in San Luis Obispo, and you stopped in one day. These two were on sale for half price, and their wooden handles looked so supple and otherworldly. Carbon steel from Japan. You knew a bargain when you saw it.

Your sink is stainless steel, dull and practical; it would be too small for a family. You keep it clean, and you have a small vase for flowers off to the side of it. Flowers make everything nicer. There's no dishwasher in this kitchen; the oldest piece of furniture in the house is the refrigerator, its handle thick and rounded, a relic of the early space age. The remaining cabinets hold a few matching white plates and bowls, and a single unmatching ceramic bowl that gets more use than any of them. When you live alone, no matter how lovingly you decorate your space, you come to rely on the things that serve you best. *This* coffee cup, *that* spoon, this rustic beige bowl that's a little heavier than the others.

The counter overlooks the living room; your space is continuous. The living room walls, forever a work in progress, are a riot of movement in your care: like a teenager, you've put up anything that catches your fancy, adding and removing according to your whim. Today, the center of attention is a drawing of a shield bearing the image of a unicorn, ballpoint and felt tip on lined paper, artist unknown though you have your suspicions: your students' desks at school have brown metal pockets attached to the frames, and every day things get left behind. On your desk, at the front of the class, there's a lost-and-found basket to which you occasionally draw the class's attention. But no one had claimed the unicorn shield, even though the curves of its emblem seemed a labor of love, the mane especially, dozens of gentle curves with real motion to them. Potential, you want to say. Maybe something more. Other teachers complained about students doodling in class, but you understood that attention works in funny ways, and considered a find like this evidence that your students were comfortable enough with you to let their imaginations venture outward a little in your presence. So you brought it home, and affixed it to the living room wall with clear tape: a crest for your chambers, an insignia to mark them as your own.

On the day next week when your living room gets photographed, the unicorn shield will still be sharing wall space with a mounted panel from Beatrix Potter's *The Story of a Fierce Bad Rabbit*—the page showing the nice, gentle rabbit who nibbles a carrot—and an inexpensively framed publicity portrait of Myrna Loy in *The Gypsy Minx*, her knee drawn up to her chin as she sits on a rough-hewn bench attached to a tree, playing solitaire or possibly reading tarot. Her eyes meet the camera: she's almost smiling, her mouth closed. The shot feels electric. They had something special, the stars of the silent age. Every expression had to contain multiple shades, to stand in for all the missing words and inflections. It's easy to read a lot into a single frame.

†††

IT WILL ALWAYS SEEM CRASS TO ME to enter your bedroom. Nothing that ever happened in here is anybody's business: not the judge's, not the jury's, certainly not mine. But investigations turn up what they're bound to turn up. It's the way of things, and besides, once we're inside the building, there really isn't any point in leaving stones unturned. So many investigations run aground precisely because somebody overlooked something—out of carelessness, yes, but also from misplaced ideas about propriety, or fruitless reverence. It's good to respect the dead, and to stay out of the way of an investigation in progress: but it's also good, when the dust has settled—on the grave, on the desks of the investigating detectives—to widen the lens, to take in the bigger picture.

Still, I cringe reading through the testimony of Albert N., called to the stand in support of the prosecution's theory regarding ritual sacrifice. He is no expert witness; he'd met you at an outdoor concert in a park in the summer, and you'd exchanged numbers. He was almost comically earnest when you met for cocktails one Friday a few weeks later. He spent that Friday night at your apartment. It hadn't been especially memorable or regrettable for either of you—this was a new age—and you'd parted amiably, hardly thinking of it later. Under questioning, asked to describe the wall-hanging in the bedroom, he first says it was "a tie-dye thing"; pressed, he recalls the design:

It was like—and I don't want to say this is what it was, *be-*

cause it was sort of abstract, you know? But to me it looked like a spider.

A spider? the DA asks, as recorded in the trial transcript. *Do you mean a small—you know—a small spider like you'd see around the house?*

No, sir. It took up the whole middle of the—

—of the tapestry.

—the tapestry, right. Or the sheet. Like, it was just a purple-colored sheet with a giant shape in the middle that looked to me like a spider.

The prosecution moves to introduce Exhibit 3-L, says the DA. It's a batik wall-hanging. Albert N. is right: it's an abstraction, the sort of thing an artistic child, under pressure to describe his work to a schoolteacher, might call "a design." There are craze-lines like the cracking finish on an old guitar all over it; at its center, there's a rounded shape where these lines seem thicker, six of them uniformly segmented, angling in toward the center from either side.

It's not a spider. It's an accident. You don't belong to an order of witches that venerates the spider, and the batik wall-hanging isn't in your bedroom because you think the spider will afford you protection from enemies. You bought it at some crafts festival in a park, and it looked like a pinwheel to you, and you hung it up in your bedroom.

How, in this age, are grown-ups still afraid of a witch? Spells, curses, bloody sacrifices: none of them really believe in any of that, do they? It's just for fun, that stuff. You had assumed everybody knew that. It seemed obvious, self-evident. There aren't any witches. There are just the stories people tell each other, who knows why. But when you finally go to trial, almost a whole year from now, you'll learn better, and feel trapped. Four days from now you'll do what you have to do, and, when your story is assembled by the powers that have agreed to do the telling, meaningless details will be woven into a tale that would seem absurd to everyone if they weren't all proceeding backward from its bloody end.

The wall-hanging is long gone by the time I set foot in your old apartment, of course, and so is the God's-eye you'd thumb-tacked above your window frame. Times have changed. It's hard for me to imagine something like it here in the college student's bedroom where I stand, years later, trying to picture you and Albert N. one Saturday morning in 1972, a meaning-less shape overlooking the scene like an omen neither you nor your weekend lover were capable of heeding. Laurie, the student who lives here now, stands in the room with me, waiting for me to leave; I'm only here by her good grace. I am an intruder trying to see what the intruders before me saw just before they saw nothing ever again.

You can't do this kind of work unless you're willing to be an intruder once in a while.

†††

IT'S MORNING: Wednesday. It's a little grey today, those coastal clouds that cast long shadows and then usually clear out while you're checking on the traffic in your rearview. You drive to school with the expectation that things will conform to their observed pattern: it shouldn't really rain today, you think. But it does; the warm asphalt of the high school parking lot smells sweet, the rain splashing hazily on it as you walk, purse held in both hands over your head, to class.

You call roll; no Gene Cupp again. On your desk, to re-mind yourself, you leave the attendance book open, and it distracts you throughout the period. Are the kids distracted, too, by this meaningless variance in the expected order? Do they even notice the studied tidiness of your desk, how it looks the same each day? Probably not; they're kids, you think, and when you hear yourself think it, you notice how easily the thought comes to you now. Your first year as a teacher, you struggled to think of students as people living in a different world from yours: you still felt young, just as you still feel young today. Just no longer *that* young.

Teaching high school means facing daily reminders of the exact distance between your present-day station and the days of your youth. Some people get a little bitter about it. You haven't yet. You position yourself by the door just before the bell rings, so you'll be able to stop Jesse on his way out without making much of a show of it. Young men are very sensitive about how their teachers treat them when their peers are looking.

"Jesse?" you say as he's about to pass you.

"Miss Crane?" he says, stopping. Several other kids bump him as they pass, without excusing themselves.

"You're friends with Gene."

"Yeah?" He looks suspicious, or scared, you can't tell which.

"Well, I'm a little worried about him. He hasn't been here in over a week."

Jesse purses his lips; he's suppressing a laugh there behind that downy attempt at a mustache.

"I think he's, uh, done," he says.

"Done?"

"Well, they sent him a, an, uh, they said he wasn't going to pass algebra again so he has to do it in the summer if he wants to graduate."

"OK," you say; you feel like it's a delicate moment: you wait to see what else Jesse has to say.

"So, I think he's done," he says again.

"Oh, but he—he shouldn't just quit, there are ways—" You're not sure what to say; you should probably be having this conversation with Gene's parents.

Waiting to see if you're done with your sentence, Jesse watches your face with the sort of curiosity you'd expect from a lepidopterist wondering whether a butterfly he just noticed in a familiar setting is actually new. When he realizes you're waiting for him to answer, he says, sounding a little old for his years: "Oh, I know there are. His old man told him, 'You have to get your diploma,' too. I'll tell him you asked, but—"

"You think he's done."

"Sorry," says Jesse Jenkins, and you hear in his voice what it might sound like if he really felt sorry: it's a distant echo. It is distinctly possible that you are only imagining it.

"Sorry to keep you," you say. "Will you tell him he's welcome in class whether he's going to graduate or not?" You're doing your duty: trying to give your students as much as you can give them in the time allotted to you as their teacher.

"You got it," Jesse says, the way you might promise a child that you're checking for monsters underneath the bed.

4.

YOU ARE SOUND ASLEEP. It's one in the morning. In the parking lot of the Taco Bell over in San Luis Obispo, Gene and Jesse are sitting side by side in the front seat of Gene's blue Ford Torino. Gene is too high to drive, but nobody can tell Gene anything when he's high; Jesse hopes that the bag of tacos they're working through will help him drive less erratically, and then maybe Jesse will mention that Miss Crane said he should come back to class, that it's no big deal.

Taco Bell is closed now; Gene is a cook there, and he worked closing shift tonight. About an hour ago, he turned the OPEN sign around at the window and scraped down the grill, washing the spatulas and serving spoons afterward in the tiny sink in the back. Then he went back to the line and, gloveless, assembled twelve tacos, heavy on the ground beef and light on everything else: any leftover beef he has to throw away, but the lettuce and the olives and the tomatoes and the sour cream will go back into cold storage for the night. If he hits the reserves too hard, he's supposed to charge himself for an extra meal on his time card, so Gene's after-work tacos consist of hours-old seasoned ground beef ladled into a hard shell and given a cursory dressing of two other things apiece, varying it from taco to taco to minimize the amount taken of each ingredient. Sour cream and olives. Tomato and lettuce. Lettuce and olives. Olives and cheese. Some of the combinations don't really taste good at all without the other stuff that'd usually be on there, but Gene doesn't seem to notice. In the front seat, later, a joint in one hand and a Marlboro Red in the other, he identifies each taco by whatever two-topping combination it happened to catch: "You like tomato and cheese? I got two tomato and cheese."

Jesse is scared of Gene these days, who seems to be getting worse. He smokes so many cigarettes. It makes him look like one of those people who hang around outside the public library but never check out any books. He's smoking right now, a sour cream and olive taco in his free hand.

He's talking about moving to Oregon. He does this a lot. Gene's never been there, but one of his dad's biker friends moved to Bend last year: every time he's back in town, he gets drunk with Gene's dad at their kitchen table and talks about how nobody gives a shit what people do up in Oregon. Then, for the next week, without fail, these are the stories Gene relays to Jesse. "All the pussy you can eat up in Medford," he says. "Even the Oregon cops smoke pot," he says. "Super-clean microdot coming out of a lab in Eugene, they sell it to you in little vials, you can just drop it on your tongue and you're flying," he says.

He sticks his tongue out when he says this, pointing at the tip. He's like this all the time now. It's weird and uncomfortable to be around. Jesse doesn't really have any other friends, so he hopes he can be a positive influence on Gene, but, at the same time, his own natural stance is a sort of half-paralyzed neutrality: his positive charge is weak. He likes how hanging out with Gene seems to make him care less about stuff that usually bothers him: moving out, for example. Jesse really wants to get out of his house and live somewhere else, by himself, and he knows he's going to need money to do that: first and last and deposit, that's what everybody says. But to hear Gene tell it, there's a million ways to get first and last and deposit together.

"You just say the word, little brother," he says now, drawing on his cigarette, still chewing. "People act like money is such a big deal, there's a *million* ways to get money. Nicky comes down here with everything he needs in a brown bag and leaves town with *thousands* of dollars. *Thousands*. Sits in the kitchen talking on the phone for maybe ten minutes, some other people come by a little later, and he's good for two months. Three. Barely has to lift a *finger*." Nicky is Gene's dad's biker friend; because Gene's dad's apartment is such a shithole, Jesse wonders if Nicky the biker who lives in Oregon now is exaggerating a little to impress his friend, or if maybe Gene's just making stuff up. It could be either, but there's no point trying to find out, when Gene's like this.

"There's some new apartments over in Los Osos," he continues, Jesse still waiting out the storm. "Not even expensive.

We could talk to Nicky, get the work done, pay all the up-front on one of those, and—shit!—can you even imagine? Right out there on the fucking *bay*. We can totally put this together. Nicky can probably get us a stereo, too, he hooked my dad up with one. Big, loud speakers."

The way Gene talks about his dad paints a picture of a household in which father and son get along famously, but Jesse knows that this is not the case; he doesn't understand why Gene puts so much effort into keeping up this fiction. Gene's father is worse than Jesse's ever was. The magnitude of his presence in Gene's life can hardly be measured. Once, when Jesse was over at Gene's watching television, Gene's dad came into the room, looked at the two teenagers sitting on the floor, and then, to his son, said: "You always gonna be a piece of shit?"

When Gene didn't answer, his father laughed and went back down the hall to the bedroom, where a radio was turned up too loud. The living room with the television is also Gene's bedroom; he sleeps on the couch.

"We should just tell my dad to tell Nicky to find us the biggest speakers he can get," he says now, in the car, wiping his mouth with a handful of napkins. The tacos are gone; he's slowing down a little. "Big honkin' cherrywood housing like in that one magazine, remember? I can get money."

Jesse does not remember that one magazine. There's a part of him that thinks he should try to steer the conversation someplace else, just in case Gene's serious one of these days: there was the time he shot at the windows of Cork 'n' Bottle Liquors with his BB gun. Nothing ever came of it, but it had been frightening, sitting in the passenger seat watching his friend pull the trigger in the dark, the BBs bouncing impotently off the glass, leaving a bunch of little marks. But the greater part of Jesse is too numb to act. It's how he is.

"I know exactly where I can get money," Gene says, his gaze out in the oleander that edges the parking lot.

† † †

YOU'RE HAVING LUNCH. There are seven class periods per school day, each teacher carrying a six-class load: you're expected to take lunch at the same time the students do, after fifth period, and to spend a floating open period either grading papers or holding office hours. Some teachers try to game their schedules to allow them to either sleep in or clock out early, but this year you've opted for the long lunch: fifth period's your off period. You could drive home if you wanted, as long as you kept track of the time—you wear a wristwatch from Japan, a Seiko. Its face glints so brightly in the sun—you could use it to flag down a plane. But then, just as you're clearing the parking lot, you think: *What about fish and chips. Sam's. Why not?*

The drive along the water today is hypnotic in its beauty: the sun, the sea, the brush growing along the roadside blurring green and reddish brown at forty-five miles an hour. It was drives like this that led you to buy the convertible: other teachers tease you about it a little. It's a Mustang with plenty of wear on it—the newer models all look cooler to the kids, and the older ones won't be considered collectibles until long after your name's passed into legend. You bought it used last year; it's a little like an oversized hat on you. Kids who see you driving do a double-take: *Is that Miss Crane? With the top down?* You relish these reactions. They keep you feeling young.

Sam's sits directly on the bay; they have a seal in a tank on their boardwalk, which is a little sad, but the seal himself seems happy enough, and you'd never get to see one close up otherwise. They sell raw fish you can throw to him. Sometimes he snaps it right out of the air. But today you don't buy him any fish, because he's lazing on the concrete that abuts the tank; you don't want to wake him up. He looks so peaceful, as long as you don't think about the ocean and about how he has to smell sea breeze all day without ever getting to swim in the sea.

You've brought the *Telegram-Tribune* with you, and you do the crossword while you wait for your lunch, gazing out at the bay when you're stuck for an answer. You finish about half the puzzle waiting, and then the food comes: the breading is a little heavy, but crisp, and the chips are steaming hot. When the waiter asks if you want more water, you ask if they have 7 Up; when he says, "Sure," you smile like a little kid who's just learned about Christmas presents: "I'll have that, then," you say.

We know about this because the waiter remembered.

†††

THE DRIVE BACK to school is even better than the drive out—the bay right there outside the driver's-side window as you leave, the sun just beginning its descent into the western hills. The top down, the smell of the sea. People still pull up roots and move to California on a whim all the time, and days like these are why—to find light like this in the early afternoon, you'd usually have to travel to Crete, or to the South of France, but here in Morro Bay, every time the clouds clear, you feel like you're drifting through a golden moment that might never end.

The rest of the day drifts by weightlessly. There isn't much to think about: tying up loose ends with students who are over-concerned about their grades, reviewing basic concepts for final exams. Nothing really new to the students who've studied all year, and nothing the ones who are behind will suddenly be able to grasp. You'll be easy on the ones who've tried and come up short; you see their faces as you go over material from two months back, their exaggerated concentration, as if the right attitude now might mitigate the disaster awaiting them when you place the exam booklets on their desks next week. There are some teachers who hold cram sessions at their own houses this time of year—University of Chicago grads, people who're going to change the world through secondary education; they're a little much sometimes. One has to keep one's boundaries pleasantly firm, you think. What if the students just started following teachers home for free tutoring? How would you re-draw the line, once you'd let them smudge it? But nobody follows you back to your apartment from school today, because they don't need to: they've already looked up your address in the phone book.

This is something that will make your story harder for later generations to understand. Why is your address right there in the phone book? You're a teacher; public school teachers have targets painted on their backs. If a student gets mad about his grades, "Better safe than sorry" is the watchword. You never know what these kids will do. Some of them have guns. Didn't you hear about that one teacher in Massachusetts? Just twenty-four years old.

But no, you haven't heard about Colleen Ritzer at Danvers High. Philip Chism will not slit her throat with a box cutter and stuff her body into a recycling barrel until 2013, forty-one years from now. Jennifer Paulson won't be shot walking to work at Birney Elementary in Tacoma until 2010. You haven't heard about Toby R. Sincino, who shot two teachers and then turned the gun on himself at Blackville-Hilda High in October 1995.

You haven't heard of Neva Jane Wynkoop-Rogers, sixty-two years old on the day she was killed alongside eight others and five wounded at Red Lake Senior High School, on the Red Lake Reservation up in Minnesota. You wouldn't think to take any measures to protect yourself from your students. Occasionally a few will confront you about their grades, but these are usually college-bound seniors, worried about future prospects. The idea that any of them might try to hunt you down with the intention of killing you is absurd. They have a hard enough time focusing on social studies for a single class period. They're not killers. They're just kids.

There's a little pastrami left, so you have that on a sandwich for dinner with some roasted potatoes. It might look modest to the outside world, a sandwich and some plain potatoes with butter and salt. Some feast! If there were an especially sensitive poet walking past your window, he might muse awhile about the quiet pains of solitude, maybe bleed you for a few good lines— "the woman at the table, reading alone," something in that vein. But in fact you're quite pleased with yourself: while the potatoes were roasting, you've toasted the bread, steamed the pastrami over boiling water for a minute or two, and then dressed it with a little cheese and mustard. It's a joy, a little sandwich like this, the potatoes on the side a little oily, steam rising from them when you break the pieces open with your fork.

You burn a little incense afterward, skimming a chapter in the Carlos Castaneda paperback you found in the laundry room last week. You ran across it halfway through a stack of books that had been left on the folding table with a little note beside: "Free!" *The Teachings of Don Juan: A Yaqui Way of Knowledge* is pretty wild fare, but it's entertaining enough. It reminds you of a more grown-up version of the fantasies you used to indulge in as a child, dreams of leaving the world behind and going off to live in the desert among the wild animals; or maybe up in some cave in the mountains, surrounded by mossy trees and cool, running streams.

It's lovely to think of, though for you these reveries only last for the time it takes to burn a stick of incense while idling awhile on the sofa. But people entering adulthood seem to hold tight to childish dreams nowadays, even carrying them into the lives they make for themselves. Might the future hold, for you, some unmooring like the one your divorced neighbors seem to be having: new and unknown horizons, unexpected spiritual awakenings? Did you have plans for the summer, plans that could have included some personal inventory like the one all your fellow grown-ups seem so invested in at present? I don't know; it seems unlikely. At any rate, the Castaneda book in the laundry room, whatever else people might have made of it later, could have meant something or nothing. In order for us to know, someone would have needed to explore the foggy territory of your unremembered daydreams, and these aren't the avenues people pursue in the wake of a catastrophe. One thing seldom asked of those on whom disaster has laid its hand is what their future plans were before the flood.

†††

THEY PULL INTO THE PARKING LOT after you've gone to bed. Seen from the outside, they'd almost seem comic: first they have to find your car, and then they circle the parking lot arguing about whether parking next to it is a good idea or a bad one. Then, when they've agreed that it's probably a bad idea, they argue about where a better place to park might be—on the street, or a block away, or across the parking lot next to some other cars whose owners don't figure into the story at hand.

Most of the argument consists of a running monologue from Gene, but as Jesse begins to apprehend the reality of his situation amid the unusual sticking power of Gene's pipe dream from the previous night, he raises objections or notes possible complications. "Anywhere you park, somebody might see," he volunteers, interrupting, and then, a minute later: "They built most of this in the last couple years, it's all going to have streetlights." Jesse has a fear of consequences whose constant presence at the periphery of his consciousness is a sort of tribute to his father.

This irritates Gene, who likes Jesse for his passivity, his use value as a sponge: he soaks up the runoff from Gene and never seems to saturate. "If you wanna puss out, say the word, little brother," he says, pulling up abruptly near the enclosed swimming pool, whose lights shimmer dreamily through the window. "I'm only doing this for you, anyway."

"Gene, I'm just saying, a lot of people live here, probably somebody's going to see." Gene, staring through the windshield toward the swimming pool, is plotting points on a line whose arc is really only a rough guess. "You know? Just, probably somebody."

Gene has made up his mind. "So?"

Jesse laughs, despite himself. "So nothing she's got in there is worth anything to us in jail."

Gene punches Jesse on the shoulder—not hard, but hard enough—and smiles. "What do *you* know about jail?"

"What do *you*?" says Jesse, punching him back, but tentatively: there is an order here, one whose terms Jesse understands instinctively. These constraints are comforting, known parameters. It's good to have someone to mark out the boundaries, to keep them consistent. Some people wait their whole lives for such a person.

"About as much as I'm *gonna* know," Gene says, suddenly parking the car in an available space and killing the engine. They remain there for quite some time, smoking cigarettes with the windows down and watching your building like amateur detectives on stakeout, waiting until the last light in the last window has gone dark.

5.

THE KNICKKNACKS, the found art taped to the wall, the modest assortment of paperback books; the cutlery. You had so little to protect, so few things you chose to call your own and keep as tokens of your passage through this world. Mothers protecting their children are expected to act with ferocity: society demands this of them; it's one of many requirements women are encouraged to absorb and internalize, selves they're supposed to envision themselves growing into. You? You were a high school teacher in a one-bedroom apartment a block from the bay. Few could have looked on your life with envy, fewer still with scorn: your days were like leaves. Why, then, did you defend your domain, such small holdings, with lethal force? It was this line of questioning, unfair and unfeeling, that would eventually put you on death row, but when the moment was alive and present, none of them were there. Only you know. Only you remember. Only you, alone among your inquisitors, know how it feels to have a place of refuge defiled, to see the barrier breached, and to know for certain that only ruin will remain unless you act.

Today, you arise unaware of the little drama that played out in your parking lot while you slept—the boy behind the wheel tightly coiled and ready to strike, the one in the passenger seat gently planting seeds of doubt, clearing a little space for light and nourishing the tender sprouts until his companion, Gene, turned to him angrily in the near-dawn, and said: "Fuck it. Tomorrow."

But tomorrow's here now; school's out for the day, and you're at Jordano's again. In the lounge this morning, skimming the newspaper, you ran across a recipe for fried oysters in sauce, and it sounded so decadent—what a thing to do, just on impulse, to whip up some oysters and eat them, by yourself, on a Thursday evening in May, in sight of the very waters from which the oysters had been harvested. Maybe pile them high on a French roll, head down to the shore alone for dinner. Spread a tablecloth on the sand and watch the sun set. And with a glass of wine from just up the coast? Why not? It's the small favors we do for ourselves that we'll remember when we're older. A little pampering, insurance against the unknowable tides of the future, maybe. It seems that way from here, today, anyhow. You can't be sure that it's true, but it *feels* true.

The man behind the seafood counter is older; he wears a name tag that says BILL in white letters debossed in a red field pinned to his white smock, and he makes charming small talk with you while wrapping your oysters. "This one spit in my eye when we dropped him onto the ice!" he says, holding one up; you picture the scene and smile.

"Can you blame him?" you say.

Bill cocks his head and wrinkles his lips, which causes his already bushy greying mustache to bunch up; it looks like an animal with its back turned to you, nestled just beneath his nose. "Guess I'd do the same, in his shoes!" he says, breaking into a wide smile. He must have been at this job for years: without drawing any attention to his hands, he's wrapped every-thing up in butcher paper, tied it with twine, and written a price on the outside.

"Fresh is best!" he says when you thank him. "If you don't eat them all tonight, just put a damp cloth on 'em in the fridge, they'll keep!"

"A damp cloth, right," you say, smiling and nodding as you turn toward the dairy aisle: the recipe calls for buttermilk. Maybe you'll make biscuits or pancakes tomorrow. Maybe you'll just drink a glass of buttermilk with breakfast, like your grandmother used to do. Does anyone still do that: drink but-termilk? At the checkout counter, again your eyes catch those little booklets. *Secrets of the Chinese Zodiac. Modern Needle-point. Hollywood by Night.* They call to you—bright colorful designs on their covers, whole worlds of unknown possibility for forty-nine cents apiece. They'd look lurid on your coffee table: red lines drawn between stars to trace the shape of a monkey against the night sky. Quaint bright patterns. A cloak-and-dagger motif. But you leave them where they are, because everything's already in order. You have a date with a tablecloth on the beach.

†††

WHO KNOWS HOW the children who will tell your story in the future retain the detail of the radio on the counter? It sounds like something made-up, an embellishment from one of the older kids on the playground whose sense of detail demands a still focal point. But it's true. The radio spends most of its time in a drawer: it's a simple handheld transistor, the kind your father might take to a baseball game to listen to the play-by-play. When you come home from the supermarket, you wash your hands at the sink, take the shucking knife down from the knife rack, and, riding the inspiration that's been with you since your morning cup of coffee, take the radio out and set it on the counter.

It's clearly visible in photographs from the scene, a palm-sized silver faceplate with a round bubble in the upper right corner like a porthole where the dial is. The housing is shot through with perfectly round circles, die-cut and looking for all the world like the work of a very attentive child with a hole-punch. The top four holes are decorative rather than functional, framing a colorful pattern: red, yellow, yellow, blue. Why two yellows instead of a four-color spread? Who can say?

When Jesse and Gene let themselves in through your unlocked front door, the radio is playing "Hold Your Head Up" by Argent, a hard rock band. You remember this because it's not your sort of thing; it's a type of music you sometimes hear coming through the open windows of cars in the school parking lot. That it feels somehow aggressive seems, to you, a sign that you're getting old; pointless to resist, it seems. The chorus is beginning to grate on your nerves as you work away at the oysters, prying their shells open and pulling the soft flesh loose, but this work requires focus, so you're waiting the song out, hoping they play something mellower next. But at trial, later, you can't remember what came after. Whatever it was, it has not been able to rise above the memory of the panic, and the chaos.

Neither of them announce themselves when they enter: they aren't seasoned thieves, but they know that a doorknob turned gently enough makes hardly any sound at all if there's ambient noise to mask it: a stove fan, a countertop radio. Everyone was a child once; everyone's moved stealthily sometimes, either at play or from sheer animal need. Your awareness of their movement in your peripheral vision is sharp and sudden, the momentary flash you get just before an especially large bug hits your windshield: *thwap.* Just like that, the huge abstract splatter of guts and carapace across your field of vision. The wind widening its spread, rippling in the splotch.

When Gene covers your mouth with his right hand and pulls your body tightly against his, your fist reflexively tightens around the handle of the shucking knife, and your eyes go wide. You can't stop your mouth from trying to open, to scream, to call for help: it's pure instinct. "Easy, easy," he says in a hot whisper, just next to your ear; you feel his arm against your right breast as he moves his hand to your wrist, intending to squeeze hard enough to make you drop the knife. Jesse, per his instructions, is already heading for the bedroom, since Gene has told him several times that the valuables are always in the bedroom.

But Gene, although a very dangerous person in many ways, has not planned for resistance. His assumption that there won't be any is based on his own experience: every time he resisted a blow as a child, it only made things worse. Other people know that, too, he imagines; how would they not? The teenagers he shakes down for small change at school all lend support to this theory; his menace, the immediacy of the threat, is enough to dissuade them from putting up a fight. But here, at Oakside Court, he is on new ground—just as you are, but in a different sense; and, although he's spent several days convincing Jesse that he's thought all the angles through, he hasn't. When he hears Jesse pulling down shelves in your bedroom closet, he jerks your body in the direction of the hallway. You fall into him; you are being dragged. A clear view of how things will play out if you fail to act explodes across your inner vision like a sped-up movie reel.

You jerk your right hand free, going against his thumb, as an article in a magazine once told you to do. Gene grabs your hair and pulls, hard, and the pain burns, but your motion now is natural, fluid if desperate, full of purpose. You don't see the knife pierce his eyelid, which has only squinted itself to cover the eye in the split second before the blade arrives: Gene's mind is on subduing you, not protecting himself, and he doesn't register the threat of your right hand until you've thrust it forward with a terrified, needful strength, and then jerked the knife free.

You scream, and the sound that comes out of you is low, more roar than shriek, a single vowel with no markable beginning or end; it degrades into panting and grunting as you rise to a standing position. Gene is screaming, too, a panicked falsetto, both of his hands covering his left eye, blood flowing down his cheek. He has to move his hands back into place over the eye, because they slip. You scream again, not as loud, and not for any reason you can later state—it just happens—and then you stab him in the neck. He hits his head on the kitchen counter as he falls, and he says, "Fuck, fuck, fuck," landing on the floor as blood begins erupting in spurts from the wound in his throat.

Jesse is not prepared for this. He has one foot in the hallway between your bedroom and the kitchen when he hears Gene's scream; he freezes. He needs Gene to tell him what to do; he's afraid of making things worse, and he's afraid of the unknown. The sounds reaching him while he ransacked your bedroom closet, looking for jewelry, locked boxes, or things that shine, began as unpleasant distractions from his work: Gene had warned him that you weren't going to like this. But he hadn't said anything about an actual fight, and he hadn't gone over any contingencies: he'd sketched out a clear timeline that made no allowances for bumps in the road. Over the course of several minutes, the noises made it impossible for Jesse to focus on his task. You're just a teacher. There are two of them, young strong boys. How dangerous could you be?

Gene is crawling toward the front door, trying to drag himself forward with his right hand while keeping the left pressed up to the wound on his neck. You lunge, stabbing him again, the blade entering this time at the base of his skull; this is the blow that will be most damning at trial. Pulling the knife loose for the third time proves hardest, but you manage it; he falls, face-first, onto the carpet, and his limbs begin to twitch.

Behind you, Jesse's shock has finally spurred him to action: he grabs the nearest thing he sees, your vase, and hurls it, with all the strength his skinny arm can muster, at what he hopes will be your head. It connects instead with Gene, whose body does not react to the insult. Jesse's eyes widen when he sees the vase land on his friend; he is terrified. He dashes for the door now, escape his only thought, but there's so much blood, just everywhere, and he slips and falls, landing halfway on top of Gene, who is technically not dead yet.

Jesse cries out, just as Gene did when his moment came. Your mind is telling you that more noise will attract the attention of the neighbors, though in reality you're the only one on your floor of the building at the moment; everybody else is still at school, or work, or out getting an early dinner. But Jesse, unlike Gene, does not scream in shock: his brief speech, at high pitch, is hastily calculated to save his own skin. "Please, Miss Crane," he cries, his eyes shut tight, his hands crossed in front of his face. He's lying on his side, his face on the floor in a still-forming pool of his friend's sticky blood; his legs, supported by Gene's torso, are in the air, his ankles crossed. He's getting louder; his cries settle into an incantatory, desolate rhythm.

"Please, Miss Crane, please, no. No. No! Please, Miss Crane. Please, no."

You stab him thirty-seven times in total. The third strike, the one that enters his throat from the left side, is the fatal one, but you succeed in puncturing his lung during the ensuing overkill. There is blood on your hair, in your mouth, all over your face. On the floor of the kitchen, the oysters, some still in their shells, sit in pools of it.

You stand over the bodies of Jesse Jenkins and Gene Cupp until you feel certain neither of them is moving, and then you sit down in the still-gathering pool next to them, trying to think.

6.

CALIFORNIA'S IN BETTER SHAPE than a lot of places when it comes to labor laws, but protections don't generally extend to part-timers like the line help at Taco Bell. At the San Luis Obispo location, Angie Gessler, the shop's general manager, writes out the weekly schedule like a failing student filling in bubbles on a Scantron, making everything look tidy without much thought about what the markings might otherwise mean. Few of his workers complain, because most of them don't expect to be around much longer. Angie'd been one of them, too, a few years ago, but then corporate promoted him before he got around to thinking about what else he might do with his life once he finished his BS at Cal Poly, and now here he is.

Within a generation nobody will be calling boys "Angie" anymore. Even now, people sometimes sound a little surprised, on the phone, to learn that the man speaking is the Angie they were calling for. It happens today: Gessler's alone in the restaurant, wondering where Gene is. Gene was scheduled for the opening shift. Gene being late for an opening shift is nothing new, but it's twelve-thirty now, and the lunch crowd is getting thick. Gene's dad even called to see where he was, and hung up as soon as he got an answer; the interruption just increased the tension. It's all too much to handle, especially for someone whose days on site are usually spent in a tiny office at the back of the building, filling out the schedule and monitoring the walk-up window. When, from the order window, he hears the office phone ringing, he's immediately aggravated. *You can't call in an hour past the start of your shift,* he thinks. *It doesn't work like that.*

"Be right with you," he tells the next customer at the window before dashing down the thin corridor alongside the grill to his office. When he gets to the phone, he assumes a managerial stance—it's like an actor putting on his face. This is how you get the promotions, he knows. Days like these.

"Taco Bell," he says cheerfully into the phone, "how can I help you?"

"This is Detective Haeny with the San Luis Obispo Police Department," says a voice on the other end, sounding for all the world like he's reading from a script. "Do you have an employee named Gene Cupp there?"

"Well, normally, yes," says Angie Gessler, "but he hasn't turned up today."

There's a pause. "Am I speaking with the manager?"

Gessler laughs. "Yes, and also the cook and front window man as of right now," he says. "If Gene comes in I'll be back to just being the manager."

Another pause. "If he does turn up, would you please call me at this number?"

Haeny gives Gessler his direct line. "Sure," Gessler says. "Is he in some kind of trouble? His father already called once."

"He called us, too," says Detective Haeny. "At this point that's all I can tell you. Do give me a call if you hear from Gene, all right?"

"Sure thing," says Angie Gessler, trying to picture what a kid like Gene Cupp's father would actually look like, and then trying to imagine him as the sort of father who'd call the police because he was worried about his son's whereabouts.

†††

RONNIE CUPP, as you have always suspected but could not confirm, is not that sort of father at all. The reason Ronnie called the cops about an hour ago is that his son's blue Torino is still missing from the driveway, and he needs it for the beer run. His biker friends will be turning up again sometime later this afternoon; it'll take two runs to bring enough home if he ends up having to use the trunk bag on his Harley instead of the trunk of the car.

His assumption on seeing the empty driveway is that Gene is in the holding tank again. Gene has not yet learned to avoid the radar. Records show no sign of his having been booked last night, of course, but Officer Quinn, Detective Haeny's partner, is new to the job, and eager to do everything according to procedure. Twin miracles of youth and naivete, usually unsought-for graces in this job, allow him to lead Ronnie through the process of filling out a missing persons report over the phone.

Quinn brings the form to Haeny, who looks it over. Even for a sleepy town like this, it feels like a stretch. "You've got to be kidding," says Haeny.

"Sorry," says Quinn.

"It's all right," Haeny says, scratching the back of his head, ready to get to work. "Get me the number of the—what was it? Taco Bell."

† † †

AS THE LINES CRACKLE between substations and stucco apartment complexes and cramped fast-food managers' quarters, you swim upstream against a tide of panic. It ought to have ebbed by now, you think, but its approach feels endless: each wave feels new, and you don't seem to be building up any resistance. You've managed to keep your body working while your mind revolts by thinking of the two as separate, only coincidentally related entities; and so, when fear and revulsion rise in your throat, you're able to brook them without stinting from your labor. The work feels needed, compulsory. Your mind meets any complications that arise automatically, instinctively: Tools? There's a garden shed at the edge of the property. Waste disposal? There's a wheelbarrow with a garden hose in it by the pool, you can dump the hose against the building and no one will know, it's the weekend. Cleanup?

Cleanup will be last, because it will take longest. It is a pattern with you: save the hard work for last. Just last spring, through a friend inside the DA's office, I got my hands on the last stack of papers you graded before the disaster. Your habit of signing and dating your remarks at the end of each one suggests, to me, that you took your work seriously: that you envisioned real futures for these students who fumbled their way through essays about the rise of mercantilism or the Second Great Awakening. You addressed them by name in your comments, as a college professor might have done, and afforded them more dignity than any other person in your position might have felt obligated to do.

But there are few virtues that can't be turned against a person who's been charged with murder. "MOREOVER, that DEFENDANT did willfully and maliciously cultivate trust between herself and victims CUPP and JENKINS, in spoken and in written communications [Exhibit L], with a view toward gaining their confidence and allaying suspicion about her motives in grooming them to seek her approval," reads part of the text pleading for special circumstances. I felt visceral anger the first time I read through it: it didn't square with what I already knew about you by then, and I couldn't imagine the charge being made in earnest. It seemed to come from another world.

Once the suggestion had been placed in the mind of the jury, though, it established residency, and never once wanted for décor. Even the testimony of your students about your mild, almost passive classroom manner could be cast in an ominous light; your lovers hinting discreetly but insistently about your appetites could be made to seem part of a larger tapestry whose secondary shades were all threat and menace. It only took the initial read-through of the charges to plant the seed of suspicion. After that, vines sprouted and grew wild, and proved hardy against attempts at pruning by your competent but outmatched defense.

And, in fairness, the cleansing of the bodies would be hard to cast in a flattering light even under the most favorable circumstances. It was necessary for you to do it, because you had to dispose of them somehow: that's clear to anyone. But a jury of your peers will find this work hard to stomach. The details have a way of obscuring their context in cases like these. Your multiple trips to the gardener's shed as the need for specialized tools became clearer. The haphazard spreading-out of the garbage bags around your living room, intended to prevent further spillage: needless, as it turned out; blood thickens when it's stopped circulating through a body, and doesn't gush so much as ooze—you can catch it before it hits the carpet, but you can't put the garbage bags back into their boxes. They're new evidence now. You reuse the ones you haven't nicked with knife or saw, stuffing them half full of lean muscle shorn from bone like steaks from the carcass of a steer: your thought had been to make the flayed remains collapsible, portable, and as inconspicuous as the primitive conditions of your labor would allow.

It's a mess. It takes all night, a night during which panic causes you to black out several times: you'll wake up to find yourself still sawing through cartilage, breathing through flared nostrils oblivious to the stench. There's so much cartilage in a body, and it's all so slippery: your kitchen gloves are useless; you have to work bare-handed or you can't get a grip on anything, and it makes you sick to have to keep plunging your hands into everything; and the sickness doesn't ever seem to lift, except when the effort you have to put into pushing the saw forward and drawing it back is enough to require all your focus. In those moments, which are plentiful across the span of two nearly grown bodies, the force of the work engages you sufficiently to allow the nausea to abate for a moment, and it's nice, until it dawns on you how this process is working: how your body and your mind have joined their strength to help you complete this task. How there was something already inside you whose purpose was to help you through a time like this if such a time ever came. You apprehend it at once, midcut, and then the sickness returns. This process repeats itself, again and again; after the first time, you don't make it to the bathroom. The garbage bags you load into the wheelbarrow at day's end contain skin, and sinew, and bone, floating in a broth of blood, and fat, and sweat, and the vomit you've repeatedly emptied onto the bodies of Jesse Jenkins and Gene Cupp as you worked, on and off, all day until the sun went down.

†††

JANA LARSON is standing by the wall phone in her kitchen, cupping the mouthpiece with her hand, trying to make herself heard over the outbursts in the background that occasionally make it hard for the operator at the substation to understand her. Some beef stew from a can is bubbling in a copper-bottomed pan on the stove; she holds a wooden spatula in one hand, stirring while she speaks to keep the gravy from burning. It's too early in the day for beef stew, but Michael is always content when he has a bowl of it in front of him. She would like to distract Michael for a few minutes while she gets her bearings.

"Ma'am?" says the operator. "Do I understand you, that this is for missing persons?"

"My son didn't come home last night," she says. She is trying without success to keep her voice down. "Please find him, please find him, you have to find him."

"I'm going to put a stop to this shit," yells Michael from his recliner in front of the television. He turns his head toward Jana, to make sure the dispatcher hears. "Tell him this shit is going to stop *right now.*"

"Please," says Jana Larson, who went by Jana Jenkins until just a few years ago, when she'd succeeded, for the first time, in getting away from the man she'd married as soon as she turned eighteen. He's four years her senior; he'd been nineteen when they first met in the parking lot of the A&W. Two years later she'd given him a son; they'd named him Jesse, after nobody in particular. They both just liked the sound of it. In the years since then, which feel long and hard, she has fled from Michael Jenkins several times; a few years ago, she even succeeded in completing divorce proceedings. But nothing is ever really over, she thinks sometimes.

"*Right now,*" Michael repeats, at or near the top of his lungs, who knows why.

"Can you tell me where you last saw him?" asks the operator; her low voice has a steady, calming resonance.

Jana draws in as much breath as she can manage. Jesse left a note the only other time he ran away.

"He was getting into his friend Gene's car. He plays—*pinball* while he's waiting for his friend to get off of work," she manages, though she chokes on the word "pinball." Jesse has never been good at sports or excelled in school, but he is very good at pinball, and she used to take pride in the way all the other kids looked at her son with admiration whenever she picked him up from the arcade.

The operator pauses.

"Ma'am?"

"Are you going to let him treat you like this?" Michael yells without looking away from the commercials. "Just let him treat you like shit, like this?" There's some spit or phlegm caught in his throat, which gives an ugly granular quality to his voice. Jana stares at a fixed point on the carpet.

"Yes?" she says.

"Can you tell me what kind of car Jesse's friend drives?"

She scowls; there's more in this question than she's able to parse before answering. "Yes, I think so. It's a blue—it's a Ford. It's a nice blue Ford. It's kind of a race car," she offers.

"I'm going to hand you over to Detective Haeny," says the operator.

† † †

IT'S A LONG WAY FROM THE DUNES to the shore if you're pushing a heavy wheelbarrow across the sand. It has been a long day of desperate errands and hastily improvised solutions. The interior of your apartment is a catastrophe: the carpet, the walls, the kitchen and bathroom sinks, all that smeared and sticky linoleum underfoot. You have vague plans for cleaning: a vision of your home's restoration to its earlier state has occasionally brought you mild comfort throughout the day. Mopped floors. Clean cutlery. A relatively spotless couch.

You try to hide yourself somewhere within the folds of these visions as you drag your burden down to its destination, hoping that no one notices the woman alone on the beach who might be searching for treasure or cleaning up trash but seems bent by her labor, stopping every few feet to catch her breath, and leaning, when she stops, pointedly away from the wheelbarrow she's pushing ahead of her. Of course, this is not a private beach, and your being alone on it means that certainly someone will see you, at least in passing. You have no spell of invisibility to cast. You are nobody's witch.

When, at last, you come to stand in the water, physically exhausted, sobbing aloud, the moon is high. The Pacific Coast is such a beautiful place, this far outpost that's always made room for the exile, the fugitive, the wanderer. You are none of these. Your position is primary, absolute. Outlaws and desperadoes are stock figures from story and song; you are a young schoolteacher who has had to defend herself using deadly force, and who now must try to dispose of human remains. You ache. You feel it in your forearms the most, but your entire body is stiff, sore, racked by tension. You need rest. You have needed rest for too long now. You can rest when this last leg of your journey is done, you think. And so you stand in the surf holding a leaky garbage bag, sobbing aloud for what feels like the forty-eighth consecutive sleepless hour, trying to calculate how to empty the bag without once again letting its contents splash onto your clothes, your skin.

It's such a simple problem to state, but the physics of it, at this late hour, are too much for you. When you hold the bag away from your body, it sags, and you lose control of it. It feels important to remain in control. But if you should undo the knot in the bag and empty it out too near to you, its contents will likely splash against your body as it empties, the solid pieces catching the current around your legs. You want to avoid that, but you can't untie the bag with your arms at full extension. You stand in the surf trying to come to a decision: it will only take the effort of the first try; after that, the remaining bags in the wheelbarrow back on the shore will be easier. The byways of your life have not prepared you for this passage.

You are not strong enough.

Today you have summoned strength from reservoirs you hadn't known were present in you—strength whose nature you'd never had cause to contemplate; strength whose character had been, until these days came, a subject of idle contemplation, of outward wonder. People tell passed-down stories about mothers lifting up school buses with their bare hands to free their children pinned under the wheels. The foreman in a mine single-handedly holding up the beam that allows the men in his charge to escape before the walls collapse. From an early age, every kid on the block knows stories like these, and swears she got it firsthand from her mother, or an uncle, or a close friend of the family. You know these stories probably aren't true: but you also know that you've sawn through more bone today than the hacksaw from the gardener's shed might otherwise have been thought capable of splitting, hoisted more weight than anyone might have guessed your slight frame could bear.

It has not been enough.

They find you at the shore.

7.

THE FLASHING LIGHTS down in the Oakside Court parking lot draw several early risers to their windows; were you looking up, you'd see them looking down at you through gaps in their curtains, but you're not. You're looking into the eyes of the arresting officer, your hands cuffed behind your back; you are asking him for the third time if there will be food at the station. They will use this against you in court. But you're light-headed, confused by hunger and exhaustion. Officer Quinn, mindful of how lost you seem, has told you several times that you don't have to talk to him until you've called a lawyer. "She seemed like she was in another world," he will say, later, under oath.

There's seldom any action around this place. Who knows how the rumor begins floating through the building this early in the morning, but gradually people begin to emerge from their apartments. They keep their distance from the squad cars, and at first they seem also to be avoiding each other, like congregants observing a rite or trying not to break a spell. Through these mainly silent ranks, officers are leading you down the asphalt to their cluster of cars, whose blue and red lights dance across your face and body; having arrived, you stand, still as a statue, awaiting an answer from Officer Quinn. He has stopped responding to your questions. He's waiting for radio dispatch to tell him whether to proceed without further backup. The circumstances of your arrest are unusual. He wants to be mindful of protocol.

"It's that teacher from the high school," someone says when the quiet has grown oppressive.

"What did she do?" someone asks.

Everybody gazes out into the wash of red and blue light, wondering, their imaginations seeking out and finding places they would normally never visit.

"They sent a lot of cars, whatever it was," says the first voice. It's Don from your hallway. He's a little tipsy from the night before, and he can't believe his eyes. He thinks briefly about how nothing like this ever used to happen in the neighborhood where he used to live when he was married.

He and the others all watch as you are helped into the back of the cruiser, hands behind your back. In the absence of any information to work with, the onlookers begin asking themselves what they know about you, and using what answers they find to tell themselves stories about what they've just seen.

People are awful, even when they're not trying to be. None of the stories they tell themselves are good.

†††

IF YOU'D LIVED IN AN EARLIER TIME, who would remember you? Your name would be known only to students of esoteric crimes, your face seen alongside Lizzy Borden's on dust jackets designed to attract a very specific readership who know exactly what they want from the books they buy. Maybe some singer in the early nineties might have splashed your mug shot on a T-shirt and worn it to the MTV awards, but probably not. For every iconic pair of murderer's eyes staring blankly into a police photographer's lens, there are unremembered dead in small towns across the country going back centuries. Murder seldom inspires much lasting interest beyond the houses it strikes. You used to have to really work at it to make a name for yourself.

But this is a new era. Americans have been more or less glued to their televisions since the Tet Offensive; that was four years ago now, and nightly drama coming out of the nation's capital has only intensified the bond between average people and their screens. Print reporters have always known it's good to have somebody on the inside; their colleagues in broadcast news are learning as they go. KSBY's office in San Luis Obispo started sending crews around to talk to people about the missing teenagers yesterday; the head of the news department heard about them from a station clerk he knows. Occasionally he's sent her movie passes to the Fremont; these cost him nothing—they're a perk. They have netted him a huge score this morning.

The news van captures your face in the back of the car as it leaves the parking lot. The anchor describes your "evidently expressionless face" to his viewers as he wraps the segment, but what expression suits a person whose keep has been fatally breached, whose safe harbor, until days ago a place of idle peace, now suffers its second invasion in the space of days—a parking lot teeming with strangers, a chatter of voices.

"We'll have to wait and see if there's more beneath the surface," he says, handing the broadcast back to his colleagues at the station. "Back to you."

"'More beneath the surface,'" echoes his counterpart, her cadence dark, suggestive, and inconclusive as she pivots to camera two to change her tone. "And you can be sure KSBY will be there to cover it. Meanwhile, more details on the historic agreement signed this week in Moscow, and, for those, we head over to Tom Brokaw at the national desk. Tom?"

†††

MOMENTS LIKE THESE are notoriously hard to reconstruct—the mundane aftermath of a signal event whose import isn't yet clear, the muddy beginnings in which legends are conceived. Whole histories got wiped and recorded over by TV stations all the way up through the late 1970s. But I got lucky. Frank Haeny'd worked on missing-kids cases locally for years, and in the course of his work he'd learned that there's no such thing as an insignificant piece of evidence. He Mirandized you personally through the grating that separated the front seat of the car from the back—and then he asked Quinn for a second outside the car.

"Get her processed, get her some food, tell her we can talk about all this later this morning," he said. "I need to make sure nobody does anything stupid here."

Quinn blanched; he didn't want to be alone with this woman whose shining eyes gazed exhaustedly out through bangs plastered to her forehead by blood.

"I'll be practically right behind you," Haeny said, taking a reassuring tone. "Just dotting *i*'s here." With that, Quinn nodded and got into the cruiser; the report indicates that a junior officer named Thaler rode along with you in case there was any need for corroboration of details later. Per Quinn's report, neither he nor Lieutenant Thaler spoke to you during the ride down to the station. The sun would have been rising above the bay by the time you got there. The report indicates that you sat down in the first chair you saw inside the station, and that you slumped there, and were slow to respond when asked to get up.

At Oakside Court, Detective Haeny went back and forth between your apartment and the parking lot, keeping an eye on clean procedures in the one and the camera crews in the other. He knew it was better to make friends with them than to antagonize them; you never know who you might need to call for a favor later. When the crowd had thinned down to a few stragglers, he waved all the newspeople over to him; there were three of them left along with their crews, lighting rigs and fuzzy boom mics in hand. They'd been interviewing bystanders for at least half an hour.

"I know you have to get your broadcasts together," he told them, "but when all that's done I'd appreciate it if you could get all of what you just got here to me." He made a circling measure in the air that indicated he meant the footage they'd just shot, and then he handed out business cards. "I'll get it back to you."

The oldest of the camera operators didn't like the idea of just handing his footage over to the police; he never called the number on the card, and anything he shot is lost to history. The other two did as they were told. It was from this raw footage that I was able to assemble an account of the genesis of the White Witch. I got it from Detective Haeny, and I wondered aloud to him why no one had ever reported on it before. "No one ever asked," he told me.

Neither the prosecution nor the defense used any of the unaired tape in court. Several of its principals were in fact called to testify, but their voices got lost in the squall. By the time you came to trial, the tales people told had, through repetition, assumed shape. Confusion gave way to conjecture; friends would ask one another how something like this could have happened, and would keep right on asking until they came up with an explanation that could be passed along. The cautionary tale that came to stand in for the facts of the case belonged to the familiar type of legend in which the greatest possible menace to a community lies just beneath the skin, its portents only readable, in retrospect, by those lucky enough to have survived its eruption.

†††

GARY LOGAN (NEIGHBOR): Well, I didn't really know her much. At all, really, I guess. I live downstairs. She's a lot younger than me. Most of the people here are younger than me but I like it. I'm retired, always wanted to live by the water. No old folks' home for me! Anyway, we just said hello sometimes. One time she helped me with the groceries because she saw I had three bags. There was nothing really different about her as far as I could tell. She seemed nice.

MARY ZAVALA (NEIGHBOR): I don't know her! But she was at the beach earlier, I saw her out there. I went out for a swim. What? No, over at the pool. Nobody ever swims out in the bay almost, you know? It's too cold! But I have trouble sleeping and we have a pool key so I went for a swim and then I thought I'd just kind of, you know, you're up late, just look at the sky a little while before trying to go back to bed. And I saw her out there! She had a wheelbarrow and she was standing in the water. I didn't know who it was. I still don't know. I live in the other building, right over there, it's all the same apartments but there's three buildings. Do you know what they say she did? I don't really know anything but they sent all those police cars, you saw 'em. She doesn't live in my building, I don't think. I know pretty much everybody who lives in mine. But I knew something was wrong! Like I told you I have trouble sleeping and I'm awake a lot, there's never anybody else awake but there she was. I wanted to go ask her: Is everything OK? But you never know with people. And then I seen her throwing things in the ocean and I said, Oh, I don't want to know, you know? I went back inside, it's not my business.

DANIEL REED (PARAMEDIC): We got the call about—was it two hours ago, Vince? Two hours ago. Hour and a half. Severe bodily injury was all we heard but when we got here they told us just to sit tight. I can sit tight here as easy as I can anyplace else, they can get us on the radio if they need us, so I sit tight. When they brought her out, from what I could see, a lot of blood, she looks hurt, possibly in shock. I wanted to put a blanket over her but I didn't want to get in the way and she was in handcuffs. To me she looked like one of those crazy—what were they—

VINCENT ROSSETTI (PARAMEDIC): Manson girls!

REED: The Manson girls! You seen them? All whacked-out on something, all dressed up like—

ROSSETTI: Halloween, man.

REED: Halloween, you know? Anyway all I know, the two injury victims, the two—

ROSSETTI: The two alleged victims.

REED: Right, the two alleged victims, thank you, we were supposed to take them to the hospital, but they didn't end up going to the hospital, because—

ROSSETTI: We can't do anything for them, is what he's saying.

REED: We can't do anything for 'em. You know what I mean? I don't mean to sound hard-hearted, but you see a lot of stuff on this job.

EITHER THE CHYRON OPERATOR DIDN'T GET AROUND TO inserting the names of the three people whose conversation makes up the last frenzied minute-plus on the tape—three people talking to the camera all at once, finishing one another's thoughts, framing questions for themselves in order to make sense of the scene before them—or somebody forgot to pass their names along to him. They stand in an undecorated frame; they could be anyone. They are a nameless chorus whose song the censor didn't see fit to pass along to the public. It took me two days to locate the spot in the parking lot where they'd been standing; everything's different now, so I had to go by shadows and light at the exact right time of the early morning according to the paramedics' log. It seemed like a pointless effort in the end. The turnover inside the complex was total by the time I got there. Their brief testimonies stand apart from the case as it went forward. There is no way to compare their reporting to the matters in question, save asking you. It was too late for that by the time I got here.

WOMAN 1: She was always nice to me!
WOMAN 2: That is a nice lady. This can't be right.
MAN: There's no way. People are saying she cut up those guys and sacrificed them or something. There's no way.
WOMAN 2: She's just a teacher!
WOMAN 1: I don't believe it.
MAN: Somebody was saying she did it right there on the beach. In the middle of the night, they were saying. It sounds so awful but there's no way.
WOMAN 2: There's no way.

WOMAN 1: She tracked blood all the way down the hall, I heard. Bloody footsteps. I don't believe it, but here we all are.

MAN: What kind of person does that?

WOMAN 1: This is a safe place! What kind of person?

WOMAN 2: I don't know. They say it was her, but I don't know.

WOMAN 1: And she was always so nice.

WOMAN 2: I know! And it's safe here, like you say. I don't believe it. I just don't.

3

Devil House

1.

KNIGHTS REALM

Derrick didn't have a regular shift at Monster Adult X. His arrangement with the store was informal but reliable: he showed up when he could and helped out where needed. Anthony Hawley wanted to help Derrick out, because Derrick's presence haunting the racks had lent an agreeable energy to the often otherwise empty store back when it sold comic books. Then he'd persuaded Hawley to let him do busywork for store credit now and again—straightening up the racks, or running a vacuum over the dingy carpet. Hawley could still remember the frustration, in his younger days, of getting turned down for easy jobs on the grounds that he lacked experience; before he made the shift to dirty movies and magazines, he told Derrick he'd be welcome to stay on if he wasn't bothered by the new stock. "You're eighteen, though, right?" he asked feebly when he'd made the offer. Derrick laughed and said something about September birthdays, though he wouldn't actually turn eighteen for several months. But vice economies avoid the radar. Anthony Hawley wasn't going to demand to see his ID.

He felt confident about Derrick, who showed promise, with his canvas backpack smartly slung over his arm everywhere he went. In Hawley's day, wearing your backpack around town after school would have been a kind of social suicide, but Derrick made it work; once, when business was slow, Anthony'd caught him cleaning it with a fresh toothbrush, the way you might with a pair of shoes you wanted to keep new. It left an impression: Derrick didn't idle. When he ran out of tasks, he sought out more to do, and when there were no more tasks to be found, he tended quietly to his own affairs.

The arrival of the new stock didn't seem to faze him. One day, half of it arrived all at once on a pallet from Encino: several hundred pounds of pornography, tightly shrink-wrapped in plastic and vacuum-sealed. In the supply closet there was a giant stack of comics Hawley had paid cash for and couldn't return; the supply closet claimed more of Derrick's interest than the store could. Plenty of teenage boys would have been willing to risk a shoplifting charge to get their hands on the torrid stuff now glistening under fluorescent lights inside the revamped Valley News, but Derrick couldn't see himself as one of those guys who openly ogled *Playboy* at the barbershop. All this harder stuff seemed a little gross. Any reading he did behind the counter consisted of comics dead stock.

Anthony felt largely the same way about his new inventory, but business was business. For the first few weeks after the big changeover, as shipments of fresh tapes and magazines arrived every other day, he'd found some of it a little exciting—in plenty of places, you'd had to go to ratty movie theaters if you wanted to see this kind of stuff. But being surrounded by porn all day numbs you up in a hurry. After you've seen the people who can't seem to live without it, shuffling in through the door every day, struggling to make eye contact as you change out their bills for tokens, your attitude shifts; even sadder are the ones who don't struggle at all, who hang around the counter trying to make conversation. They were all friendly enough; he tried not to judge them. But it's easy to get jaded.

Derrick saw Hawley's gentle manner with his new customers as worth emulating. There was something desperate in how the people coming in always kept their heads down until the door shut all the way behind them. Everybody needs something. Sometimes a customer, mid-conversation and without any evident provocation, would start regaling Derrick with itineraries of perversions, disgusting things—acts they'd either seen or heard about, unnatural things that sounded like unpolished fantasies half the time—and then his sympathy felt more like pity. But unless they left more mess in the booths than they had to, he bore them no ill will. He couldn't understand the ones who didn't clean up after themselves, though. Didn't they know somebody else was going to have to do it?

One late summer afternoon, he found the back door stuck. He was just going to put in a couple of hours and then head home; his family had been taking great pains to treat him like an adult now that he was almost eighteen. As long as he didn't make trouble they let him do as he liked, more or less; he had always studiously avoided trouble. It was strange, this feeling of no longer needing permission; you want to grow up until it starts really happening, and then it happens. He'd been reflecting on this a little when he found that his key wasn't turning in the lock.

"Change the locks on the back?" he asked Anthony Hawley from the customer side of the front counter as he entered.

"Yeah," said Hawley, trying to appear busy with the cash

register: he wasn't a good actor. Derrick could tell there was something he wasn't ready to say yet. After a minute of deep concentration, he drew his hand out of the till; there was a molded plastic *Monster Adult X* key ring looped around his index finger. Derrick knew there were boxes containing hundreds of these key rings on a shelf in the supply closet, but the keys on this one looked shiny and new. "Here. Put the extra someplace safe."

"Done," Derrick said, nodding his head as he stuck the pair of new keys into his pocket. "Anybody in the back?" He meant the arcade.

"Not just now," said Anthony, but Derrick was already retrieving his mop and bucket. It was true, the daily routine at Monster Adult X was gross. But it gave him pocket money, and a chance to prove to himself that he knew how to be a good employee, the kind who was loyal enough to stick around even when things changed. The kind of person who shows up on time and goes right to work, and the kind who knows better than to ask the boss annoying questions about things he doesn't need to know.

He headed back to the arcade. Mop-up was the worst part, and it had to be done several times a shift. It was best to get the first one out of the way early.

MINOANS I

Hot and Ready. Hot, Young and Ready. Hot and Young. Hot Young Punks. New Wave Hookers. Backstage Pass. The Devil in Miss Jones 3: A New Beginning. Café Flesh. Night Hunger. On Golden Blonde. Rush. Bolt. Crypt Tonite. Pig Poppers. Secrets of the Orient. Deep Chill. Anal Assassins 5. Motion Lotion. Emotion Lotion. Mr. Prolong. Lady-hunger. Sex Fiend

Firemen. Sex Fantasy. Sex Orgy. The Training of Rose-Marie. Curious Co-eds. Co-ed Surprise. Topless Co-eds. Sex Hideaway. Sex Dungeon. Private Orgies. Secret Dreams. Night Visions. Night Shivers. Dungeon Slaves. Deep Chill. For the Love of Blondes. Young and Blonde. Blonde Agony. Whipped and Restrained. Captives of Lust. Apartment Babes. Tijuana Tingler. Swedish Fly. Parisian Nights. Ball Gaggers. Hogtied. Swedish Erotica. European Special #5. Secrets of Japanese Bondage. Just Over 40. From Sex to Sexty. Never Too Old.

These, such as they were, were the assets of Monster Adult X: VHS tapes, their housings on display in the store and the tapes in translucent clamshells behind the counter; sex toys packaged in brittle, yellowing plastic; inhalants marketed as fuel additives or liquid incense; magazines of unknown vintage, probably trading hands multiple times en route to the rack, where they gathered dust. Most suppliers had a very strict no-returns policy, although one or two offered limited and very modest discounts if you sent back exhausted stock with your new order—what use they might have found for all that dead weight was hard to imagine, but the policy was there if you had the pluck to try them on it. Send back five old tapes nobody rents, see if a new one doesn't have better luck. Ten dust-gathering toys sealed in their original packaging invoice, five dollars off any order. The stuff in the bottles and capsules under the counter wasn't returnable but somebody had to want it. It would be possible, if he sold the store, to turn all or some of this into cash somehow, Anthony thought, but the math on it felt like more work than it was worth. He spent half an afternoon working out a few possibilities for it on paper after he learned he'd have to vacate the building, and then he decided to cut his losses.

"Probably closing early tonight unless something happens,"

he said to Derrick out of the silence that had gathered between them as they sat on their stools behind the counter after the arcade was clean. Derrick's nose was in a copy of *Epic*, one of the old science fiction magazines from the Monster Comics days.

"Yeah?" he said, sensing that something was different but not wanting to seem nosy.

Hawley looked up from his ledger. "Yeah," he said, turning to Derrick and looking him in the eyes. "And I think I'm kind of short here generally."

"Short?"

"I think I'm going to do something else," Hawley said. "I read about how you can open an office and do phone sales. No monthly overhead except for rent and the phone bill, clock out by five every night. No more booths."

"No!" said Derrick, reflexively; he didn't know what else to say. It was weird to feel sentimental about his time in the arid, creepy darkness of the store. But it was nice to have a job with downtime for reading; he knew sketching in his notebook was a luxury few other jobs would offer. He dreaded the prospect of job interviews, having to dress up for them and answer questions: "Why do you want this job? Do you see yourself staying with it?" The people asking these questions—at restaurants, at convenience stores—were barely older than he was. Most of them still had wispy facial hair. It was embarrassing. The store job was perfect, in its way.

Hawley laughed. "Derrick, it's just a dirty bookstore," he said. "Places like this come and go. Every job you get after this one will be better than this one."

Derrick considered this for a moment in silence. He tried, but he couldn't find a counterargument. "Well, no more booths, then," he said finally; he ventured half a smile, trying to guess at his boss's feelings.

"I'm sorry," said Hawley. "There's just not any money in it, you know. Been doing this three or four years now on my end. It starts to get to you."

"I hear that," Derrick said, but he could tell there was something else. He wanted to know; he wondered if he could help. But he decided to wait it out.

"Besides," Hawley said, and then he paused for a moment; what he wanted to say was more a feeling than a thought, but he felt like he might miss the chance to do Derrick a small favor if he held it back. "If you look around—I'm not in any position to judge anybody, but just for myself, you know, when I go home and think about this place, sometimes I remember how when I was a kid it was a diner. You know? Or even when it was a normal newsstand."

"Yeah?" Derrick wasn't sure where Hawley was going with this idea.

"Well, and then I think about"—he extended his arm from his chest, like a master of ceremonies introducing a beauty contestant—"all *this*."

It was in Derrick's heart to disagree: "All this," to him, looked like money in the bank and the right to say you answered to no one. What was more, the people who came in here weren't going to suddenly get religion if they showed up one day to find the place closed; they'd just go get the same thing six or seven exits farther down the highway. Why not keep taking the money, if it was just there for the taking?

He understood the bit about some weird tension between the interior of the store and the world outside—stepping into the sunlight after being inside too long was always a little like returning to Earth from space, or passing through a portal between conflicting realities. But that feeling, for him, never followed him all the way home. He hadn't considered how it might be different for Hawley, who worked here seven days a week, and who stayed until midnight on weeknights and then even later on weekends, changing twenties for whoever came to a place like this that late.

"Guess I can see what you mean," he said. "If this was a business you loved, it would be different."

"It would be different."

"Still, like, I don't know," he said. "It'll be weird when it's gone. I get a lot of reading done in here when it's slow."

The screen door in front of the front door was opening; it triggered an electronic doorbell. "We'll talk more. It won't be right away," Hawley said, turning. He nodded to the customer as he came in, a man in a baseball cap who looked nervous, but he offered no verbal greeting and didn't look directly at him. Etiquette. Wait for the customer to say hi first. It's not exactly a *rule* in stores like this, but it's a good idea.

HAD THEY WANTED GOLD

Derrick left his shift after a couple of hours; he was always home by dinner. He wasn't attuned to currents in town gossip, but he wondered if there weren't a few people getting ready to register their displeasure with the fate of Valley News; small towns are always looking for something to make a big deal about. As far as he could tell, though, Hawley had managed to duck the radar since making the switch.

Still, he wondered if his father knew. Plenty of men who didn't look that different from his dad came and went daily.

Every teenager who gets a job knows the leverage it suddenly affords them with their parents: even the most loving mother and father in the world are a little glad, after seventeen or eighteen years of raising a child, to have the house to themselves in the afternoon for an hour or two.

He crossed two creeks on the way home: he did this on purpose. He knew the line that cut the straightest distance between the doomed bookstore by the freeway and his family's duplex, nested tightly among several dozen other identical ready-mades, but it pained him. There was nothing to see, and it made his life feel boring. Taking a few extra turns allowed his mind to wander, and allowing his mind to wander was one of Derrick's best-loved luxuries.

There was a lot of construction lately, or it seemed that way. Old buildings getting renovated. Apartments turning into condominiums, jazzy landscaping out front and ridiculous new names like "Falcon's Landing." Derrick had seen these places before all the computer people started putting down roots; he knew what they really were, no matter how anybody tried to dress them up. Still, sometimes, at the right time of day, he sensed a little glamour in the modest boomtown makeover everything was getting. He'd have renamed plenty of places around town, too, given the chance—there was an old building that looked like it must have been a real estate office once but was a church now, and he liked to call it the Ghost Temple, which was a shortening of its actual name: Spirit of Prophecy Church of the Living God.

There were a couple of people standing on the grass in front of it talking to each other today, he saw as he passed. They were dressed in business clothes: a woman in a plain brown skirt and matching jacket over a cherry-red blouse, and a man in a plain grey suit and lavender tie. He was near enough to them to catch some of their conversation as he passed, just enough to know that they were realtors.

"Zoned for retail or rental or really whatever you want," he heard from one of them, and something about permits from the other, and then they were behind him. They'd been standing in front of the church's modest, sun-faded marquee, which presently cast a shadow over an even more modest FOR SALE stuck into the grass, WILL BUILD TO SUIT. He'd raised an eyebrow, reading it silently to himself; it paired, in his mind, with Hawley's news about closing the store.

He tucked it away, continuing homeward. This was grown-up stuff, dull real-world stuff. He was now grown-up enough himself to be interested by it, but still young enough to think of it as somebody else's affair.

SOUGHT AND HIGHLY FAVORED

But the best thing about the long walk home was that extending it didn't make it feel less purposeful. Any additional zigs and zags represented an alternate route, not idle distractions. Wandering around is great, but it's better to have a destination.

This distinction was one of many like it that Derrick had been quietly filing in his memory since childhood. Reckoned together, they didn't quite amount to a creed. They were more like a list that had taken on mildly dogmatic aspirations: 7 Up over Sprite; short story anthologies over single-author collections, but novels over both; space opera over sword and sorcery; but dystopian future earth movies over both of these and over alternative history science fiction, if only by a little—and all four of these better than epic fantasy, which was sword and sorcery without the swords and with worse sorcerers. Night over day, late afternoon over morning, but morning over dusk, long sleep over naps, midnight over noon. *Twilight Zone* over *Outer Limits*. Shields over armor, castles over forts, turrets over towers. By the end of his walk, he sometimes found he'd argued himself out of a position he'd thought immutable at its beginning; there was real pleasure, even joy, in the process.

There were three manila envelopes on the coffee table when he got home. His mother had put them there, trying to make it look casual; the stack had a studied splay to it. But Derrick knew what they were, and that they'd been placed on the table specifically for his eyes. They were college brochures. It was expected that he'd apply to in-state schools first, out of practicality, but his mother knew her son wanted to see more of the world.

She hadn't had the chance herself. She'd gone straight to nursing school from high school; there'd been a very persuasive recruiter on campus who said an associate's degree in nursing would travel with you wherever you went. A license that worked like a passport to decent jobs anywhere in the world sounded very appealing to young Diane Coleman; but, during her clinical rotations, she kept hearing that the real money was in overtime pay, which was there for any nurses willing to work it. She remembered this when she landed her first job out of school, and she never looked back.

The overtime crew at any work site is an invisible elite. They settle into their work as if it were part of them, and cash in unused vacation pay not out of greed but out of habit. She'd picked this habit up early, advancing from floor nurse to assistant charge to shift charge over just a few years; once she ran out of promotions to seek, she starting working toward her bachelor's degree. Marrying Bill (he worked in medical records; their courtship consisted of two years' worth of lunch breaks), having a child with him: it only slowed her down a little. As private hospitals around the valley closed or consolidated, she learned to land on her feet; new hospitals actively recruited her before they'd even admitted their first patients.

She had worked her entire life, seeing hard work as the price she paid for the things she liked best about herself: her independence, her experience, her authority. Derrick was more like his father, a bookworm who'd found that high-ceilinged rooms full of medical files were peaceful places to read if you got ahead of your work early in the shift. She didn't begrudge Bill his books; Bill with his books was a joy in her life. The palpable energy of his focus in his chair by the bookcase as he leafed through shiny paperbacks with spaceships on their covers. The pleasure he took in just being there. But she'd tried, without making a show of it, to infect Derrick with some of her ambition. It had served her well.

Derrick picked up the envelope on top of the fanned stack and physically suppressed a laugh. "Where am I going to college now?" he said. His mother was in the next room.

"You're going to college at whichever one of these offers you the best loan package," said Diane, who was in the living room, on the sofa; at work, save for the hour she spent charting and another half hour at lunch, she spent the whole day on her feet.

"Kenyon!" Derrick said, opening the envelope. "Isn't it kind of cold in Ohio?"

"It gets cold most places," said his mother, coming in and picking up the other two envelopes. "There'll be some more of these. I tried not to overdo it, but they say to apply to as many as you can. I'll send everything in if you just fill out your forms. You have the grades."

Derrick thought about Anthony Hawley, setting up a clean but grim office somewhere in San Jose where he'd try to sell God knows what to old people over the phone; he hated to think of Hawley's life as a cautionary tale. People liked him well enough, didn't they? He lived in a nice enough duplex, didn't he? But his mother's aspirational zeal had a sort of glow to it. Other ways of thinking about the world tended to look a little bloodless in that light.

He looked at the return addresses on the other envelopes she'd handed him: New York University. Wesleyan. These were among the schools his friends in AP English would be applying to, the big names his advisor had recited to him just a few weeks back during their obligatory "what's next for you" talk. September wasn't even over yet. It felt like things were moving fast.

"I do have the grades," Derrick said, measuring his response; his mother's vigilance about his college applications felt a little smothering, but he knew this was important to her. He slipped the envelopes gently into his backpack. "We're *real* early with these."

She gave him a hard look. "Early bird gets the worm," she said.

He smiled. "I got it, Mom, I *got* it," he said, already heading down the hall to his room with the posters, and the stereo, and the notebooks, and the box full of Sharpies.

She exhaled only after he was safely out of sight. She had no desire to put her only son on a flight bound for New York or Ohio or Connecticut next August; the house would feel empty, and her life would require a new ground plan. She wouldn't go idle when he was gone: she'd find things to do. She always kept busy. But all versions of her life, for almost nineteen years, had involved Derrick: if she'd been absent from the house more than she might have liked, that was because she was in the process of building something special and safe for his future.

That future was almost upon her now, she knew. She saw his potential; he could already take care of himself, if he'd needed to. But teaching your children to take care of themselves and letting them do it are two different things. The former is a long labor of patience, and focus, and forbearance. The latter requires skills you never have time to learn when you're busy practicing patience, maintaining focus, and picking battles. Most parents are unprepared for the time to let go; even if they've managed to find time and space to contemplate the arrival of the moment, it seems to come too soon. Diane Hall was different from many parents in a lot of ways, but not in this one.

TRIBUTE

A few days later, Derrick pedaled over to Monster Adult X on his bicycle; a breeze cooled his face as he rode. He vanished into the feeling, the action of his legs pushing the bike over the blacktop, the blur of the world going by. Would there ever be a day when this feeling didn't evoke fond memories of childhood—his father teaching him to ride a bicycle on the playground at school in early January; telling his friends, on the first day back after Christmas break, about his new bike, how he'd arrived at the foot of the Christmas tree at 5:30 a.m. and seen it there, foil garlands wound around it, light from the tree sparkling in the foil like magic; the day some time later when, at last, the training wheels came off. These images rode with him every time he began to work the pedals; they set the stage.

He mulled over Hawley's news as he rode. He was privately a little relieved; he'd felt certain more than once that his parents were ready to call him into the living room one evening and tell him they knew everything—about the store, the hours after school, the money under the table. *We're disappointed you'd try to keep secrets from us*, they would say—that would be Dad's word, delivered slowly and with resonance handed down over generations: *disappointed*. His mother would be angry, but anger was different. Anger passes. Disappointment vibrates.

The bell dinged when he opened the door; Derrick noticed that Hawley looked oddly chipper for a weekday afternoon inside a dark bookstore where people came to do things in secret. "Hey, now," he said.

"Hey, now, yourself," said Hawley. He smiled broadly; he was never unfriendly in his aspect, but this felt like an unusual look.

"Everything all right?" Derrick asked. He was already headed for the supply closet, but Hawley stopped him: physically stopped him, gently but firmly putting his hand on his shoulder.

"I don't want you cleaning up back there anymore," he said.

"Come on," said Derrick. "Nothing I haven't done before."

"No," said Hawley, "it's not like that. It's just—I want to be out of here by the end of the month. I don't trust them to prorate me if I'm still here even a minute into October. And I'm not taking anything with me. So it doesn't matter if we take care of this place now, and there's no need for you to give everything the Cadillac treatment like you do."

Derrick raised his eyebrows more pointedly than he generally allowed himself to when adults were present. "It will get nasty back there," he said.

"I'll mop the halls. That's it. They raised the rent on me four times in the short time I've been here. Four times, you know?"

Either Hawley had been carefully masking real anger over the whole affair, or it had taken a little while to surface. But Derrick could see it now: resentment. Spite. Maybe he'd spent a few days thinking about it.

"So they can just clean that shit up themselves," Hawley concluded, looking back down at the counter the way he'd often done to indicate that a subject was now closed.

Derrick sat down on one of the two barstools behind the counter, the one he considered his: it had a maroon seat cover made out of leatherette, attached to the cushion by hexagonal gold-colored metal studs so old they boasted a kind of grimy patina. To Derrick, this chair had always looked like a prop from a scene in a low-budget movie: a crew of medieval nobodies at the tavern, sitting around drinking before the guy who's come to wreck the village shows up.

"Landlord's gonna be mad," Derrick remarked, getting out a sketchbook.

"Then she can *be* mad," Hawley said, his tone mild but conclusive. The landlord's pleasure was no longer his concern.

The bell sounded again as a pair of customers came inside: college students, from the look of them, a man and a woman, both visibly trying as hard as they could to not look nervous.

SOLO I

In its brief operating days, the Monster Adult X arcade boasted seven booths in total: six for single occupants and one couples booth. You had to select one specific movie to watch if you wanted the couples booth, and you paid eight dollars to watch it in the comfort of a booth with a long bench seat down the back and a small love seat to the side of the screen. The other booths, minus their screens, might as easily have been confessionals: dark, austere, private. All were lockable from the inside by a sliding bolt latch; these locks may or may not have been legal. Had the store lasted longer, somebody from the city might have taken an interest in the question.

But nobody did; Monster Adult X barely pinged anybody's radar. Its flickering existence had been a brief detour on Anthony Hawley's travels through entrepreneurship. Beyond the business license, the only outward sign of the life inside had been an advertisement in the Yellow Pages, under "BOOKS—NEW AND SPECIALTY": set off by a bold black border, and featuring a small clip-art portrait of a clean-cut man with a very firm jaw, it stood out from the more demure ads with which it shared space on the page. PRIVATE BOOTHS, the text read in part. When I talked to him, Hawley seemed amused by my interest in the details.

"I know it was seven booths because of the whole thing with Derrick's friends later," he said. "I remember that. And I remember the couples booth because the couples cleaned up after themselves, unlike the guys in the solo booths, who . . ."

He pursed his lips. "You wouldn't believe what some of these guys get up to in there. It would make you sick. And they write on the walls, or carve designs in there. Who does that? Gets out their pocketknife while they're watching the porno movie and just carves something in the wall."

But these carvings, occasionally, either by virtue of their sheer crudeness or because of some detail that grabbed the imagination and wouldn't let go, made cleanup—the worst part of the job, and also its most recurring, reliable function—a little less degrading, and a little more interesting. Derrick judged them like entries in a competition. The first solo booth, just to the right of the arcade entrance, had had two carvings, both predating Devil House; neither would have made his honorable mentions list. One looked like an eyeball but was probably supposed to be a breast. The other was unmistakably a penis drawn by a person whose feeling for the organ was one part wonder to two parts revulsion; none of the later work done to improve it could wholly mask the veins that had once popped out from under its skin, or the sinewy detail of the frenulum.

Still, one evidentiary photograph shows how a later-arriving artist had tried to improve upon it, doing his level best to transform the glans into the head of a sea serpent that looked like one of the Godzilla knockoffs who used to show up on late-night TV. The batwing-like ears jutting out from it are stark, and striking; the urethral meatus is now only one pupil among three gazing out from carefully rounded, menacing eyes.

No one familiar with Derrick's hand—his gently wavering lines, the slumping biomorphic shapes—could mistake this work for his. Derrick's work awaited the onlooker's attention; it repaid the eye wise enough to dwell on it with detail and nuance. Even his most garish pieces had a softness, and doted on line and curve that seemed to soften their content. The penis-monster in Solo Booth I is also quite detailed—its scales are meticulous, the claws at the ends of its bulbous feet are of uniform length. But the hand that drew it feels driven: the point of the piece seems not decorative but communicative.

It has to be Seth. Seth wanted to say something to the outside world when he drew, even if the chances anyone would see it, or care when they did, were infinitesimally small.

Often, if you have an exact enough description of the primary source you're looking for, you can follow its movements—you can find out when it changed hands, and for how much, and how heated or tepid the bidding was during the auction. Once in a while, when buyers or sellers get sloppy, you can even find out their names and cull their contact information. All it takes is someone whose hurry was too great to check the "keep this information private" box on a single click-through screen, and many auctions end in a short flurry of click-throughs: people get impatient. Archaeologists have determined that the earliest written records in existence were sales records; if you can get your hands on a bill of sale, or, even better, a ledger, the data you harvest tell a vivid story provided you know how to connect the dots.

In the case of Derrick's notebooks, however, the buyers have been on their game, and cannot be tracked. I've got alerts set in case either book should come up for sale again, but I'm not hopeful. The people who raid the Internet for relics like these aren't investors. They're collectors, and if this were Derrick's notebook, it would be in their hands, not mine. It's Seth's. When it came up for auction, only dumb luck and decent search terms brought it to my attention. The blind-lot grab-bag the seller had found left him grasping for straws:

£ΩΩK! *RARE* ∞MURDER SCENE∞ ARTICLE NOT RE-COVERED BY POLICE. NOTEBOOK FROM FAMOUS DEVIL HOUSE CASE IN THE 80s, *VERY FEW* EVER TURN UP . . . SAFE SHIPPING GUARANTEED OR ADD INSURANCE. CHECK MY REVIEWS FOR OTHER CRIME FINDS AND BID WITH CONFIDENCE

Technically, it's not really a notebook at all. It's a loose-leaf binder with three sturdy spiral rings holding forty-seven pages total, the last sixteen of which are blank except for a few stray marks: somebody testing a ball-point to see if it still has ink. It's a sketchbook, for the most part, though the detailed, murky monsters of its pages are occasionally interrupted by sloppy paragraphs in a crimped hand, lines sometimes running past the red margin and sometimes stopping well short of it.

Save up bus fare to (SF or even Seattle???) bcz this won't last, the first of these interrupting pages begins. *Is there a safe behind the counter?? Otherwise keep in _r_____ _n____.* I spent an hour working out possibilities for the blank spaces here, but couldn't come up with anything conclusive—"broken [something]"? "Trick [something]"? "Green knapsack"? Probably not "knapsack." You can really spend a lot of time with things you're not ever going to nail down.

I think they Know, the next one starts. There's a picture of an eyeball underneath these words. It's not identical to any of the eyes on the penis-monster in the first solo booth, but the harshness of its line—the way the rounded curves darken as they progress toward their meeting point; the reinforced thickness—seems sufficient. *Ang saw people snooping around and warned me. Everybody worried now. Feel like shit. Ang says I shouldn't feel bad it's nobody's fault. Knew this couldn't last forever but oh well.*

"Knew this couldn't last forever but oh well." If the true crime goblins cruising the web for rare finds had actually known what this unassuming-looking binder actually was, I'd never have even learned it existed. But I did, and its contents awakened my first suspicions that Devil House, and in particular the story of Derrick Hall, was something wholly apart from any old news stories Ashton might have run across on his lunch hour: the reality of it was something different from the story told by the local press and, eventually, by the national news media. It would be a disservice to the living and the dead alike to rehash these stories; it would be beneath me, I thought, which was saying something. I haunt dreadful places and try to coax ghosts from the walls, and then I sell pictures of the ghosts for money. I'm not ashamed of my work—I think it's good, when it's good. I won't apologize for that. But I also can't argue too strenuously against several cases that might be made against it; and this notebook made me pause, in the stillness of a summer evening in this ridiculous house, where nothing much ever happened save occasional knocks on the door from speculative realtors. I wondered how much of the story I'd come to tell was something I'd brought with me, more outline awaiting shades than a blank page seeking figures who lived in three dimensions.

It was a moment. I made note of it. Then I reflected that I'd already claimed half my advance against royalties, and returned to my work.

2.

YELLOW MOLD

It took ten minutes from his doorstep to school if he rode his bike: he'd timed it. Most days it took a little longer, but the direct route—north, then west, then north again—could be done in ten flat if he set out at a clip and didn't let up.

The other way from his house to school cut south through Cardoza Park, crossing under the cloverleaf before riding up Escuela Parkway. There was no good reason to take this route;

it cost a few extra minutes, risked more stoplights, and didn't boast better scenery than the quicker path. But he left early for school and rode south from his door all the same, both because the empty streets in the early morning felt free and peaceful in a way that had always appealed to him, and because the longer way around would take him past Monster Adult X. He was curious to see if anything had happened to it yet.

It didn't look any different. Gates hadn't even gotten around to putting up a sign. The grass in the useless little side yard was uncut and ragged, and there were beer cans and empty potato chip bags in the entryway. Freeway detritus, eternal. Out of habit, Derrick picked some of it up and carried it around back to the Dumpster. And then, leaning into a different habit, he took the key he still had on his key ring and opened the back door.

It felt weird; Milpitas was a sleepy town, but police sometimes parked under the on-ramp. He punched in the alarm code, which still worked—maybe nothing would have happened if he hadn't, since he knew Hawley wouldn't have paid the security company a dime past September, but he didn't want to chance it. Inside, things were unchanged. If there'd been any prospective buyers stopping by to survey the property, they'd left no trace of their visits.

He sat down in his old seat behind the front counter; it was dark inside, but a little morning light seeped in through the painted-over windows, just enough to sketch by. He got out a notebook, and he spent fifteen minutes working on his coat of arms. It was an idea he'd been sporadically refining ever since first hearing about shields and crests in the fourth grade: trying to squeeze a true representation of himself into a single image appealed to him on an almost basic level. It was a task whose

culmination both beckoned and threatened; every new itera-
tion of his crest gave both the satisfaction of having arrived
somewhere new and the possibility of greater refinements
down the line.

Derrick's crest as it presently stood had four quadrants, up
from three in childhood. The balance appealed to him. The
concepts he hoped to depict had grown denser and more abstract over the years, and would have been hard to explain to
outsiders, but he didn't talk about them to anybody but Seth,
who, of course, had dozens of crests of his own, each wilder
than the last: The Shield of Unbreakable Perfection. The Great
Flag of Blood Warfare. Death's Herald.

The upper left quadrant, Derrick had lately considered,
should be the thing everybody knows about you, because it's
the first one the eyes land on; but he also knew most people
considered him a nice guy first and foremost, which was fine,
but not exactly the sort of thing you hold up against a renegade
knight in battle. So he was working on images of speed: wings,
horses, lightning bolts.

He could work for fifteen minutes, maybe twenty, before
he'd need to leave for school. Each of these minutes felt like
stolen treasure. Time to work in the quiet: free of obligation,
free of future plans. Free of questions that needed answers.
When he finished, he thought idly about leaving his notebook
behind; maybe he'd be more certain to come back later if
he didn't. But he didn't like to be without his supplies, so he
packed everything away, reset the alarm, and left the way he'd
come. There was still nobody around. The world felt like a
movie set, or like a carbon copy of itself with fewer people and
cars gumming up the works and getting in the way.

Derrick's last class of the day was Spanish 2, which he considered easy; he'd taken Introduction to Spanish freshman year and aced the weekly tests without studying much at all. Some students were struggling with verb tenses in second year, but for Derrick it was simple stuff: memorize five endings, tack them onto the roots, half of which gave you a pretty good guess at their English equivalents.

Derrick sat in the back to keep Seth company; Seth sat in the back because he probably should have repeated Spanish 1. He was a mess today. There'd been pizza in the cafeteria for lunch, and the cooks had burnt two pans' worth of it and then thrown them into the trash before lunch period ended. At any high school in the U.S., this is an error in judgment unless the school's trash bins are housed behind a locked gate. At Milpitas High, the cafeteria's trash bins stood on a concrete dock; it had a gate, but it usually wasn't locked.

The pizza fight had been short—somebody saw a proctor coming and everybody scattered in time to avoid getting caught—but Seth had been at the center of it, lobbing slices rapid-fire like a medieval soldier flinging half-pikes. His insistence on landing as many clean shots as possible meant there'd been no attention left for defense, and in just a few minutes he was coated from head to mid-chest in tomato sauce and sticky, coagulating cheese. He stopped by the bathroom—it still said BOYS on the door, which felt weirder every year—to soak his shirt with water and wring it out in the sink, but it hadn't really helped. Seth hunched even lower than usual at his desk, avoiding the radar.

"Man, what is wrong with you?" Derrick whispered while Mr. Martínez was writing down irregular verbs on the blackboard, his back to the class. Seth didn't answer verbally but punched Derrick sharply in the thigh. Derrick smiled with his mouth closed, trying not to laugh.

Martínez turned around. "Derrick, could you conjugate *volver* in the preterit for us just to get us started?" he said.

"I can do that," said Derrick: "*Yo vuelvo, tú vuelves, él o ella vuelve, nosotros vuelvemos, ellos vuelven.*"

"Pretty close," said Martínez. "It reverts to the stem for the first person plural. So."

Derrick scanned the list of verbs on the board. "OK, so, *volvemos?*"

"*Volvemos,*" nodded Mr. Martínez, turning back to the board just long enough for Seth to hit Derrick in the leg again.

In the hallway, after class, Derrick quickly claimed his payback, connecting a sharp, straight jab to Seth's upper arm. "Ouch," said Seth, and then: "Fair, though." They'd known each other since junior high; they'd grown apart. Derrick didn't know what Seth did with his free time these days. But in class their old bond held firm. Like Derrick, Seth drew in his notebook when his mind started to wander: lines with sharp edges, monsters with claws. He gripped his pencil so tightly that there was a permanent callus on his middle finger; over the years, they'd seen each other's styles grow into formed aesthetics, and known the pleasure of growing together, of becoming adept at a craft they valued. They'd grown together in this nearly invisible, almost private pursuit. Derrick felt physically protective of Seth, whose body seemed stunted, like a tree afflicted by some mild blight, and he knew that leaving for college would fix Seth in his past, maybe permanently. But in the pages of their notebooks, they were equals.

They walked across campus together. They talked about people they knew, and people they used to know who probably weren't going to graduate; Seth mentioned Alex, but Derrick didn't like to think about Alex. Alex was considered "missing." "Missing" is a hard word to hear said about somebody whose friendship had been, in your younger days, a great joy. People drift, even friends who used to go to the matinee together every other Saturday when they were kids; that's just how it is. But after you lose track of them, Derrick was learning, it hurts.

"Wanna ride someplace?" Seth asked as they arrived at the bike rack.

"*You* wanna ride someplace?" Derrick asked, smiling cryptically.

"What do you got?" said Seth.

"Follow me, young warrior," Derrick said, pedaling back toward Monster Adult X.

MINOANS II

"Yo, I never really went into one of these places before," Seth said as they entered the darkness of the back hallway. "You sure this is OK?"

"Relax," said Derrick, laughing. "This really isn't technically 'one of those places' anymore. It's closed." He flipped the lights on; the store with the lights on and nobody inside it was one of the strangest sights Seth had ever seen, like the Yellow Brick Road gone degenerate.

"Whoa," he said.

"It's weird, right?"

"I don't—" Seth grabbed a VHS shell from the nearest rack. The cover art was blurry, and in black-and-white. "*The Whore Next Door.* Is this, like, homemade or something?"

"Yeah, he had all kinds of crazy stuff in here."

"Had?"

"That's why we're here, dude. Store's closed. He's leaving everything here for the owners to clear out because he's salty about having to leave. They haven't even checked in, as far as I know. Until something happens, this is basically, like, my treehouse."

"Whoa," Seth said again. He began strolling around the store, scanning the walls and floors like a foreman sizing up a building site.

"Yeah. I've been using it as my, umm, my *studio*," Derrick said, putting on an upper-crusty accent and pulling out his sketchbook. "If you can get over the, uh, *décor*, it's nice."

"*Décor*." Seth laughed, taking down another tape. "*Neighborhood Pussy*."

Seth was a quick study; although teachers and other interested adults worried a lot about whether he was learning the right skills to help him survive in the big world of adults and jobs and responsibilities, his wits were sharp. He reached into his backpack and retrieved a pen-style X-Acto knife, the kind the journalism class used in paste-up.

"If they ever search your backpack you're gonna get expelled for that," Derrick said.

Seth rolled his eyes. "Dude. Watch," he said. He gripped the VHS case in his left hand about half a head below eye level; working quickly with his right, he carved out the eyes of the model on the front cover. Then he sliced a couple of snake-like s's into her forearms, and a perfect equilateral triangle into the center of her midriff. It took him only a minute, maybe two; his casual speed with the blade was like a magician's sleight of hand.

He flipped it around so Derrick could see. Just three modifications to the naked woman with the girl-next-door face made her look like a demon priestess. Lowering his voice to a demonic gurgle and making a face, Seth growled: *"Neighbor-hood Satan!"*

"Dude, stop," said Derrick, but he couldn't keep a straight face; Seth had known how to get a laugh out of Derrick since playground days.

He put the case back on the rack. Face-out, the changes on the model's body registered just enough to cause a double-take. Seth was happy with his work; he scanned the other titles on the same rack, wondering if a second one would spoil the effect of a single defaced picture. And then he turned to Derrick and said: "We can seriously have all this, though?"

His normal voice was so earnest, so young, Derrick had to laugh again. There wasn't anybody really like Seth in this world; it'd be a nicer world if everybody could have a friend like Seth.

"All this can be yours," Derrick said in his rich-butler voice again.

KNIGHTS ENTRY

They spent an hour or so together in the store. It felt strange to both of them, two young men in a place usually visited by older men who almost always arrived unaccompanied. But Seth saw all the possibilities; they were visible on his face, and palpable in his energy. He cased the place like an artist pricing out supplies. When, after a while, he joined Derrick behind the counter, he found a roll of Scotch tape on a shelf underneath the cash register and began assembling a collage on notebook paper. From the *Neighborhood Pussy* housing, he taped the eyes and stray *s*'s to the page; they looked lonely there, so he headed out into the racks to grab more materials. "You're sure this is OK?" he said.

"Everything's gotta go," Derrick said. "I can't stay long, though. Now that it's early-acceptance season Mom wants to talk every day." Seth didn't respond; Derrick knew he'd collected several failing grades over the years—in PE, in civics, in history. Things Seth didn't care about. When he didn't care, he couldn't focus.

The silence gathered for a moment, and, in it, Derrick had the kind of melancholy realization that lands on people repeatedly during their senior year in high school. *Whatever happens next, this won't be part of it.* He tried to think of things he'd miss about Milpitas—bike rides on known streets, people he'd known half his life, the many perks of familiarity that only feel like burdens if you fear never being relieved of them.

"You could stay here and draw if you make sure and lock up," he said.

"Yeah?" Seth said.

"Yeah," Derrick said. "But you gotta punch in the code. You have to promise. The cops will come otherwise."

"Is it—"

Derrick picked up a pen and wrote it at the top of the page where Seth was presently sketching a tall tower with half a dozen small, dark cave entrances ominously dotting its height.

"Five-seven-five-seven-one-star," he said as he wrote. "OK? Five-seven-five-seven-one-star. The star is the lower right. Come have a look." Together they went to the back, and Derrick armed and disarmed the alarm several times.

"That number seems pretty easy to guess," Seth said.

"That's because you're ignorant," Derrick said, ducking Seth's punch in response. "That's because you're ignorant" was a phrase left over from a brief phase Derrick had gone through in grade school when he and all his friends had been trying out meaner aspects than the ones most would eventually settle into. It was a shared memory of long ago; calling back to that time made their connection vivid, immediate.

"Now you," Derrick said. Seth passed the test on the first try.

"There's a hundred thousand ways to make a five-number combo," Derrick said, standing in the doorway to the outside now, the setting sun behind him. "Nobody's ever going to guess it. I'll see you tomorrow. Remember to lock."

"Got it," said Seth.

"No, man, seriously, though," Derrick said. "Seriously. I don't mean to be all like this, but if you don't lock up, trouble for everybody. Lock up like I showed you or all this will be gone."

"*All this will be gone,*" Seth said, lowering his voice and gesturing dramatically behind him with one hand, toward the clamshell cases and the racks and the as-yet-unexplored alcoves of the arcade.

THE ANCIENT ART OF ASTROLOGY

[*Interior: a small office in the 1980s; MARC BUCKLER, a young man in smart business wear—grey blazer, crisp pink shirt—at his desk, atop which sit period-appropriate cosmopolitan desktop accessories: sleek black-and-silver multi-line phone, miniature "magic window" sand toy on a clear plexiglass stand, etc.*]

[*CHYRON lower screen center throughout scene. Text, yellow or red, all-caps: DRAMATIC RE-CREATION*]

BUCKLER [*mid-conversation*]: . . . perfect. Perfect. And it's how many square feet? [*pauses*] How many subdividable? [*pauses, listens*] Great. And, making sure I'm correct here, zoned commercial? [*pauses, laughs*] Well, OK, I hear you, but I have to be honest, "zoned commercial" makes us nervous down here. Not really our area. At all. They will ding you down here if you screw up on zoning. Just ding you. Just six blocks from where I'm sitting, one violation can tie your business up for— [*pauses, listens*] Sure, no, you're right, you're right, but I've seen it, people get cold feet. I'm just telling you. I have a colleague from up closer to you who says there's some towns where nobody really cares, but I— [*pauses, listens*] Sure. Anyhow, no real reason to get ahead of ourselves. I can't make any promises until I see the property. But I feel good about this! We had some good experiences last year expanding into, you know, Arizona. When's good? I'm not in a hurry, but at the same time I could be there whenever.

[*As he hangs up, PAN around office. Aside from the desk, décor is sparse. A corkboard on one wall with motivational phrases in Sharpie on lined paper, stuck to the board with colorful pins: BELIEVE IN THE RESULTS. REPRESENT WHAT YOU PRESENT. STAY OUT OF YOUR OWN WAY.*]

FLAGSTONES

The architect's name has been lost. The man or men who designed Lonnie Roberts's diner, who planned its rise from pencil-on-paper to brick-and-beam, left no record of their instructions: they did their work, then vanished forever from the scene. There's no record anywhere of anything that preceded the luncheonette, it's true—but see, here, this walkway leading up to the door? These are old stones, old bricks. They were transported here in a time predating most of what we know about this plot of land. It's hard to imagine anyone, even some-one who didn't have to do all the hard work himself, going to all that trouble for something so small as a luncheonette.

Sorting through available views of city streets—streets as they originally appeared, in the early days of the automobile, and earlier, even, than that—supports this thought, of a house preceding all. Businesses rely on foot traffic to survive; they abut the street as nearly as they can. Demanding that a curious cus-tomer cross the lawn just to get a good look at what's behind the front window: Who does that? Not people who plan to build a business from the ground up. No. These flat stones whose jagged path arrives at Devil House's odd, unnecessary porch suggest that, in its final guise, it finally succeeded in reverting to its original form: a place where people gathered, and ate, and slept, and lived. The vision that came, briefly, to possess it—this was no innovation. It was a return, a retracing, a rebirth. A rad-ical, not to say new, form of excavation.

Whether the team that did the digging knew what business they were about doesn't matter much, in the long view. Whether tidy or sloppy, planned or haphazard, restoration seems to come to its own aid, given the right hands to help. But you have to wonder what they felt, looking out through the worn patches in the painted-over windows: whether they sensed that they'd brought back something from a past no one remembered, to sit impudently in the light for a short while, proud to be itself once more, a shelter again at last.

Seth did not go home that night. Once Derrick left, he stood for a moment looking in from the back entrance, surveying the scene: the narrow arcade entrance projecting from the back wall, the tiled rows of wire racks along the floor, the display case up front. He headed up to the front counter and picked up the phone to check for a dial tone; it hadn't been disconnected yet. Then he called home, telling Mom he planned to spend the night at Dave's. Dave had a cool mom; she was young, and never ratted anybody out for anything. She let Dave smoke cigarettes inside the house. It was wild.

Seth Healey had a cool mom, too, according to most of his friends. Derrick especially had always been a little jealous about how it didn't seem to matter what time Seth got home. For Seth, it was more complicated than that; he was an only child, and had been called "hyperactive" by his teachers from an early age. He'd gone through several different prescriptions intended to help him focus over the years, but he hated the way the medications made him feel. By the time he turned thirteen, he'd learned how to hide a pill in his cheek, and could hold it there until he got the chance to spit it out someplace—down the drain of the bathroom sink, or into a gutter while walking to school.

His adolescence seemed to exact, from Maria Healey, a greater measure of forbearance than she had left to give. Raising a child without a partner is hard enough; if the child in question needs extra care, it's harder. Seth's father was only good for two weeks a year, in summer; when Seth came home from Dad's he was usually worse for the wear. Irritable but needy, moody but aloof. When, sometime during freshman year, he began spending more time away from home in the afternoons, his mother didn't ask too many questions. Of course she loved her son; everybody who knew Seth wanted the best for him, she more than anyone. But if he was learning to make use of his own time, that was good, wasn't it? And her job kept her out of the house until four. A little quiet allowed her to put dinner together in peace, to steal a little time with the TV or radio by herself.

"If you're sure it's OK," she said over the phone. There was a pot of beef stew bubbling on the stove. "Call if you decide you want to come home early."

"I'll see you tomorrow, Mom," Seth said. The sun was setting; it would be dark inside soon. But he could still see, in his mind's eye, how things had looked in that moment when Derrick flipped the light switch on: all the fantastic angles, the dozen little projects a boy like Seth might make from a space like this. Showing off with a razor on a VHS case was just a toe in the water: now he would swim. He headed back into the arcade, precious felt-tip pens already retrieved from his backpack, a whole fistful of them: red, purple, black, pink, orange. When he crossed the threshold and saw the seven booths, their doors standing open, he felt the uncomfortable ache of inspiration. It made him want to jump out of his skin, but it wasn't unpleasant. Just a little overwhelming. This was going to take all night, he knew. He figured Derrick would understand.

When he finally ran out of energy, with only an hour left before daylight, he set the code on the back door and curled up inside one of the booths to sleep. It was a tight, cozy fit. To Seth, it felt a little like what he imagined camping was like—drifting off all by yourself inside a small, confined space with nothing to distract you beyond the walls of your tent. It wasn't comfortable in a physical sense, but there are many other kinds of comfort worth seeking out in this world.

3.

MINOANS III

The threshold to the arcade was changed. Curling strips of sturdy paper now hung from either side of the portal, affixed by tape, glue, or maybe staples—something slight enough that its presence could be entirely concealed by the scale and care of the greater composition. Derrick hadn't hit the light switch after closing the door behind him; it seemed better to keep the place dark now. But the display cases, whose fancy interior lighting had always been dim when the store was open—nobody cared about the displays; no bells and whistles were required for the people who needed the things inside the displays—were lit now, and the light was enough to set reflective effects off throughout the store. It was like the inside of a dark ride: just enough light to make you ask questions about what you were seeing.

He headed toward the arcade entrance. As he approached, he saw that its fresh decorations consisted of repurposed glossy stock: shards cut from VHS cases, twisted into corkscrews. Someone—Seth—had spent an hour, possibly two, transforming the grey entryway to the arcade into the mouth of a cave as it might appear in a dream. There was a color scheme to these cascading curls: dominant shades of silver and white at the arch, darkening as they traced a path to the floor, resolving midway down into something gaudier—red, orange, the brown of high-teased hair and the obligatory pink of human flesh. The bottom went blue and yellow, faceless primaries that framed the frenzied, nearly ecstatic middle. Linking these fields were the body parts and flimsy lingeries favored by almost any printed surface to be found in the store—bits of skin, eye, and camisole insinuated themselves, more as suggestions than as whole visions, as Derrick considered Seth's work.

On the way home the day before, he'd wondered how things might pan out in the hours following his departure. Seth tried to stay out of his mother's hair these days, he knew; it was one of the sweetest things about his old friend, how conscious he could be of the toll his company sometimes took on others. But he also knew Seth was easily distracted, and needed reminders for even the most basic tasks: To shower when you needed a shower. To zip up your backpack before you slung it over your shoulder. To follow through on promises you genuinely mean to keep.

He'd even thought about turning his bike around halfway home, to double-check, but he didn't want to be a nag. Now he stood at the arcade gate, admiring his childhood pal's initiative. Close up, you could see the care that had gone into this arrangement: the miserly space allowed to peek through the cut strips, the gradation of the color field.

"Are you back there, you crazy person?" Derrick hollered through the entrance, his hand cupped around his mouth.

MOAT

"Don't be mad" was the first thing he heard from somewhere inside—down the hall to the right somewhere. Derrick took in the changes as his eyes adjusted to the relative darkness of the arcade, and smiled: he could see how Seth might have been worried he'd gone too far, but how could Derrick—or anyone—have felt anything but wonder in the face of a vision as vast as this?

Movies were playing in every booth—you could hear them

going all at once. Their doors stood open, and the screens inside flooded the otherwise unlit hall with shifting patchwork patterns of light and dark. The scuffed-up floor looked like a bubbling stream underneath his feet: flashes of snow, gestures of grey.

On the rare busy day in the store, Derrick had heard what several movies playing at once sounded like from behind those doors when they were closed. Moans, gasps, and dirty words repeated with increasing urgency and rising pitch—a cacophony drawing on a common tongue, a roomful of people who weren't aware of one another's presence all making noise at once. The sound in the arcade now was different. "Seth?" he called, laughing now, the blurred sound too loud to let him think. He picked out the pornographic note from somewhere— some oohs, some aahs—but amid them, other notes, other voices: here dialogue, here music, here revving engines.

Seth emerged from the couples booth. "Your dude had a shelf of normal movies in the closet behind the counter," he said. "I loaded 'em up. That whole chain of tape players under the counter is *wild.*"

Derrick leaned into the nearest single booth: he recognized *Game of Death*, Bruce Lee's final picture. "Son of a bitch! Goddamn bastard!" he said, pointing his index finger stiffly at the screen and trying to make his lips move like an actor's in a dubbed movie.

"I know!" said Seth, relieved; he'd spent much of the morning fretting about how Derrick might react.

"You skipped school to set this up?" Derrick said.

"They're not gonna let me graduate anyway," Seth said.

"They told you that?"

"Last year they said I'd have to take summer school to get enough credits."

"So?"

"So, summer's over, I stayed home."

Now the squall of the screens became intrusive. Derrick wanted to tell his friend he still might make it to graduation if he started dedicating himself to his schoolwork, if he talked to the right people, if he made some kind of a deal. But none of that was true; Derrick would only have been describing how *he* might have dealt with Seth's problem if the problem were his. He didn't like to think of how different Seth's path was going to be from his own in the future, because the future was almost upon them both. Derrick had worked very hard for almost four years. Seth probably had, too, in his own way, but the world beyond school didn't seem like a place with tons of extra room for people who did things their own way.

"Man," Derrick said.

Seth scowled a little; Derrick was ruining the moment.

"Look inside the booths, dude, there's more to it than just the movies," he said, finding his register. He was proud of his work. That it wasn't going to last made it even better. It was just something cool to do while waiting for the next thing to come along.

Derrick ventured into the *Game of Death* booth. Its walls were covered in a canvas of flame through which peered cross-contour drawings of half-human faces arrested mid-scream, a vision of hell in red and blue Magic Marker. Fluctuations from the light on the screen obscured or illuminated the details. Anguished faces would resolve into clarity, then recede into the dark, only to reemerge again, as if asserting their own existence against the elements conspiring to keep them hidden.

"Dude, this is amazing stuff," Derrick said.

"That's only one!" Seth said, spreading his hands wide like

a state fair pitchman saying, *But wait, there's more.* "I worked all night!"

Derrick took in the six other open doors at a glance, and then he felt the contagion take hold. Seth was right. There wasn't any point in letting a chance like this go to waste. He could find an hour or two in the afternoons. Anthony Hawley was done with this place. Senior year was when you finally got to have a little fun, right? People said that. No more summers, not like the ones you'd been having since you were a kid. Make this last year count.

THE SHIFTING PRICE OF DISCRETION

There's a chance that, someday, I'm going to be the guy at the convention teaching the How to Succeed in True Crime workshop; I've known some of the guys who do these workshops, and they say it's actually fun, that it can really give you a jumpstart if you're feeling stuck—young faces looking up at you like you might be carrying the philosopher's stone in your pocket, scrutinizing your expression for signs of secret knowledge. There's no end to the different ways you can do these workshops: you can talk about how to follow up on inspiration, that's an hour all by itself with plenty of things to say in the one-to-ones afterward; or you can talk about structure, or plotting, or outlines—everybody needs technique; or you can talk about the Responsibility of the Author to His Subject, which nobody wants to hear about but which might come in handy later, and so on and on and on. No end. You can get down into the thorny details: how to talk to a stranger whose brother got killed by some maniac, what to look for in a crime scene photograph. But for me, the sticking point, the thing I'd want to talk about except that I don't know how, is what to do about the people you can't get close to because they're completely gone. The conversations no one ever heard, the events you have to imagine, the unknown thing you have to bring to life and present as something real that came and went and left a small mark on the world.

That's Marc Buckler, for me. I didn't know him; I'm never going to know him, because he's dead. I can't ask Evelyn Gates what it was like to talk to him, either, because she's dead, too; plenty of people remember her, but there's nobody up here who knew Marc Buckler. I could call his parents; I'm not going to do that. For them, he is the central figure in this story; from where I sit, he's collateral damage, and, unless I really wanted to put on a show for them, they'd know that. What's worse, they'd know that I'm right. Marc Buckler could have been anybody. Somebody was going to call Evelyn Gates at some point and ask what she wanted for the property by the freeway. Somebody, someday, was going to follow up; there's no surer investment than property. Whoever called Evelyn Gates was going to arrive at the mouth of Devil House and be surprised, and then things were going to unfold as they did, because people, even and maybe especially young people, feel a need to guard the things and places they hold dear from becoming polluted. Buckler, as detectives would have it, was just in the wrong place at the wrong time.

Nobody really cares about Marc Buckler, including me. I have to breathe a little life into him so that when he dies you'll care enough to feel bad about it, even if you feel, as you might, sympathy for his killer, who was only protecting his home. Or hers. We don't really know, and we're not going to know.

There's a lot we don't know.

But I had a dream, anyway, about Marc Buckler's first trip

to Milpitas. We know he came here twice. The details of that first trip are recoverable—I know and have already mentioned some of them; his airline, his rental car, his drinks with Evelyn Gates. I have a few receipts. What I don't have is the look on his face when he and Gates take the Milpitas exit, and he sees, over there on the other side of the windshield, a smaller town than he's ever visited in his life. Did he get that half-frightened, half-condescending look cosmopolitans get when they pull over for gas at some last-chance stop? Did he begin spinning fictions about people who'd live in a town so small, imagining them as being like country folk in an episode of *The Twilight Zone*? I know that when I first got to town, I felt surprised by how modern it seemed, for lack of a better word: there are fewer old buildings here than there are in San Francisco; there's less of the past angling for room in the frame. But Marc Buckler didn't come from San Francisco; down where he lived, raze-and-renew had been the rule for as long as anybody could remember. Maybe he didn't take any note of details like these, thinking instead in spreadsheets, in projections, in the possibility of the easy score.

In my dream, though, he notices something as they ease down the off-ramp. It's the change in scale, the nearness of things. It's the feeling that, not so long ago, there were hills and dirt roads here: in Southern California, you have to strain to imagine such days, but up north their aura has a half-life. It's fading, and it'll fade even further as the march of progress continues, but in the right light you feel like it's only receding a little, gathering strength, waiting for its time to return.

It's a feeling you get sometimes, pulling off the highway once you get away from the city. It seeps in through the windows, even when they're rolled up and you've got the air-conditioning up high.

In my dream, Marc Buckler notices this feeling, and then swats it away like a June bug.

MISE EN ABYME

Now came to this abode while that the days of this compagnye were yet grene, this noble knight ALEX, known to both Sir Derrick and Sir Seth from schole; and the wise in whiche he arrivèd ther, a wonder was for to tell. For inside the howse, on that day, passing their noontide in gode earnest as had been their wyl lo these passing days, stood noone oother thanne Sir Derrick and Sir Seth, busy upon the errands that semed mete to them.

Now Sir Derrick had taken up unto himself in recent days, a quest, to wit, a cote of armes, the which might best bear forth, to the world at large, the good name of the castle in which both he and Sir Seth found themselves ful many an afternoon; and his grete scheme was, to emblazon above the castle door the legend *DEVIL HOUSE,* and upon the door, its shield, in colors most bold and with symbols to bear forth the soule and character of the compagnye. But, syne that as yet they numbered only two, his effort was somedel slight; and he did question himselfe, how best to assigyne the quadrants of the shield, or if agayn he might survey some noue style with which to say unto the passing throng: *We, who do goe through your world somewhat unknown, are within; and behold, we too have a tale.*

To this end he hadde placed, in the upper quadrant to one side, a figure in the likeness of a Spirit: so as to say, the ghost within is no dream upon the midnight, but a thing both of your world, and not. All in white, as a laundered cape, stood the figure of the ghost, its eyes pierced black and raggèd, its round mouth in mid-cry; and the field upon which it stood was sky-blue, to say in plain, these are the waking hours in which this vision does walk, and not the night to which he had been formerly consigned.

"Hark ye, Sir Seth," callèd he from behind the counter where he sat with his boke, "see how liketh you our cote"; and Sir Seth, busy with scissors among the library halls again, arose and considered his goodman's work.

"Behold, Caspar," replied Sir Seth, in jape, but continued: "But fine, those thynges of our childhood have grown vast and fearsome while we slept; an fittynge, for will we not defend this castle if need be; and, should fortune find us in defeat, will we not pledge to haunt the dayes of those that laid us low; upon my troth I swear it, I favor no rest in the afterlife unless I am avenged upon those who would oppose this howse!"

Sir Derrick heard, in his companion's voice, his troth; and thoughte unto himself, *What we are, we are; a noble howse, but small.* And behold, a silence came upon the compagnye, into which, all unexpected, intruded the sound of a hand knocking upon the door from the outside.

Both knights jumped as men awakened by thieves, so deep was their reverie; and then did both laugh as men helpless, until of a sudden they stopped again, and fell silent. For no visitor had been sought or called for, and none were expected; and who, then, of a day, should presume upon this fortress? For its ramparts in those days were as yet meager, and the walls without most modest, to speak truely.

Then heard they both, from without, a voice meek and familiar.

"It's Alex," came the voice. "I saw your bikes."

Seth and Derrick exchanged a glance of unsoundable depths. It wasn't that there was anything necessarily wrong with Alex; it was just that no one had seen or heard from him at all in several months. He'd gone missing from his foster family's house in the middle of July. He didn't leave a note or let anybody know he was leaving. People at school were starting to say he was probably dead. The few who'd known him well enough to care didn't want to believe it, but it was hard to know what else to think.

An indispensable architectural feature of any adult bookstore is that nobody can see the inside of it from the street. By the mid-eighties, security cameras had become part of the standard package turnkey contractors offered bigger markets. But Monster Adult X never made it that far. There were safety mirrors in the two back corners of the store, and another above the front door, but there was no way of seeing outside the front entrance when the door was closed.

Seth had a hunch. "Weland?" he yelled, his hand cupped against the door. "Quit fucking around."

"It's Alex," the voice said, no louder than the first time, with no real force or urgency.

"I told you quit fucking around," Seth said. "Last time Alex was in town this place was still a comics store."

"I don't have any place to stay, man," Alex said, and now both Seth and Derrick heard it clearly: the need, the resignation. Key suddenly in hand, Derrick rushed toward the door.

"Get in here, man," he said, ushering Alex inside with one arm like an army nurse in wartime, trying to hurry the patient to safety before the enemy gets a chance to reload the cannons.

He didn't like it. His family had been affording him so much space and range this year; he already felt a little guilty about the time he spent inside the former store in the afternoons. Anthony Hawley probably wouldn't have cared either way: but he didn't know, and that was where the ethical question lay. There was no "probably" in the other half of the equation: his parents would not approve. They didn't ask him to account for his hours between school and suppertime, but he knew if the truth ever surfaced, they would put an end to these afternoons; and these afternoons, with Seth, at this time in his life, as he prepared for the uncertain journey that lay ahead of him on the other side of high school: they felt special. They *were* special. He wanted to guard them. And so the matter took on several facets, some of them more inclined toward self-preservation than he would have liked to admit.

As he listened to Alex's meandering accounts of his time away from town, though—stories that passed through numberless streets and shelters where he'd slept sometimes, tales without lessons, jokes without punchlines—and listened, in the silences between exchanges, to how his heart went out to his old friend whose path had run out into the wilderness so early, sovereignty began to seem like the only question of real import. Whatever the former porn store was now—whatever you call a shuttered store that will probably be razed in the near future—did he have the right to tell Alex it was OK to sleep there tonight? The next night? Until he figured out what he was going to do with himself, how to take care of himself, how to keep himself safe?

He didn't think he did. Cutting up the posters and the glossy boxes, scribbling in the booths, reprogramming the VCRs: this was all essentially invisible work. None of it mattered. The only people who'd ever notice any of it would be the crew who eventually came in to tear the place apart. On the day that crew arrived, would any of them bring expectations about what they were or weren't going to see inside? It didn't seem likely. They'd get out their crowbars and start prying doors free from their hinges, and by the end of the day they'd have loaded everything into bins and driven them off the lot in forklifts. What the place they came to destroy looked like when they got there was none of their concern.

But to offer the space as a shelter: that was another thing entirely. He and Seth had covertly assumed shared stewardship of the store, it was true; and any place friends spend time together eventually starts feeling like a sort of home. They'd logged long hours in the half-dark together for more than a month now, drawing pictures and shooting the breeze. He knew of a couple of nights Seth hadn't gone home, it was true. He'd let these occasions pass without comment.

But Alex was homeless; when he talked about his situation, "homeless" was the exact word he insisted upon to describe himself, much to Derrick's distress. Derrick didn't want to be a person who turned his homeless friend back out onto the street. He didn't want him to have to go back to San Jose, or San Francisco; he pictured Alex at the on-ramp with a sign in his hands, waiting for somebody to take pity on him, and he couldn't stand it. It didn't matter how long ago they'd lost track of each other. His own self-image required him to offer his help.

"You look pretty bad," Derrick said after Alex took his parka off: it was a puffy army parka, too warm to wear in the fall. His face was dirty, and so were his hands.

"They took me downtown a couple of times," Alex said in the slow, clear cadences people sometimes teased him about.

Derrick and Seth waited for him to explain further, but sensed that no further explanation would come; he stood with his head half-hung, looking like he expected to be insulted, or rejected, or attacked.

People said his mom was Vietnamese, but nobody really knew. He talked like a guy who'd grown up in a suburb someplace, but the only place he ever mentioned living in besides Milpitas was Washington, D.C.; when people asked him where he was from, "I'm from D.C." was always his answer. But he never elaborated any further about it, and he'd been no older than seven when his family moved to town. Seth heard that young echo in Alex's voice now, the sound of a child grown older under pressure, and wondered how much he'd never really known about Alex.

There wasn't much certain about who he'd been before he ended up in the foster system. Alex himself was unreliable when it came to information about his birth family. In grade school, he'd often made up stories, trying at first to keep them all straight; but it gets exhausting after a while, and you learn to just stick to whichever story you find yourself telling, whether it contradicts some earlier version of it or not. After years in the system, he wasn't really even sure himself about what he believed. But it was hard to discern even the outline of that vigorous storyteller in the gaunt figure who stood by the front counter now, trying and failing to make conversation with a couple of old friends.

"You all right?" said Derrick. Seth was subdued; when he looked at Alex, he knew he was seeing a version of what people expected he himself would end up looking like, sooner or later.

"I'm always all right."

Seth couldn't take the tension. "We thought it was Weland," he said. "Weland fucking around."

Alex found Weland in his mind's eye and looked like he was about to smile, but he only said: "Nah, man."

Derrick pointed at the grimy backpack slung over Alex's shoulder. "Is that, like, a mattress pad in there?"

Now Alex did smile. "Factory-fresh from behind the Kmart," he said.

"There's two bigger booths back that way," Derrick said, pointing very demonstratively at the arcade; he wasn't sure of how conscious Alex really was of his surroundings. "You could go get some rest."

I wonder if anybody who's never been trusted with any kind of responsibility can understand how it must have felt to be Seth in that moment—to be part of a mechanism that would afford a friend shelter, to have even partial responsibility for a space of comfort and relief. To provide safe harbor for a comrade in need. I try to imagine it, and I picture a young man suddenly seeing that the body in which he lives has grown bigger without him noticing it. I imagine him looking at his hands, just a passing glance, and thinking momentarily about his redecoration of the arcade just a short while back. I see him leading Alex to the arcade to help him find a place to sleep, and I want to tell him: *Seth, in this moment, you are exactly who you think you are—a helper, a minister almost. The keys to the fortress are yours; in the right light, to the weary traveler, the luster of their gleam is almost holy.* But of course I can't tell Seth that. I can only hope he had a brief glimmering of it when the moment came, a sense of how sweet the face of the one who lowers the drawbridge appears to the one whose need for passage to the castle, for a home within its walls, has become critical.

Seth on the roof of the building by moonlight, enchanted to learn that its surface is a sheet of black rubber tightly attached to the frame. Seth with buckets of paint from somewhere, working with salvaged brushes, maybe, or with a broom, possibly, or with his hands. Who knows. Alex inside, asleep or just staring off into space as he does now, his childhood friends unsure of how to react, wanting to help, not knowing how. Derrick at home, asleep, sleep has never been a problem, he rests well even when he has things on his mind, when he hears people talk about how they have trouble sleeping he always thinks, *I feel bad for you*, but in his waking hours now he feels uncertain about several things, almost as soon as he wakes up he starts trying to wish them away because they can't be resolved: the responsibility he feels about his friends, the difficulty he has reconciling that responsibility with what comes next. The intersection of now and what comes next: it's visible from his front porch, a little closer every morning now as he sets out for school. He and his friends in his AP classes all seem to have noticed it at the same time, the fragility of their shared nexus. The spaces they've cultivated together will shortly undergo a seismic change. There is nothing for them to do at this point but wait.

Seth's canvas, about which his surviving classmates will unanimously later claim to have known nothing, is vast but simple: it makes good on the promise of Derrick's work on the MONSTER ADULT X sign by filling in the details. It is an enormous inhuman face. It looks a little like the Master from the TV adaptation of *Salem's Lot*, and a little like the Creature from the Black Lagoon. It's in three colors—white, black, and green—but that black is of course the black of the rubber underneath, Seth making use of negative space to complete this vision of a monstrous guardian for the house, a house whose existence the face proclaims to the heavens above it and to no one else. Its ears are webbed and leathery, its forehead high and pale, its cheeks sunken and greenish. Its thin-lipped mouth is agape as if to receive Communion. Its eyes are wide. It has seen something.

Adorning the portrait, some simple white clouds to the right and left, establishing the face's unearthly origin firmly enough for those who saw or heard about it later to put a name to it. A monster, a specter, a fiend. A ghost. A devil. It's easier to rely on familiar things when you're describing something different than to imagine a context whose parameters require faith, and vision. It's a sure bet that when people see the easy way across such differences, they will take it.

4.

FROM ST. EVROUL

I should be clear about there being nothing left. On the property, I mean. It would be terrific to describe how I found access to some secret attic space behind a loose panel in the ceiling, and how, inside, I discovered ledgers or receipts or remnants of Derrick and Seth and Alex's weeks-long redecorating spree—anything at all, really. Prying up the floorboards for primary sources, peeling back the paint: it might have made for a great hook, but, at the time, I couldn't see any point to it. I'm fairly certain I have greater access to a wider range of contemporaneous artifacts than anyone who's ever studied the case; I'm diligent in my research, and I've learned to be patient. I don't need to use force to get to the story. The good stuff always surfaces in the end.

But as to the house itself: the refurb job was comprehensive. Try though I might, using my photographs, articles, diagrams, grim memorabilia, primary and secondary sources, and the method of inhabiting a space which is my signature, I'm still essentially living in a new house. Only the outer walls remain: the shape, the view from above. The fortress that this place became in the days following the demise of Monster Adult X was a moment in time, and its destruction, when it came, was total. I sit on my sofa and look out the window, having grown attached to the house in my time here: I feel a ghostly kinship with the lives once lived atop the same ground that now cradles me while I sleep. Sometimes, in quiet moments, this mood seems ready to gather an almost tidal force; I feel like the place is something handed down to me instead of something I bought outright and must vacate when my work is done.

But it's impossible to squint hard enough to see all the way back to the era before the coming of the age of change, whose beginnings were heralded by the arrival, in San Francisco, of Marc Buckler, aboard PSA flight 295 from Los Angeles.

ATMOSPHERIC DRAG

The further you go back into the past, the more you have to extrapolate about details and specifics; try though you might, you can't get around this rule. If an aspiring real estate speculator were to fly from Los Angeles to San Francisco today, and, later, for whatever reason, we needed to trace his journey, he'd leave data everywhere: Checking in with the airline. Buying mints at the newsstand. Drinking a vodka tonic at the airport bar.

This was true in 1986, too, but the entities gathering the data weren't as well-organized as they would later become, and the market for consumer data was still relatively elite. Over time, as the storage space needed for vast troves of memory shrank to microscopic sizes, the detail available to data hounds has become almost obsessively minute: behaviors too trivial to recount are lovingly enumerated. Every transaction locked, every point of contact recorded. There was a time, now hard to imagine, when you had to rely largely on self-reporting to know what people were up to.

For this reason, the dead from the distant past—even if you frame "distant" at fairly close range; even if the ever-advancing present seems, each year, to exist at further remove from the days that gave it birth—tend to look, in the mind's eye, like ghosts who don't know they're dead yet. The impressions they left on the world, great or small, seem to outline a prophecy, one consisting of hunches you can't verify and stories largely woven from inference and innuendo. Even once you've collated as much real evidence as you can collect, the ends they met enshroud and obscure their remembered figures, as if gathered, rumpled at the shoulders, like a cloak.

Marc Buckler met Evelyn Gates at a Morton's Steakhouse in San Jose—the venue had been her choice. If she was impressed by him, I don't know about it. If she found him ridiculous, as I do most days, I don't know about that, either. She'd probably changed into some fresh clothes: simple sales instincts. She wasn't a real estate agent, but hiring somebody to sell a building she owned would have struck her as silly. People want to own property; her father, in so many words, had drummed the lesson into her all her life. All you have to do is tell people you have something and they want it. They want it already; they learn what they want when you show it to them.

As the lone steward of the properties her father'd left her, she considered herself rich, just as she'd always considered her father rich: collecting rent every month on places whose tenants didn't have enough leverage to demand repairs, tenants who lacked the social standing to assert their right to a plumbing upgrade or to functional wiring in every room. At Morton's, her focus would probably have been on the strong monthly cash flow her properties represented, and on ways one might increase their yield if he felt so inclined. Cosmetic improvements— subdivisions, even, if he felt up to it. Pay for themselves in a year, two at most. There was a whole side yard adjacent to the book- store, big enough to build a second property on, an easy sell depending on what kind of client you found for the—

"I looked it up," he might have said. "The porno store, right?" I know from the books his parents had to retrieve from his office later that he'd been reading up on the importance of establishing yourself as fearless in business.

"It's closed now," she might have said with a little irritation. "Do you want to give it the once-over? I haven't had a chance to see if they moved everything out."

These are possibilities. We know that Evelyn Gates paid for dinner, tipping twelve percent, and that they then drove to Mil- pitas. His hotel was near the airport, but I'm not sure if they left his car at the Morton's parking lot or drove in separate cars. I'm not sure it matters. I just want to be able to get a clear picture of it, because they were both in here once, and my need to see what that looked like has become sharper since I moved in.

KNIGHTS QUEST

The brochure had a detailed map showing Kenyon College as it related to nearby cities and counties. Derrick couldn't stop studying it. Some of the best science fiction books, he'd found, feature maps of imaginary terrain on their opening pages. He always found himself going back to the map as he read through them, trying to situate himself within the fictional space again and again, until it seemed as real as the outside world. Knowing where the rivers were, the names of the lakes. Anything short of full immersion felt like a cheat.

People his age often feel trapped by the towns they grow up in, he knew. They complained about it all the time, even if plenty of them were born elsewhere—Seattle, some of them; San Francisco, several more; Colorado, at least two he knew of. A couple of sophomores at school, two years back, had come all the way from Florida; they'd been welcomed with that mixture of awe and suspicion usually reserved in America for visiting royalty.

The other side of the coin, however, never seemed to merit much thought from his classmates: the comfort of living in a place you'd always known, the ease of knowing your parameters. Derrick's bike ride from the store to his house, for example: he'd never once had to plot it out. Even when they tore up the street to put in fiber-optic lines, the grid beneath remained familiar. Second nature. Sometimes these days they'd pave over a whole cluster of old buildings to make way for an office building, but it made no difference to Derrick's sense of his own position on the map, because the coordinates didn't change.

He knew how people felt, though—he couldn't imagine not having an urge to travel, to see new things, to encounter the unexpected. Those Florida sophomores hadn't been able to hide how alien the California landscape was to their eyes, how small differences cropped up everywhere once you started looking for them: in the trees, in the air at dusk. There's something appealing about being a visitor. The whole world's a new thrill.

Ohio. A world away. Cold winters, wet springs. The brochures from the schools were, themselves, a kind of science fiction. They represented the possibilities he'd only vaguely known he was working toward over the past four years, urged on by his mother, and, more quietly, by his dad, who saw, in his son, a kind of resolve that seemed miraculous to him. He hoped some of it was down to good parenting, but it felt bigger than that, and better, too. He didn't want to go spoiling it with awkward comments and observations.

As the pile of envelopes from the colleges grew higher, the feeling of new possibilities became general within the Hall household. It felt more like spring than autumn. Something new was under way for everybody. Who can resist such a good feeling within a family?

He let that feeling ripple for a second, and then reflected involuntarily on the question of Alex. It made him sad. Why shouldn't Alex, who was as smart as Derrick, also be setting out into a new and exciting chapter of his life instead of just trying to secure a safe place to sleep? There were so many things to consider in this world. The scope of it all seemed too great to grasp. Maybe it got easier as you grew older, or maybe you just got numb. Either way, it was probably worse for a guy like Alex, whose options seemed to be sealing themselves off daily, like a long hallway interrupted, every few steps, by a new door, each of which locks itself behind you as soon as you've passed through it.

He looked again at the picture on the cover of the Kenyon brochure as he considered all this. Everybody in the picture looked sharp. They were walking across a campus in autumn, huge orange maple leaves underfoot. All of them were smiling. It was a hard image to resist.

"This is some weird shit," Buckler said as they entered the building. It was a planned line; he'd read in one of his how-to-succeed-in-business books that delivering a mild shock to the seller was a prospective client's best leverage. Establish your ground. Make them inhabit *your* space, not the other way around. Evelyn Gates hadn't even flipped the lights on before he said it, and she recognized the desperate cadence of an over-rehearsed opening.

"Excuse me?" she said. Her practice in business predated Buckler's grade school days.

"Weird *stuff*," Buckler corrected himself, making eye contact with her quickly and smiling. He had a lot of faith in that smile. "Weird stuff, I mean. No offense intended."

Gates understood, then, the extent of the wetness behind her client's ears. Her father had taught her how to spot a novice; now she began calculating markup, contemplating which structural anomalies she'd now frame as features. Her eyes would have been on Buckler, not out among the racks—a failed porn store didn't interest her. She was a little annoyed that all the sordid merchandise was still there in the building, but not terrifically surprised. A tenant who can't afford to make rent probably can't afford to hire movers, either.

But Buckler—young, nervous, and out of his natural habitat—blinked once, and then again. To be in a place like this in the company of a woman old enough to be his mother was uncomfortable enough. Trying to find the least self-incriminating spot for his gaze to land made matters worse; no line of sight seemed safe. So he settled on some magazines, since their outer sheen seemed moderately less trashy than the big, glossy VHS cases lining the walls. He tried to diverge his gaze, to make it seem like he was lost in thought instead of scrutinizing a skin mag; but then some grainy break in the shiny surface would catch his eye and draw him in.

It was mainly Seth's handiwork, one of his earlier pieces from the first day he'd spent in the store with Derrick. The magazine had originally been called *Sinful Sluts*. It had a parochial school theme. The model on the front, facing the camera naked from the waist down, now boasted curling ram's horns drawn in ballpoint on either side of her head; Seth's curling interior lines, simple but effective, made these horns look gnarled and ancient. On her thighs were tattoos of swords, their tips and hilts reversed to face one another from either side of the gap between her open legs. Her right hand had originally held an erect penis, jutting from the body of a man whose remaining parts were all out of the frame; Seth had shaded the shaft and sketched wire mesh across the glans to turn it into a microphone. Finally, with the X-Acto, he'd removed her eyes—a recurring and reliable motif in the renovated Monster Adult X; any face in the world looks creepier if you cut out its eyes.

Derrick, adept at lettering, had contributed the title. Using Seth's pen and some Liquid Paper, he'd settled on the title *Satan Sings*; it fit the modified picture, and they both laughed after they put it back on the rack. You had to look twice to see where he'd altered the curve of one letter or the angle of another. That was the whole point.

"Don't mean to offend again, but what the hell is *this*?" asked Buckler, turning to his host, who had no ready answer.

SOLO III

Alex heard the key turn in the lock just in time. He'd been sitting at the front counter, resting his head on his hands. Hidden away inside the store, he'd located a few places where, in waking hours, the energy felt less malevolent to him; the counter was one of them. His sensitivity to energy fields had grown quite acute during his time sleeping on the street. The crazier guys you meet out there talk about this kind of thing all the time, but if you listen past the crazy you begin to see their point. Every corner has an angle. Every room's got a shape. The front counter felt warmer than the dark, claustrophobic booths. Warmth matters.

He jumped up; he'd been sleeping in the arcade for at least a week now, possibly more. His sense of time was pretty shot, but maneuvers in the dark were second-nature instincts by now. He made it back to his booth just as the front door opened; settling in, imperceptibly silent, he began hearing the sounds of people out in the store.

There were two of them, a man and a woman. The woman was older. The man was nervous. Alex wished he could form a picture of them inside his head; he was very afraid of being found out, all five of his senses sharpening in preparation for flight, and he wanted to know what he'd be up against, if it came to that.

They talked; they both seemed to be asking questions, which felt off. Was there somebody else with them who wasn't talking yet? Derrick's boss, maybe? Away from the world for some time, Alex struggled to conceive of realistic scenarios that would explain the muffled tones drifting down the halls to his hiding place. Curiosity gave way to obsessive, dark thoughts, real fear; he gripped his elbows in his hands, breathing in and out through his nose as slowly and evenly as he could.

One of the people outside knocked on the arcade entrance after a while. His heart jumped. At this distance, he could make out what they were saying.

"These are the TV booths," Evelyn Gates said. "There's seven of them. I can have all this stuff emptied out at my expense if you like, this was really the previous tenant's responsibility."

Buckler sensed the advantage; she hadn't been any better prepared for the scene inside the store than he had. She was trying to smooth over it by talking through her pitch. He recognized the rhythm of it.

"No need," he said. "Maybe a little break on the price for the effort, though?"

"Comes out the same," she said cheerfully; she knew more about the costs of moving abandoned belongings than he did. "The building's sound; the roof's original, but it's got a protective rubber cap on it, so no water can get in. The previous tenant installed an alarm system, and that conveys, since they didn't give notice. The neighborhood is zoned—"

"Residential and retail," Buckler interrupted. "That's why I like it."

Evelyn Gates felt the hook sink cleanly into the mouth of the fish.

"Residential and retail. We'll need to walk through it again before we finalize," she said, her deal-closing voice growing fainter to Alex as the two interlopers walked back toward the store's entrance. They stayed awhile longer, examining fixtures and furniture, but their words were a muddy drone in his ears again, too muffled to make out. After a while, he allowed himself to accept that they were gone; still, he waited another half hour before emerging from the booth. He was a smart kid. This place was doomed. He knew the night's visitors, seen correctly, were raiders making land on the shores of a crumbling kingdom. They would be back, and, when they came, would bring more of their kind with them.

But they wouldn't be back tonight. He fetched a bag of potato chips from under the counter, something Seth had left for him earlier, and went back to his booth to sleep. When you feel like you're safe for an hour or two, you sleep. You never know if you're going to get a chance to later. This was another thing he'd learned from the friends he'd made in his time away from town.

MINOANS IV

Sleep was deep and dreamless. He lay motionless for an age; he didn't know what time it was when he finally woke up. The absence of natural light in the arcade offered no clues. It's said of Alex that he could remain in the company of others without speaking for hours at a time; perhaps his sleep in the empty store lasted ten or twelve hours at a stretch, or more. The comfort of the booth offered security the outside world couldn't match.

He stayed there the next night, too. Derrick told him it was OK. He felt almost safe—an unfamiliar feeling for him; even in well-regarded placement facilities, the threat of some fellow resident getting aggravated could keep him awake and alert until late. Roommates were the worst; the booth was cramped, but its walls were solid.

He came out to say hello when Seth stopped by in the afternoon on the second day; they talked a little about his time away, and Seth, a better listener when the occasion called for it than many of his friends would have suspected, told him things would be better soon.

Somewhere during his time in the darkness of the booth, Alex carved his initials into the wall. The markings people leave on walls aren't usually dated; contextual clues can take you a ways, but stop short of specifics. When Alex carved his initials into the wall of the booth, did he mean to say: *I'm here. Find your own booth*, or did he mean, *Here is where I slept tonight; in case I don't come back, I'll leave this mark*? Did he use his pocketknife to carve it as soon as Buckler and Gates left the premises, sensing that time was probably short? Or did he wait a few days—until, as it seemed to him, the threat had passed, even though Derrick, when he finally heard about it, made it clear that everybody who spent time in the store was now at risk.

"Those people don't care" was how he put it; he stood on the service side of the counter while Seth and Alex leaned on the glass from the customer side. "Miss Gates used to charge interest if the rent check was ever a day late. I can't believe you waited this long to tell me."

"What are they going to do, arrest us?" Seth said. He was grinning; the prospect of trouble remained irresistible to Seth, no matter how many times he learned anew that real trouble and the threat of trouble were two different things.

"Sorry," Alex said. "I was pretty out of it that night."

"Think about it," Derrick said, gesturing generally at the interior of the store. What is it about senior year that makes some people suddenly talk like parents? Seth couldn't understand it. "They saw all this stuff. They already know somebody's been in here. The next thing they do is send the police. If the police come in here and hear anybody, what are they gonna think?"

"They're gonna think it's crackheads," Alex said. "Get their sticks out before they even reach for the light switch."

Derrick pointed over at Alex while looking Seth dead in the eyes, a game-show host who's decided not to let anybody down easy. "We're done," he said. "There aren't any crackheads in Milpitas, but he's right. It was fun, and we're done."

"Come *on*," Seth said, whining a little; he couldn't help himself. "They only came once. We don't even spend that much time in here but an hour or two a day."

Alex didn't flinch, but could feel Derrick's eyes on him. He was a problem again. "I can go someplace else," he said. "It's OK. Angela used to help me when I needed help." He meant Angela West; she'd be going to Central next year.

"Come *on*," Seth said again. "Nobody's going to buy a porno store with all the porno still in it! Your boss was right!"

"Mr. Hawley only meant to make trouble for whoever came next," said Derrick. "Because he was mad. We shouldn't even be here right now. It's dangerous here now."

Seth stopped objecting, both because he knew his friend was right and because his anger was already giving way to sadness and resentment. No matter who you are when you're young, you always notice how the adults wreck everything as soon as they show up on the scene. To Seth, it seemed like this was especially the case if you already had a few problems and needed help. It wasn't fair.

"I can take care of myself if they show up again," offered Alex. "I can find exits in the dark and I'm pretty quiet." He didn't want to ask, directly, for some more time to figure out where else he could go.

"This is chickenshit," Seth said. "They only came once."

Derrick looked at his friends: of the three, he was the only one heading in the general direction of the adult world. A run-in with the police would expose him to anger from his parents, and possible consequences that might cause Kenyon to look twice at him if things went the wrong way.

Monster Adult X had been a safe place when the responsibility for anything inside lay on someone else's shoulders. It was no longer safe.

"We can't be here much longer," he concluded. "We probably shouldn't be here at all. It could get bad."

But he stopped short of insisting that his friends clear out entirely, and he left some drawing supplies under the counter. He could come up with a better plan tomorrow. Maybe that was the night Alex carved his initials on the wall of his booth: to leave an indication of a short time ending too soon, a sign by which generations to come might glean a little of a story they'd never hear.

We can't know. It's hard enough to make out the initials among all the other marks that came a little later. But they're there, in the picture, if you look.

A BEACON IN THE WEST

In his bedroom, atop the dresser, Derrick found a stack of twenty postcards, all with stamps tidily affixed and delivery addresses filled out in his mother's handwriting. The addressee, of course, was herself.

She'd been thinking for weeks about how to go about it—not obsessively, just idly, but with steady focus. At first she'd considered something fancy; it might seem more like a present than a motherly prod if the envelopes had something Derrick liked on them. Superheroes, or movie stuff. But at the office supplies store, there were only two types of stationery: sets that looked fussy and overdecorated, and kids' stuff. The superhero stationery, especially, made her feel both sad and a little embarrassed: at one time in his life, Derrick would certainly have loved these envelopes depicting a transparent three-color image of Iron Man in flight. But that time had long since passed. Remembering that children are older than you think they are is one of the most reliable errands of parenthood, and one of the hardest.

So she settled on simple postcards—a set of twenty with California scenes on their faces: mountains, redwoods, the Pacific Ocean. As soon as he saw them Derrick's throat got tight and he wanted to cry; but he checked the impulse, just in case Mom was already on her way down the hall. He forced himself instead to focus on how few of the scenes in the pictures spoke to the California he was going to miss next year: a place where you could ride your bike downhill past auto repair yards whose rusty corrugated rooftops would probably never be replaced, a place where on the wrong day you could get lost trying to find your oldest friend's house because every other house on the block looks just the same.

"Got those postcards," he called through his bedroom door, his smile audible in his voice, a small ache behind it for Alex, and for Seth, too, fellow travelers whose paths he would only be sharing a short while longer, good friends to whom the entirety of this small, sweet moment would have seemed foreign, alien, unknowable.

5.

PROVISIONS FOR THE JOURNEY

"Your mom made breakfast."

It was Dad's voice on the other side of the door, speaking in a light, cheerful tone. Derrick was awake but still sleepy, and the sound of Dad calling him to breakfast made him feel like a kid. He waited to reply, luxuriating momentarily in the indulgence of his morning mood. The way our worries seem like they were smaller before we grew up is a universal feeling, or nearly so.

"Let me get a shower first," Derrick said through a broad smile, stretching his arms over his head.

There was a brief silence. When it broke, his father's voice had deepened—just a little, just enough—and he spoke more slowly.

"Your mother made breakfast," he said, and Derrick understood then that he was being called to the table rather than invited.

But if there were some pressing matter, it lay on the other side of some formalities Mom and Dad seemed to feel were essential to what lay ahead. The breakfast small talk seemed to go on forever—Dad asking Mom about work, which he never did, Mom passing along the sort of innocuous coworker gossip that her husband and her son both knew she hated. He waited it out. His last autumn inside the house where he'd grown up was proving full of oddly staged moments like this.

Maybe people in different sorts of families were teasing their parents this year about how awkward they'd become with their nearly grown children; some of his friends talked about their mothers and fathers with a condescension that made him feel a little sad. He understood, because he felt it, too, sometimes; the planet all parents occupied seemed to be growing ever more remote. He'd told a few stories, too. Still, it seemed miserable to fault them for trying. His parents had given him a lot.

"This time next year you'll be somewhere else," his father said, finally, and this, to her own considerable surprise, was the thing that caused Diane Hall to burst into tears. She'd rehearsed this breakfast in her mind for days, but when she looked at Derrick and imagined his chair empty in twelve months' time, a feeling of profound helplessness descended upon her. She lowered her head, focusing on her pancakes, but neither her husband nor her son were fooled.

Dad said then how proud, how very proud, he was to have raised a young man now college-bound; Mom talked vaguely but sternly about the importance of avoiding distractions, of keeping your goal in sight. They went over simple stuff for far too long: punctuality, diligence, time management. They had a short bit about getting enough exercise; out of sight, underneath the table, Derrick had to dig his fingers into his thighs to keep from laughing. He'd been faithful to a daily exercise regimen of push-ups, pull-ups, and sit-ups ever since first seeing those corny Charles Atlas ads in comics back in junior high.

The big reveal was a savings account Dad had opened for Derrick, years ago, without ever telling him about it. He slid the passbook across the table; its cover was worn enough to suggest that Dad had visited the bank many times over the years. Derrick didn't know whether he was supposed to open it or not. He waited.

"I opened that account when you were very small," Dad said, clearing his throat, "and I put a little something in it every month except in December, every year, so if it's not enough, you know—blame Santa Claus."

Derrick remembered a December morning years ago when he'd gotten up early to find a shiny bicycle under the tree, and a lump formed in his throat, which he chased down with a mouthful of food. Then he discreetly put the savings passbook into his back pocket, nodding at his father as he did so.

"I don't know what to say," he said. He raised a too-big final forkful of pancake to his mouth; so many recent occasions had been attended by an unfamiliar but not unwelcome gravity, and it seemed to him that the best way to meet them was to remain in the moment. Be yourself. Plenty of his friends never even got a chance to think about this kind of stuff. "Thank you, Mom. Dad. Seriously. Thanks."

His parents smiled at each other, each grading themselves a little in their minds: points for poise, points for focus.

He saw his opening in their exchange. "Guess I can go get that shower now," he said, rising to his feet, clearing his dishes and taking them to the kitchen, wondering as he walked at how serious adult life seemed from the outside: the outside, whose distance from the inside kept growing shorter every day, erasing itself as it went.

PLAGUE SEASON

Whisper networks among the young are subtle and sophisticated technologies, better than any state spying apparatus: they leave no paper trails, and their points of contact seldom retain any memory of their own agency. People just talk, that's all. How Angela West heard that Alex was back in town is anybody's guess. Alex avoided daylight, and Derrick never talked to anybody about the store.

Unless there are some names still missing from the record, which remains possible, this leaves only Seth. It's easy to blame Seth; where there's trouble, he always seems like a possible suspect. He was proud of the daylight fortress he and Derrick had made of Monster Adult X, and probably talked about it if the opportunity arose. But Seth had never been popular at school; the only confidant he had was Derrick, from whom he had no secrets. It's hard to say who else Seth would have talked to if he'd wanted to tell someone about Alex.

Alex himself makes a marginally better suspect. He had a key to the back door, given to him by Derrick. He'd learned, during his time in bigger cities, how to find a handout. And he knew where Angela lived; they'd been close friends before he got sick. She'd done her best to keep up with him through his sad changes, more than most of his friends had done. She'd tried to ignore the way talking to him was like trying to have a conversation with someone inside a plastic bubble, his voice muffled and hard to hear over on the open-air side of the membrane. Angela might have appeared to him as a beacon of safety here in the boredom and floating paranoia of his present days. There was a phone at the counter; hours inside the store were dead and empty. Time, opportunity, and motive.

These are the facts: Angela left her shift at the 7-Eleven one evening and got home late. She told her parents that a high school football team had shown up all at once for Slurpees just before closing, and that she'd had to ring them all up individually before she clocked out. None of this was true. She left at eleven on the dot; from work, she drove her mother's Toyota to Monster Adult X, where she was granted entrance by the keeper of the key. And in that place she was straightaway bade good welcome, which welcome she returned with cheer; and behold, in their hidden glade deep within the forest, far from the reach of stern authority, the noble knights did then hold conference, to honor old friendships thought lost, albeit in the absence of Sir Derrick, who yet tarried at home; Sir Seth, out late, regaled the company with tales of the quests on which Sir Derrick intended, shortly, to embark: those journeys ahead, to lands unknown. And lo, while that he spoke, a quiet spirit of despair did descend upon the house, a known familiar whose name none dared invoke, lest its presence oppress the noble knights yet further; and Dame Angela, in the stillness of her heart, did rue upon the fickleness of time, whose hand grew stronger with each passing day, for which no remedy seemed apparent.

Inside, Seth was holding court. He stood in the middle of the racks, gesturing excitedly as he spoke. He'd had an idea, and now he had hands to help.

"Derrick's serious that we can't hang here anymore," he said. "He's going to call time on this whole thing, today or tomorrow. I *know* he is. We ran together since we were little kids, I know when he's serious."

Angela felt like a parishioner in the wrong church. She'd only come to see Alex; she had no personal stake in the future of Monster Adult X. She found the porno tapes disgusting; she didn't like having to be around them. Seth's tales of marauding interlopers profaning the sanctuary held no resonance for her. Who would want to spend their afternoons in a place like this?

But she looked over at Alex as Seth's exhortations grew louder and more animated, and she saw something stirring in his eyes: the look of someone drawn to a purpose, the look of someone with something to defend. He'd called the back arcade home for a week now, maybe two; he told her during the half hour they spent talking before Seth turned up. "It was nice to have a regular place to stay," he'd said, and she heard the yearning in him when he said it, the need for a center. She'd worked as a candy striper in a convalescent home back in the summer of her junior year; she knew how much small comforts could mean to people. And she hated to think of Alex out on the street.

"This is our home," Seth said insistently at one point, his pitch ascending the scale.

Alex laughed. "It's not really anybody's 'home,'" he said.

"It's your home right now," Angela said.

"It's my *spot* right now," Alex corrected. "Sometimes you just have a spot."

"Any other spot we find isn't really going to be ours," Seth said. "Fuck this."

"I knew some long-timers in San Francisco who used to shit in their tents if they got cleared out of an underpass," Alex offered; Angela winced.

"That's no good, though. You know? Nobody can tell one person's shit from anybody else's," Seth said, a vision upon him, the sort of thing that made him feel like when he finally found his life's purpose it would be something special the whole world would understand. "We just have to show them something that says this place is ours no matter what else they do to it, something they'll remember after they see it even if the next thing they do is tear it all down."

Angela pursed her lips against a smile; Seth sounded like he was quoting something he'd seen on a Saturday morning cartoon, sprinkling it with dirty words to make it more applicable to the moment.

"That's a good speech, Seth," she said.

"Thanks," he said, already headed for the far wall. He shrugged his backpack off and reached into the top pocket, retrieving an X-Acto knife and a red Sharpie. For a second Angela felt panic: Was he crazy? Was he going to try something stupid?

But instead he did that which is recorded both in the Polaroids and in the tabloids which would describe the details of those renderings in future days, that act of wonder from which proceeded the great days of the castle, candle-short days marked both by mad revelry and the solemn raising of the ramparts: those thin but fearsome fortifications meant to guard the Knights of the Broken Mirror, who bore but few arms, if any, against those intruders then clearing the near horizon.

He slashed the number 7 into a section of the wall with his

knife, then drew a circle around it in marker. Then he traced the 7 with the marker in one quick, intentionally sloppy movement, bringing it into harsh relief.

"They'll put this place on the TV news when they find out," he said in triumph to the gentle assembly.

MINOANS V

Seth was off to the races. In his mind, he imagined Alex and Angela joining in with abandon, caught up in his vision of turning the inside of the store into a scarecrow for the authorities. He was like this whenever an idea took hold of him. It had been causing him trouble all his life.

They watched at first. It was fun to watch Seth when he got wound up about something. Everybody knew it. After a while, Alex joined in; it would have been bad manners to sit and stare, even if his feeling for shared activity had been blunted by too much time alone. Awkward in his movements, he approached Seth's backpack, leaning over it and asking: "Is it just pens?"

"There's some cans in the storage closet," Seth said. "They're Derrick's." This was an untruth, if a harmless one: the spray cans belonged to the store, its quickest remedy for the regulars who kept writing their phone numbers and local meeting places in ballpoint on the walls and seats of the viewing booths. Angela saw Alex register Seth's words and then turn toward the counter: first the turn, then the onset of forward motion, slow, mechanical. He moved his body like it didn't belong to him. It was hard to watch.

All the while, she did her best to ignore the many parts of the store that were still exactly as they'd been before Anthony Hawley turned the OPEN sign around for good. She didn't consider herself a prude, but the more of the interior her peripheral vision picked up, the less she liked it. After the homecoming dance, at the curb in front of her house, her date had tried to show her a glossy European magazine with brief text in French captioning explicit pictures of people having sex: *Douce Maîtresse*. It was vile; she was relieved when her father, inside the house, flipped the porch light on to let her know he'd registered their arrival and was marking time. "I had a good time tonight. My father will kill you if he sees that," she said to her date, opening the passenger-side door before he could lean in for a kiss.

She was a good student; she never skipped class, and she signed up for all the extracurriculars that were supposed to help you get into the universities—debate team, student government. She was hoping to make assistant manager at 7-Eleven before she left for college; she'd been told that colleges loved to see first-year students who arrived trailing a list of credentials. It had made for a lot of tension thus far, trying to make her last year count; two months in, she was feeling the strain.

She looked hard at the entrance through which she'd come after convincing Alex, her hand cupped to the door, that it was really her; she noted the double crossbar now reinforcing it in case somebody breached the dead bolt.

She decided to use broad-tipped permanent markers instead of the spray cans, because she didn't want to get any paint on her clothes.

HUGH THE FAT

In Hollywood for the weekend, staying at his friend Keith's rental on North Hayworth, Marc Buckler treated himself and his host to a half gram of cocaine. It was the weekend, and he was on the cusp of what felt like a big step forward. Locally, his property bids kept getting undercut by buyers who could afford short-term losses for the sake of increasing their holdings. He'd tried making moves in places where he couldn't imagine any real action—Rowland Heights, Baldwin Park, Walnut—but most of the time he came away holding the short straw. He liked to think of himself as a renegade, a little guy trying to knock a few jewels loose from the collars on the big dogs.

Keith did data input for an investment firm and talked a lot about how much action there was in the job. Seated next to Marc on his sofa, occasionally leaning over to snort from a small mirror on a coffee table, he kept telling his friend that the entrepreneur game was "very small-time stuff." This didn't agree with Marc's image of himself, but Keith made a persuasive case.

After a while, Keith got up and went to the kitchen to fix gin and tonics. He spoke rapidly and animatedly as he worked. The plan was to kill time until it felt late enough to hit the bars.

"If you can get rich in property, God bless you," he said, returning to the sofa and raising his glass. "If I get even the tiniest sliver of my company's nest egg I'm set for life. For life, you know? Let somebody else assume the risk."

"OK," said Marc, returning the toast, "but if I flip two properties in this tiny town nobody's even ever heard of, I can buy four more. Six more. Whole blocks. OK? Now you tell me. What's the only investment that never, I mean *never*, stops increasing in value over time?"

"Real estate," Keith said, closing his eyes and leaning his head back a little. The gin rush hit, cold and bracing. It was good to feel young, it was good to feel like you were getting a clear view of the bigger picture.

"How much you pay every month for this place?" Marc asked.

"Too much."

"My point exactly. In other markets it's even starker. Just incredible, you know? The return on just a little paint and spackle, you wouldn't believe it. Assuming I can get the price I want for the place I saw last week, I—"

"I'm just saying, job security," Keith said. "I know there's no glamour in job security, but there's no glamour in unrecouped losses, either."

There aren't going to be any unrecouped losses, Marc Buckler thought but did not say; in his heart, he worried that his time in the self-made-man lane was growing short. But all his sources told him self-presentation was paramount. What he said instead was: "You have to make your *own* job security."

"Better men than me have tried," Keith countered, while allowing himself a brief vision of his friend Marc as a jet-setting real estate magnate, processing payments from several states every week, renting space in mirrored Century City office buildings for the sole purpose of governing his small empire.

Marc didn't have access to this vision. He was just hoping to close the deal in Milpitas next week. He imagined it as the start of something big and beautiful.

THAT THE GOSSIPS MIGHT REJOICE

It was on the afternoon of the following day that Derrick beheld the work; he'd come by to tell Seth and Alex that this was it, that their autumn clubhouse was closed, that everybody had to keep moving. They weren't used to having people in their lives who told them what to do, he knew. Not his problem. As he pedaled to the store from school, he tried out different ways of saying it: he didn't want to be mean, but he needed to be sure Alex and Seth knew he meant it. Time to go.

The initial shock of entry gave way to total glee as the scope of Seth's project revealed itself to Derrick's near-speechless gaze. Hawley had left all the porn behind on purpose: forfeiting his cleaning deposit, money he could have used, for the pleasure of inconveniencing a landlord who'd raised the rent on him four times without any explanation during his brief tenancy. It's a helpless feeling, paying rent to people like Evelyn Gates. You remember their names for years. But Hawley was beyond her reach now; the interior of the store, a cardboard-and-wire-frame nuisance boasting hundreds of practically useless videotapes and magazines plus seven heavy arcade screens in the back, had been his goodbye note.

This note now had several anonymous cosignatories, whose work both clarified and complicated the message. Think about it: If you owned a property, and you arrived on the premises one day to find that your tenant had just left everything behind, what might your assumption be? That they couldn't afford to hire a moving company. That they were in a hurry. That they, who had to rent their storefront from somebody who owned dozens like it, lacked the means to clean up after themselves. Arriving at a vacated property to find old dishes still in the cabinets or nonreturnable stock still on the shelves was not unusual for Evelyn Gates; she had a couple of guys who helped her clean up when it happened.

Her guys would have their hands full when they got here. A sort of porn angel oversaw the great hall now, a seraph whose body, made up of disassembled cardboard VHS sleeves stapled together, hung by its hands from the ceiling. Its head slumped down over its chest; Angela had tried to help Seth and Alex find a way of keeping the head upright, but, after three efforts, they decided that the nodding angel had a unique sort of menace of its own. "It looks hurt," was how Alex had put it.

The angel was immense. The images that formed its bones ranged from solo shots of San Fernando Valley models in leotards to garish collages of graphic sex. Oral, vaginal, anal, gay, straight, group, and solo, stylized and raw, slick and no-budget, the entire imagined commercial spectrum represented in patches torn roughly or cut carefully from sleeves whose black splashes of all-caps text popped like word-bubbles from the covers of comic books: *XXX. NO DIALOGUE! FOUR HOURS OF HOLES AND POLES.*

If you circled around to the back of the angel, overkill gave way to understatement: white cardboard, the insides of the sleeves, framed the shape of the body a little more plainly to the eye, imparting a mood of helplessness to the figure. About a foot short of the floor, its feet dangled; any slight disturbance of the air caused them to sway, as if trying to kick themselves free of their staples.

Even as he examined it, admiring its balance—both legs the same length, a color gradient that could only have indicated a heavy hour in the Seth zone where attention deficit and deep focus were two sides of the same coin—he felt all the action out on the walls in his periphery, dozens of details begging to be noticed. "You gotta be kidding me here," he said, his eyes finally reaching the carpeted floor, where the outlines of bodies, seven in all, had been drawn in chalk, adrift in a sea of trigger-words written in frenzied capital letters: *ANGEL* and *MURDER* and *PRINCE* and *PLAYPEN* and a half dozen others, a confusion of voices, a great chord of terror.

Seth emerged from the arcade. He'd forced himself to stay hidden all morning in case Derrick came by.

There is an entry in Seth's journal about all this, in the journal I believe to be Seth's. Like all the other entries, it's brief, to the point, and undated. It says, *Derrick had to admit we did it up right.* Beneath, there's a sketch of the angel in silhouette. Stripped of its lurid skin, rich with menace, it dances on the page like a lesser tormentor in an aberrant book of hours.

FOR KING AND COUNTRY

There are no army surplus stores in Milpitas. It's too small a town to support one. There aren't any over in San Jose, either; in San Francisco, you can find secondhand stores with decent supplies of outdated military stock, but you have to know where to look. In all likelihood, given the need to return inconspicuously with unwieldy cargo in tow, San Francisco is too far afield.

But 1986 is a long time ago. Might there have been a local source for weird army stuff back then, someplace that's gone now: a storefront, a counter inside a hardware store? If you want to reconstruct local retail histories, contemporaneous materials are your safest bet—old newspapers, phone books, ledgers if you're extremely lucky. Thrift stores, flea markets, any used-books place whose street-facing windows are caked with several seasons' worth of dust and dirt: you learn to view them all as libraries operating under more modest auspices. Free from the obligations of outlines and dramatic arcs, you dig through documents whose faces never offer any eureka moment; you have to open them up, you have to go down the columns line by line. Sometimes you strike a vein and learn two or three things nobody else was ever going to remember: the storefront office that sold magazine overstock by mail order for a few months before closing up shop, its proprietor forever anonymous now; the fire somebody set in the same office, who knows why, just a week after the magazine guys moved out. But no matter how deep you dig, you'll still probably have to guess when it comes time to say where a teenager might have gone to buy an old sword.

I have pictures of it; anybody who cares at all about the case has seen pictures of the sword. It looks heavy, though most swords weigh less than people think. It looks ancient, but cheap materials can bestow a kind of crude antiquity on their subjects. Its outsized handle looks like a movie prop.

It's not a prop, though. In fact, when the forensics team retrieved it from its place atop the crushed bodies of Marc Buckler and Evelyn Gates, one of the technicians, betraying an adolescence spent in hobby stores and library multipurpose rooms, said, a little louder than he meant to: "Whoa. Two-hander. No wonder nobody heard anything."

I don't know whose sword it was, and I don't know where it came from. There are conflicting stories. They cancel each other out, amounting to anecdotal evidence, only useful to people who've already got a story to tell. To get this kind of detail exactly right, meticulous care has to be taken with the initial investigation.

It happens sometimes. People take extra care, they bother to fill out the paperwork before their memories start to rust. You get lucky. But in the case of the Milpitas teenagers accused of plotting and carrying out the murders of a local property owner and visiting real estate developer, you don't.

6.

MINOANS VI

The first thing Derrick said after Seth and Alex emerged from the arcade was "It's beautiful." He looked at his friends, and then back at the immense, terrible angel overseeing its new domain, the total repurposing of practically every item and surface in the store.

"You like it?" Seth was smiling broadly, his face tense with pleasure.

"It's incredible," Derrick said, circling the angel, watching it sway.

"Wait til you see the booths! Every booth is different! There's a witch booth, there's a wizard booth, there's the Son of Sam booth. I saw something about him in *People* when I was a kid and I just *went* for it," Seth said, unable to contain himself any longer, audibly catching his breath and then beginning again. He described how he and Alex and Angela had spent half the night working, making it all up as they went along; the characters he'd improvised and the symbols he'd assigned to them, all the half-grasped mythologies he'd been trying to invoke on every surface and in every corner. To every booth an angel or a demon, its face gazing menacingly out from plexiglass screen protectors, slogans and symbols clustering riotously on the walls and ceilings.

"On the floors, too!" Seth said, in triumph. "On the *cushions*! It's crazy!"

Alex stood by him but didn't look up; he was still good at drawing, and, given the right tools, could still lend form and shape to his ideas and visions. The night's work had been a team effort; after Angela went home, Seth's intensity had escalated, and Alex had managed to keep up with him. Something about the solitude of the project, its hermetic boundaries, allowed him to remain present to the moment instead of disappearing into the interior fog that called to him whenever things got quiet. But this feeling, which he'd harbored all night, didn't survive Derrick's arrival; the severe discomfort in just talking to people, even people he liked, remained. It wasn't that the presence of others was intolerable; their bodily presence was actually nice. Space, left empty too long, might start to hum. But when those bodily presences began to talk—asking questions, getting animated, complicating matters—their need for some kind of response caused the pressure to push against the inner walls of his skull. The pain cut through the haze. It demanded relief. Seth was a perfect foil in these times: he never stopped talking. You could use his shadow like a blanket.

"I gotta see those arcades," Derrick said. "It's . . . it's just beautiful, you guys. You did something great. They're gonna hate it, and they'll never know."

"Never know what?" Seth said.

"Who it was," Derrick said.

"I hope they *do* know!" Seth said, too loudly. Alex had caught a catnap in his booth at around 5:00 a.m.; Seth was still going. "I hope they see this and think: *Better just leave whoever did this shit* alone!"

Derrick flashed on Anthony Hawley's last phone call with Evelyn Gates: How he'd tried, and failed, to ask for his key deposit back. How he'd hung up the receiver in silence. How he'd had to swallow his anger in the end, leaving behind thousands of dollars in wasted inventory because it felt like the only counterpunch available to him.

"Landlords don't think like that, dude," he said, trying not to lecture. "The last thing they think about is leaving people alone."

"Wait til they see the *booths*!" Seth said. "They will shit themselves! They'll never come back!"

Derrick looked at Seth until Seth returned his gaze.

"They will come back and clear everything out," Derrick

said. "That's what they'll do. If anybody's inside, they'll be cleared out, too. We have to get out of here."

Alex scowled. "At least they should say it to my face," he said, with audible effort; when he paused midsentence, he felt like he might never arrive at his destination.

"They'll bring cops," Derrick said. "Miss. Gates will definitely bring cops. Come on, you both know this. You could get killed. Think about it. Put a tent under the freeway and be safer than in here."

Alex returned to his silence, which was now clouded by bad possibilities.

"This is our house," Seth said.

"It's not anybody's house," Derrick said, sounding like his own dad. He felt bad after he said it, but it was true. "Nothing personal. But this isn't your house, it's not our clubhouse, it's not anything. It's just an old store where we were fucking around after Mr. Hawley bailed on it."

He was trying to look at things the way adults would look at things. But Seth and Alex watched him as he spoke, awaiting the moment when he might attend to their expressions, to better divine for himself their meaning: for in their faces lay this news, that a castle in which one finds shelter, be it the meanest dwelling place in all the land, is home and hearth to those it guards from harm; and that the right of those within its walls remains, to defend themselves from the intruder, and from the thief, and from those who would encroach upon their rightful domain.

"It's kind of my house," Alex said. He sounded healthier than he had just a moment before. Seth's mania was getting contagious.

"You know he has to sleep here," Seth said, nodding in Alex's direction.

"I don't know what you want me to say," Derrick said. "When they come to take their place back, it's going to be too late. Please, you guys. Don't be stupid."

"I'm not stupid," Seth said to his childhood friend, who dreaded the possible consequences of neglecting to argue until he'd gotten his point across, but who also, after so many years, knew better.

THE EVIDENCE OF SULGRAVE

Behold the first chamber: the depth of black ink, the white spaces between those deep alleys too narrow to afford the fugitive escape. Behold the writing along its three walls, in script too crimped to parse save those few words that leap to the eye through the pure splendor of their desolation, *devil* and *grave* and *witch*, *blood* and *fire* and *sacrifice*. Behold a lone image, a monster arising as if from the depths of the sea, only to drown again in the disordered frenzy of waking dreams. And behold the subsuming totality of the Word, every surface flowing with it, betraying and perverting the human function of language— to share, to bridge a distance—and setting, in its place, this labyrinth with no center, this maze with its blocked exits. *Set up here devil time in 48 bitch when they come for me been here better than you*, it said. *Gave blood 1x military hospital 3x First Baptist hopstial 10x Mmeorial hospital checkt your sacrifice records bitch. Fire kingdom lord of the seventy-ninth degree to the unknown and still too good for this world*, it said. It went on like this forever; had anyone read the whole of it, which in its execution took two hours to complete, they could not have come away without pity. Pain leapt from its lines. But in truth, these lines bore hidden testimony to Alex's empathy: the whole of it was a performance, one drawn from men he had met on the street, men who transcribed their screaming internal monologues onto empty cereal boxes and discarded newspapers as though driven by an irresistible need, scribbling late into the night until they passed out from exhaustion. He wondered, as he worked, if his ability to embark upon such labor so easily meant difficult days for him down the road. He marked, as he ran out of empty space on which to write, that this indeed had been his home and hearth this short time, and that his true presence here had now been disguised: the spare handful of things he'd already written in the preceding days was, now, buried beneath the outpouring of this imaginary tenant, this conjured spirit, to confound the coming invaders.

Behold the second chamber, its colors ablaze: red Sharpie, white correction fluid, and oily orange paint meant for indicating where it's not safe for construction crews to dig. Monstrous features emerge from great blobs of Liquid Paper—gaping maws, weeping boils, clusters of eyes. There are seven of them in all—Seth and his attention to detail—and each bears its number underneath it, marked with a pound sign: #2 has no eyes; #5 boasts fingernails that look like scythes, some fluid dripping from the index and middle digits of its right claw. The numbers scatter: #1 and #3 are on the right wall, staring across the distance of the booth at #2, #4, #5, and #6, whose gored scalp is infested with small worms. Surveying them all is #7, who takes up the entire back wall of the booth, his body the shape of a great stone fortification, a single eye peering out from a small aperture near the top and crude flames shooting out from either side of his face. Beneath him, the only words in this chamber, terse flowing cursive in heady contrast to its disordered, loquacious neighbor: *BEAST KINGDOM*.

Behold the third chamber, form without knowable function, shape without evident purpose, symmetrical waves flowing down each wall from ceiling to floor, dazzling to the eye, not painted but carved, like ancient symbols from cave walls in the deserts of the West or on the surfaces of planets as yet unconquered; yet bearing, if the onlooking eye survives the maze, along the ascending lines of several peaking points, a name, in pencil, *David Hell-son*, distributed six times throughout this labyrinth of jagged and increasingly frayed waves, and a final time in careful capital letters upon the plastic protector of the television monitor. Behold the hypnotic sway of David Hell-son's chamber on the eye, how he beckons from within, a deceitful oasis from the arcade's horrors; yet behold the pornographic tape still playing in the booth, casting its light onto the design around it and emitting its distorted squall into the blue air, a garden of bleached perversion handpicked by Derrick for its purpose before leaving for aye. "The worst tape in the store," he'd said, assigning it to the booth with a grimace.

Behold the fourth chamber, the witch booth, upon which the luxury of spray paint has been bestowed! Alex is no apprentice, but has known one or two in his travels, seen them bestow their hurried work onto the sliding back doors of parked semitrailers in rest stop lots. From them he has borrowed a quavering line, an easy slope to his turns; the witch is bloated and her breasts sag. Over them hang the strands of her long, white hair, crossing each other in loose braids all the way down to her spindly ankles. On the floor of the chamber, stray symbols—stars and planets and letters from imagined alphabets. Her eyes are red X's within black circles; from her place on the back wall of the booth, she surveys her domain's original graffiti, lewd offers and phone numbers. Alex with the natural touch. Some things are scarier when you leave them as they are.

Behold, then, her mate, lord of the fifth chamber, namesake of the wizard booth! A new hand announces its presence herein, meticulous and excessive; she means to distinguish herself, to leave her mark in the moons and stars of the wizard's robes. Behold the terrible demons in the skies around him, mouths agape with sorrow, drifting among white outcroppings of stardust that threaten to bury them but from whose caked, clotted smears they yet emerge, in eternal servitude to their lord, whose beard teems with six-legged insects. See, scrawled in cribbed, hasty felt-tip, the word *Satan*, inserted here and there amid the tableau, clumsy, awkward, effective. Note the slashes in the cushions, grouped in twos and threes like the marks of a nesting animal that hopes to return to its lair. Behold the work of Lady Angela, fair knight among knights, game for the hunt, there when you need her, tight-lipped when pressed for confession.

Behold the sixth chamber, repository of congealing paint left in supply closet cans, the very face of disorder: paint poured onto the vinyl seat, paint smeared on the screen, pools of spilled paint on the floor, their surfaces muddily reflecting the blackness of the ceiling above, and words, yet more words scratched into it while still wet, seeming now ready to recede into the lakes that gave them voice: *HURT*, alone on one wall; 7 alone in the screen, a clue, a sign, the tail of the red herring. Behold this obscure and unreadable signal to the coming invaders, curling question marks splashed onto the ceiling, a dozen of them at least, jumbled, mocking, senseless.

Behold, finally, the seventh chamber, the glass house, the room that gives the castle a name by which to be remembered: for someone has succeeded in shattering the screen, and affixing broken shards to the walls of the booth with glue, and nesting more of them in dug-out crevices here and there, so that everywhere one looks, one sees a partial reflection: enough to direct the eye toward the ceiling, where, behold, in marker, a portrait of a man in profile, five-o'clock shadow dotting his jawline, a swarm of flies around his balding head, a jagged line where his neck terminates suggesting rough decapitation; and, indeed, this caption beneath him telling the tale: *ANOTHER ENEMEY OF THE HOPELESS ONES*. Framing all, on the back wall, written sidewise, in evident haste, unadorned, a farewell to the onlooking eye:

> *look in the mirror and what do you see?*
> *Bloody Barry, five of his friends, and me*
> *those who knew us knew us well*
> *those who didn't SERVE IN HELL*

And finally, on the single surface remaining, the inner door, Seth's masterstroke of misdirection: the jewel in the crown, the christening of the shrine, in dripping script, the menacing starkness of its expression ready-made for the local camera crews, and, later, the nationals.

NOBL NIGHTS R WE

SOLO IV

"What do I even say," Derrick said when he emerged back through the entrance, shaking his head, a huge smile on his face. "It's . . . Seth. Alex. Ang. Man, you did it. You guys really did it." In Seth's heart, the glee of Derrick's speechless awe clashed with the finality of the moment; the work was done. They would not return.

"I knew you would love it!" he said. "Did you see the mirror chamber, all that Son of Sam shit?"

"I saw it," Derrick said. "Man, I saw it. When those people come back and see all this, there won't be anything but a big puddle of piss underneath them." For a brief moment, an ugly vision of interlopers in business dress pissing down their legs made everybody smile at once, a welcome break from the gathering feeling of departure.

"Let me go get my stuff," Alex said. It hardly takes any time at all for a person to get used to packing up and moving along every night; he'd met plenty of people out there younger than him who'd been at it for years. Some of them get proud about it during bullshit sessions late at night, claiming not to know where their families live or to remember their last fixed address; many of these are probably telling the truth, except when it comes to saying how they feel about it.

For Alex, the notion of feeling proud about one's station, however high or low, seemed alien. Some foster homes are good, and some are awful, and most are better than group placements except for the ones that are much, much worse; and some group placements are preferable to hospital units, though occasionally there's a therapist who hasn't yet given up hope, and who tries to help, and in so doing almost makes it worth living behind a locked door with no shoes on for a month surrounded by strangers who all think their problems are bigger than yours. A few nights in a shuttered porn store with some friends had been nice. But he'd harbored no illusions about it. He hoped to stay in town somehow; he'd heard that several people he knew from before had jobs at a car wash, and he thought he could maybe do that long enough to save up some money.

Derrick and Seth both knew that the loss of the store meant uncertain days ahead for Alex. Nobody knew what to say to make it better.

"Hey, man," Derrick said.

"Hey," Alex said back. "It was nice."

"There's probably not a big hurry, though."

"I just have my bag."

"I feel like all of us leaving together is a bad idea," Derrick said. It was still very early in the morning, but people would be out and about soon enough. Seth was used to being the first person asked to leave; he grabbed his backpack from its place inside one of the chalk outlines on the floor.

"All right. I might wait until tonight," Alex said.

"You going back to San Jose?"

"Maybe." Alex knew telling people you had no actual plans made them feel sad. He was exhausted; his only real hope was to find someplace to rest after staying awake all night redecorating the store with his old friends from another life, from school.

"This sucks dick," said Seth.

"It's just how it is," Derrick said; the sound of his own voice in his ears, saying those words, made the adult world ahead of him seem cold and ugly.

"I bet if you come to school one of the counselors can think of something," Seth suggested, knowing from personal experience how useless the counselors at school were but having nothing better to offer.

Alex wanted to let them off the hook, and he didn't want them to see him if he started getting loose, as usually happened when he didn't sleep. "Maybe I'll see you at school," he said.

Derrick and Seth took the cue. "Probably doesn't matter if you lock up when you leave," Derrick said, heading for the back door.

Alex laughed and said: "All right."

For the last time, now with a heavy heart, Seth followed his friend out through the back.

"School called," Maria Healey said to Seth when he got home that afternoon, earlier than he'd been home in the afternoon in several months.

"I went to school!" Seth protested loudly, as if he'd already been arguing about the question for several minutes.

"I *know*," said his mother, slowly, carefully, trying to look her son in the eyes. "They called because you fell asleep in class again. You're not in trouble. They are *worried*."

"I'm fine!" Seth said.

Maria took a deep breath.

"I'm worried, too," she said. "I don't know where you go at night. By myself, I can't really do anything about it. You're too big now for me. If you won't take care of yourself, I—"

"Mom, I'm *fine*," said Seth, wholly exhausted and in need of sleep, responding to the emotion in his mother's voice like a sponge soaking up water until it can hold no more, feeling some of what she felt: changes just up ahead, the end of something.

"Well, I hope so," she said, wishing she had something stronger than hope on hand, knowing better than to look too hard for whatever that stronger thing might be.

FOREIGN INFLUENCE

He looks for signs of construction as he's landing this time. From the air, sites look like something out of a Lego kit— uniform geometric spaces identical to one another in shape if not always in size, interrupted occasionally by yellow cranes in their wet clay pits, the search like a scavenger hunt whose rewards are great but as yet intangible, and then the plane gets cleared for landing, at which point he takes note of the occasional swimming pool. The presence of people who can afford swimming pools is a great sign, he thinks—people who'll spend their money on luxuries won't hesitate to buy an improved property in a developing neighborhood. He takes a confident attitude toward the future prospects he intends to finalize on this visit; he's done his research. The Bay Area is on the move. All property appreciates over time. Real estate, held long enough, is immune to cycles of boom and bust. Progress is real. It's the chances you don't take that you'll remember.

But the cashier's check for "earnest money" that's in his briefcase in the overhead rack keeps interrupting his reverie. You can't get that money back; once you hand it over, it's gone. If anything goes wrong down the line, it's a sunken cost. And Buckler, as they'd put it in the churches near the property he intends to buy, is stepping out in faith. Back home, he's walked through plenty of properties, and he talks a good game: but he's an amateur. It nags at him. He knows that once he turns that crucial first property around it will be easy; he has friends who say it's like taking candy from a baby.

Up late at night, he's watched hour-long infomercials whose hosts speak to him from the decks of yachts, surrounded by women in bathing suits and well-wishers hoisting flutes of champagne.

He looks at the buildings below as they grow larger, the plane descending, and imagines owning whole developments, selling them off by parcel, outbidding every over-educated asshole on prime locations in the market until everybody knows his name.

I'm too smart to be doing this, Derrick thought to himself. *I'm too smart and I have too much riding on me staying out of trouble. I'm too* old *to be doing this*, he thought to himself, still working patiently although he'd assured his parents he was only going out to ride his bike: remaining aware of his surroundings, sauntering casually around the corner of the building from time to time, trying to blend into the general scenery for a minute or two if he happened to spot an idle interloper walking nearby; and then, when the danger seemed past, ambling gently back to his station, as if attending to some quotidian duty. Repeating this process several times as the afternoon progressed to dusk: at school everybody had ideas about when it was safest to be out and about doing things that might get you noticed. Guys who'd run into trouble once or twice said lunch break and dinner break were your best bets.

Trying not to be seen while still getting it right; staying focused but remaining on guard—the handicap gave an edge to his work. Every time he returned to his station at the door, that edge sharpened some, leaving direct evidence of its bite. Seth and Alex and Angela hadn't had time for the facade of the property; they'd been too busy all night attending to the interior, where the chances of getting caught were lower. Slowly, now, Derrick was finishing the job, using the worn stub of chalk left from a piece Seth used for the outlines on the floor.

For his contribution, Derrick meditated a moment on the things that make people afraid to enter a place. In his literature class, when they did Edgar Allan Poe, they spent almost the whole time talking about fear of the unknown; to him this was a sort of training-wheels fear. The unknown is too vast and shapeless to be a threat. To Derrick, harm, the prospect of it, was the deciding quantity: the possibility that something inside will hurt you. That's the stuff that makes you cross the street to avoid a house. It's the chance that there's something inside that might leave a mark on you. You'd be even more scared if you knew what it was.

So he sketched a devil's head, its mouth open as though to devour; it was a version of one of the monsters from Seth's numbers booth. Seth had littered the booths with repeating motifs—"People are idiots, they never see anything," he'd explained—and the impulse to overdo it seemed like a good one. Sometimes you have to hit people over the head with your visions to get them to notice anything.

But when the shape was complete, he wanted something more: to leave his mark, to really put the fear of God into whatever dumb fish Evelyn Gates had wriggling on her hook. So he dragged the chalk in a straight line down from the devil head's chin, angling it deftly so that no eye could miss it. A head on a stake. Alligators in the moat. A torch that burns not in welcome but in warning.

He then wrote the following:

SICK SATAN SENTRAL FAITHFUL 4EVER! BY THIS

SIGHN CONQUER BY THESE LIGHTS COME TO

SEE

and painted, underneath, sidelong-gazing googly eyes that mirrored the ones overhead on the store's sign. The echo of the unseen, the exacting feel for detail: he kept it all in there, even working at speed. A risky choice for a simple embellishment, which is how you know Derrick was the one who made it. Anything worth doing is worth doing right. You hear it all your life. When the hour comes to remember old sayings, you learn a little about how they've managed to grow old without dying out.

INSTEAD THERE WAS THIS TUFTED ROCK

The strip of developed land in the shadow of the freeway wasn't a total eyesore—it had served a purpose, once—but it stood out, and Anthony Hawley's porn store had made that worse. People noticed. Of course, there were a few who, privately, were glad to find a place like it that didn't require them to drive all the way into San Jose. But most people quietly hoped it would go away. On its best days, it looked ratty.

The police fielded several calls that day about the broken glass and the animal bones. These were recorded as "reports of vandalism," but none of them were from the owner of the property, and no vehicle was dispatched to investigate. Secondhand reports of vandalism are data points, not priorities.

The store itself, the old building that had been many things over the years, waited uncertainly for the people who would come, that evening, to help it cross into the next phase of its long existence.

7.

GLOSS MYSTERY

Angela and Seth spotted each other in the halls at school the next day; they nodded and exchanged greetings, but quickly moved along on their own errands. Secrets require care and nurturing; they die when they hit the air.

Seth was accustomed to adrenaline letdowns. Staying up all night, held firmly in the pincers of some momentary obsession, was almost routine for him: in his bedroom, alone, he often watched the sunrise creep in under the shades, wondering how long he'd already been awake. His sleeping medication's window of effectiveness was about an hour. If he toughed it out past that hour all bets were off.

Angela, on the other hand, was sorting through the events of last night carefully in her mind, working overtime to compartmentalize them: everybody does crazy things in senior year. Her friends talked about it all the time; it was something they'd all noticed together during their first few weeks back after summer break. There was something in the chemistry among the incoming senior class that felt unmistakably new. Anything seniors did together felt like some ratings-grab cliffhanger from the season finale of a TV show—not just the big moments, but the small things: going out for ice cream; standing in the lunch line together; showing up at a pep rally. Everything took on some pathos. Even the most practically minded seniors—Angela counted herself one—had started letting their hair down in case they never got the chance to do it again.

Had she been Alex, rationalizing her part in the rededication of Monster Adult X might have proved a more difficult task. Alex was attuned to the frequencies of life-changing moments. He'd heard that high tone droning all night, and felt the current traveling between himself and the others, an unmistakable circuit. He recognized its vibration. Angela felt it, too—the first twelve bottles of amyl nitrite she'd arranged into a cairn on the counter hadn't felt like much, but after stacking six more brightly colored pyramids atop the glass display case, all separated by brand and tiered into a color spectrum from dark to light, she began to feel personal investment in the work; the shape she and her friends had begun imposing on the interior of the store felt like a personal expression, something privately satisfying, a confidential matter. In front of the seven pyramids, she'd placed a jumbled arrangement of letters cut from VHS sleeves to spell out *MYSTERY?* She especially liked the question mark. It made you stop a little longer, but even then, after you'd given it a whole extra minute, it didn't give anything extra back. Before leaving, she made a point to regard the counter carefully: a mental snapshot of something for which no evidence was expected to survive.

For her, that snapshot was meant to be the whole of it. A captured moment in time, something crazy she'd done when she was young. One of a dozen oddball things she expected to do this year before she took her diploma and headed out into the world to see how the future looked.

Arriving to class that morning, she saw several of her friends already at their desks—Rhonda, from drill team; Rudy, who drove a Ford Mustang and was always offering her a ride somewhere. The life she'd dabbled in last night returned to the shadows of memory. She settled into the comfort of her daylight self, its ease and familiarity helping last night's work slide into the acceptable context of the preterit. Even when we don't find ourselves doing something wild, we sort out several selves along the line as we're becoming the people we will be. It's a constant, half-conscious process.

Most of the time, it's hardly even worth trying to remember how it happened. Most of the time, no one will care.

THE BLESSING OF GOODLY COMPANY

To Anthony Hawley, it was a little surprising that Evelyn Gates had never given him at least some small indication of outrage about having to clean out his failed porno store. He knew she'd probably seen worse in her time; her targeted clientele, like her father's before her, were the perennially at-risk, people with bad credit who knew when they signed the lease that cleaning deposits were a scam but who lacked the standing to object. Gates would have seen some hostile gestures in her time: rotting food left in refrigerators, or dirty old furniture abandoned in haste. Hawley figured it would take a lot to get any response out of her after she'd seen the last of his money. But a whole storefront full of hard-core porn, a video arcade with the floors unmopped? He'd've thought these would merit at least an angry phone call.

But there had been nothing. No letter announcing she'd be keeping his deposit, nor certainly any check for the remaining balance on the rent. It was as if he'd only existed for her until he stopped sending her a check every month.

He got up from behind his desk and went out into the office, where his three employees were all giving the pitch: tickets for a pancake breakfast to help the Firefighters' Fund. They'd do this for three weeks and then move on to whoever wanted to pay for some phone solicitation next. The job was commission-only for the people working the phones. Hawley's pay came from whoever owned the business, which was housed in a dingy grey building in San Jose; he didn't know a lot about it and it seemed considerably shadier than the porn store.

Still, he got to go home at five, and nobody tried to talk to him about their personal business like it somehow involved him, and at the end of the day he didn't have to feel shitty about sending the nice teenage kid who only wanted a quiet place to read back into the arcade to mop up the booths. It was good to have Monster Adult X behind him. Maybe some people were cut out for that kind of work; who knows? But every day he felt happier to be a little further away from those days. Phone sales wasn't exactly the road to riches, either, but at least he didn't have to think up creative ways to tell people what he did for a living.

MINOANS VII

By now Alex would have been awake. He'd gone to sleep around dawn; people who sleep badly know that the hours between five and eight may be your best chance to ramp down into a little of the restorative sleep that keeps madness temporarily at bay. Over time, sleep deprivation changes the texture of sunlight into a mild narcotic, a lilting force of such gentle, persuasive power that it can cause the terrors of night to withdraw their attack. Alex had thought long and hard about this. At the first rays of dawn he repaired to his booth.

The paint was still wet inside. He slept in the couples booth, the one on whose walls he'd spray-painted a witch last night. The paint still smelled, and he could have fit himself comfortably into one of the smaller units, but routine was a luxury for him, one whose comforts would shortly be receding into the distance.

Whether he turned on the multi-arcade tape machine before he went to sleep or much later, possibly not until after dark, I don't know. A lot of people sleep with some kind of background noise, like a transistor radio or an electric fan. Vested interests in establishing the working status of the video tape machines that fed the arcade would have been of great value to a prosecutor, but I am not in the business of aiding real or imaginary prosecutors. I can only offer guesses based on available data.

Still, it's likely that Alex's auditory hallucinations would have been acting up again. The less you sleep, the worse they get. Ambient noise can help a little, sometimes; it makes me sad to picture Alex like this, asleep in the glow of a screen upon which naked bodies writhe, their distorted moans filtered once through the monitor's cheap speaker and again through its protective plexiglass housing. His backpack on the floor, stuffed too full to zip closed. The handle of the sword visible, even down there in the dark.

I would greatly prefer to see Alex breathing deeply, untroubled by dreams in the quiet of the dawn becoming morning. I'd like to see him wake up and elect to leave while the day is young, perhaps seek out a counselor as Seth suggested. I'd like to see that counselor follow through on the protocol, still vague and unstandardized but finally developing now, for homeless adolescents at risk. Maybe there'd be a mentor for Alex, someone who could relate to his station in life. They could talk about job training or the importance of some basic daily living routines. I'd prefer, in all cases, for Alex to leave this place, which had served its purpose for him. But there's a considerable distance between the things we're called to bear witness to and the things we'd prefer to see. I learned this, late, from a friend in Morro Bay.

A ROYAL WELCOME

Evelyn Gates saw the damage as soon as she pulled up to the curb, but it was too late for excuses; Buckler was riding in the passenger seat. Where, before, he'd seen a porn store that reminded him of the parts of Southern California he generally tried to avoid, he now saw something wrecked, grubby, despoiled. There was an enormous pile of broken bottles on the sidewalk just in front of the store. Down the walkway, an assortment of empty tin cans, used diapers, old cereal boxes, and the contents of ashtrays: someone had emptied one or several trash cans behind them while walking out to the street. Where a person might have placed a welcome mat just in front of the door, crushed pieces of another bottle or two had been mounded into a shining amber heap. The jagged edges caught the late sun like low tide.

They approached the door, its chalk-white text successfully framing for them the bottles and the broken glass, a story behind the squalor. The lettering was neat, and tall enough to be read from a distance; its message was brief enough to be taken in quickly, even by eyes hastily surveying the scene to scan for present danger. Buckler looked around, and then at Gates: he was trying to gauge how aggressive a tone he should take when, at the end of all this, he lowered his offer.

But she was in shock; the hallmark of any Gates property was its constancy over time. These lots she'd inherited from her father had relaxed into shabbiness and disrepair, but they resisted substantial change. Their motif was neglect, the subtler cousin of outright abuse. The sense of ownership, of entitlement, that she'd been raised to feel about her family's holdings was a world apart from pride of place, but the sight of the entrance to Monster Adult X both outraged and intimidated her. Somebody was trying to assert their own claim to her land, in terms to which she had no ready response.

"Neighborhood kids," she said, turning the key in the lock while trying to affect, despite herself, a tone of clarity amid the murk and disorder of the scene before her.

In later years, establishing the whereabouts of a person would be a lot easier—cell phone records, browser histories. If you needed something more specific, you might seek a special warrant compelling an ISP to release their data, but after 2002 resistance on that front was pretty weak. You could snoop in broad daylight without your target ever even knowing he'd been under surveillance.

In any case, though, then or now, you'd try to find probable cause, or something you could frame as probable cause; and to get that, in the absence of any direct evidence, you'd have needed a previous record, something you could point to that backed up your suspicions. As of the afternoon of November 1, 1986, there were no crimes on record involving any of the people who'd been spending their spare time, and sometimes sleeping, inside the building formerly known as Monster Adult X.

If you are questioned as to your whereabouts on a given day, you should immediately ask if you are being arrested. If you're not being arrested, you should invoke your right to remain silent. What you were doing with your time on a given day is nobody's business but yours, but I want to state for the record that Derrick Hall spent the afternoon and the evening of November 1, 1986, at home with his parents, both of whom can account for his presence in the house at dinner and aver that they all dined at the table together that night—turkey sandwiches with gravy; Derrick had seconds. More importantly, a few days later, neither Bill Hall nor his wife, Diane, allowed the detectives who'd arrived unannounced on their doorstep to "have a word" with their son.

"I don't know anything about any of this, but my son is not available for anything without a lawyer, and neither am I. You have my phone number," Bill Hall said, in as amiable a tone of voice as he could stand to feign while closing the door. "Have a nice day."

THE STRONGHOLD AT CORNWALL

Alone in the store, he found a copy of *The Last Starfighter* among several general-release movies in the supply closet near the counter. Seth had left the store's usual fare playing in all the booths—the light was needed to showcase all they'd done to the walls, and the seats, and the screens, and the floors—and had hand-selected the most unpleasant fare he could locate. But Seth wasn't here now, and he wanted to watch something fun. He'd seen *The Last Starfighter* on the big screen two years ago; it felt like an eternity now.

The comfort of a story line he knew and could follow without difficulty was profound; before long, he dozed off, awakening only during a loud battle sequence. When the tape ended, it automatically rewound; he watched it again, staying awake this time. Known quantities help situate us in contexts that anchor us to ourselves; he'd had very few chances to confirm this over the last several months, but the second run-through of *The Last Starfighter* made him feel alert, undistracted, palpably alive to the present moment. Even when he reflected, during a lull, that the present moment found him in a wrecked porn store with almost all his worldly belongings in a backpack—not much to brag about—the clarity of that moment's particulars felt like a triumph. He'd read once, in one of those books you always find in the lone bookcase in a corner of the overnight shelter, that your mind could be your best friend or your worst enemy. It was true. By himself in the booth with a movie whose plot he already knew, he felt on good terms with his mind. It was a good and comforting feeling, one whose integrity went slack and then unraveled completely the moment he heard voices outside in the store again: speaking, this time, not in the voracious tones of buyer and seller but in registers of shock, and panic, and fear.

He readied himself to defend his home. He felt steady in his resolve; the moment held great clarity for him, as if all this time in the store by himself, drifting in and out of sleep until day and night became a smudged continuum, had been necessary for the gathering of strength, for the conservation of energy. The time of gathering was at its end, and the energy would now find its purpose.

A person has a right, perhaps a duty, to protect himself and his stronghold from invaders. There are laws on the books about this, very old laws. They're there for a reason.

597

When the castle door came into view, as her car approached the curb, Lady Gates saw straightaway that aught was amiss, and said unto her companion, But steady, for these woods are not as they were; and sometime among them run bandits and drunkards. Then bethought she to say also, *I'm sorry, I don't know what's going on*: but called she then to mind an old counsel of her upbringing, to wit, that she never express regret before regrets are sought. Howsobeit with these old counsels and their sway, which ever arise before us like shadows at noon, their strength did wane as she assayed the walkway, and the excrement strewn down it, and the broken glass, and the ashes:

I'm sorry, she thought again, and yet again did check her incli-
nation, scrutinizing instead the countenance of her companion, whose face betrayed no special outrage. For if a man, at
cards, cries out when dealt the queen, all will know his fortune
and fold their hands; and while still green and young and indeed in the bloom of his youth, not for nothing had Marc
Buckler at his studies been thought one who might succeed,
were he to learn patience, and to favor the small gain over the
grand sack, the lined pantry over the glitter of the counting
house. Yet alack! for further ventures to the counting house,
and for errands to the pantry, as the great door of the castle
gives way to Lady Gates's key, the better for her to behold the
Great Angel of the Transformation before her, its limbs all
atwitch, the iridescent colors of its skin revealed in the glint of
the late sunlight. For this was the time of early evening, when
shadows grow; then did Lady Gates, mindful of her client's
presence, and thinking on her feet as befitted her station, reach
for the light switch while closing the door behind her in a single movement; and all was revealed.

Jolly in the face both of danger and an advantage to press,
saith Marc Buckler, What the fuck; nor could his Lady protest,
for, under her breath, a language better suited to the common
knave did issue in whispers; for all was ruin; yet not the ruin of
the vandal but the cunning of the imp; spells on countertops,
racks rearranged into shapes better suited to the coven than to
an empty property awaiting one young enough to pay the
markup; wares all about repurposed as if to confound evil spirits; and behold, the dam breaks, I'm sorry, says poor Lady
Gates, these neighborhood kids, I didn't know.

See, then, the throb and ebb of light from the entryway to
the chambers of the knights' council; and a moment of mutual

understanding between Lord and Lady, that they are not among their own, but have breached some castle grounds whose customs, to them, seem strange; and behold, upon the floor, the outlines of bodies, mockeries of life, blind oracles; which both do regard overlong, Marc Buckler remarking upon them, What happened here, and his Lady in response, I have no idea, I'm really sorry; and he seeing the words AN-GEL and PLAYPEN and perhaps feeling, in his coward's heart, the turn of the play; and she seeing BEYOND and ETERNAL, and bethinking herself to return to the surer safety of the outside; Come, says she, obviously something happened here, again betraying the careful stewardship of her father, never apologize for anything, they smell blood; it is too late; I'm really sorry, I had no idea, and him a-following, his visions of wealth all a-glitter with the youthful vigor of un-knowing; and, from the darkness, unseen, emerging, lo, a brave knight, his sword mighty, his strike sure, a swordsman forged in the fury of self-preservation; and as has been seen on battlefields for as long as men have done battle, he who fol-lows last is first to fall; and behold, this ocean of blood, the sword-point hath pierced the neck; he falls retching; see now Lady Gates gaze in horror upon this young knight all mad, his mail but rude, the outfitting of the peasant; Get away from me, you son of a bitch, she cries, but finding the door closed, fumbles; Where is the Goddamned doorknob; and does the blade fall once, or twice, or three times sidewise upon her skull; yet living, Marc Buckler beholds; the blows that fall like rain; the careful silence of he who wields the sword; nor can Lady Gates cry out, her head struck by iron; she has found the doorknob; yet but one blow from the flat of the blade and her hand retreats; the doorknob knocked from its housing; she must join her companion upon the floor; and in the dusk remain where she lies until some deeper grave be found, if the cunning of the knight who guards the castle gates can abide but a short span longer.

NORTHUMBRIAN WHISPERS

The initial reports went out over the airwaves; cases like these are godsends to local radio. Something lurid to make drive time pass more quickly between work and home, something so juicy it makes Dad turn on the TV news as soon as he gets in through the front door. Bill, what? Shh, listen. Some kind of satanic thing. That stuff in New Jersey? No, down near the freeway. The freeway here? What other freeway is there? Shh. Well, you said it last year, whole lot of new people lately. *Too* many, last time I checked, this is just, wait, shh, here it is.

Rumors began to spread as soon as the news hit the wires: on the campuses of the middle and high schools first, filtering down a day or two later to the elementaries. These would grow distorted and bizarre as they traveled, the inevitable process of myth-building in an age of print and video: seven kids in a pact with Satan to kill, unrepeatable atrocities visited upon the bodies, old corpses dug up from the lawn. Signs and symbols to describe with fear and wonder. Nocturnal rites inside the dirty bookstore. Younger kids, hearing, genuinely frightened but too proud to show it, would, when they passed the stories along, embellish new details from the reservoirs of their dreams: I heard they lit the bodies on fire. I heard one guy was covered in oil but he didn't burn. My friend lives near there, he saw the burning bodies. For real? For real. My brother said there was a lady inside whose right leg was twice as long as her left one, she had to drag herself around by her hands. How did she kill any-body if she couldn't run after them? Somebody held them down for her right there on the floor.

The detail of the lady with one leg twice as long as the other is one I found in an openly skeptical news report, one of the few pieces about the killings to be broadcast beyond the confines of California during the week that followed. A teen-ager, whose name the paper, citing general policy, had declined to publish, said he'd heard it from at least three people, includ-ing somebody who claimed to have known Siraj personally. Siraj? Siraj, yes, with a *j*, new kid, everybody at the whole school knows he was involved, he's crazy, he can't shut up about all the shit he gets up to, excuse me, all the *things he does*—this as fellow students nearby, also unnamed, erupt with laughter and then try to compose themselves. Find him, though, for real, he knows all about it, swear to God.

Dana Reid, the reporter of this story, seems to have re-quested and been given access to the enrollment records; I was unable to locate a court order granting her access, but these were looser times. Finding nobody named Siraj, she remarked, parenthetically: "Action News found no student by this name on the rolls for the 1986–87 school year." She touched then on competing theories of the case—former tenants with an ax to grind; criminals occupying an abandoned property; crack is mentioned several times: in the eighties you could get away with blaming almost anything on crack—before returning the broadcast to its anchors.

There's a lot I'd like to ask this student whose name Action News couldn't find, but he's lost to us. It's almost impossible to get clarity on early details like these, especially when the facts have been so successfully obscured by Siraj's later life within the febrile imagination of the public—or within, I should say, that small slice of the public that still follows stories like these after they've dropped off the front page, the people who can't help but be curious about details left out of the news reports; and who, denied such details by miserly detectives and cowardly reporters, fill in the blanks themselves as best they can.

4

Song of Gorbonian

the life and works of
Gorboniaw map Morydd,
known more generally as Gorbonianus, but
called, by Geoffrey, in his History of the Kings of
Britain,

Gorbonian:

that good king who, in his time, defended the
husbandmen against the oppressions of their
land-lords; who ruled his kingdom with right justice, and did show mercy to the poor of this land;
who shunned adventuring over-seas, preferring,
to such sojourns, the happy haunts of his youth,
those green boughs and pleasant meadows deemed
greater by him than all the exalted halls which
house the kings and lords of this world; and who,
in the strength of his days, did, of his own enterprise and will, restore an ancient temple, in those
groves of mystery which he had loved since boy-
hood with honor and reverence, a spirit he honored
until the end of his days.

1.

Now the birth of Gorbonian was as follows. His father the King, having defended his counties against the Flemish invaders, brought upon the land a time of feasting and plenty; and tribute did issue from the land all round, in gratitude to King Morvidus, who, though his mother had come from some far country, none knew which, did now guard his kingdom from marauders. And the people did say, that there was none so worthy as King Morvidus; and in the richness of his reign, commerce prospered, the town around the castle growing great, and newe fangled habits did arise among the young and old.

But after a time the people did say, that the old customs were gone out from the land; and that, with the coming of the new, the old had been washed away. Greatly did folk rue the passing of their customs, saying, that a kingdom ruled by thankless men, would, in short measure, become a kingdom unremembered; and men did complain, when they gathered, at how few remained who yet could call to mind the noble names of the gods. Those gods, they said, had once sustained this land; but they might forget as well as be forgotten, as would be seen.

And then did the rains begin: those long rains, of which it was sayd, their like had never fallen; and the streams did overflow their banks, and flood the fields. And the ditches filled with mud, overflowing onto the roads, that none might pass in safety. And vermin did breed in the still water by night; and many infants were delivered still-born, for that the rains had so drenched the roadways, that mid-wives might by no means traverse them in their ladies' time of need. Which seemed a very omen; and some did wonder, how best to please the gods who had served them so.

In this time was delivered of her nine-months' burden, good Queen Argoel, who in time would bear King Morvidus five children. As the rains battered the castle wall, the child began to kick within her womb, saying,—Mother, my time is come; yet, with the storm still upon the land, she lay abed unattended in her toil.

Alone in her labor, and sore afraid, Queen Argoel gave over her heart in prayer, that the baby might be safely delivered; and she cried out, seeking in her suffering those same gods, whose names she had learned at her grandmother's knee. Especially, did she call upon Arawn, ruler of the other-world; and no sooner had the goddess-name gone up, but the dam breaks, and the babe is born, and straightaway lets forth a great cry, nor hold-ing back its force. And Queen Argoel, her eyes full with tears, did raise the child to her breast, saying,—The babe too remembers Arawn; hear, how he names Her by Name. And the babe was calmed, and did sup, and then take his rest; where-fore it was sayd thereafter of Gorbonianus, that oft-times he seemed ill at home in this world, and longed for the next.

But lo, above the din of rain pelting the roof-top, the cries of the new-born babe were heard, yet only by some cooks who tarried yet within the walls of the castle; and by these were the Queen and her babe attended. And some do say, that husband-men from the stables, did also come, for that they loved their Queen. And the night did pass; and thereafter, Queen Argoel did enjoin all who were present, not to speak further regarding the humble circumstances of the child's birth, on pain of exile; for he alone would be heir to the throne, and, if the mean manner of his appear-ance in this world were broadcast more gener-ally, it might give rise to rumor.

When the rains had abated, the child was taken in to King Morvidus; who, seeing the babe so hale, its face a very likeness of his own, was heard to say,—Behold, mine own son; he has come to bring cheer to our castle; all that I have shall be his.

And then did the King call for his men, to see his son all pink and round, a-mewling in his mother's arms; brave Kaswallan did he call, saying,—In all your days my general, have you seen one such as him? And Kaswallan in reply,—No, my liege; he bears the brow of the warrior born; and who would know it but I. Then called the King to his chamber two more: Seisil, who kept the counting-house, and Madauc, his magi-cian; Eadman the strong, who guarded the castle gate, and Saewulf the navigator; and many more did he name, saying, let them come, to see my good prince. And when that his men saw their King all red-cheeked for joy, they clapped their hands together and joined their voices in song, to welcome Prince Gorbonian.

Now Morvidus was greatly moved by their merriment, and listed to them with keen ear; and at last he bid them be silent, saying,—Long will I remember my friends, who came to share this day with me: nor will they want for aught, while I draw breath.

2.

Now shall I tell how young Gorbonian was learned in the ways of piety. As a boy he showed reverence always to gods of the hearth, be they ever so strange; for oft had his mother sayd to him, that a custom only is strange, if that it be one unfamiliar. And she told him, truly were the gods of this kingdom once afoot in these fields; and instructed him in lore long lost.

To the boy, who did love to go all a-wandering, his mother's words would often return. For sometime in the forest, and betimes by the sea-coast, where caves with bone-white walls did beckon, he might encounter a nest of birds unknown to him, or some fire-pit dug by none knows who, the sand beneath it charred black, or such stones as might be used to scry the shape of future days. And should those stones gleam, or the fire-pit seem to tell some tale, then would he say,—I know this not; and yet does it please me; and so his pockets were often heavy with sticks, or clay, or scraps gathered from along the wayside.

Befell it on a day that Gorbonian sought adventure, and called to his friends in the castle-town,—Ho, good Braith! Come away with me! Ho, Hedyn! Wouldst seek treasure hidden in the hills? For his mother was a good Queen, his Queen a good mother; no child was of too low estate to prove a playmate for her son. But none came, that day; for, they said, the signs were for rain. The spoils of adventure be mine alone! Replied the Prince; and so saying, set out alone, as, to tell plainly, he oft did, wondering that the secrets of the world did best reveal themselves in times of solitude.

Ere long, as shadows grew upon the land, he came upon a path within those low-lands, ascending to the place called Witches Keep. Now this place looked inward to the kingdom, its back to the brine; and long had the Queen forbidden the Prince to venture sea-side, for that he was her only son.

Now tales told of Witches Keep were many, and long had he sung their strains; for oft will young boys gather, to trade in lore and legend. But the Prince did doubt the better part of these; For, said he, if there were giants, where then are their bones; and, if there are fairies, what becomes of their wings.

Thus did he regard most idle talk of those haunted hills; but, at bed-chamber, when his nurse-maid Meri would regale him with fables of her people to the east, then would his mind set all a-wandering. Most did he marvel, when she sang „The Clan of the Ogre's Cave"; for it told of a place where people of old had lived, who now were gone.—They were known in their time, she did sing, but they are no more; they were known and they are no more, and all in the ogre's cave, while that the young Prince did drift into dreaming.

Came he now as the late sun sank to the cave by Witches Keep; and the cold of the evening did creep, and his skin shiver. Then by the cave-mouth, to speak truly, did the son of the King tarry: For the telling of tales is one thing, and the turf of the telling another. And yet, from within, it seemed a voice, or, as may be, an echo, did call, saying,—Come, see how we are.

Then, peering in, he saw the late light cast upon the wall, as a lantern lights a stable; and said,—What things are these? For all about were old cloaks, eaten by moth and mold; and among them, blackened torches brake in half, and bones besides: not those of men, but of pigs, and hens, and fish. Mean fare for an ogre, bethought the boy; but the empty air within did say to him, that all inside had long awaited one coming, to see that which would fade from memory, save that one might venture forth who dared to witness. And so did his eyes follow the light all around, in wonder at these remnants of times unremembered.

Then did the rains begin. The cave grew dark, and without the thunder cracked; and Gorbonian saw that all was as in the days of Noah, and, pressing back into the cave, said,—J shall wait until the rain has passed, and then return home. And so did he continue inward, the better to keep dry, should the storm increase.

And at the cave-end, behold, a free-standing stone, howso conveyed therein, none can say; but there it stands, its smooth surface, notches scored into its sides. And he nears to find what might these markings mean; and some are in the shapes of men, and others like giants. And, atop the stone, a tool, sharp-edged and shining.

To the Prince it seemed his dreams had crossed the breach; wherefore he brushes the dust away from the stone with his hand, to lay his body flush atop it, pressing his ear against this level rock, to test if it might sing with the voice of the fields, or echoes of the sea.

And there he lay, a-waiting. And when he awoke, the rains had passed, and the light of the morning was upon the cave. And it seemed to him that he woke as from the slumber of ages: Re-called he now names from his nursery, heroes of old; and within him some spirit sounding music, its melodies strange but not newe fangled. And attending to this song within, his eyes filled with tears, a mist of memory; but then did he dry these tears with his sleeve, saying aloud, that the shades might hear,—When that J arrive to the shelter of my rightful chamber, be it ever so many years hence, then shall J make known these things kept hidden.

3.

When that Gorbonian came in view of the castle, he saw that the rains of the night had been hard on the land. For the sea lay upland, and the village in a dale; the flood had run straight through til morning. Now men and women of the town stood in the road, hanging their clothing in the branches of the trees to dry; for the flood had unhoused them quite. But good Queen Argoel did espy him from her high window, which looked out upon the town; and cried out,—My son is returned; and fell faint then, and must needs be revived. Whereupon, finding young Gorbonian in the entry-hall, she did lay hold of both his ears, and grip them full sore, saying,—Where hast thou been, what hast thou done.

To this Gorbonian, head hung, replied,—To the sea went I; and there fell into a deep sleep, to be visited by dreams; and I repent of your worry, and would beg of you your pardon.

Now it is said everywhere, that boys do love their mothers yet fear their fathers; wherefore Gorbonian did ask,—Is also my Father full wroth?—As to this, the Queen replied,—If he but knew, your fate were sealed, but alas; and began she then to wail, saying,—I have seen him not, nor since he hied him to the stable, to save his horses from the storm.

For the King's horses were his delight; and, when the storm brake, some did bolt, and were drowned; and to the stable ran King Morvidus then, making great dole the while. For but that his servants had raised the goods in the counting-house above the flood-line, and all in the castle were safe, yet for his stables there seemed no remedy. So sent he word to his Queen, not to expect him until the rain was passed; for he would remain with his steeds til they were safe; stood now Gorbonian before his mother, and said,—I will hasten to him now, to see how I might help.

But when, at the muddy stable-door, he called a-loud,—Father, it is I, no reply did issue. Within that place a ghastly peace now reigned; no horse remained, nor stable-hand; and the Prince did hie from stall to stall, to find his father. Yet the search is short: for long had the King favored a bay horse called the Woodsman, the terror of the tournament. And to him had he run.

Now some tell how Morvidus met his end in battle, to die in glory, as befits a king; while some speak of a great beast that made menace upon the people, feasting on sea-faring folk in the Irish sea, and say Morvidus did raise arms against this monster, and was killed. Of these tales I hold my tongue; they are as they are; but see, now, how in the stable of the Woodsman does the young Gorbonian find his father the King, all life gone out of him, his crown crushed, the blood of his body all out upon the straw. See the Prince all in panic, the stable-walls his prison. See again his eyes return to the cause of their wildness; no more shall the King draw breath; the flood has found him; yet it is the flood not of heaven, but of human villainy. For the Woodsman, too, lies dead beside, its saddle and its shoes torn from its body: and from his father's feet, the boots are stripped; and see, now, the mutilation of his hands, for he wore upon his finger the insignia of the throne, now finger and ring cut away. For into every storm intruders venture, hoping to sack that which they can while wildness and disorder reign: and the thief has come to the kingdom, and who shall restore that which he has taken?

Thus in his young arms does Gorbonian lift the body of his father the King from the mire, holding it to himself, and crying,—Woe is me, and woe unto the kingdom, for today a great tree is felled.

Then did this noble Prince make such dole as never was heard in those humble halls, wailing as he were wood; and all hastened to the stables, each calling back to each, saying,—Come and see, the King is dead. Dead, says one, the King, say not so. Killed, saith another; and so, as birds in the bush all a-chatter, do they prate, the cry gone up and into the streets beyond. Thus was this direst of news made known; and when his mother arrived to his side to grieve with her son, saith she unto him,—This day is thy Father gone; grieve well and wail away, for he is no more; this day didst thou arise a prince, and go forth a king.

4.

Now Morvidus was wrapped in fine cloth, according to custom, and laid atop fresh earth for all to see; and garlands were strewn in fragrant heaps atop that noble body. Around him were placed jars filled with wild honey and oil; and among the people who came to see the King in state was one, yclept Kenir, who earned his keep thinning scrap-heaps day to day. He foraged among waste; and some he did sell, and some did keep for use. In rags he went about, for no fine clothing was his; he stayed in his dwelling somewhat away from town and upland, where that he did find shelter from the storm.

Now seeing the people all in mourning, he did espy the body of his Lord, dressed for the grave, and cried,—My Lord and my King, whose land this is, what shall we do? And bitterly did he wail. But the folk around did comfort him, saying,—Behold, Gorbonian, his son, shall rule us.

Now this Kenir knew the old ways, and did keep them well; and so, turning to them, he cried,—Was this the work of human hands? And all around did say it was. Then straightaway he began to draw with his finger atop the grave-mound, fine symbols, the meaning of which none knew. But, wild in his grief, young Gorbonian did approach, saying,—What dost thou upon my father's grave! Gird up thyself, for I shall slay thee.

And old Kenir replied,—Slay me if thou must; but your father knew me; and this would he will, that his friends, and, yea, his heir, if thou will'st, would avenge him as men of old were avenged, with the aid of signs and portents. Whereat Gorbonian wondered, and did withdraw with the scrap-scavenger; and spake they of the old ways, those now dying from the world: of the passage of the dead, and the duties of the living, as in this case, to exact from the robber such tribute as might be bitterly pried.

Then did the young King wail aloud, crying,— My father, guide you mine hand, for I am your son, and must needs have counsel. And behold, upon the burial-mound, a raven alights. And the new King did rise, and order sheep and oxen brought in from the fields, to be laid atop his father's body and burned; and for days of sport and game to follow, as men had practiced in days of old.

Now all was done as the King decreed. And when the body was burnt, then did he bury his father's bones, made pure by fire, deep in the earth; and, coming away from the graveside, said,—Let us be done with mourning; and games were held, and men made merry: yea, at riding, and at jousting, and with sword and shield, crying,—Long live the King!

Thus was Gorbonian made glad in his grief; but within him, his heart grew hard, a-wondering at the wickedness of men.

And so, to seek the butcher of his father's body, Gorbonian called up men of rank, to establish his court; but sought he also men of the common kind, friends from town, heart-fellows. And the first he called was Kaswallan, a general greatly loved by his men; his army was the envy of the whole world, though he despised a bath, and his hair as a clump of river-reeds did hang from his head; but except that they fear him in battle, and pay him well thereafter, he cared not how he seemed before men, and for this had King Morvidus loved him well.

Next came Seisil, a man but small in aspect. It was said of him that no hair on his horse's head escaped his notice; of tributes taken and costs accrued, he kept count for the King. In fat times and in lean had he served the castle, having known King Danius before, and King Kimar before him. Wherefore he knew better than any the needs of estate, and served in the counting-house.

And next to come was Madauc; he was a magician, and all did pale at his power. By cards and by the casting of coins, he told of times to come; oft had he strengthened the hand of the King, with potions brought to battle; from which, victorious, full many a time would Morvidus return, saying,—Ah, Madauc, in truth my sword is thine. He did live even within the walls of the castle, in a small corner room reserved for himself, to enjoy the pleasures of his station. He held his weapon well, but sang with soothing voice, his beard gone grey and fit to house a nest of sparrows. But time was short for men such as Madauc, though few or none did know it.

Now a king without friends is a king in name only; and so did Gorbonian call to his court, two friends most dear to him, to advise and instruct. First did he call Braith, his companion since cradle-days; to them were known the hidden haunts of the castle, and what trees of the orchard bore sweet fruit in spring; and, pardee, how in stealth to take such fruit, if that the overseer slept.

Next named was Hafren; and to many this did seem, in sooth, great scandal, for her mother was the witch Seren. But others did attest that women such as she had long served, in village and in castle hall; and that only with the coming of new men to the land, had any seen cause to shun such care. To Morvidus in his afflictions had she come in aid, restoring him to health with wild roots, and with poultices pounded from none knew what. Wherefore the saying of Morvidus, still remembered,—I know not whether by cunning or by physic I am healed, but I arise and walk.

She was comely, though her hair was raven-black. She was tall, with womanish manner; and oft would she say to Gorbonian,—Recall I our first meeting, though you do not; for I am older than thee, and found thee at play in the rocks and the wild weeds, and asked,—Small friend, seek'st

thou some salve; and you, but a boy, looking up,—
I shall know if I find one.

To her were known the names of the birds in
their sky-bright wanderings, which to the boy
was a great delight; and fast were they friends,
these two, despite the low murmurings of the
gossips.

Now came them all to court, to see what must
be done. And a rough slab of quarry-stone did
serve at court for table, with chairs set all around
it; and the shape of this arrangement appeared to
the eye like the face of some great beast, emerging
heavily from the dark. All took their places now;
and, when they had gathered, the King did survey
his court with aspect most grave, saying,

—In sorrow have we gathered; but we are men,
pardee, or maids of power; and now we shall see,
in this time, how we might set right the wrong our
eyes have seen. And knew they all that he spake
of his father, and of the bloody scene in the stable,
and that he would true the wheel so wrongly
turned.

6.

A sailor forbears to row against the tide, said
King Gorbonian to his company. My father the
King is dead, his body burned. May the smoke of
his body be an offering to the gods! Yet sons must
to their fathers cleave: thus shall I follow that
current where it carries us, until justice be served;

and thus shall we ride, affirmed the King, we seven.

Then did the chambers of the King buzz like a humming hive, for each man did have his mind as to the question; for, as to the affairs of court, some did say that to survey the land were more pressing, for the tribute to be increased; and others did remark, that to leave an empty throne while that His Lordship's reign blushed yet green, were a great risk, even unto the kingdom. But as to this King Gorbonian said,—It does me no force; and he laid before them the vision of his father's body, broken upon the straw, left to die without e'en the noble horses which had been his heart's delight in life; and who shall remember him if he be not avenged, saith the King; and what shall they say of me, if that I fail to visit swift vengeance upon those man-slayers, who, when that the rains were hard upon us, and e'en the mighty were reduced, did creep in; and in so creeping, visit calamity upon me, yea, and upon us all? Thus spake the King, that none might gainsay him; for, in this world, to leave a blameless body unavenged, is a deed most dire.

They assembled in the early dawn; and there they stood, each considering the other; and Braith saw Hafren all in white, and the King clad in mail, and thought unto himself, *Now we are grown, we three.*

So set they out, seeking first the forest yclept Gwydion's Woods; for, as Gorbonian said,—My mother, long may she live, did enchant me in my cradle with songs of these woods; sweet melodies to me, yet warnings to the keen; for villains nest therein.

7.

And as they rode through haunts ancient and green, the young King remembered his time as a babe in these woods; and said, that he should like, should fortune see him to't, to restore those temples of old which were said to stand in the forest in days of old. Thus discoursed he in such manner as they rode, until, at some hour, they knew not which—for into that remote place fell but little light—behold, a great oak obstructed the path, a great gash in its trunk in the shape of a half-moon. Now this ancient sign was hewn by human hand, a clean cut, a hand's-breadth deep shining wetly in the shadow.

—See here, saith the King, the mark of an ancient temple.

—My liege, says Madauc, and I hope to remain ever in your favor, 'tis but a tree marked by some hunter.

—Nay, says Hafren, if I may make bold to speak, my liege speaks aright; for these woods belong to the spirit of the forest, and its people serve him still. Touched she then the mark within the wood, as a merchant might caress a jewel most dear.

—We shall restore this place, saith Gorbonian, drawing his sword. For these old ways are forgotten in this land, and should be remembered; and these hidden places must be made whole. My father's fathers worshipped in these woods; and long shall be the life of he who honors this temple, but woe betide the man who defiles this altar anew.

Then, walking backward and dragging his sword before him, did the King trace a circle about the trunk of the great tree. And when he had completed the circle, he retraced it again; and yet again, seven times in all, until its depth spanned half the length of a man's leg. Then did good Hafren retrieve, from her purse, a powder of her mother's, bright blue; and circled she the tree in like wise seven times, dye trailing from her hand before her. And the King did bid all kneel.

I shall avenge my father, said he; and men of great station in latter days shall tell, how my friends and I set out from this darkened place to uncover the hands of a killer; and to set right the wrongs we have all seen done, in our time; such wrongs as never were, in simpler times; then rode they on, til on a day

5

Devil House

ANGELA

At the end of a winding gravel road just a few miles outside Richmond, Virginia, there's an old house with a new coat of paint. You can't see it from the highway; if you could, its renovators might have been instructed to use a less arresting color combination than these several shades of purple—darker for the doors and window casings, lighter for the eaves, and somewhere in between for the siding.

It's a charming house, one that's been standing on this land since 1931, when its original owner, Marlee Stuart, who traced her family line clear back to Mary, Queen of Scots, built it atop a plot of land she'd inherited from her father. It belongs now to Angela West, who's taught graphic design at Virginia Commonwealth University, a brisk drive up the road and into town from the Stuart house, since 2014.

"Out where I grew up, houses don't usually have their own pedigrees," she remarks as we stroll past a grape arbor on the property—one of several; it's weathered but sturdy, and came with the house. "It's an adjustment, to a native Californian, to feel like you're part of a longer conversation with the ground underneath you."

Silence governs for a moment as we walk toward the house,

or near-silence: I hear the movement of squirrels in the trees, birds in the bushes.

"Maybe less of an adjustment for me, I guess, or else you wouldn't be here in the first place, right?"

†††

INSIDE, IN A SHADED PARLOR ROOM, the faint but sweet smell of old tobacco seems to govern the pace of our conversation. In languid, long reflections, she answers all my questions directly, volunteering long tangents rich with such details as can only be found in a primary source. Sometimes she stops, and doesn't pick up the thread again for several minutes; in those minutes, we might sit quietly, or she might get up to make tea; or she might remark again, as she does several times during the course of our afternoon together, how far from Richmond Milpitas is, in many important ways.

"I was a kid, and it was a huge deal at the time, of course," she says. "But there's a gulf between the girl I was then and the person I grew up to be; when people want to talk to me about it, I feel like I'm telling them a story from somebody else's life."

I ask her to start at the beginning, and she does.

†††

ANGELA WEST ENTERED her senior year at Milpitas High School with a feeling of hope: she'd worked hard for three years, and could see a path opening that led to her future. Her grades in high school wouldn't win her admission to the Ivy League, but she'd talked to a counselor who believed in her; that counselor, Beverly Benton, had seen a lot of students pass through her office, and knew how rare second appointments were. "When a kid wants to see you again to make sure they understand their options, it kind of makes your day," she told me by phone the week before I headed out to Virginia. "Angela hadn't set the world on fire academically, but she felt like she'd be able to shine if the stakes were a little higher."

Together, they developed a plan: Angela would apply to state colleges and even look at community colleges, with a view toward transferring as a junior. She kept a perfect attendance record for September and October, hoping that a good first senior semester would stand out on her applications. She reckons these times as the dawn of her adult life; the habits she developed in the foregoing years, she says, were prelude, but these were the days in which the person she'd become first felt like an entity with real flesh on its bones. A hard worker, a self-starter, a team player who knew how and when to bring her own visions into the big picture: these roles, and several others that inform her pedagogy today, saw their first rough passes that fall. She did paste-up for the yearbook, and saw how page design was more than a formality—or how formalities, when carefully tended, quietly congregate to make form, without which all one's good ideas go wanting for a roof above their heads. The idle sketches with which she'd decorated her notebooks since junior high now followed a practiced aesthetic: a small line design like an insignia at the upper center, a slogan or a lyric from a popular song running corner to corner like a banner, its block lettering rounded, effervescent. "Of course, I didn't have the vocabulary yet to talk about it like this," she says. "But from here, I can see what was going on, how my interests were becoming coherent."

And then it was Halloween; and people in Milpitas may not

remember where they were on October 31, 1986, but most of them remember where they were on the morning of November 2, when the news broke.

†††

EVEN IF YOU DON'T KNOW Angela West, there's a good chance you know her work, if you attended any but the most cloistered of American high schools in the early 2000s. Those splashy notebooks whose iridescent colors displaced the Pee-Chees and Trapper Keepers of generations past? Angela was first on the scene with the style; fresh out of college, she took a job with a design firm in Boston, and her first assignment was for Mead in Pennsylvania. "Cross-branding was really big—licensed designs—but they wanted their own line of splashy covers so they wouldn't have to pay the Hollywood studios or the Lisa Franks," she tells me with a laugh. "At the same time, everybody's afraid of getting sued, so they wouldn't tell me, you know, *Do something Rainbow Brite.* We'd sit in meetings and they'd dance around the point until I gave them a nod and told them I thought I had it, and then I'd scare up a knock-off Rainbow Brite with enough wrong to make for plausible deniability."

Mead sold a huge amount of notebooks with her charming if generic fantasy horse outline gracing the cover; it was her idea to print the design as a gold or silver silhouette, and it was her proposal that they be printed on neon covers instead of the simpler tones that were Mead's bread and butter. She insists that they're nothing special—all in a day's work—but their success helped her up the ladder in her trade. By the mid-nineties, she'd started her own company; she had a keen eye for good new talent.

"I knew some super-talented people in high school. None of them went on to work in design, but just being around them—" She breaks off, looking for the right word. "If you see good things early, you know what to look for later."

††††

ANGELA LOOKS SURPRISED when I ask her whether she remembers which of her friends, if any, might have triggered the alarm at Monster Adult X: the piercing siren whose keening wail got someone in the neighborhood to call the police, who, on the grounds of possible imminent danger, then entered the property, where they found the bodies of Marc Buckler and Evelyn Gates surrounded by pornography and paraphernalia, all of it repurposed to look like the inside of a haunted house. "We never triggered any alarm," she says. "That wasn't the idea. We just wanted the landlord to freak out a little when she tried to sell the place. Maybe ask herself, you know: 'Whose place is this, really?' So we stayed up all night with scissors and paints and markers and glitter and felt-tip pens, and then we left, and that was the last any of us knew about it."

There's a short break in the flow; she's seeing whether I'm skeptical. She has cause to wonder. She and her friends were the focus of an intense investigation that brought together the police departments of three cities—Milpitas, San Jose, and Charter Oak, a small town at the other end of the state, where Marc Buckler had grown up—and spanned six months, resulting, finally, in no arrests.

"That was all any of us knew," she says again.

††††

SCISSORS, AND PAINTS, and markers, and glitter; felt-tip pens, and, possibly, a sword. That's the item missing from Angela's account of the night she spent inside the store with her friends; according to the timeline established by detectives, sometime after the redecoration of the store but before the morning of November 2, 1986, two people were murdered on the premises of the adult bookstore whose doors had been shuttered for at least a month. One of them was the owner of the building, a local slumlord named Evelyn Gates; the other, Marc Buckler, an aspiring real estate investor from Southern California. Their skulls were split, and their bodies had been badly mutilated, the sort of repeated insults to a corpse that experts in criminal science call "overkill." Seventeen stab wounds is the threshold for overkill. Evelyn Gates's corpse boasted twenty-nine discreet insults. The probability that her attacker meant to express some degree of personal animus was high.

"We didn't really know the details," Angela recalls. "Everybody said they knew, you know. The gossip mill was grinding night and day. Night and day! We almost had to laugh, Derrick and Seth and me, some of the stories people told. Things we knew about the scene, things we knew for a fact were made-up. But we didn't laugh, because it was serious, and we were scared."

They were scared because they knew pressure on local police to make an arrest would be intense. Just five years earlier, in a case that had made headlines nationwide and was later turned into a successful movie, a disturbed local teenager had murdered his girlfriend and shown her bloated body to their mutual friends. The small town that would later become an outpost of Silicon Valley had no intention of becoming the focus of national news for a second time; the local department consulted with experts, contacting investigators from Long Island, and from Boston, and from Oklahoma City—any place that had seen occult-related crime, any crime whose details had been lurid enough to attract the attention of the national press. "I thought they'd arrest Seth for sure," Angela tells me. "They would have arrested Alex, too, if he hadn't disappeared again, but as far as I know, we were the only ones who knew he'd come back to town."

We were the only ones who knew. She means herself, and Derrick Hall, a college-bound senior known to all as a bookish kid who kept his cool, and Seth Healey, a class clown raised by a single mom. Their connection to the store would have been difficult for the authorities to establish; but teenagers imagine that authorities have mystical powers of insight, and know, too, that when adults are looking to pin something on a kid, almost any kid's a potential target. The three of them spent several weeks waiting for a shoe to drop, feeling both relief and dread as suspicion gathered around a transfer student from New Mexico.

"I didn't know him," she says of Siraj, the child born to college-graduate spiritual seekers from back East, around whom the community's suspicion gathered. "Nobody really knew him. But I didn't think he could have done it, for a lot of reasons. It felt like everybody was looking at Siraj because he was so weird, because he was new, because he had a strange name.

"But none of us wanted to say anything. We had our whole lives ahead of us," she concludes.

I say she sounds worried, and she says it's not worry, it's guilt.

"Or shame, maybe," she says. "We didn't do it. But neither did Siraj. Sometimes I wanted to say something, but—our whole lives, like I said. Just our whole lives."

††††

BUT IT'S THE *WE DIDN'T DO IT* I'm here to learn more about, not Siraj, whose story has been told and retold; so I have to press her further, even though it's clear to me, having interviewed dozens of people whose experiences mirror hers to greater or smaller degrees, that she's reached the point in the conversation where she'd usually shift to the after-all-that stage: her life beyond the moment when it felt threatened by forces beyond her control, the self she became when the waters of chaos ebbed. Communities where these types of crimes occur form bubbles, and the air inside gets humid; when the membrane finally dissolves, people who lived inside emerge with stories they can keep, or tell.

"Usually it's Siraj they want to ask me about," she says when I ask if she feels the case is truly cold. "I tell them I didn't know him well, and I hope wherever he wound up, he stays there and they never find him, because I know he didn't do it."

I tell her that my examination of the evidence—the interviews, the crime scene photos, the ephemera I've collected—concurs with her claim: that there wasn't any real case against Siraj; that the gaze of suspicion with which the community began to regard him, which grew so intense that his father moved the family to Menlo Park, was miscast.

"That doesn't do him a lot of good now, wherever he is," she says. "Can you imagine what it's like to be the guy who 'everyone knows' killed two people so savagely that it made the paramedics puke? That was another thing everybody talked about, how people at the scene had to see a psychiatrist about it." This, of course, is unverified lore of the sort that crimes like this produce voluminously, without aim or effort; some of it sticks, and that becomes the story for future generations.

I can't imagine what it would be like to be that guy, I say, but it seems to have been hard enough on him and his family that they've placed themselves entirely beyond the reach of the radar. It's my job to track people down and get their stories, but I've been unable to find the family after several years' searching. I also wonder what it would be like to be the guilty party, knowing that the authorities and the public are all looking in the wrong direction.

"It probably wasn't even somebody from town," she says in response, in a tone that tells me she's quite certain neither one of us will ever know the name of the person or persons who killed Evelyn Gates and Marc Buckler, and who never faced charges for the crime. "I think about that sometimes, about how anybody could have just pulled off the highway and done this and gotten back into their car, and no one would have ever known.

"It's a scary thought," she concludes, and then she looks over at a showpiece clock on her mantel, with, I think, an almost theatrical ability to convey her meaning without having to say it out loud.

SETH

"Welcome to the cage!" are the words that greet me when I enter Gym Rats, presently celebrating its fifth year in business by offering six-month memberships at half off. It's located in a strip of modular buildings off the Golden State Highway in Fresno, abutted by an auto shop on one side and a place called Import/Export, Inc., on the other.

I remember Import/Export, Inc., because it's the first thing Seth Healey, owner and sole proprietor of Gym Rats since its opening in the summer of 2002, asks me about when we meet. "Did you go into Import/Export, Inc.?" he says, visibly excited to hear my answer.

I say that I didn't, that I saw the sign for the gym and followed it. He looks disappointed.

"A lot of people try the Import/Export door first, by accident," he says. "But there's never anybody in there. Five years I been here, there's never anybody there. No idea. I'm always waiting for somebody to solve the mystery."

He holds the door for me; inside, there are a handful of men pumping iron, jumping rope, or working heavy bags. There's no music playing; just the sounds of bodies breathing and weights clanking.

"Most of these places are loud as hell, right?" says Healey, leading me toward his office at the back of the barn-sized room. "Can't even think. So when I built the place and they tried to tell me I had to spend a bunch of money on speakers, all I could say was: 'For what?' You know. 'For what?' Not me, that's for sure. I knew I wanted my own kind of place."

He smiles when he speaks, a smile that seems to come from a deeper place than the smiles you sometimes see when you've only just met someone. But it only takes a minute or two in the company of Seth Healey to see that he's different, and to begin understanding how he's managed to survive all these years, braving setbacks and roadblocks that would make many of us want to throw in the towel.

†††

WHEN I VISITED Angela West in Virginia, she made it clear that the murders at Devil House were only part of her story. She spoke with me in the hopes that her story might help people closer to the beginnings of their own tragedy-adjacent timelines feel freer to put the past behind them, to shape their own lives along trajectories of their own choosing. Our conversations touched on her work, her teaching, her travels—I tried to follow where she led, and to only take what she was willing to offer. Even after two mornings and one afternoon in her company, I had to supply several conclusions myself; like many who've brushed the edge of the spotlight, she'd learned the value of the carefully chosen word.

Seth Healey is cut from different cloth. No subject is off-limits; his long monologues are wide-ranging, but never incoherent, though you can see how inattentive people might think so. He knows why I'm here, and, if it's not fair to say he's excited about it, it's only because a state of excitement is his default setting. Nor is this my personal observation; as soon as we take our seats on facing weight benches, he points it out to me.

"I can be pretty intense," is how he puts it. "It used to be a lot heavier, and they had me on medication for it for half my life, but that wasn't the answer for me, which is something I figured out for myself after I got into exercise. I could tell the medication was holding me back, so I talked to a doctor about it and he leveled me down and I learned that if I just never stopped pushing myself, I'd never feel out of control. That's the thing when you're like me. You get bored, you lose control, you do something stupid. But, like I say, I fixed all that for myself, and that's why I'm here. But it's not why you're here. You're here to talk about the gruesome murders in the sleepy suburban town of Milpitas, right?"

I laugh; Seth is a funny guy.

"OK, right. So. There's a lot of levels to the whole thing, and I'm not sure what you know or don't know, because people have so many different stories about it, and none of them really get all of it and most of them miss pretty much all of it, which is partly because we planned it out that way. Although 'planned' is a little strong of a word to use there, you know, it's more like 'we got an idea and ran with it.' But that still works out as 'planned' to me, that's one thing I've learned about responsibility over my life, if you did something on purpose it doesn't matter how committed you were to that purpose. I'm always telling the guys I train here. You need just enough dedication to get started and then you get a little momentum. Some of us work up the momentum in a hurry, and that's me. And that's what we did, that's why you've heard about it. We'd read all the serial killer stories about guys like the Son of Sam or the Manson murders, what have you, wild crime scenes in all the pictures, and we said, let's make this a crime scene, and then we got a plot together about seven chambers, right, because there were seven booths in the store, and . . . this is what you're here for, right?" He looks a little nervous.

Yes, I tell him, this is what I'm here for—I've dutifully collected any and all details that haven't vanished into the tides of time. I know about the seven chambers, and the story they succeeded in telling, and how the local media ran with it for a cycle or two, tying the case to rumors of satanic cabals around the state and the Southwest; and that there were other theories headed in the other direction, up into Oregon, where Anthony Hawley had gotten his start.

"Hawley!" says Seth. "Do you know I never actually met that guy, I figure he's still around here, people tend to kind of settle once they land here, I've noticed, though that won't be true much longer if the rent keeps rising. Whole different subject. But I felt so bad for him, you know, they kept sending news crews to his house, to his office, if a news crew showed up here to talk, well, I mean, I guess there's you, but that's different. Did you talk to Derrick?"

I haven't, yet. "You might want to put on your kid gloves," he advises me. "It was different for Derrick, because Hawley told them he'd had Derrick working in the store, and so some of the cops started to get a lot of very sick ideas about the whole thing, which then of course became rumors, small towns are like that, and then people started to look at Derrick like his whole life was just a front for something seedy. And he didn't really need something like that in his senior year with all the big things to be thinking about, you know? I mean college. Life after college. All that stuff. And he's thinking, *This is going to ruin my chance with the colleges, they'll find out, what do I do if I don't go to college.*

Seth Healey grows quiet; as I'll learn over the course of our day together, this is something that doesn't happen very often. There's a window in his office overlooking the gym; he's gazing through it, maybe taking stock of the scene, so far from the place we're talking about—even if, physically, it's really just a short drive away.

"Not everybody has to worry about the same kind of things Derrick had to worry about back then," he concludes when he picks up the thread. "It took a toll."

††††

WE'RE AT A CHAR-BROILED BURGER STAND half a mile from the gym, seated at an outside table; there are fewer and fewer places like this left in California, but once they were everywhere—fast-food stands before the big players gobbled up all the little ones, relics of an earlier time. Seth has ordered a double patty, no bun, covered in the works and with special sauce; slopped onto translucent wax paper in a plastic basket, it's a giant, lurid heap of color with steam rising from it. Seth attacks it studiously, without looking up, his lean, wiry frame wholly attending to his task.

People are sometimes offended if you make observations about how they eat—most people don't think about it much, and some would rather not—but I take the chance, and ask him if he's always this quiet over lunch. "Always," he says, wiping his mouth with a paper napkin. "If I don't devote a hundred percent of my attention to something I'm likely to abandon it halfway through. It's my brain, right? My brain is like that. I can't focus and I can't focus and I can't focus and then suddenly, bam, there's something I care enough about to really give it my time and energy, and for that period of time, it's the only thing I care about. Almost the only thing in the world. Meals, conversations, work. It means I have to warn people, don't try to tell me two things at once, even though, when I'm the one doing the talking, I can keep almost an infinite number of plates spinning. But it looks different from this side, I guess."

I wonder aloud whether the intensity of his focus feels like a blessing or a burden.

"Well, it's both," he says. "When people don't understand you, they don't even try, they just write you off. So you have to really sell yourself. That's something I had to learn. But the internal benefits of being your own man, it's something I teach at the gym. For example, I have one of the best memories of anybody. Because I'm all over the place when I talk, people assume my memory's like that, too, but it's not. Once I take note of a detail"—he taps his temple with his forefinger, twice—"it's in here forever."

The police thought you had an active imagination back in 1986, I say.

"I do have an active imagination," he says proudly. "But also, I know what I know, and if I say I saw something, it's because I saw it."

†††

THIS, FOR ME, IS THE HARDEST PART of talking with the exiled knights of Devil House: they all know that suspicion coalesced around Siraj, both among the investigating officers and out in the community; they all know that, as a figure in the public imagination, he became a spectral presence, a name that evoked fear without proximal cause. A bogeyman. But Siraj, as they also all must have known, could not be connected to the crime scene in any way. The people who'd pointed fingers at him were busybodies looking for an outsider to blame, long-standing locals eager to shift any blame from their own. Had the Devil House Four talked among themselves, at all, about the net that was closing around Siraj and his family in the days and weeks after the news hit the wires? If anyone could answer, it would be Seth; he would remember.

"I know Derrick felt bad, but that's just because he's Derrick," Seth says, back at the gym. It's empty now; Seth teaches a class at four-thirty, so I'll need to make the best use of our time together. "He knew enough to get people to leave Siraj alone. We all did. But he also knew if the finger started pointing at me, they'd send me away again. Once you've been in, they're always looking for an excuse to send you back."

He's talking about his time in care facilities—brief stints both times, but acutely unpleasant experiences, brought on by manic episodes when he'd gotten his medication schedule mixed up and his mother hadn't had the time or the energy to keep it straight for him. Several of the boys he'd known on these wards would only be graduating to even more restrictive environments, and knew it; his old friend knew it, too.

"It would have gotten really bad if they started looking at

me," he says, getting up. "Or Alex. Derrick and Angela could handle the heat, but if anybody'd gotten their hands on my notebooks, they would have made a connection."

I actually have some of your old notebooks, I say, and he breaks into a smile so big it could power a naval substation.

"Did you bring them with you?" he says, sizing me up, wondering if they might have been in the room with us the whole time, and I tell him they're in my car.

†††

WITHIN SECONDS we are halfway through the gym, headed for the parking lot. I'm not quite sure how to read Seth's eagerness to revisit his younger days; as he's told me himself, they weren't always the happiest times. There wasn't a lot of money left over after his mom paid the monthly bills, and people who've spent time behind the locked doors of treatment facilities seldom return with good memories of their time inside. But Seth leads the way back to my car, his monologue gathering steam: "You had these on you the whole time? Wow. Just wow. We were at that table eating burgers and these were just sitting there? Man. Wow."

I retrieve my backpack from the trunk of my rental car— I always stash it in the trunk, just in case; Seth reaches for it as soon as I have it in my hands. I follow his lead, even though sitting down at a desk or a table away from the wind and the weather feels like the obvious move when handling what are, essentially, antiques.

Each notebook is individually sealed inside its own Ziploc bag, just as they were the day I got them, when I took pictures of every page before returning them to safety. Treasures like these are vulnerable to wind and weather and sunlight and air;

they'd been safely stored in a cabinet at the Milpitas house ever since.

In Seth's hands they are living entities, not artifacts but vital presences in the present day. He grows quiet when he extracts them from their housings; the shock of his silence is considerable, as I've been listening to him and making few interruptions for several hours now. He leafs through the pages roughly, his eyes scanning down each one, searching for something. If there is something specific he's trying to find, it could take ages; Seth's style back then was a riot of detail, and almost no blank space emerges from the dense thickets of line, shadow, angle, curve, accent, and annotation.

But it only takes him a minute. "There," he says. "I did this one just a day or so before. Wow. It's all coming back. It's like—it's like the whole experience was highly negative for all four of us, but when I see this, I think, even then I was a guy who knew how to plan something and make it happen, I just didn't know it."

He is quiet again, and he's stopped turning the pages. He stands still and concentrates. He's looking at a gigantic block-letter 7 that takes up a whole page by itself, drawn in a comic-book style that makes it look three-dimensional, like one of the letters on the Hollywood sign casting its own shadow against the hillside beneath it.

"Hardly even feels real," he says, staring into the block 7 like a fortune-teller looking for shapes in the crystal ball.

†††

WE'RE ALONE IN THE GYM, sitting on the apron of the boxing ring; Seth says the time after lunch until his afternoon class is pretty slow most days. I get the feeling that there is no point in trying to hide things from Seth, who reads moments accurately while they're still developing. His focus may wander, but his mind is very sharp. I tell him that one thing that struck me about his notebook is how closely its contents correlate to some of the reimagining of Devil House, right down to the deployments of symbols and sigils.

"Man, I was living and dying for Devil House," he says. His voice, almost hushed, sounds like it's coming from a distant world, some permanently disappeared planet whose hills and valleys he walked when it was real. "It was a special time. When the thing happened in there, no disrespect to the dead, of course, but it hurt us more than it hurt almost anybody. Or maybe I just mean me. I needed a place to hang out, a place to be with one friend instead of in a crowd, a place that felt like I belonged there. *Needed.* You'd have to be me to really understand."

In his hands are two of my crime scene photograph finds— not the gory stuff, I don't have any of that, but the aftermath of the transformation. You can see the porn angel, and the words painted on the walls, and a chalk outline somebody drew on the floor: Seth, or Angela, or Derrick, or Alex. The outline must have seemed especially jarring once the investigation got going—if there are two dead bodies on one side of a room and a chalk outline on the carpet right next to them, the fair assumption is that there's a third body somewhere. I say to him that I think I get it, at least a little: the care they took to make their work seem real, the cooperative spirit of the enterprise.

"No offense," says Seth, "but it's like you're trying to describe a flavor that you've only ever heard about but never tasted yourself. Like, look at this." His finger rests just above the left lower corner of the shot; all I see is something crumpled-up, nothing that seems to merit real description.

What is it? I ask.

"Alex's notes," he says. "He was super-careful about all the words and pictures. All night he stayed focused. I felt like it was a present to me from him: because he knew he was leaving, because he was only half-there a lot of the time anyway but the store had given him life. I freaked out when Derrick said we were going to have to leave, but Alex almost apologized to him. He just seemed sad. I didn't have much, you know? But he didn't have *anything*. So when we started in on the whole thing, Alex gave it one hundred percent, and he's such a great artist, you know, he always had the touch. Me, I paint first and ask questions later. Alex outlines everything first. Here—"

He snatches a notebook from the small stack of them that sits on the apron between us.

"All this stuff. Page after page. Plans, outlines. I saw him doing it all night while I was just running wild, doing whatever seemed wicked to me: there's Alex, eyes all screwed up on a fixed point on the page, making sure it's going to come out as cool as it can be. Throwing it away if it's not exactly what he wants. First time I'd seen him all the way awake since he turned up again."

He points again at the crumpled ball in the frame.

"When you see this, it tells you a different story than the story I know. All the stuff you have, the story you're going to get from it is different from the one I know. From the one we all knew. From the one you're probably going to tell no matter how hard you try to tell the real one. All this stuff, to me, is something only a few people can understand, and some of them, maybe all of them, aren't even the same people they were back then, you know? It's like this stuff can only really be seen by people who've already seen it."

He looks up at a big clock on the wall, and then back at me.

For a man who had to teach himself most of the social graces from scratch, he's a remarkably effective communicator.

"No offense."

†††

ONCE, WHEN I WAS IN SECOND GRADE, somebody stole a pencil sharpener off Mrs. Mangano's desk. There were thirty-one of us in class, and things got chaotic sometimes; she was nearing retirement, and knew to pick her battles. But the missing pencil sharpener had struck a nerve, and she shut down class until she found the culprit, which she did by asking everybody directly, one at a time and in front of all the others, if they were the guilty party.

She kept her calm when she did it; this was the genius of Mrs. Mangano's art. She didn't look mad, but she had to've been furious, to sweep the day's lesson plan aside just to recover an item that the school probably bought in bulk, that the supply closet probably held whole boxes of in reserve all year-round.

"Robert, did you take the pencil sharpener?"

"No."

"Thank you, Robert. Christine, did you take my pencil sharpener?"

"No, Miss Mangano."

"Mrs. Mangano. Thank you, Christine. Gage, did you take my pencil sharpener?"

I hadn't, and I said so; it was Patrick Long who'd done it, and by the time she got to him, he was almost grateful to crack. He cried in front of the whole class, and his pranks never again attained the destabilizing character of their pre-confessional days.

So, when I decide it's time to put the question to him directly, I do it in my best Mangano voice, hoping to harness some of her deceptive ease and confidence. "Hey, just because I have to ask," I say: "Did you kill Evelyn Gates, and her client, the visitor—Marc Buckler, right?"

He fixes me with a cracked smile. "'Her client,'" he says. "This case is your whole life right now, and you're going to make money off of it like a lot of people have over the years, and Marc Buckler's name is just slipping your mind sometimes, right? Right, OK. Well, Gage, I had a good time showing you around, and I hope I was able to help you a little; and also, I never killed anybody in my life, and I don't know anybody who did, and I wish you all the best."

We both stand up; the formalities of the interview have a sacred rhythm almost everybody respects.

"Sorry if that was a sore question," I offer as he holds the front door for me.

I'm on the sidewalk; he could let the door close, but he waits.

"I'm not sore," he says. Seth is a very believable guy, and I believe him. "But when I start to see which way something's going, I usually check out if I think I'm not going to be able to control it. I spent a lot of my life not being in control. Now I know that if I want control, I have to take it. You know?"

He gives me an extra second to study his face; I feel like if there were a murderer behind those eyes, I'd see him now.

"Good luck," he says, as the door swings gently shut.

DERRICK

"It was different, but it wasn't a gigantic shock," Derrick tells me when I ask him what he thought of North Carolina at first.

"Pensacola right after Milpitas, now, that was something else. Can you even imagine?"

He's the spitting image of everybody's favorite professor: easygoing, good-humored, insightful, inviting. But the tenure track, he decided somewhere along the path to a master of arts degree in maritime history, wasn't for him. Once you've spent enough time inside the academy, it can be hard to imagine life outside of it; but Derrick Hall has never been short on imagination.

"I was working on my thesis, working really hard, when I had this realization: I didn't want to be talking about all this stuff in the abstract. I wanted to be next to it. I'd be revising a section on distinguishing between two types of anchors and there'd be doodles all up and down the margins. I realized I was most interested in the stuff I could see with my own eyes, this stuff I could really get close to."

We're standing on the dock out in front of the North Carolina Maritime Museum at Beaufort, a wooden-shingled building on the Beaufort Sound; it's just a week or so into the off-season, the middle of the week. Derrick looks out at the docked catamarans and cruisers gently bobbing in the water; the calm of the view is intoxicating,

"Can't get much closer than this," he says.

†††

BEAUFORT IS MY THIRD STOP; my trek to the heart of Devil House enters crucial waters here. Derrick had arguably the closest connection to the property, having frequented Valley News before its decadent days, and worked inside the building when it was still a functioning store; he spent many long afternoons within its walls after Anthony Hawley abandoned it wholesale as a kiss-off gesture to his landlord. When I asked Angela and Seth for information, there were several limitations already in place: they only ever knew so much, and neither ever stood at the center of the storm the way Derrick did.

"I'm not sure that's true," he says when I suggest he's the best authority I have encountered so far. "Seth's memory is amazing. He calls me up once a month, we have it on our calendars, and his recall for details—you met him, right? So you already know."

We both laugh; Derrick's natural, easygoing manner is immediately comforting. I feel like success, on whatever terms he might define it, was always awaiting Derrick, wherever he ended up.

"But I know what you mean," he continues. He pats the dock, dappled by the shadows of the pines; he has an office inside the museum, but it's windowless, lifeless. Dockside, it's peaceful. "I'm the man, right? They didn't charge any of us, but I was the guy they wanted."

There is a very long pause; there's a shift in the tranquility of the water and the shadows on it, one that I think I see Derrick try to wish away.

"I was the guy they wanted," he says again, and the mood lingers.

†††

THE MOOD LINGERS because Derrick was, in every sense, the guy they wanted. The killings at Devil House hit Milpitas hard, resonating with a deep and menacing tone; *River's Edge*, the movie dramatizing the murder of Marcy Renee Conrad just five years earlier, was due to hit theaters next year; it was already on the festival circuit, and, around town, people were talking. There was burgeoning local resistance to sensational-ism of all stripes, and front-page images of the ratty storefront with caution tape around it provoked immediate and bitter re-sentment. "People felt like, *Why should we have to go through all this again?*" is how Derrick puts it. "Everybody wanted to fix the problem as fast as they could. Simple explanations are what people want when they're scared."

The simple explanation that would have scratched several itches was that a cabal of Satan-worshipping teens had sacri-ficed a couple of innocent victims to the devil for kicks. Stories like this had been generating high Nielsens ever since the Manson killings in 1969; a small industry had grown up around cult coverage: pockets of evil sewn under the skin of the sub-urbs. Hidden infections waiting for the right host. There'd been the Ripper Crew in Chicago, and the unsolved Jeannette De-Palma case in New Jersey. Father Gerald Robinson in Toledo and Ricky Kasso on Long Island. Whole legacies of grief, texture-warping events in the life of a community. Milpitans, collectively, decided that one was enough, and the police department—with, Derrick suspects, the help of some outside advisors, though he's unable to offer anything more concrete—developed a strategy to quash interest in the case beyond the city limits.

The first peg of the plan was to lock down all photos of the crime scene. Photographers gathered all the evidence that might be needed, and then the cleanup crew arrived: the police themselves, but also several trusted helpers from town. In one day, they scoured the inside, took down the sign out front, and threw a tarp over the roof to cover the gigantic portrait of the ghoul. Overnight, one of the most sensational crime scenes imaginable became an unremarkable remodeling project in progress: orange cones, drab scaffolds, thirty-gallon garbage cans. It looked like plenty of places by the freeway in any small California city, and the absence of a focal point for cameras went a long way toward dampening out-of-town enthusiasm about the case.

The next thing they needed was a suspect, or so they thought. As soon as they had a suspect they'd be in a position to fast-track the whole affair. But they were wrong about that, Derrick insists. "They're very, very lucky they never arrested me," he says. "My mom and dad worked very hard to give me the best chance they could, and they were mad as hell about my little secret life inside the store, but they stayed focused. They told the police to charge me or let me go, and then they hired a lawyer, and they didn't blink at the price tag.

"If there'd have been an arrest," he says, "that's all the national media would have needed. A name on the logs, a kid with a face to splash onto the pages. Without that, what do you have? The same thing I get from recovered ships' quarters. Salvaged relics. People look at them once and maybe they have some kind of reaction, but minus the story behind them, hardly anybody cares.

"But in town they didn't know this yet, and it was very hard for a few weeks—"

He stops; he looks worried, or frightened. Is he trying to compose himself, or searching for the right words?

"It will be hard for you to understand what it was like during that time for me," he concludes.

†††

THE MILPITAS POLICE DEPARTMENT interviewed Derrick at least eleven times over the course of eight days. It was his senior year; according to Derrick, he kept his mind on his coursework inside all the cacophony. "I was pretty focused on college," he insists. "There's nothing wrong with Milpitas, but when it's the only place you've ever known and you start to get the feeling there's a whole world out there for you, you lean pretty hard into taking your shot.

"And it was exhausting," he continues. "Just absolutely exhausting. I think they brought me in for follow-ups twice in a single day at least two times." He's right, and errs generously; on three occasions over this span of time, his presence was requested for an interview at the police station twice in a single day—the second day after his initial interview, three days after that, and once again a week later. These interviews grew more confrontational as public pressure increased, and Derrick remembers wishing he could make a public statement of some sort.

"Just something, anything," he says. "I mean, when you're the one in the crosshairs, it's like you don't have permission to be going through what everybody else is going through. And that's just an awful feeling, because you *are* going through that. You just have to do it alone. My dad tried to help, my mom tried to help, I'm lucky I've always had a very supportive family, but in the end it was just me. I couldn't call Seth and I couldn't call Angela, and Alex was gone again and the police didn't even have him on their radar, thank God, and I was— you know, when you're a kid, and you hear adults talking about whether they slept well or not, it's like, what are these people talking about, you know? But suddenly it's me, I can't sleep at all, and I want to just say something to clear the air. To clear the air, and for me personally, just to be seen.

"But the lawyers weren't having it," he says. "And they were right. No smoke, no fire."

But there was a little smoke, I suggest, knowing from experience that you can't miss these small moments when an opening appears. The scene itself, I mean, the writing and the arrangements and the decorations: that was you.

"Yeah, but I didn't—"

He appears to be sizing me up anew, trying to get a different angle on me. Am I a tabloid reporter disguised as a guy who writes real books?

But he smiles again, a smile he's very fortunate to have been born with, I think. "You saw the crime scene photos, though, I know. Seth told me.

"You already know none of us could have actually done that."

†††

I HAVE, IN FACT, SEEN THE CRIME SCENE PHOTOS, probably several more of them than Derrick has. I've exhumed more evidence connected to the crimes at Devil House than had been previously supposed to exist: relics and primary texts, case notes and bagged exhibits. I know where people in town pointed the finger at first, projecting their unease over the ever-present prospect of Silicon Valley sprawl onto the site of the unspeakable— there were those, at first, who'd said that this is what happens when homeless people from neighboring cities get word that there are places to sleep nearby where the night patrols don't reach. There were those, as there still are, who suspected that, whatever the real story was, they were only hearing a part of it. And then there were the voices that were easiest to amplify, because their ranges were familiar from similar stories around the country. The kids are out of control. They grow up faster and bigger than they did in our day. They lack the moral grounding of generations past.

"Yeah, yeah, 'the moral grounding,'" Derrick says; his smile holds, but we're out on the open water now. "People looked at me like I had demons inside me, and I was grateful for how my mother'd always coached me to hold my tongue if I didn't have anything useful to say. But when you have your neighbors thinking you're a monster, you know, a demon from hell—I'll be honest, there was a part of me, and there will always be a part of me, that sort of carries this, that would feel a stranger's eye on me and want to call them on it to their faces. To just say to somebody: *You, there. Staring at me. I see you! You don't know anything about me! Everything you think you know about me is a lie!*"

What stopped you? I ask.

He pauses, and I see him returning to the familiar ground of himself: the person who's still alive, and reasonably happy— on the worst day, still content with the way things turned out for him.

"People already know what they want to believe," he offers, returning wholly to his comfort zone; I feel almost like I'm watching a ghost reenter a body. "I see this even in my daily errands here, when it's busy. People want me to tell them about pirates, but I know that if I told them what pirates were really like, it would ruin their day."

I don't quite follow you, I say.

"Well, you know, *Treasure Island*," he says. "Long John Silver with a parrot on his shoulder, the push and pull of good and evil, the romance of the high seas. The integrity of the thief, all that stuff. Whereas if there were even one photograph of the aftermath of a real pirate raid on a ship, you know, it'd turn your stomach. There's a reason they hung pirates without a trial."

The sun is setting into the Beaufort Sound; I don't want to

wear out my welcome. Derrick's been very generous with his time.

"They didn't see me, and you don't see me, and nobody's ever going to see me except the people who actually know me outside of that whole story," he concludes—there's no rancor in his voice, no anger. He's just laying out the facts on the ground for me, making his case. "Unless you were actually inside, any story you end up telling will be some distortion along the lines of, *Four teenagers killed a property developer and a landlord with a sword, then disposed of the weapon and deflected attention from themselves onto the new kid in town until the case went cold.*"

People do end up pretty invested in the stories they tell to explain how, and why, some awful thing happened in their community, I offer.

"That they do." He laughs. "But I feel like they settle on whichever story eases the burden a little."

The burden?

"The burden of the story they don't want to tell."

ALEX

I didn't find Alex.

I asked Angela, and I asked Seth, and I asked Derrick, and I even sent follow-ups to Angela and Derrick—I hadn't gained Seth's trust; there was nothing tangible on the other side of any further communication between us—and I parsed their responses for hints that they might be hiding something from me, trying to protect their friend. I liked this story, because Alex had means, motive, and opportunity, and that's the trifecta. If there were people trying to keep others from picking up the scent, from following the trail that led to Alex, that alone would have drawn me nearer to the horizon-line of all cases, the place where we begin to state our conclusions.

But they weren't lying. I meet a lot of liars in my line of work, and I do a lot of lying to get the information I need. Most people consider themselves good judges of character, but for me it's a job requirement. Angela didn't know where Alex was. Derrick told me directly that he'd shield Alex from scrutiny if he had to, but it wasn't necessary. Alex belonged to the wind.

One of the first rules of detective work, especially the historical kind, is that nobody really disappears without a trace. The term is empty poetry. Everybody leaves traces. There is no lost colony; the bones of every pilot downed over the Bermuda Triangle rest peacefully under silt at the bottom of the ocean; every city that ever was can be excavated if you have the right tools, and time, and patience. If you come up empty-handed, it only means you were digging in the wrong place.

I talked to Joey Macias. That was as close as I could get, and it wasn't close at all. He worked as an orderly on the night shift at a shelter in San Jose during a span of time that overlapped with the Devil House days; he runs a treatment center for drug addiction now. I found his name, without any further identifying notes, in a police log from the investigation. My call to Joey was the last cold call I made to anyone regarding the murders at Monster Adult X.

"That was twenty years ago," he said.

Right, I said, they never made a collar.

"They called the shelter and I took the call," he said. "Asked me if anybody showed up who looked like he was on the run from something."

And?

He laughed. "All my guys were on the run from something," he said. "Don't get me wrong, every one of them had his own story, and some of them it would break your heart to hear it, it just gets harder when you realize how many of them there are. In cities everywhere. It hurts your head to imagine it."

I waited; if you stay quiet sometimes, you get something.

"The shelter was a safe place," he said. "If I'd seen anything I wouldn't have told them, but I didn't see anything. Which doesn't mean anything, I guess. Nobody likes to talk about it, but a lot of these guys, they just disappear. It's sad. It's really sad. But they just stop showing up to the places they used to show up and—"

"Yeah," I said, and I thanked him for his time, and wondered what to make of Alex, how to give a decent burial to a man whose body had never been found.

†††**6**†††

The White Witch

1.

YOU FOUND ME IN MILPITAS. I had taken no pains to obscure my location, since I usually don't have a lot of people looking for me, but, for you, the process of finding me had been long and arduous, and the human cost of that process was reflected in your first letter. You spent most of your first two pages on this theme: how you had written to me at my mother's house, because finding that address had been easy enough: the public library still kept old phone books, you said, and it had them all; all the various little local ones, anyway. Los Osos and Avila Beach, and San Luis Obispo. You had looked up my last name for the year Jesse died, and there it was, the same name as the one on the cover of the true crime book about the woman who killed your son.

"The woman who killed my son": this was the phrasing you used, heralding the first of your long asides, to which I would grow accustomed over the course of our correspondence, and in which, I would learn, though not as quickly as I ought to have learned, you would often give voice to your truest thoughts and feelings. I say that I didn't learn this quickly enough because by now, for me, after half a life at this work, I would usually recognize it as a familiar dynamic. We bury the things we need to say under a flood of narratives, counter-narratives, details, and clarifications. People slip hard truths into casually dropped interjections and conditional clauses. Detectives know this, too; it's something they go over in their training. Watch for the thing the suspect says that he doesn't notice. Watch for the part he assumes you agree with him about, and exploit that. It's free.

But I was taken by surprise when your first letter came through the slot in the front door of my rented house in Milpitas. I'd been in there for the better part of a year, assembling the story of Derrick and Angela and Seth and Alex, of the fortress they'd built that went wrong. I spent a lot of time on the floor, which is part of my process, trying to get close to the places where my subjects lived, and I was burrowing down deep into my dreamscape when a manila envelope, stuffed fat enough to require a little manual help from the mailman in pushing it through the slot, squeaked in past its own midway point and then landed with a *thud* a few feet away from where I was sitting.

I assumed it was a galley. People send me books; I don't imagine that my blurbs sell many books, if any—"Chilling . . . A grisly look into a mind on the far side of the mirror"—but agents and publicists insist that they're useful, and I want to be a good sport. I'd developed, by then, a practice of looking at galleys as soon as they landed on my desk: I'd know within a chapter or two if it was a good fit or not, sometimes just from the cover letter alone.

So I went over and retrieved your envelope from the floor, and I saw the hand-lettered URGENT with asterisks on either side of it underneath the Milpitas zip code, and I felt the heft of whatever lay within, waiting, presumably, for my approval to help it on its way through the world: but it wasn't that at all.

But it was you. You had found me. "At last," you said. There were several other addresses to which you'd sent the same letter, or a version of it; when you didn't get an answer, or when your letter came back marked *Addressee Unknown*, you concluded that I didn't realize you were looking for me. You drew this conclusion, you said, because you remembered our conversations from the mid-seventies, and you trusted your instincts now in a way you wished you'd known to trust them when you were a young girl: and your instinct then had been that I cared, about you and about your son, and about the truth of the murders in Morro Bay that had so captivated the national news media for a cycle or two. You believed that I would want to know how my book had affected the people in it who were still living: who had, daily, to deal with the ripple effects of the events and outcomes upon which, you said, I had built my reputation. I'm paraphrasing here.

What you said was: *You made your money off this, but I need for you to know what it has been like.*

I had already begun redecorating the living room when I read your words that day: the moment I read them has imprinted itself in my mind. I wasn't quite sure who you were, yet—I'd seen your last name on the return address, but I've written several books, and all of them have necessarily involved telling several stories at once. Perpetrators, victims, commentators, bystanders—a whole chorus whose various melodic strains I sift through to find a theme. So you could have been anybody, really, but your point, in part, was that you were not just anybody.

You were Jana Perez now, though I had known you under

the name Jana Larson, and you didn't feel right saying that I owed you anything, but, at the same time, you felt it was fair to say that I owed you a hearing, because I had done so well writing about the woman who killed your son.

Maybe it was my environment that made me receptive to your letter, which I might otherwise have put into a pile of things to be dealt with when I had time: the pile where the galleys often go, the pile where the pitches for movies whose directors haven't found a source of funding yet end up. Maybe it was something more. But I sat and I read, and, sensing something immense beneath your patient detailing of the pain with which, you said, you would live forever—not anger, but not *not* anger; not resentment, but grievance, something with a fair claim on the space it sought to hold—I asked myself several questions.

What happens when somebody tells a story that has real people in it? What happens to the story; what happens to the teller; what happens to the people?

†††

WHAT OTHER BOOKS MIGHT I HAVE WRITTEN about the murders of Jesse Jenkins and Gene Cupp? Would those books have been made into movies, or gone quietly into a single paperback printing after their initial run?

Who were my readers? What did I really know about them, about what the stories I sought out and brought into the light did for or to them?

Why did I always flinch when somebody asked me to write a sequel?

This was not the first time I had asked myself these questions, or questions like them. They were familiar friends, after a manner of speaking. Take that any way you want—as an indictment of my character, as a complicating factor. As nothing.

What had I missed in Morro Bay?

†††

WHEN YOUR LETTER CAME through my mail slot, I was preparing to shift gears on the book. I'd moved to Milpitas, gotten a feel for the town: for what it was like now, and for what it had been like before the tech boom changed it the way it changed a lot of places. I'd spent a long time doing preliminary research, and then I'd gotten granular: I'd conducted interviews, scouted important locations, and dug around in the microfiche at the public library. I had primary texts and secondary texts, and now it was time to move into my next phase, where I try, for better or worse, to gather together the twin spirits of time and place and make them real. In my line of work, you have to have something that sets you apart from everybody else: a feel for time and place is the corner on which I set up shop, years ago, when I first started writing about a locally famous double murder whose legend still haunted the town where I grew up.

Like all legends, it felt eternal to me, as non-negotiable as the scenery: the hills, the missions, the coastline, the White Witch. In writing about it and bringing it to life, I'd touched a nerve—not everywhere, but somewhere. I felt confident about my methods in the wake of the White Witch's success, and had taken those methods elsewhere, with similar results. People liked to read true crime books that brought them inside the house or hospital or garage or basement where it all went down, to feel as though they'd breathed in a little of the menacing air they imagine circulating or hanging stagnant around a crime scene. I got better at what I did. I sharpened my focus and broadened its reach. I didn't hurt anybody; the proof of my goodwill was in the results.

You sure got San Luis Obispo right, you wrote. *I guess we were both there at the same time so that shouldn't be a surprise.* You elaborated on this theme for a number of pages, mentioning places we both might have seen in those days—me as a child, you as a young mother trying to leverage enough control over your life to make the effort feel worthwhile. The Madonna Plaza: you remembered taking Jesse to a petting zoo there one Easter. You remembered that it was unseasonably cold that spring, but that Jesse had loved the animals so much it hadn't bothered him at all; you recalled all the other mothers huddling together outside the wooden stiles set up in the great parking lot, many of their young children clinging to their coattails, and Jesse inside running wild, touching all the animals and yelling their names. "The llama! The goat! The sheep!"

You remembered discovering that it wasn't too expensive to take Jesse to see a movie at the Fremont Theater, and doing that when you could: the westerns, the musicals, *The Incredible Mr. Limpet*. Sitting in the dark with your son, watching a movie and eating popcorn: these were precious memories for you, pearls of incalculable price. When the horror of his final hours on this earth came for you in the middle of the night, as it still did after all these years, you turned to these memories for comfort, and knew you had done what you could to make his life a good one.

But I had made his childhood sound like a nightmare, you wrote. I had saved the worst for Gene Cupp, and you couldn't say I'd been wrong there, you said; but, by the same token, you couldn't say I'd been right, because who really knows what a person is going through with their child? In their home? With their family? That was the problem with my book, you said. Everything about it was real except for the people, who could only be one way for me because I had a story to tell, but the story was bigger than that, and the people were real, not characters in a movie whose lives were only important when they were doing something awful.

But there's a lot more to it than that, you wrote. *I get it, though, you probably think I don't but I do. A story has to be about something, it's not just about the people in it and everything else that ever happened to them. See? I understand.* And then you explained—patiently, in detail, a teacher trying to spell something out for an especially dense pupil—that, however insistent the demands of narrative and convention, there were things beyond and beneath those demands that were just as important, and perhaps more pressing, in the final analysis. You took pains to make it clear that you understood your position wasn't impartial; you had real skin in the game. Your exact phrase: *I know I have skin in the game.*

I felt my heart surge in my chest when I read it: even in the early going, it seemed plain enough that you were being careful, so you had to know how that sounded, didn't you? But I knew you, a little, I thought, and struggled to imagine you intentionally reaching for the harshest metaphor available, the word that would sting most. I wanted to rush ahead through the letter, to find out if you'd undergone some immense transformation in the years since I'd last thought about you. Were you a professor now? A writer? Some sort of spiritual practitioner? I remembered the arresting officer's account of the arrest of Diana Crane, the one he gave to me personally: *It was just dripping through the bags*, he'd said. *Not just the blood, but, you know, parts and pieces that came off.*

And so, you said, ten or so pages in, you had spent a number of years working on this letter, which you knew was long, but you figured that I, as a writer, would understand that sometimes a story takes as long as it takes to tell it, and while you no longer felt like I owed you a hearing—*nobody owes anybody anything*, you said—you hoped I was honest enough to give you the time you were asking for. The earliest drafts of your letter had been short and angry, with only a few details about your son, how special he had been to you when you were a new mother: those had seemed most important at the time. You were glad those versions hadn't reached me; you didn't believe in fate, but each time your envelope returned to you, you'd taken the opportunity to revisit your theme, to try to make it as clear as you could; and now, if this worked and I was still at this address, you felt you'd gotten to the center of it, and that if I would do my part now, that would be nice. Again quoting: *That would be nice.*

There was a tack hammer on the floor near me; I needed it to pull up the carpet. I looked up from your long letter to catch my breath, and I thought how it's not every day that a writer like me has a primary text just land on his living room floor like this; and then I looked at the hammer and thought about the work that lay ahead, and I returned to you.

2.

YOU MET MICHAEL JENKINS in 1953, in the parking lot of the A&W where you worked as a carhop. He rolled up in a Dodge Custom convertible with its top down; there were a couple of guys driving newer convertibles around town, but he kept his clean. It looked cool to you.

A lot of people don't remember how nice you had to be to everybody back then, if you were a young girl working at a diner, or in an office, or at a soda counter. They don't remember, or they pretend it was different. But it was exhausting: smile all day, get slapped on the ass a few times when you turned your back on them walking back to the kitchen with their orders or after taking dictation at their desks—younger guys, older guys, they all did it. Even your own mother had told you, as soon as you took your first job, that you should be cheerful about it: nobody likes a complainer and it doesn't do any good.

So you did as you were told, and, as a consequence, didn't much like your job most days. It gave you a little walking-around money and sometimes your customers were friends from high school, so that was all right. And then Michael drove up in his Dodge, and even though everybody said he was a bad guy, he seemed sweet on you. He spoke gently and asked you questions, and, after a few more visits, he asked you out to the movies.

I don't understand, you told me in your letter, because I couldn't understand, what it meant to you when Michael Jenkins asked if you wanted to go with him to see *Blood Alley* at the Fremont Theater. You'd been serving him burgers and floats at his car about once a week for at least a month; he'd been so polite and friendly with you that you wondered whether it was all a gag. But it wasn't, and he'd been a gentlemen the whole time at the movie, too. Which, you said, was a little weird; you had already done your share of making out at the movies by then and it wasn't usually a big deal. Your mother always made sure you had a small, sharp pair of scissors in your handbag—another of her lessons—just in case. But Michael had to be goaded into kissing you good night for the first month or two.

It changed after you turned eighteen. You mentioned to him, one day, that you'd gotten a portable radio for your birthday, and he said he was sorry he hadn't known, and that night, before you got out of his Dodge at the curb, near your house but not near enough for your parents to see him from the front window, he kissed you on the mouth, hard, and kept going when you didn't offer any resistance. His hands didn't wander, but, you said in your letter, they could have, you were all softened up by then.

I already knew much of the story that followed: How fast things seemed to move from there; how jealous of you all your friends were; how much your parents hated him. How he'd been careful, you saw in retrospect, to stop short of getting you pregnant. How this had only served to strengthen your resolve. Your other dates had been fumbling high school boys; Michael was full grown, and acted like it. Being part of the grown-up world, riding around with Michael, stopping by the garage where he worked, watching TV with him at his apartment on his couch: it felt both more real than the high school life you were preparing to leave behind, and like a dream.

You got married in a civil ceremony without your parents' blessing shortly after graduation. As it turned out, you weren't pregnant yet, but the way things were going, you figured, it was only a matter of time. You were right about that. After you moved in, all caution went out the window. Pregnant, you wondered whether Michael would start looking for a house, since the apartment seemed so small, but you didn't want to be pushy. He'd begun showing a meaner side of himself—irritable, short-tempered—almost as soon as the wedding was over.

††

YOU DID NOT WANT TO MAKE THIS A WHOLE SOB STORY about yourself, you said, because that was not the point. The point was Jesse, your baby, who came into this world, and who, you thought, might bring the sweetness you knew was still within his father back out into the light. That sweetness had been hard to come by until you got pregnant; the first months of married life had meant getting yelled at a lot, for almost anything, it seemed. When he yelled, he would put his face up so close to yours that you could feel his breath, and hear the sounds, wet static and raw wood splintering, that a human throat makes when it yells. He yelled when you said something wrong, he yelled when you hadn't said anything at all. He yelled at the black-and-white television when the sound was bad, and he yelled at you if you talked when he was trying to hear it. But he yelled less after you got pregnant. You noticed, and remembered the presence of Jesse inside your body as a time of reprieve, a more peaceful renewal of the happy times you'd known before you got married.

You found a bigger apartment before the baby came, and that meant Michael had to work longer hours at the garage, but he didn't seem to mind. He slept hard when he slept, and treated you like a glass toy that would break if he treated it roughly. He paced in a waiting room while you were in labor, as was the custom then; he smiled so big when they brought him back to meet the baby.

The baby was a boy, of course, and he made you feel like your life wasn't just a lot of waiting around to get yelled at some more. Like many women of your generation, you'd learned to sew on an old machine your mother had inherited from her own mother, and you had a cheaper, more recent-vintage machine you kept in your closet. You sewed bunting into printed patterns for stuffed animals, and you sewed darling little pants. Nothing is cuter than your own son in his fresh new pants that his mother made herself. You pushed the baby in his stroller around town, down the sidewalks of the newly sprouting malls and by the fountains of the mission. You were always home in time to heat something up for dinner; Michael was not a picky eater and was easily satisfied on that front. You ate what he ate, and the baby graduated to jars of pureed carrots or peas. There were a few other mothers in the apartment building, though Michael did not like to have company over, and preferred that you keep to yourself. Still, you made a friend or two, and had coffee in the morning with them, sometimes, at their kitchen tables.

These had been happy times, for the most part, and they did not last.

†††

JESSE WAS TWO YEARS OLD—two and a half, to be precise—the first time Michael yelled at you loud enough to make him cry. The moment is still vivid for you, because you have sometimes wondered how things would be different now had you responded differently to it. You had served a dinner of cube steak with a baked potato. The cube steak was fine, but the middle of the potato was cold, and Michael was tired from work, or he hadn't slept well, or something else was wrong. When he got to the part that hadn't heated through, he spit it back out onto the plate—like a baby, you remembered—and threw his fork: not in your direction, but across the kitchen counter with such force that it broke a glass when it reached the sink. "Even I know how to bake a potato!" he shouted, which was a funny thing to hear, even in frightening circumstances, so you smiled.

You were confused, you remember, and began acting on instinct immediately; you were already smiling, so you thought you might try to sell him on the idea that he was somehow joking. "Some potatoes are colder than they look," you ventured.

He paused, looked at his plate, and then back up at you. "Are you talking back to me?" he asked: a note of angry disbelief in his voice, an audibly present threat.

"No, dear, I—"

The yelling wasn't new. It was just a fact of life, like disease, or traffic. But some days, like today, it seemed louder, even if it wasn't. Maybe the cumulative effect of it had eroded your ability to withstand it. It was impossible to know how to behave with a person just an inch from your face like that, yelling.

"Don't you talk back to me!" was all he said that time, because Jesse—two years old, in his booster chair—began to cry, his young eyes wide and filled with panic, clutching his oversized spoon so hard in his fat little fist that his knuckles went white. Both of you looked over at the baby, who began repeating, through labored sobs: "Mommy!"

You got up from the table, picked him up, and left the room with him. Michael, his loud voice following you into the hall, yelled after you: "You're gonna use the kid against me now, is that it?" From Jesse's room, a moment later, you could hear the sound of a dinner plate hitting something, which turned out to be the wall he'd been facing in the dining room. It did not break, but it left a stain.

You did not see the point, you said in the letter you sent to me that finally reached me in Milpitas, of dragging the story out any further; the scene more or less ended there on that occasion, but there were worse scenes to follow. I could probably guess what they were, you said, especially since I had already read a lot about them in the trial transcripts. It didn't do any good just to keep going over the same old hurts, you said, but I wasn't as sure as you were about that, then or now.

†††

IT JUST KEPT GETTING WORSE, you said. A year passed, and then another. Sometimes it was so bad. You hadn't told your parents, though you suspected they knew; they seemed to be avoiding you. It made you angry and resentful; weren't things bad enough? Michael drank too much; mainly beer, but a lot of it, after work, every night. He broke things and he yelled. He played with Jesse sometimes, but he didn't seem to think the way he acted around his son mattered at all. It did.

At preschool, Jesse sometimes threw toys: not merely in frustration, as children will, but at his playmates. He would panic if one of his friends got hurt, and would cry; you had to conceal this from Michael, who had markedly different ideas about what sort of person his son ought to grow up to be. Mrs. Wright, his teacher, a kind lady who had been teaching for twenty-five years, told you in conference that she was worried for Jesse. She tried to get you to open up, saying that the more she knew about Jesse's home life, the better she might be able to help him; and you knew she was right, and you wanted to tell her everything, but you were afraid. Michael had told you directly not to go around telling stories about him. You had learned that a little foundation was useful for concealing bruises and scrapes. It can get to be like a game, you said, seeing how well you could hide it. Your life as it had turned out wasn't much fun. Even the saddest games seemed worth playing.

The one thing you had going for you was Jesse, who loved you, and who you loved more than you could ever imagine loving anything, and it hurt you deeply to hear Mrs. Wright wondering out loud about what might be done to help him. Didn't she see you were doing the best you could, that old bitch? Did she think everybody lived in some happy house where everybody treated everyone else with kindness, like in fairy tales? Did she imagine that you were rich, that you were keeping Jesse in that house because you *wanted* to?

You knew it was wrong when these feelings bubbled up, but you were only human. Nobody can know, you told me, what's going on inside another person, even when they're sitting there right in front of you. People have their ideas, and then there's what's real. It's hard to get them to see the difference, especially when there are things you can't talk about.

††††

IT'S NOT CLEAR TO ME what happens next. The paragraphs that follow the meeting with Mrs. Wright are opaque. You say that Michael was in a really bad mood "after that," but I don't know whether you mean "on that particular day," or for a span of time afterward. You say that you didn't want to sit there and be treated that way, like an animal, but again you don't specify a time frame, and "that way" has, as a referent, only the pages that precede it.

Yet the missing information, as is often the case, speaks fairly vividly for itself. The sense I get from these paragraphs is that your pain, in defiance of time, is still fresh: that it still wields the capacity to wound you, or that it feels that way. I scrutinized these murky paragraphs and I pictured you, mother of a two-year-old child with whom you had developed a lasting and important bond; and I pictured the child, soaking up the unspecified chaos like a towel set down near a leaking pipe. I imagined that, if the situation were allowed to get bad enough, the energy needed to store vivid memories might find itself conscripted in the service of more urgent errands: self-protection, or the protection of your own flesh and blood.

It's only a guess. Several things might have happened over a period of weeks, or months. I know enough, now, having been at this business of telling true stories in which people—good people, bad people, complicated people—do awful things to each other, to say that the extremes implied by your missing data are, for me, quite lucid. I even find myself growing attached to best-case scenarios, because you seem, from your letter, like a good person who has been dealt a bad hand. But at some point, anyhow, you moved back in with your parents: when the pressure, or the threat, or the danger—one of these—proved too great.

In those days, you wrote, your savor for life returned. Your mother seemed more sorry for you than angry, and you were relieved about that; you had been prepared for lectures, for penance, for pointed remarks at the dinner table. Your father, meanwhile, took great delight in his grandchild, bringing home penny candy from the corner store and doing magic tricks with pencils and coins.

Jesse thrived. He talked more, telling stories, singing songs. He asked about his daddy—all children love their daddies, even the ones whose daddies don't love them back—and you didn't know what to tell him, but it's easy to change the subject with children, even if it makes you feel like a villain. You thought, and people tended to agree, that he was still young enough to forget about Michael entirely, which was your hope for yourself, too. You were too old for that to be a real possibility, but hadn't you heard something about children not forming any real memories until they were five? It was a hopeful thing to imagine.

But Michael came by one day when both your parents were out, his face cleanly shaven, his clothes laundered, his voice full of regret; and Jesse was home at the time, and he ran to his father, and the two of them played like father and son. And you felt trapped, a rat in a maze unable to turn around and retrace your steps, wishing for a gloved hand to lift you out and set you back down at the entrance, and three weeks and a few similar visits later—*I took my time. It just wasn't enough,* you wrote—you were a family again, in the apartment a mile and a half across town.

We will keep the door open for you, your parents said. Jesse hugged his grandfather as you carried the last of the few things you'd brought with you to the trunk of Michael's car.

3.

PULLING UP CARPET IS HARD, but putting down carpet is harder. Still, I felt like the safest course of action was to keep doing everything myself. I found a library book about do-it-yourself home repair and copied the relevant pages, and I bought some cheap carpet studs. From the crime scene footage and photographs I knew the exact sort of carpet I needed, that sickening granite grey that paved office floors for most of the 1980s, its weave so dead that the eye registers it as near cousin to the sidewalk; I was guessing, I think fairly, that Evelyn Gates would have spared little effort in cutting corners.

The new apartment was nice, you wrote; it had a shag carpet, and little else in it when you first arrived. The new place was Michael's surprise. He'd had a lot of time to think, he said, and you deserved to live somewhere nice: he spoke to you and Jesse as he said it.

Jesse, of course, was thrilled. He ran from room to room, inspecting closets, asking questions. Where would he sleep? Where did they eat? Was there a new TV?

"I thought we could pick out some furniture," Michael said. It was plain that this was more of his planned performance, but you liked it. You wanted to believe in him, because it would make things easier. Easier like I wouldn't have to feel like such a failure, you wrote. So you went to a place that had secondhand furniture that was nice, not ratty, and he let you pick out a table and some chairs. Michael found a big, soft sofa tucked away in one corner: it wasn't in terrific shape, but it was comfortable, and inexpensive.

Everything was timed right, so that you'd see the new empty place—a fresh start!—and have the chance to make it yours. In future years, you couldn't help but wonder how much insight, if any, Michael had into his own motivations. Did he understand how cruel he'd been to his family before: cruel enough that they'd fled in fear for their safety? Was he sorry for that, or mainly sorry that he'd pushed them too far? Could he talk about any of this, or did he mean to "put it all behind us"— he'd used this phrase, and it seemed a little ominous to you.

I was stupid and tired of living with my parents, you wrote in your letter to me, your long letter which I sat and read between fits of tearing up old carpet and putting older carpet down. It's really not any more complicated than that.

Jesse was happy to live with his mom and dad again, and when, five months later, Michael yelled at you for asking him a question when he was trying to watch TV, he ran off down the hall and hid in his room for several hours.

†††

BUT IT TOOK FIVE MONTHS to get there. Five months! You hadn't enjoyed five months of continuously good days in—well, you didn't know *how* long; as you'd said, you wrote, you sometimes have a hard time keeping the order of events straight. You knew that Jesse had been at least two the first time he reacted to Michael yelling at you, and, for you, that probably meant he'd never yelled at you like that before; but now, you wondered, had you really enjoyed two and a half years of relative peace after the wedding? It seemed impossible. You hated not being able to trust your own memory; you had to go with the information it gave you.

Those first five months were like a vacation, you said. Or not like a vacation: you were still raising a four-year-old. Or five, possibly. You wished now that you had kept a diary then, but who thinks of keeping a diary when their life feels like yours: uncertain when not frightening, disorienting when not destabilizing. But if you'd had a diary of those days, you might have recorded, you said, trips to the drive-in theater as a family, and the sweetness of Jesse's palpable joy in the movie right up until the moment, midway through it, when he fell asleep; and dinners as a family on Fridays, an effort Michael had undertaken by splitting his shift at the garage, because, he said, it was good to eat dinner together. Weekend drives: these were the best of all; Michael was happy when he drove, and Jesse loved cars, too, and the ride could give you an hour or even two of peace.

He was trying so hard, and then your friend Barbara Thiedleman stopped by one morning with her Avon kit, wondering if you wanted to give it a try; it had been fun for her, she said, especially now that Josh, her six-year-old, no longer asked to play with Mommy when he got home from school.

You told Barbara you were fine; Michael had a good job, and you didn't think this would be the sort of thing you were good at. You said that just to try to sweep the matter under the rug as quickly as you could: it could be hard to explain to people why you didn't even need to ask whether you could do certain things, why the effort of the asking, even if slight, wasn't worth the risk of return.

"Oh, I know, I felt the same way," said Barbara in response; you could hear that she was reciting a memorized script, maybe with a few idiosyncratic fixes for that personal touch. "Me, sell makeup? I barely even have time to make up my *own* face in the morning! But after I gave it a try, I—"

"Barbara," you said, unsure how exactly to proceed; she knew you'd moved out for a while, but you'd only told a few friends the details—the volume, the bruises, the fear.

She scanned your face, with a sensitivity that had been missing from her pitch, you thought, and concluded: "Well, listen, you don't have to decide today. It's a big decision! Can I leave this with you, though, just so you can get an idea of the range of products? Some of them are really nice."

What were you going to say? Maybe you could tuck them into the closet, tell her later that you'd looked them over, and they were very nice, but you simply couldn't. She left them on the dining room table, where they sat for half an hour after she left, and you wondered if it wouldn't be fun, being an Avon lady.

You moved the kit from the table to the corner of the dining room, thinking that you could just mention that she'd made the offer and accidentally left the starter kit at your house. The last five months had gone so smoothly.

Nothing happened after Michael came home, but he stewed quietly about the Avon starter kit for, evidently, the next eight hours; he woke up angry about it. His response, before you could really explain yourself, was swift, violent, and deeply destabilizing. Jesse, getting ready for school, sat in the middle of the living room crying the whole time, though Michael, sky-high on his first fully unbottled rage in God knew how long, did not seem to hear him over the sound of his own voice, yelling about Avon ladies.

You felt very ashamed when Barbara stopped by the next day. You tried not to seem shaken or sad as you told her you really didn't think the Avon lady was a hat you were ready to wear just yet, but you appreciated the opportunity. She suspected nothing, as far as you could tell. Settling back into the routine was sad, but not hard. It's pretty easy, you wrote, to just do something you've already done before.

†††

ONE THING, THOUGH, WAS DIFFERENT THIS TIME. He'd always been sorry the next day after a big blowup; or, if not the next day, sometime in the next week or two. You had been trying for many years, you said, to not say things like "It wasn't his fault" or "He couldn't help himself," but I had to understand that that's how it feels when you're watching somebody change right before your eyes. One minute they're maybe mad, but in a normal way, and then it's like somebody flipped a switch in their brain. You didn't want to make excuses, and you *weren't* making excuses, but you wondered whether anybody from the outside could ever really understand. People are responsible for their own behaviors: every counselor you'd reached out to over the years had hammered this point home again and again. But to see someone lose control and then practically pass out later after the rage drains out of him, with no beers or drinks or anything: just pass out on the couch, emptied of his energy—maybe having seen this so many times made it hard for you to take the right point of view.

You think of these things, when it keeps happening, you wrote. You think harder than most people: harder, you'd guess, than the people who write books about it, even, or the people who write laws. Your perspective is unique. It's not a fun perspective to have, but it's yours, and, if you want to keep it, you can. You don't think I understood this, because I had turned Michael into a cartoon villain, beating his young wife, and, later, their child, yelling at them for nothing, terrorizing his own family for no reason. For me, you said, it was simple, because I was never there. For you and for Jesse it was not simple.

Jesse did ask you, now, about Michael's temper. These were the hardest conversations you'd ever had as an adult, and you were totally unequipped for them. Just the beginnings of them were enough to make you feel like you'd never find the strength to go through with them.

"Why does Daddy yell so much?" he asked after Barbara left.

"Oh, honey," you said, hugging him, trying not to cry.

Jesse felt safe enough in your arms to let his own tears flow freely, which made it harder. "I hate him," he said. You looked at the scowl on his small face.

"Now, honey, you don't hate him," you said, licking your thumb and cleaning around his eyes. "I don't hate him, either. He can't help himself sometimes, but he is trying."

"Even if he's trying, it comes out the same way," said Jesse, his stab at defiance replaced by a resignation so crushing that you scrambled to correct it.

You lowered yourself to a crouch so that the two of you could be eye-to-eye, like equals.

"He is trying to change," you said. "He has done a lot for us and if we can help him change, that would be nice, right?"

It causes you, you wrote, more pain than I will ever know, no matter how vividly I paint pictures of death scenes and coroners' inquests, and no matter how many movies they make out of those scenes, bringing it all to life for everybody to gawk at, making everybody feel like they know what it's like when they don't and never will, to remember the sound of your own voice trying to sell Jesse on an outright lie about the meaning of what he'd seen with his own eyes, about what the situation on the ground really was for you both.

"He's not even sorry," he said, and you hugged him close again, hoping some more crying might help you both, and might also help you get through a moment from which you could see no easy exit; and realizing, probably too late to undo any of the damage already done, that children have greater powers of observation than many people suspect, and are often perfectly capable of drawing good conclusions from the information available to them, information not volunteered by anyone in particular but circulating openly, effortlessly, in the very air that they breathe.

†††

I WASN'T SURE WHAT TO DO about the bottles on the walkway. I could just buy new bottles and use those, of course, fresh bottles of whatever soda happened to be available in glass, but I felt like keeping things as true to the pictures as possible meant avoiding substitutes. There are people who buy and sell antique bottles that vary from one another and from their modern incarnations in size, in shape, and in color, but that's a collector's market. I didn't want to run up a huge tab on bottles I was just going to break anyway.

I thought the solution I landed on was pretty clever, almost elegant. There are still some local dairies here and there who sell their milk in glass bottles; I guess some people say it tastes better that way. I calculated—guessed—that one half-gallon milk bottle would be about two Coke bottles' worth of glass; and I reasoned that Derrick and Seth and Angela and Alex had probably raided a steel trash can directly behind the store for empties. Twenty bottles? Thirty? Forty.

I drove to the dairy—not a short drive, but a pleasant enough use of my morning—and bought ten gallons of milk in half-gallon jugs, which cleaned them out; I'd have to settle for reduced bulk, but you learn to improvise. I then distributed them, still capped, among four pillowcases, and waited until it was dark and there wouldn't be much foot traffic near my house. When the time seemed right, I put on a pair of rubber gloves, set the bulging pillowcases down in a jagged row along the front walkway, and went at them all with a baseball bat.

It disrupts the flow; I had to become destructive to get the dirty glass I needed, but Derrick and Angela and Seth and Alex had scavenged from available materials. It makes the process of re-creation feel tainted by some original energy. I try to avoid that, but here I was constrained by available materials. Everything's in plastic now unless you go looking for glass.

When I woke up the next morning and came out to the porch, and saw the sun shining on the white, jagged mounds of sticky glass I'd hastily swept together last night, I felt pleased. They looked like I imagined their predecessors had looked, all the way back in 1986, after the crime scene photographs had all been taken and the yellow tape taken down, and the mess left by Derrick and Angela and Seth and Alex was finally getting cleaned up.

I looked right, and I looked left, and then I threw caution to the wind and knocked over both piles with the flat of the broom. The broken glass sprayed loudly into the air, and then all the tiny shards landed on the walkway, bouncing this way and that.

I did this until both piles were gone, and there was broken glass all over the front walkway, and the lawn, and until bits of it were glistening here and there in the light on the street just beyond the curb.

4.

THE FRESHLY BROKEN GLASS outside was soaking up the sun; on the table in the dining room was a small box of my most treasured eBay finds—the exterior crime scene photographs— and, alongside it, your letter. I resented the letter, a little, because I felt obligated to read it all the way through, even though I wasn't sure what it might tell me that I didn't already know. I had done my research before publishing *The White Witch*; I knew the break-in hadn't been Jesse's idea. He was a kid who had bad luck most of his life. There hadn't been anyone to help him, and then it was too late. There was a case to be made that it wasn't his fault that he ended up in Diana Crane's apartment, but this didn't feel like the case you were making.

I did believe you were building toward something; your letter was meticulous, even when your sentences ran on or your spelling flagged. You had been waiting for a very long time to get your message to me. Every time I turned over another page, I could feel the weight of all that time, the shape it had taken around the parameters of your life, its ever-gathering presence.

What would my work be like if I had to keep returning to the same story every time, I wondered. If, instead of hunting down sad places where people's lives had been ruined, there was only the one place, a place where, every time I told the story again, there was some new thing to learn about it, some overlooked ripple or wrinkle or speck that fleshed out the details, that brought them more fully to life: but with the provision, present in the process, that nothing could help, nothing would change, no one would be unburdened, or healed, or made whole. My methods: How fine might their focus grow if they had but the one object, a moment and its consequences? And if I were some-how drawn inside that moment, me myself, not as an observer but as someone touched by it: What then? These moments are tidal in their force, I knew from long study: those unsteadied by their flow come to think of them as inevitabilities, as natural forces, energies whose actions can be resisted no more profitably than the rising of the sun. And still, sometimes, when they can't sleep, those once visited by these moments ask themselves, bar-gaining for some vision of a second chance: What might I have done differently? Aren't there infinite possibilities present in any given situation? What was I supposed to have done?

When he was nine years old, you wrote, that was when things seemed to get a lot worse.

†††

JESSE WAS NINE when a teacher at his school asked him what he was sad about and he told her the truth. It was different then, you said in your letter: it was a different time, people had differ-ent standards, people had different ideas about how to do things. It wasn't just that people drove different cars or wore different clothes, you said; there was a lot more to it than that. People talked different, and people acted different, and people expected different things from their wives and from their husbands and from their parents and from their children. From schools and from hospitals. From the police. To you, it felt, back then, like these expectations were, if not set in stone, then certainly beyond repair as far as a person like you might be concerned: there wasn't anything, you said, that you could have done about any of it, so you did your best to take care of yourself and of your loved ones within the boundaries of the rules as you understood them. At some point, those boundaries shifted, and things got a little better, but all that was after, and too late for you, and for Jesse. You weren't sure when things had changed; you thought maybe things were always changing, but there are some changes you barely notice until a lot of time passes, you wrote, and other things where when the change comes it feels like a whole big thing. Like when the divorce laws changed in California, you said. That was a big thing that changed.

But that change hadn't come yet when Jesse told his teacher about his father getting mad over dinner. The teacher, Mrs. Benson, was fond of Jesse, who seemed to love being in school most days: he and a pod of other boys roved the schoolyard at recess, laughing and yelling at high volume; Jesse wasn't a leader among this group, but a very faithful follower. The boys played rough: they pushed each other into a ditch at the edge of the playground over and over, and they played contact football. On most days, Jesse couldn't get enough.

But lately he had started sitting out of recess entirely; he volunteered to stay in the classroom with his teacher, cleaning erasers and sharpening pencils. Mrs. Benson had taken a careful approach in trying to find out what was going on; she could see that he was bothered about something, and wanted to let him tell her about it at his own pace. So she waited a couple of days, and then a third, and then, on the fourth, when the day outside was too nice for a child to be cleaning erasers, she thought she'd prod as gently as she could, just to try to let him know she was there to listen if he needed.

Back in your day, you wrote, a teacher would have just minded her own business, because a teacher's job was to get the kids to behave, and to get them ready for a world where they'd *better* behave. It wasn't like that anymore, you said. Teachers take all kinds of interest in their kids. And that was mainly good, you said, but could also cause trouble. You didn't want to sound like somebody always complaining about people who are just trying to make the world better. You weren't like that. You were glad Jesse had somebody, one person, at least, trying to watch out for him when he was nine years old, someone who could see that something was wrong, and who cared enough to ask him why he didn't want to go outside and play with his friends. Maybe one of the kids was being a bully, Mrs. Benson had wondered aloud, trying to leave a door open in case that was the one he needed.

"The only bully is my dad," your son told his teacher, and then, she said, he began to cry, quietly but very bitterly, trying to hold his tears back, gritting his teeth until his face shook.

He stared off into space for a whole minute, Mrs. Benson said.

These days, a teacher would probably hug him, and maybe that would help, you thought, and maybe she did hug him, and left that part out of her story; you didn't know.

But she did call you at your apartment and ask to arrange a meeting; and Michael was home when you took the call, and although you'd been careful, in answering her questions, to

speak in a neutral voice and to be as vague as you could, he got
suspicious, and the rest of the night was pretty bad.

You sent a note to school with Jesse the next day, saying that
you could meet after school any day this week, and that would
probably be the best way.

† † †

WHEN MRS. BENSON HAD COME AND GONE, you gathered your
thoughts, you wrote to me in your letter, your letter which
filled a nine-by-twelve manila envelope until its fold strained
against the clasp and which reached me at my house in Milpitas, the house where my renovations were already under way. It
had been a bad visit, for you, though you had tried to conceal
your worry as best you could. You understood well enough that
Jesse's teacher wasn't trying to be a busybody; that she cared for
him, that she wanted to help if she could. But you resented her,
too, for forcing you to see the situation through the eyes of the
outside world—eyes through which you could only permit
yourself to gaze as an occasional luxury, a sad indulgence, a
hopeless sort of daydreaming that left you feeling worse than
ever.

You tried to explain your position: that Jesse and his father
got along very well most of the time, and that Jesse truly loved
his daddy, even if, sometimes, Daddy was mean. But Michael
was trying to get better, you'd said; it had been worse before;
but this was a lie, and you suspected she could see it. You could
call her to talk anytime you needed, she said as she rose from
her chair, by which you took her to mean that she understood
the full extent of how bad it was, and would help you if you
ever decided that help was what you wanted.

When you got a moment alone with Jesse in his room, you

tried, as gently as you could, to ask him about Mrs. Benson, and what their conversation at school had been like.

"She was asking why I didn't want to play outside," he offered, his head hung.

"And you told her about your dad?"

"She asked me did I have a bully," he answered, and then he looked up, and seemed to search your eyes: For what? you wondered, then, and, when you remember it, now.

"Your daddy is trying the best he can," you said.

"That's what you always say," said Jesse. Your heart hurt; your head hurt; you didn't know what to say, or to do; you felt like you had already ruined your own life, and maybe your son's, too, but you did not have any idea, you said, what you were supposed to do about any of it. You thought that if you could share with him the tricks you used to get through Michael's angry times, maybe he could learn how to use them for himself. But it was important for him to understand that if Michael found out about Mrs. Benson, and about what she knew, that would make things worse.

"It's true," you said. You were improvising. "Your daddy is trying. I know he can do better. So do you. But if we tell everybody about how Daddy doesn't always do his best, it could get Daddy in trouble."

This was a moment you remembered, you said, because out of all the moments you wished you could get a chance to do over, this was always the one that came unbidden to your mind. When Michael had come to your parents' house begging for another chance, mightn't you have told him, No, we're better off this way, get out of here or I'm calling the police? You might have, but it was this moment that you always remembered first when you found yourself going over the details of Jesse's young, wasted life, and what you might have done to protect him. Even on the very day he died, couldn't you have done something to throw a wrench into his plans that morning, even without knowing what they were? You thought probably yes, but the day of his death wasn't the thing that came for you at night when you were trying to sleep. It was the time after his elementary schoolteacher's visit to the apartment, a visit during which she had expressed concern about the conditions in which Jesse lived, and about you, and your safety, and you had tried to put the best face on the situation you could without lying out-right, because you hadn't wanted to call your son, your beauti-ful son, a liar to his teacher. The thing that haunted you was how you'd explained to Jesse, in the most loving way you could, that he wasn't supposed to tell people how his father behaved when he got angry with his family.

"He should get in trouble for hitting you," Jesse said. At nine, he was beginning to resemble the young man he would briefly become: a handsome sandy-haired boy with a perpetu-ally worried look in his eyes, an expression that suggested his expectations of both the present and the future were low.

"He's trying," you said, because it was all you had and you had to believe it, either because you didn't see any alternatives, or because you were afraid of what would happen if you tried them.

Mrs. Benson approached Jesse several times over the course of the rest of the school year to ask him if things were better at home, but he refused to volunteer any further infor-mation to her, usually changing the subject by talking about hiking trips he'd taken with his father into the foothills. You knew that this was how he answered her because she contacted you one final time before the school year was out, and she said that she was happy to hear Jesse's dad was doing better.

For people on the outside, either you're doing things with

your son and trying to be a good father, or you're a monster twenty-four hours a day, you said. They don't actually know what it's like.

If they knew, they would know, you said. Twice, in consecutive, identical sentences.

If they knew, they would know.

†††

THE OTHER THING THAT HAPPENED when Jesse was nine, besides all the other things that kept happening and why dwell on them, they are what they are, you said, you can't fix the past, was that he met Gene Cupp. Gene's family had moved from Arizona to California in the middle of the school year; it's hard for children to be uprooted from their environment and have to make new friends, though Gene, at eleven, had already been through the process several times.

He lived with his father, which was unusual. You learned about Gene and his father early on because Jesse had befriended him on the playground the week he got to school; Gene had been playing tetherball by himself in a far corner of the playground, hitting the ball as hard as he could in one direction, then pivoting on his heels to hit it back after it had circled the pole a time or two.

His father, you said, was a biker. He had a beer belly and a brown beard and a leather jacket, and a Harley-Davidson, which was what most of the bikers rode. He dropped Gene off at school from his motorcycle; Jesse thought it was the coolest thing he'd ever seen. Gene would lift the helmet off his head and hand it back to his father, who would then lower it onto his own head and roar off. Gene's dramatic drop-off routine had made him the subject of rumors from his first day at school, most of them whole-cloth playground inventions based on how bikers looked on TV.

You are pretty sure Jesse imagined Gene's relationship with his father as something really great, you said, something worthy of his young envy. As it turned out, Gene's household was even worse than yours, but what mattered more were the dreams in Jesse's head. Jesse was smaller than Gene, who had begun growing into his preadolescent body already, his arms gangly, an uncombed mop of hair atop his head like an old pelt set haphazardly down on his skull.

You knew now that there was something weird about their friendship; of course you did. But at the time, you were thankful: for a friend in Jesse's life who made him happy, and at whose house he could play in the afternoons. Because Jesse's dad was yelling more than ever. Sometimes it felt like it never stopped, or like the quiet parts were only spaces that grew shorter every week. Anything that could keep Jesse from having to hear more of that, you said, seemed like a good thing worth pursuing.

5.

BY THE TIME JESSE GOT TO HIGH SCHOOL, you were starting to panic, because it felt like you were losing him. All parents who love their children experience something like this as those children grow into adults: the loss of the child, the emergence of the person he will become. You knew you weren't the first person to feel this way. But it's different, you told me, for people who have been trying as best they can to protect their children from something, because this is the time when these moms and dads get their first chance to find out whether their efforts have been enough.

Of course, it was worse because Michael was not getting along with Jesse at all now. It was so much worse than it had ever been; for you, it was also almost a little bit of a relief, because Michael seemed to have become focused on his son instead of you, and specifically on how his son was increasingly disobedient. You felt guilty about that at the time. Nobody deserves to get yelled at the way Michael yelled when he was angry, which was at least once every day; nobody deserved to get hit, to have things thrown at them from across the room. But you had been living as a target for so long. People who've learned to live in a war zone need a break sometimes or they'll go crazy, you said.

But of course it also made things worse inside your head. The guilt made it hard to sleep; losing sleep made everything a little harder the next day, every day. You only had one child, and now you could not protect him unless you were willing to take his place. Michael didn't seem to have enough energy to focus his anger on both of you at once; it floated. At fourteen, Jesse seemed weirdly willing to place himself in the line of fire.

He still hadn't cut his hair; he kept it long and ragged in the style of the times, and you thought he looked wonderful. You were proud to have a son so handsome, who could look so stylish without really trying. He wore blue jeans and T-shirts, and he stayed away from home a lot—over at Gene's, sometimes, or out running around with Gene, who had gotten a driver's license as soon as he'd turned sixteen.

Jesse's classmates had a different view of him. He did not seek their company, and had little to say to or about any of them. Gene was his only real friend, and the way they were always together led to rumors no one dared voice in Gene's presence, because most people were afraid of him. Only the jocks ever tried their luck around Gene, and he was rumored to have pulled a knife on one of them; that he carried a knife

on his person, a big one that could do real damage, was generally understood.

As Gene's only real friend, Jesse felt privileged, protected. It
was sad, you said, but you understood how it must have been
for Jesse. How he must have felt like he had finally gotten lucky
in life. This, you said, was one of the things you were pretty
sure I had not understood, and which you hoped to make me
understand, even if it took you the rest of your life.

†††

THE OTHER THING ABOUT JESSE when he was fourteen was that
he started smoking pot. You felt like you'd noticed it early, but
there was no way to be sure; that's how it works with secrets. By
the time you know somebody has a secret, it's already been
hanging around for a while, doing its work in the shadows.

It hurts worse with your children, because secrets are how
you know for sure that their baby days are gone. Of course,
Jesse had not been a baby for a long time; you knew that. But
even through junior high, the child he'd been was still findable
in his face: he felt small to you then. Now he was sprouting up
like a tree. He'd be as tall as you soon enough. Like other boys
his age, he sometimes wore things that men of Michael's generation would never have been seen wearing: chain necklaces
with tiny turquoise pendants, cheap rings with glittering imita-
tion stones. And the expressions on his face, you said, seemed
so complicated now: sad, angry, frightened, hungry. Hungry
was the one that bothered you the most; he got plenty to eat.
Like so many teenage boys, he conducted daily raids on the
cupboard and refrigerator. But neither his body nor his face
reflected the effort: he was gangly, and his eyes darted this way
and that, as if he were scouting out the area for provisions.

Except when he was high, you said. Or so you figured. Sometimes, when he came home from school in the late afternoon, he didn't look hungry at all. He still went to the kitchen and made short work of any food available, but his whole aspect was different. He never asked what there was to eat: he lazed through the shelves like he was the only person in the house and had all the time in the world. Checked out, you said. Like somebody else was driving.

You suspected that the driver in question was Gene Cupp. Gene was repeating junior year again; he and Jesse had a couple of classes together. Jesse was good at math, but Gene, still trying to get his algebra requirement out of the way, didn't seem to care at all about sitting in a classroom full of underclassmen. He cheated off Jesse's homework, you said; you knew this because sometimes they would go over it in the late afternoon, if Michael wasn't home.

Michael didn't like Gene any more than he liked any other visitors, but he seemed oddly intimidated by him. Gene looked like he was in his early twenties: long, curly hair, a mustache more whiskers than wisp, gas station sunglasses he usually forgot to remove when he was indoors. That his father rode with the local motorcycle crew was something Michael knew ahead of time, because Michael's work was right next door to the motorcycle shop. Local bikers congregated there at all hours, and, if you were smart, you got a feeling for which of them might mean trouble. Gene's father was one of them.

"What's up, Mrs. J?" Gene said when he and Jesse came in through the door one day. You didn't like an older boy leading the conversation the way he did; you hated seeing how passive Jesse was in his presence.

Still, any company was better than none, and you were between efforts at making friends whose presence in the apartment might be acceptable to Michael. "Jana," you said, for what must have been the tenth time.

"Jana!" Gene said, his eyebrows rising above the rims of his sunglasses. "OK, then!" You smelled the stale cigarette smoke on him as he passed you; you remembered when Michael's old car had smelled like that, and how it felt forbidden and dangerous to you, a long time ago.

Jesse retrieved a quart of orange juice from the refrigerator, grabbed two plastic cups from the cupboard, and hurried down the hall to his room, Gene behind him, bouncing as he walked. "Hi, Mom," Jesse said as the door of his bedroom shut behind him, possibly with a small laugh underneath his voice, though you hoped not.

What were you supposed to do? you asked me. Stand between Jesse and his friend, when Jesse had already had such a hard time with friends: if Michael took a dislike to one of them, he'd yell about it at dinnertime until they were out of the picture; even the ones he found acceptable were likely to hear him growing agitated about something before long. If he ever got comfortable enough with a regular guest to show his true colors, then the days of that guest's presence on the scene were numbered. The reliability of Michael's equations formed a mathematical language that was easy to understand, and hard to bear. It had broken your heart at least three times during Jesse's childhood: he loved his friends fiercely, spending as much time with them as he possibly could, and, one by one, they all eventually moved on to other friends. Friends with normal families, friends whose houses felt safe. His little friend Jason, and that other one, Neal. Gone from his life, when friends were what he needed. To see your son grow into a lonely teenager when he's really a nice kid with so much to give, you wrote. Think about what that's like.

So you tried to overlook the way your instincts bristled whenever Gene addressed you by name: the way your urge to protect your son, still keen despite years of getting overruled by Michael's rage, roared into overdrive in his presence. Jesse deserved a friend, somebody who would stick by him. Maybe Gene was that friend. A lot of kids smoked pot now. Things had changed, you said. As long as Gene was gone before Michael got home, you didn't see the harm.

Both Jesse and Gene seemed to understand, like you, that their alliance would be strained if Jesse's father came to view it as a threat. They conducted their afternoons in your house like planned raids: arrive, convene, disperse. Some days Jesse went to Gene's house instead, and sometimes he didn't get home until after dinner.

Michael made a big deal about it a couple of times and then seemed to decide that he didn't really care.

Jesse was adrift like a leaf in the wind, you said.

Did I even understand what it takes to know that about your very own son? you said in your letter, whose remaining pages formed a stack which diminished a little every time I turned one of them over, and whose cumulative effect within me was registering with unignorable force.

††††

BY THIS TIME I had started in on the walls inside Devil House, which, owing to the nature of walls and their ubiquity in the visual field, were going to require the utmost attention to detail. The amount of guesswork needed to get it right irritated me; I knew that at some point in the 1980s, possibly especially in California, the chemical composition of spray paint had been altered to keep kids from huffing it. When I started replicating the photographs, would the drip come out wrong? It's an affectation, I know; I don't include any of my restagings in the books I write. But they are important to me, and the idea that a detail isn't right can fester in my brain like an unbidden thought.

Mercifully, you had begun to gloss over periods of time in your account of Jesse's life. It seemed that Michael's violence had become more calculating, and that Jesse had begun avoiding him in the evenings; Michael didn't like it, and his focus returned to you some nights. But you didn't want to dwell on this, you said, because this story wasn't about you.

When you said that, for the third or fourth time, I wished we could meet again, so that I could tell you that this story is about you: or that it's also about you; that stories in which something ugly bursts out from the confines of its sac are necessarily about every person inside the blast area. But you were patient with your point. Jesse, you said. The boy he had been, the friend to his mother, the companion you'd had on your errands. The one who did his best to keep the secrets you hated having to ask him to keep. The one who, when he grew up, would be free in a way that you probably would never be free, you'd thought: there had even been a weekend, when Jesse was fifteen, when you'd tried running away again, but after a weekend in a motel room you'd had visions of Michael finding you and killing you both, and you'd gone home and taken your lumps and moved on with your life.

Jesse was home a lot less after that time, you said. Michael seemed to sense that his time of hitting without being hit back was growing short, and eased back a little, becoming more hateful with his words.

The words were worse in some ways, you said, because you could tell they reached Jesse in a way physical force couldn't, but there was no way for the two of you to talk about it anymore, so you just watched, and hoped he'd be able to leave as much of his life with his father behind as possible when he finally set out on his own.

Then it was junior year, you said, and you knew I already knew a little about that: but you were going to tell me anyway, you said, because it was too late to turn back now.

6.

DIANA CRANE CALLED YOU, you told me in your letter, more than once. She was not a stranger to you; she cared about Jesse, and had tried to let you know that her concern for him was real. It is hard, you said, to always be getting calls from your son's teachers: kind people who tell you about the problems your son is having, with whom you always have to feign incomprehension: when, actually, you *do* understand, with a type of perfect understanding inaccessible to those on the outside, what the problems are, and what has caused them, and why their solutions, while known, feel inaccessible, walled off, out of reach. Over the years, you had fielded enough such phone calls that your response, at this point, felt rehearsed: never tell the teachers the whole truth, always trying not to see the openings they leave in the conversation for you to tell on Michael, to say something that might allow them to file a report with the police. It takes a lot of energy to listen in this way, and to playact at answering; it wears you down.

She would probably have gotten you to talk, to tell the truth, if she had lived, you said: or if the school year had been a little longer, or if you'd met with her, either at her home or at yours, as she'd requested. But you gave her some reason, you no longer remembered what, for not being able to have visitors at the house just now, and you'd said talking on the telephone was best for you, if that was all right.

You remembered four calls: that first one, and then monthly for three months; it emerged at the trial that she'd scheduled those calls on her desk calendar at school, and you imagined her placing them from a phone at her desk at the end of the day. It made you sad, a very painful kind of sad, you said, to think of Diana Crane's desk calendar, full of weekday errands from Monday through Friday, with *Call Jana Larson* written on some weekday once each month. You didn't remember whether they'd been on the same weekday each time or not. In the end it did not matter.

What was important was that Diana Crane had understood Jesse to be in danger—from the way he acted in class, from the way he answered her questions, from his weird proximity to Gene Cupp, who, as all the teachers knew, had no friends, and probably no future, and whose body, during his second attempt at completing his senior year, was now visibly too big for the high school desks. She had made the effort to connect with you, and you had resented her for it, because you had tried, more than once, to better your situation, but did not seem able to do so under your own power, so you hoped that your son would just get a job after he graduated and move out of the house, and then at least one of you would be able to live in peace.

That had been something you looked forward to, you said, Jesse getting a chance to live life on his own, because he had always been curious about the world, and hadn't had much of a chance to see many places.

The last time she called you had been in May, when she'd said that Jesse's work in class showed signs of real sensitivity, and she didn't see any reason why he couldn't get into Cal Poly year after next, if he tried; to which you had responded, as blandly as you could so as not to arouse suspicion, that you had also heard San Diego State was nice.

You were imagining Jesse, your son, now almost grown, getting far away enough from Michael to be safe.

†††

BECAUSE HE WAS ALMOST GROWN, you wrote. That's the thing about it that made it worse. Just one more year and he might have saved enough money to move out; just one more year with his eyes on the goal line. You felt personally invested in this vision, because you had missed your chance, you thought. Efforts to leave always came to nothing and made matters worse, but it didn't really matter, because you'd had your fun.

I did not feel, sitting on the floor of my house in Milpitas, that it was fair or accurate to say that you, in the years of your life since you'd met Michael Jenkins, had had your fun. You had raised a child you loved fiercely but could not protect from the violence of his father; you had learned to shrink before Michael's anger rather than resist it, because resistance carried with it the risk of disproportionate response; you had seen the careful, methodical demolition of your every effort to carve out a small space for your own personal pleasure or growth. Coffee with friends, Tupperware parties, Avon errands—their costs had all been too great to pay over and above your daily toll. You lived in waiting: for something to happen, who could say what, that might give you relief.

But it was going to be worth it, you said, to know that you had done your best, even though, back then, you often heard a voice in your head asking whether that was really true; a mocking voice, your own but meaner, that interrogated you while you lay awake sometimes. He's so big now, the voice said. Too late to help now, the voice said. You knew these were only your own thoughts, and you understood them as expressions of guilt or shame and not the judgment of the outside world: you weren't crazy. But it just felt so bad, to lie there sometimes, wondering if the mocking, dismissive distance your son now kept from you was your fault, another mark against you, an indication that the hateful things Michael said to you when he was angry—which was all the time; he never got better now— were all really true.

All of this got about a thousand times worse, you said, on the morning after the night Jesse didn't come home.

†††

YOU HEATED UP A CAN OF BEEF STEW for Michael the following morning, you remembered. The smell of it still stuck in your brain even down to the present day, a sense memory too powerful to shake. Michael was furious, seated in his chair in the living room, yelling now at the television and now over at you, preparing himself for direct confrontation. You had called the cops, both because you were terrified that something had happened, and because Michael was afraid of the police. A call to the department would leave you with at least one chip in hand, one you couldn't actually wager but which sat there on the table, visible to your opponent for as long as the game lasted. It wasn't much, but it was something.

Michael kept right on yelling as you gave them the details: that you had last seen Jesse getting into his friend Gene's car yesterday afternoon; that he'd missed dinner; that he hadn't told you he was intending to go anywhere with anyone; that there hadn't been any major changes or arguments recently— all this was true; the mood in the house had been one of relative calm, if not comfort. Yes, yesterday afternoon, you said again. Right outside, right here. He was getting into Gene's car.

The more you told them, the more agitated Michael became. You knew that part of what was bothering him was the noise; his hearing wasn't as good as it used to be, probably from all the loud machines at his work, and he didn't like to have to turn up the television, whose speaker distorted when the volume got too high. He directed his anger at the absent Jesse for the time being; he yelled that a son shouldn't treat his mother like shit. He said "shit" so many times, you said. You pivoted on your feet in the hope that you could direct the mouthpiece of the phone sufficiently out of the path of his voice, but you knew the operator would hear everything. Fear and shame and panic, the feeling that you'd lost control at last and would now be forced to bear witness to the extent of your failure. Years of trying. It was so much for you to hold.

"Please," you said to the operator, trying to tune Michael out.

"I'm going to hand you over to Detective Haeny," the operator said to you, and you felt the muscles in your jaw tighten as they sometimes did when you knew Michael was about to hit you, which was something, you said, that you had sometimes tried to get control of, because you had heard someone say on a TV show that things hurt more when you are tense, but people who say things like that probably don't know what it's like to be under any actual pressure. They are talking about something else.

You listened. Michael watched your face for signs. You put the receiver back in its cradle, conscious of your feet underneath you, holding you upright.

"They say we should go to the station. I can do it," you told Michael, mechanically, directly, like an engineer who, her instruments all indicating disaster, finds the known center where all the knowledge of her training waits. Perhaps sensing a shift in the energy of the moment, hearing you speak with uncharacteristic confidence, Michael looked at you with an alien gaze: It was respect, maybe, you thought. Or fear of the unknown. Or of the police. Who knows where it came from. It was enough to allow you to get into the car and drive.

You had learned in the years since, you said, that sometimes you get just enough of whatever it is that you need in order to go on to the next thing, no matter how bad it is.

†††

I KNOW NOW that it's never going to be possible to make you understand, you began again in your letter, your letter which I had spent several days reading and whose end, I knew, both from recognizing where we now stood in the story line and from the diminishing number of pages left to read, was near. I know this was all a waste and possibly even bad for me, you said, because I am usually OK these days, as OK as I can be, Michael's gone now, Bobby lets me talk about him if I need to, in the end I finally found someone who cares about me and wants to protect me, isn't that incredible, sometimes I can't believe it, you wrote. But now, when I'm telling the whole story, it's not making me feel better at all, it's not taking weight off my shoulders, it's putting more on, more and more the further I go, and I can't stand it, I don't think I can stand it. But I told myself when I started this that I had to finish, so I am going to finish, and if it's bad for me, then I guess I will get better. But I am going to tell you what I have wanted to tell you. Are you even still reading this? Please say yes, you wrote.

I said "Yes" out loud in my house in Milpitas, a place where two people had been murdered in darkness by an assailant with a sword, which was the story I had moved into the house to tell. My new story, my new book.

This is the thing that you have to understand, you wrote.

†††

THE FIRST CIRCLE OF HELL was the process: it was clear to you that procedures were the most important thing to the police, but they weren't the most important thing to you. What was important to you was why they had asked you to come talk to them, why they were asking about Gene Cupp's car, and what did they know about where Jesse had been all night, and where was he now. "We think we have a lead on where he went" was as direct an answer as you got from either of the detectives at first; they kept finding ways to not answer you directly. It made you feel like they thought you were stupid and couldn't see what they were doing, which was something you were used to in your everyday life, but had the effect now of increasing your agitation a little with each passing moment, of deepening the reserve of dread whose membranous confines, you thought, surely would not be able to hold much longer, as, in wave after wave, the fear kept rushing in. They asked question after question about Jesse: had he been having problems in school; did he have close friends, and, if he did, what kind of people were they; and, if he didn't really have friends, how did he like to spend his free time; what was his life like at home; had he met anybody new lately, maybe somebody he'd been spending a lot of time with; had he been acting strangely, or had anything unusual at all happened, some change in his routine, anything out of the ordinary.

It felt like they would never stop, like they would never run out of new ways to ask the same questions, one officer taking notes while the other nodded as you answered, offering a little assurance now and then as they walked you through the paces, each step of which felt like an endless, barren expanse, even if everybody was being nice enough: treating you with kid gloves, you realized, when clarity finally came.

Clarity came in the form of Jesse's necklace, a silver chain with a tear-shaped turquoise chip dangling from the middle. He wore it every day; his father hated it and made cruel remarks about it, and made ugly insinuations about who might have bought it for him, and why. You liked Jesse's necklace; it looked good on him, and, when he wore it, you felt like you were catching a glimpse of how he might carry himself when he was all grown up: when he became his own man at last, walking around in the world on his own. It was in a plastic bag now on a table in front of you, alongside a paper tag with some numbers written on it.

"Does this belong to your son?" Detective Haeny asked, and you put your hand over your mouth and screamed through your fingers, and felt, in that moment, like the best possibility available to you would be to just keep screaming and never stop, to produce a scream so great that it enveloped and consumed the evidence bag, and the officer holding it out to you, and the land, and the sea, and the sky, to scream and scream until the screaming somehow killed you; because, if you stopped, worse things than any of these would be waiting out there in the quiet, the rapidly gathering quiet that palpably stood ready to open up for you like a dark, endless cave from which you would never be free.

7.

A CAVE I will never, ever get out of, you said: your exact words. A cave that probably has other people in it, maybe a lot of them, and sometimes you think you can hear them around you or behind you or ahead of you, talking, crying, pounding on the walls, but you can't be sure because the pain is making you crazy, and to be crazy is to have more noises in your head than usual. A cave that can disguise itself as a morgue, or a coroner's office, or a courtroom, or a bedroom, or the bathroom, you said: a cave you carry around with you like a chair you have to sit in wherever you go, and, to everybody else, it just looks like a normal chair, but to you it's the top of a slide, and every time you sit down on it you head down into the depths.

It's stupid to talk about which part of anything could really be the worst part when the thing you're talking about is that somebody murdered your son, stabbed him thirty-seven times with an oyster-shucking knife, stabbed him in his face and in his throat and in his chest and in his arms and in his stomach and on his hands, which he was probably using to try to protect his face, his beautiful face, but she got him there, too, nine times there, they said. And you were lucky, you wrote, they hadn't said "lucky" but it was only obvious that was what they meant, that she hadn't been able to finish cutting both of them apart, otherwise they might not have been able to find all the pieces, the remaining pieces of your son Jesse and his friend Gene, Gene who was always nice to you no matter what people said about him, nobody ever gave him a chance, they talked about him like he was trash but how could he help it, and now he was dead, pieces of him all mixed up in the same garbage bag with Jesse, and you were supposed to feel lucky that they'd even been able to get together enough body parts to make an identification; and that was the first worst part, the part that made you begin to apprehend the dimensions of the cave: the details.

Because they were trying to spare you the worst of the details, they said; but it was also their job to tell you, for the investigation. What investigation? What did anybody need to investigate? The world is so full of people who see what's going on right in front of their faces, you wrote, but they don't do anything, police, teachers, your own family, they see and maybe they give you a sad look, but you can take that sad look down to hell with you if you're ever lucky enough to get there, to get out of this awful place and at least be free, but that was all fairy tales anyway as far as you were concerned, there was no way any of it was true, you hated to say it, on good days you didn't feel this way at all anymore but today you did, and you wanted me to hear it, to see, to know what it was like except that I would never actually know, because for me all the details were just part of my stupid story, something I did for money, or to show people how smart I was, or who really knows why, but for you the details were like markings on a blueprint, each of them indicating just how much there was to know about the space where you would have to live for the rest of your life, how many things there were to learn that nobody would ever want to learn and which would never leave you once you'd learned them, things which would give you nightmares, and headaches, and would train you to respond to stressful situations in ways that never helped, only hurt, learned responses that made everything worse and made you feel like your mind was your own worst enemy, and who could you turn to if not yourself when all you had ever had was yourself, yourself and Jesse, the one person in this world you'd been able to look at for seventeen years and say, That is a sweet person, he deserves better than what this world has given me, but instead he was lost in the cave now, and you knew you would never find him.

You would never find him: because there was no cave, it only felt like one, you weren't crazy, you said, you just felt crazy because it was too much to take, too much, you said. You screamed when the officer showed you his necklace and they brought you a blanket, that's what they do when people are in shock, they give them a blanket, do they think we are babies, but you remembered the blanket, and a paper cup of cold water, and sitting in a wooden chair sipping it while the officers bore witness to your rapidly numbing affect, too much, what next, they had already asked their questions because they knew this would happen, how were you going to tell Michael, what would he do.

You couldn't tell Michael. He wouldn't know how to handle it, he only knew how to be angry, he would be angry at you, he would beat you until he broke something, he would punch a cop and get taken to jail, how were you supposed to figure this out when the pressure inside your head was like a shaken-up soda can; but then they told you that they had already sent a police cruiser to get Michael now that you'd identified the body, easier that way, and you didn't know how to feel, because there wasn't any room for any other feelings besides the pain, and the horror, and the rage, why had she done it, that bitch, Jesse never hurt anybody in his life, he was the one who always got hurt, and now he was dead, every time you came back to it you couldn't make yourself believe it, because you didn't want to believe it, but at the same time you kept trying to get there, you didn't know why. Instinct. What good had your instincts ever done you, you wrote, they were worthless, you couldn't trust them, but you were trusting them one more time, just this once, to tell me this, to see if I was a human being instead of a monster.

Instead of a monster, you wrote at the top of a page near the end of your letter. The rest of that page was blank. I closed my eyes and tried to picture you as you might look in the present day, older, greyer, a little closer to the end of a journey whose pleasures had been few and far between: and the face that came through in my efforts seemed real and alive to me, alive in a way I found somewhat frightening, since I spend most of my days imagining people who once lived and breathed squarely within the confines of the space where I sit and write. And I think I do a good job—I have a method—but this was different.

† † †

A PERSON'S SENSE OF TIME gets turned inside out when their whole world gets taken away from them, you said, so you had a hard time connecting the dots from moment to moment when it came time to tell the story of how everything happened after that. There were parts you still couldn't write down words about, big parts, the main parts, really, and it was making you feel so small and weak that you couldn't do it, especially since you still had to see everything so vividly in your head, all these years later; but of course how could a person forget seeing the sight of their own son with parts missing, carved off like limbs from a hunted animal. They had put the parts together on a table, and you only looked at them for one split second before the screaming started again. By that time they'd brought Michael in, he wasn't so tough now, he was scared, scared of the police and the police station and the photographers outside and the reporters yelling questions at him, and he cried: you had only ever seen him so shaken once before, the first time he came back after you left, and the connection you'd once felt to him awakened just long enough for you to hold each other in a way you hadn't since you both were young: but even in that moment, you'd known it was nothing, nowhere near enough, Scotch tape on a burst pipe, not even a cosmetic fix.

You both stayed at the police station, you said, for the rest of your lives, because, when you left, who knows how many hours later, your lives were over: your lives together, and your individual lives; Michael's in a real way, because he never recovered and was dead now, cirrhosis, he had been unable to bear Jesse's death and was never sober again a day in his life, and yours, too, because you had to see everything through to honor Jesse's memory, you couldn't just pick up a bottle and disappear into it, you felt bad enough about the sleeping pills but you needed them and that was all there was to it, unless people know what it's like to lie in the dark remembering their dead child's body they can hold their tongues about what people do to deal with their own pain, but the life left to you was even less of a life than you'd had before as the punching bag for a guy you'd had a crush on in high school, because now the person for whom you existed couldn't feel or see or benefit from your efforts in any way, and yet you couldn't let go.

Did I understand what that felt like, you asked? Of course I didn't. I didn't even try to understand. For me, you were only a figure to be moved around—I was just like Michael in this way—you were useful to me when you were at the stove taking a call from the detectives, you were useful to me on the witness stand speaking your truth to Diana Crane and demanding that she hear it, you were useful to me when you screamed. You, your whole life, all the parts that went into making you who you were, were only useful to me so that I could write my book, but the truth of your life barely grazed the surface of it, just the juicy parts, the blood and the guts and the action. The parts that you wanted to forget, you said, were the only parts that counted for me.

To Diana Crane I had given my best: I named the book after her, the book was her story, and the thing that went wrong in her story was Jesse and Gene; and that was true, you said, and if I said you didn't know that, then I was a liar, but how could I ever see this through your eyes? How could I know what it was like for a teenage girl to have a baby boy and to do her best all her life for her child, but to never be good enough, never be strong enough, never be smart enough, and then to see her son grow into a teenager and begin to slip away, and to hope, you didn't want to say "pray," you knew better, that he could at least get out on his own and find a way for himself? You had gone to every parent-teacher conference, you had made his birthday special every year with wrapped presents and homemade cakes and a card you always signed *from your mother, who loves you*; you had tried to keep your connection alive. Where was this in my book? Where was Jesse at all? The same place he was in the movie I let them make: wandering around like a pig waiting to be yelled at and beaten and stabbed in the heart and roasted on a spit, living a worthless life whose only purpose was to be sacrificed for somebody else's story.

But he could have had his own story, you said. You had tried to heal yourself by telling yourself that story sometimes, by sketching out a life for him in a world he would never see. Graduating from high school. Going to Cuesta, maybe becoming an engineer. He was always a smart kid, you said. Teachers loved him and he worked hard. One more year and he would have been there, and from there he could have gone anywhere, Los Angeles or Boston or New York, any place in this whole world. And then you would have said it was all worth it: all the worry, and all the yelling, and all the bad nights, and all the bruises, worth it to see this good kid who never hurt anybody finally getting what he deserved from this world; and you could have grown old knowing that you'd done this one thing right, standing by your son, believing in him, who might not have looked like much at seventeen but who had potential.

Potential that in fact no one would ever know about now, potential erased from the world. Potential I might have at least talked about for a minute in my stupid book before leading him from the parking lot of those awful apartments up to her door like a dumb lamb to slaughter. Just a kid. He didn't know how dangerous Gene was and he needed someone in his life who liked him, somebody besides his own mother. You knew Jesse had anger for you: he was mad because you couldn't protect yourself, and you understood. You understood why he had become so distant, and it hurt so bad. The way he walked right past you during that last year or two. But what was he supposed to do, when it was you, you who had made the mess and couldn't pull yourself out of it, you who seemed to have given up on life, you who couldn't find the strength to shield him from the rancid world Michael had made of your home. And so he drifted into Gene's orbit and never came out, your final view of him that of a handsome young man who might have been headed down the wrong path, but didn't everybody have the right to make mistakes sometimes, a handsome young man only a few steps away from a future in which he might finally have been free—free to be the sweet person you knew lived within him, he whose sweetness had been a comfort in a cold world, he who only ten years before he got cut into pieces and taken down to the ocean to be dumped into the tides had still been your baby, you said, so desperate for help that he told his teachers his father was a bully, so lonely that anyone who showed him kindness became his favorite person in the world, so hungry for friendship that he was a sitting duck for a boy like Gene Cupp. Did I really think ten years was a long time, you said. It's not. It's nothing when you are his mother. It is the blink of an eye during a commercial break, you said. That's how short a time you got to know your son before she took him from you. But you knew, you said. You knew how short a time ten years is, and how easy it was for me to make that whole time, so precious to you, look ugly, worthless, pointless. But Jesse's life had been good sometimes, it had value and he deserved to live and you deserved to still have a son and I didn't care, I only cared about the bad parts, how could I, how could I, did I understand at last what I had done to you, twisting a knife that had been stuck in your stomach since the day your son was killed, how could I.

7

Chandler

1.

LIFE IS A PROCESS of forgetting: of moving old things out of the way to make room for new things, of holding faded blueprints up to light to see where vanished angles might be hiding, of recalculating wants and needs on the fly. It's not that we become forgetful as we age, though that's true, too. It's that a million things will need to be forgotten along the way if our later forgetfulness is to have any meaning.

I know the house where I was a child in San Luis Obispo was initially much smaller than it became during our time there. My father built an addition after we'd become established in town; he needed room for a piano, a stereo, a desk, and maybe some cushions for people to sit on. It was a grand room, with high ceilings and redwood beams. I remember its newness; all that fine red wood overhead, and a high window against which branches of a plum tree pressed after leafing out in summer. But I can't remember the house as it was before the big front room got added onto it, I find; there's a gap.

The same is almost true of our street in San Luis Obispo,

but not quite. It's not a long street, though, to me, it once seemed nearly endless; but all streets must seem fairly long to children, whose short legs take longer to walk from one end of the block to the other. Just past our house, it dips sharply; then it loops right onto a parallel street, which itself has another street in parallel just past a second loop, three streets like tines of a fork. Anything beyond there registered as *elsewhere* for me, even places just a block or two farther on. They repaved it at some point in my early years; I remember the day they did it, but I can only recall how the street looked afterward. The before-time is lost.

I recognize all this now as mapmaking. Improvements and modifications come and go, and all terrain shifts; we reconfigure our coordinates. We make erasures to accommodate new data; these erasures are permanent. We left this neighborhood sometime after I turned five, though my father remained; the streets I see in memory are almost certainly the streets as they looked just before the divorce. Most of their features were once new—this is California—but to me they still smack of the eternal. The plum tree, its fruit rich and sweet. The willow on the corner, whose rubbery strands we skinned and used as whips. The slope of the hill in our backyard, wild honeysuckle climbing it to the pasture beyond. And the house of the Mean Man, with its dry lawn out front and a rusty horseshoe in a yellowed window facing the sidewalk, halfway down the street.

†††

GAGE CHANDLER LIVED OVER ON RAMONA, on the middle tine of the three-street fork that made up our neighborhood. His family moved in when he and I were toddlers. The Chandlers were old California stock, and arrived to our street fresh from the other side of town, where they'd been living the simple life until, as their only child grew larger, their bungalow began to feel cramped.

My mother remembers their arrival; she was on the local welcoming committee, which delivered gift baskets. Realtors do that now, I think, and nobody does it at all if you rent, but old habits still held sway back then. Mom, Judy Miller, and Lydia Caporale gave the Chandlers a week's time to settle in, and then they all walked over and knocked on the door one morning, fresh pastries and coupon books in hand; I tagged along, as I always did.

I was two and a half, Mom tells me. Gage was my size, and only a few months younger. We spotted each other immediately through a forest of grown-up legs, and were inseparable for the next few years. He was my first best friend: there were other kids on the block, but we played together almost every day—first in parallel play, as two-year-olds do, and, over time, learning what interests we shared: windup motorcycles, climbing hills, digging with shovels. The last of these got us into trouble once: we'd wrangled a spade from a gardening closet, and dug in my backyard til we hit water. We must have gotten into some trouble, but I remember the incident of the big hole in the backyard as mainly a success: Gage got excited watching the water bleed in as we dug. It was contagious.

It was Gage who, when we were a year or two older, passed on the legend of the Mean Man to me. I suspect that the reach of this legend ended about three blocks away from Gage's door, but it held the allure of ancient myth: when we'd walk past the Mean Man's house, Gage would find some detail to indicate the threat that lay within. His gifts for locating new features in a relatively drab landscape were considerable.

The house itself was unremarkable—California ranch, like

almost everything else on the block, slapped-on stucco in simple earth tones: sun-bleached yellow, mustard-brown. The lawn in front was also brown: creeping dichondra was popular on our street, and whoever lived in the Mean Man's house had gone with the flow at some point, but hadn't kept it up. The dead vines made a sort of fairy-tale carpet leading to his door.

We all knew about the White Witch from talk on the playground. But the White Witch was two towns over and a world away. The Mean Man, on the other hand, was practically right next door. If a threat could be conjured, then that threat would seem real. We avoided stepping on his dead lawn; if I was walking alone, I'd cross the street to avoid it.

Whatever specific acts of meanness were supposed to have earned him his reputation were shrouded in mystery; the meanness was a specific threat in itself, an energy that might land on you if you failed to take precautions. Don't trick-or-treat at his house. Don't dip your bike in and out of his driveway like you might with any other wide driveway on the street. Don't try to read the bumper stickers on his car. I was a bookworm; telling me not to read something guaranteed that I'd read it: GET U.S. OUT OF U.N.! the sticker said. Gibberish; a profound mystery.

I was afraid of him. Everything about his address throbbed with menace. Every time Gage would reveal, or invent, some new detail—*he yelled at me for stepping on his newspaper, it was right there in the middle of the sidewalk; a baseball rolled into his yard and he came out through his door in a robe, picked up the ball, and went right back inside with it*—the tension between the Mean Man's aura and the mundane nature of his malevolence would rise. Fear, at the right reach, is delicious. Once, through the front windows, I saw someone inside, possibly in a reclining chair, watching television. I averted my eyes and quickened my pace. I had this idea that Mean Men hate nothing more than finding that someone is staring at them.

Gage and I were fast friends, sometimes almost insepara-ble, and I luxuriated in his visions of shadowy threats never farther off than our voices could carry. If you let Gage set the terms of engagement, you could ride currents of myth all day, and dream terrifying dreams when you fell asleep. It was a fun way to be a kid on a sleepy street.

My parents divorced when I was five, and my mom remar-ried and we moved away, south of San Francisco; and that, until recently, was the end of those times for me.

2.

OUR HOUSE IN MILPITAS was a duplex. One of its rooms had an electric fireplace, with a plastic log that glowed orange when you flipped a wall switch. Inside the log was some rotating element to give the illusion of the movement of flame, but the entire appara-tus was for mood: it didn't generate any actual heat. On the day we moved in, I was thrilled by its novelty; I remember my mother and stepfather exchanging glances of pity over my excitement at this chintzy feature of the best place they'd been able to afford.

Gage's letters arrived about once a month for the first year of my two-year tenure in Milpitas. It is a strange feature of the partial amnesia that blots out stray spans of time in my mem-ory that I remember nothing about my sixth birthday except a card from Gage. I'd made new friends in town; there must have been a party, my mother was a natural at kids' parties. But the whole day, in my memory now, exists only for the remem-bering of Gage's reports from home.

He always talked about a time when we'd meet again, when

we'd be able to compare notes on our lives: which TV shows were cool (the *Planet of the Apes* weekly series) and which weren't, no matter who said otherwise (*Emergency!*); what candies were keepers (Fun Dip, also known as Lik-M-Aid; Wacky Wafers) and which ones you traded for the keepers because some people had bad taste (Jolly Ranchers, excepting, occasionally, the cinnamon and watermelon flavors). I would write back, hoping my life seemed more exotic than it was.

I lacked Gage's gift for the through line, but I scored a few points here and there. The monster movie being filmed in town, about a creature who ate all the garbage cans (*The Milpitas Monster*); the 45 rpm record of its theme song that I played on my small stand-alone record player. My orders from the Scholastic Book Club, always aspiring a grade or two above my actual comprehension. The small black-and-white TV that my mother and stepfather allowed me to keep in my bedroom after they bought a color TV for the living room.

The TV was a big deal. I considered myself a book person, but every kid in the seventies knew all the action was on TV. I wrote Gage about the obscure pleasures of staying up late with the sound down low, discovering movies like *The Crawling Eye* and *Twisted Brain*; he told me about *Ellery Queen Mysteries* and *Night Gallery*. After a year, a month between letters became six weeks, and then eight. We kept our connection alive, but childhood is a busy place, and my new town had stories of its own to tell.

†††

I MET DARLA when she was even newer to the block than me; she lived in the duplex opposite mine. Her father was in the military, or had been; I have only the vaguest visual memory of him, standing in front of their unit on a sunny day, his hair neatly cropped. Most of the grown-up men in my orbit looked like professors or hippies. For me, Darla's dad stood out.

We walked to and from school together sometimes. She loved to tell stories, tall tales in which everybody or almost everybody died. I remember most vividly one in which a curse, or possibly a ghost, ended up causing a woman's leg to swell to twenty or thirty times its natural size—a woman who'd heard one day of the curse, or the ghost, and said aloud to all who cared to hear that she didn't believe in it.

The next morning, she was found dead, her gigantic leg having broken down the door to her house from the inside. That was all there was to it—the rumor of the hex, and its effect; Darla's stories tended to orbit one or two gruesome details, and she insisted that this one was local, a woman who'd lived down the street.

"That's not true," I said on the morning she told me this tale. "That thing with her leg, that didn't happen."

"All my stories are true!" she said in response, making sure I saw the fierce determination in her eyes; this is among my most vivid recollections of Milpitas, of its sidewalks and rounded curbs in grey concrete, the secluded feel of its neighborhoods imparting just the right air for wondering whether a thing had happened this way, or that way, or some third way not yet imagined, or perhaps not at all.

†††

OUR HOUSE GREW CHAOTIC; not all houses are built to protect the people inside them. For a season we lived with my father in San Luis Obispo again, weighing our options. I was old enough to get an allowance—a quarter—which I spent on two-cent candies and packages of stickers or trading cards. Wacky Packages were new and hot. Any boy whose bike didn't sport several stickers was out of touch.

Gage even had the big poster, the one you could get by saving up twelve wrappers and sending in two dollars; I admired it the first time I saw it after moving back to town.

"I know," he said, "but they had something even cooler than Wacky Packages a while ago. Check it out." He dug around in a bulging box of old toys and Super Balls until he found a repurposed Band-Aid tin. Inside were cards with scenes from horror movies—vampires, mad scientists—captioned by Borscht Belt one-liners ("Look Ma, no fillings," a vampire's mouth agape, her fangs dripping blood). There was a woozy gravity in the moment. I'd been away for almost two years, but we were still the same boys who used to play "Frankenstein's Revenge" in the driveway—a game in which one plays the monster, pulling at imaginary chains that bind him to the garage door, while the other plays the scientist or his misshapen assistant, mocking and tormenting the creature until all hell breaks loose.

"I've never even seen these," I said.

"They're from England. They had ten packs at Rexall. I got three."

It was only a shared exchange between old friends, still young, but it confirmed that our growth had traced similar arcs in my absence. I did not, at the time, have the language with which to describe what the renewal of this bond meant to me: how it connected me to a safe place beyond the disorder that had stealthily taken over the reins in my family's life.

We were gone by mid-August. I am unclear on the details; I was a kid. Gage and I kept up correspondence for at least two years; we had both grown old enough to be dropped off at a movie theater for a couple of hours on a Saturday, and we'd send each other reviews of what we'd seen.

At some point we fell out of touch, and somewhere along the line I lost his letters. Of course, I heard all about his success later on. At supermarket checkout counters nationwide, his name, for several years, was a hard one to miss. It was a welcome beacon from lost years for me. In the flashy typography of his books' titles and in their eye-popping front covers, I sensed that he was the same person I'd known back then; and this was a comfort to me. Our visions may flare or recede according to the errands of our lives, but they remain.

It would be years until we met again. My family moved, then moved again: five times in eight years. Gage became a remembered figure from early childhood. That our friendship had been hardy enough to survive the initial sundering was something of a miracle, I see now. Making new friends grows harder when you don't stay put; I learned, at my third new school in three years, that I had formed a mistrust of groups. I preferred the company of one friend to hanging around with a bunch of classmates. Your earliest friends hold a place of privilege in memory. As I began pursuing a solitary path heading into junior high, I would remember Gage, and wonder how he was: what sort of friends he had now, and whether we'd still be friends, given the chance. I always pictured him in the same house, safe and secure. Leaving and returning from the same doorstep, days turning into years. Growing into the person he'd always meant to become. A figment of my imagination, I understand now, but we imagine things because we need them.

3.

IT WAS ABOUT ELEVEN YEARS LATER. My life had no discernible direction—I was drifting. Sometimes the drift went nowhere, and sometimes it headed for dark waters; there had even been a point, just a year or two earlier, when it would have seemed to any onlooker that I was idling haphazardly toward any of several early graves. Every affirmative choice I made whittled down my options a little. Every good chance I got I squandered.

It was like that for a while, and then it wasn't: if we get lucky, we emerge from our valleys. One autumn there was a movie in theaters called *River's Edge*. A time of moral panic was in ascension, and *River's Edge*, though a good and complex movie, heralded the rising of the curve. It was about a teenager who strangles his girlfriend to death and leaves her body in some brush by a river; his friends, who all knew the dead girl and numbered her among their own, see her body with their own eyes but tell no one.

Any teenager who sees *River's Edge* begins registering objections as soon as Samson tries to purchase a lone can of beer instead of a six-pack, but most viewers will overlook a botched detail or two in the service of having their biases confirmed: *the youth of today have no values; moral rot consumes them.* There is, among the public, a perennial urge to believe the worst about the generation that will eventually replace them.

I knew about this urge firsthand: Diana Crane's case had been hot currency on the playgrounds of San Luis Obispo. Those days had been on my mind. Browsing in a Montclair mall bookstore recently, I'd seen, prominently displayed, *The White Witch of Morro Bay*, by Gage Chandler. The byline seemed to sort of float in the air in front of me when I saw it. I'd only ever met one person named Gage in my entire life. It had to be him.

I couldn't afford the hardback, so I made a mental note to check out a copy from the library. But I was not, at the time, a person often found browsing the stacks. Various other errands on which I spent my days had a tendency to erase any other thought not directly connected to them. So I didn't think about *The White Witch of Morro Bay* again until a few years later, when they made the movie. It premiered on a Friday night after an extensive ad campaign of billboards and thirty-second TV spots around Southern California. By Monday morning everybody everywhere was talking about the movie based on a book by my childhood friend.

† † †

THE OTHER THING I knew about *River's Edge* was that the crime that had inspired it took place in Milpitas, the small town where I'd lived for two years as a child. I remembered reading about the murder of Marcy Renee Conrad; I was fourteen years old when it happened. Milpitas had receded into the mists of childhood. Still, sitting at the dining room table in Claremont, leafing through the *Los Angeles Times* and feeling sophisticated about it, I wondered: What if, in some imaginary timeline in which staying in that house had been not only viable but safe, we'd stayed? Would I have known these kids who'd seen the body of their friend and agreed to keep it secret? What might I have done—turned tail and run to the cops, or stayed safe with the pack?

I wrote poetry as a teenager, endless poems—the poems themselves were terrible, but writing them made me feel powerful. I'd sit at a manual typewriter in my room, staying up late, lighting candles or incense, and generally cutting quite a figure. The day I read the newspaper story about the murder of Marcy Renee Conrad, I wrote five poems, all from the imagined perspectives of her friends—the Circle of Five, I'd dubbed them; there was an Arthurian echo in the story for me, friends who hope that their bond will protect them from the wiles of the world.

I threw these poems away twenty years later when I ran across them in a folder full of old writing, of course. Their only value was to connect me to my younger self, and my need for that connection was dwindling. I did not hear about the other Milpitas murders—the ones at Devil House in 1986, the ones that occurred just as *River's Edge* began making the festival circuit—until many years later. The town had, of necessity and in a very short period of time, developed a reflex for dealing with eventualities. They knew to turn away inquiries. People had learned how to say "No comment." They circled the wagons.

A little research reveals that the case did get a drizzling of national coverage, but these years were busy times for ugly spectacles. In Southern California alone, the McMartin preschool case started staking its claim on the top of the news hour as early as fall of 1984; Richard Ramirez, meanwhile, was drawing pentagrams on the walls of tract homes in Monrovia, and in Glendale, and in Monterey Park. In the Aztakea Woods of Northport, Long Island, there was Ricky Kasso, high on blood and angel dust, heaping dry leaves over the mutilated body of his friend, Gary Lauwers. I remember hearing about Sean Sellers in Oklahoma, stripping down to his underwear before shooting both his parents with a handgun; and about Robert Berdella, the Kansas City Butcher, who kept logs of the tortures he inflicted on his victims across extended periods of time: days, weeks.

I was emerging from that time in my life when I would have enthusiastically immersed myself in the details of stories like these. Such enthusiasms are like the tides; you can't usually fight them effectively, but you can learn to wait them out. I had learned. Gage's book did not pull me back in.

†††

SO I DIDN'T ACTUALLY SIT DOWN with *The White Witch of Morro Bay* until a few years later, when the movie they made from it came to broadcast TV. The stations treated its arrival to the airwaves as an event; the panic years were ebbing slowly, and television people had been among the first to note that nostalgia and an addiction to the news cycle were two sides of the same coin. I watched the broadcast—both nights; they divided the film at a key point in the action, and tacked on half an hour's worth of archival footage at the end of the second night.

I recognized the terrain in the background of that footage. It called out to me from behind the action—those low, brown hills of Central California, those tall palms that shaded the wide, lazy boulevards. This milieu, which the movie had tried without success to reproduce, had passed out of existence and could not be brought back to life, though the conjuring of it in set design seemed to awaken its memory in me like dormant bacteria.

The teenagers talking, passing their rumors along to the newscaster, shooting knowing glances at one another: these might have been the older brothers and sisters of my preschool classmates. Their secrets were my secrets, not in substance but in weight. The coded messages of their shared glances spoke, specifically, to me: not about the specifics of my life as it was playing out in its particulars, but about the architecture within that life, about the frame within which all the action occurred. We were from the same place.

Gage's book had been reprinted in anticipation of new interest; I bought a copy from a wire rack at a Thrifty. Several loose strands came together for me as I read. Most of what I took from it was tangential to its central aim, but that didn't matter to me. It was more talisman than treasure—I'm reasonably certain I only read through it from cover to cover twice—but it became a constant and familiar presence on my bookshelf, no matter how many times I moved house. The sight of it tethered me to something real in myself. The fashioning of an anchor is, for some of us, a lifelong errand. Mine traveled with me.

†††

THE WHITE WITCH OF MORRO BAY is a nostalgic book, and a personal journey. When I thumb through it, I'm looking for signposts: landmarks I half remember seeing from the backseat of my father's Chrysler, street names that might offer me a road back into the easier days of early childhood. These totems, when I find them in Gage's book, resonate at a frequency I find almost nowhere else. The Taco Bell with its outside firepit. The sign out in front of the Cork 'n' Bottle on Foothill Boulevard. Jordano's. The beach.

The scenes at the beach, especially, seemed to stick with me. Gage's family and mine had been to that very beach when we were both freshly out of our toddler days; I had fading Kodaks of the day in a shoebox somewhere, totems of a disappeared age. Gage's book, and any reemergence of his name in my field of vision, served as a conduit between where I'd landed in the world—grown-up, en route after some lost time to somewhere hopefully fairly uncomplicated but rewarding—and the times before in-between times, the Edenic glaze we often superimpose onto our memories of childhood.

I wondered if these scenes rode similar currents for Gage, and so I wrote to him. Why not? There was a New York address opposite the title page, I figured somebody must be in charge of forwarding mail. I didn't want to seem weird or intrusive, so I thought carefully about what to tell him—I limited the present day to a few details about my work and my family, and sketched a broader outline of the paths I'd traveled in the intervening time. Places I'd lived since he last heard from me. Chicago, Grinnell, Durham; Bavaria, briefly.

Gage wrote back about a month later to say that he'd actually spent several years living in the very town from which I used to write him all those years ago. He had stories to tell, he said, that he thought I might like, if I was at all like the kid he'd known long ago. He invited me to meet up with him sometime, if I should ever have an afternoon to kill in the Bay Area and didn't mind making a detour: he was back in San Luis Obispo, could I even believe it? He signed the letter with his name, an odd symbol that looked like a shield, and his phone number.

As it happened, I traveled through San Francisco at least once a year for business. It was a reliable stop, and I usually spent several days in town. And so I looked at my calendar, and we talked briefly over the phone to set coordinates, and I began making plans.

4.

ON THE MORNING I WOULD DRIVE down to see Gage, I left my hotel early and took a long walk. When I'm in San Francisco I stay in Japantown; I ambled down Post to Fillmore and went left, in search of a coffee shop. I was a kid the first time I went walking around in the Haight; that would have been 1979 or 1980. To me, at that time, the whole place felt like Shangri-La in eclipse: I wore my hair long, and favored loose-fitting shirts in dyed cotton. The vanishing age spoke to me, and the one just dawning looked a little too cool to hold an invitation with my name on it.

Of my younger time in the neighborhood, I remember record stores offering drug paraphernalia behind beaded curtains; stores that mainly sold incense and Tibetan imports; movie theaters that had couches instead of chairs, and whose concession stands offered brewer's yeast on your popcorn for an extra quarter. These places are all gone now; you can maybe make out the shapes they used to occupy if you squint.

I found a café where the menu was written in yellow and green chalk on an immense blackboard above and behind the front counter. My phone buzzed while I was thumbing through the *Chronicle*. It was Gage. He was in town; he had an idea. Specifically, what he said was:

couldn't sleep. drove up. I have an idea, where are you at

† † †

IT WAS GOOD TO SEE HIM. Seeing old friends address nagging questions about which we sometimes otherwise feel uneasy: Am I the same person I was when I was young? Are my earlier selves still safe somewhere inside me? Is there a thread somewhere that connects the past to the present, or is everything more chaotic than we'd like to think?

Everything is not more chaotic. Our younger selves are still around, waiting for somebody to invite them out to play. Our conversation hit a manic note early and stayed there; it was intoxicating. We remembered monster movies, and we remembered the regal stature of *Planet of the Apes*, above any other media franchise for an easy six months. He dredged up a few details I hadn't carried with me on my own journey—some game he said we played in his backyard that involved a moat and a defensive line of guards whose spears were tipped with poison—but there was, between us, a note of the real. I get paid to inhabit personae; it was nice to feel like I was easing into something whose outer existence could be confirmed by another living soul.

His idea, he said, had been that we'd go to Milpitas together, and I could show him the place from which I'd written to him when we were young, and he'd tell me about his own time there a little; and from there we'd continue to San Luis Obispo, and catch each other up on the events of the last— thirty-five years? Forty?

I had specifically left leeway in my schedule to extend my time; it takes years working a job that involves travel to learn what a gift flexibility can be. Why not, I said, it will be fun.

†††

IT IS DISORIENTING to inhabit, even momentarily, any space that has played host to one or more primitive drafts of the self you've now become. There can be pleasure in this, as in a reunion. There might also be fear, dread, horror: soldiers seeing old barracks, freed convicts driving past the prison on their way to work. To have left a place once is to have left something behind; by staying away, you can have the question of whether you do or don't want to see that thing again answered for you. But learning to stay away is a discipline; and I was reminded, as I set my navigation for the address of the duplex in which I had lived when I was seven years old, that the essential quality of any discipline is consistency in practice. It's easy to undo the entire effort. You just have to relax.

And, in fact, I had no problem remaining calm as we rolled down the freeway to Milpitas in my rental car. Gage navigated from memory, peppering me with questions about the brief season I'd spent in the town about which he'd written his next book—the book he'd been working on, he said, for quite some time now. Was I there when they built the freeway expansion? Did I have any recollection of any local scandals? Had I known a guy named Anthony Hawley?

The only people I knew were kids, I said.

Yeah, kids, Gage said.

I had no sense memories of the off-ramp, or of anything we saw on our way into town—or, if I did, they were strictly general: a vague feel for the terrain, an odd variant of déjà vu that didn't feel entirely trustworthy. It wasn't until he saw the name of the street I'd lived on when I was seven and told me to turn left onto it that the jolt landed. Although our time as a family here had not been a happy time, I had good memories of the place; I'd known a few close friends. We remember our childhood friends with fondness.

He pulled up in front of the place. The streets in Milpitas are slow, and my rented Toyota didn't really stick out. So this is monster theater? Gage asked me. Where's your bedroom?

It's in the back, I said, we can't see it from here; and I

flashed briefly on nights I'd stayed up late, watching movies I'd write letters to Gage about the next day. In the shelter of a glowing screen, after everybody else in the house is asleep, you can imagine yourself shielded from the hard realities of the outside world. Sometimes, if the movie you're watching is good enough, you can even suspend disbelief entirely, and discern some mystical quality of protection in the doings of the good guys, and the bad guys, and the monsters.

I have to say, I said, I hope this isn't too weird, but this is kind of special. Those letters about the monster movies, they were a connection for me back then.

Yeah, he said. We looked at the old duplex through the windows of the car. It was kind of ratty, but no worse than that. You learn to find the stories you need when you're a kid, right? You learn to find the stories you need.

†††

I CAN'T SAY what that moment meant for Gage—maybe something, maybe nothing—but for me it positioned us in relation to one another. For him, Milpitas had, until recently, been a place he'd only known about from secondary reports—secondary reports from the distant past, at that—and from the one time it made national news. For me it was a childhood home, albeit one inhabited only briefly. To gaze upon a childhood home through adult eyes is to engage in an act of disenchantment. Great doors grow small. Turrets vanish. Emblems fray. Even if the time spent within any given set of walls was, when the days are reckoned together, brief, it's in the nature of childhood to gild all surfaces it touches, to magnify things. One should revisit such places only after having done some hard calculations: What are we willing to trade for a clear view of things? What are the chances we'll regret the bargain later on?

These were my thoughts as we hit the highway again, bound for San Luis Obispo. Three hours to go. Three hours is a long time to spend in close company with someone you haven't seen since you were six, and if we hadn't taken the detour through Milpitas it might have been weirder: but now we had a nexus through which to direct our conversational passes, and the time flew by. We spent the hours establishing timelines, trying to trace a coherent arc across our paths. When Nixon resigned, were you still in Milpitas? No, that was during that weird summer when I was back in SLO, I only saw you two or three times: but was that the same summer when Evel Knievel jumped the Snake River Canyon? No, that was before you left. Before I left! I said. We saw that together? Neither one of us saw it, it was closed-circuit.

But I could swear—

Gage appeared to be listening for a specific frequency as he waited for me to finish my sentence.

It's weird, he said, how many things you might swear to, right? When it was actually different from what you remember, when you don't really know at all.

†††

GAGE DIDN'T LIVE ON OUR OLD STREET. He had his own place now; his mother lived a short drive away, still lived in their childhood home after all these years. He lived in a part of town of which I had retained no childhood memory: maybe I'd seen this neighborhood back then, but it wasn't part of the San Luis Obispo I carried around in my mind, so it seemed oddly unreal to me, like a simulation of a place I knew, a place newly hewn from a known quarry and dressed up to look vintage.

Behold the, uh, perilous keep of Chandler Castle, in all its, you know, pomp and splendor, he said as we got out of the car, in the same dry tone that seemed to be his governing note as an adult. It was somewhere between self-deprecating and grandiose, and his sentences tended to run together, riding a speech rhythm always a little ahead of its own beat. I'd noticed, as we spoke on the drive down, that I tended to agree with him reflexively whenever he came to a stop. Some combination of tempo and register seemed, tacitly, to demand this. It was a neat trick, if that's what it was.

I didn't really have a sense of what sort of pay scale a true crime writer could expect, but the job seemed to have panned out all right for Gage. Two bedrooms, a big living room with stone walls and redwood beams, and a backyard with a firepit. The movies buy this or do they pay writers better than I think? I said, kidding a little but also a little jealous. It was a nice place.

He laughed. Well, he said, I got this between booms, I guess, anyway it wasn't worth as much then as it is now, property's nowhere near as expensive here as it is in the city, but you're right, I do all right, they start cutting you bigger checks after you write a book that gets made into a movie, for sure, that's where the real money is, those guys get to call their own shots.

Still, I said, California real estate, the way I understand it there isn't really any cheap California real estate.

He sat down in one of his modern but comfortable-looking chairs and gestured for me to do the same. Yeah, that's about right, he said, on my beat people tend to stay close to home base, it's like there's a home field advantage to keeping your focus on places you already know a little. I got lucky with this place and my agent gets me pretty decent advances, we'll see if that trend continues if we ever come to an agreement about the monster over there. He pointed at his desk, nestled up against a window that looked out onto his backyard. Atop it were big piles of paper—printouts, it looked like—and several mini-towers of bulging manila envelopes stacked four or five high.

The monster, I said.

The thing I've been working on, he said, it's a whole thing, I'm at sixes and sevens, really, I was kind of hoping to talk to you about it, maybe get a, you know, second opinion. He made quotation marks in the air when he said "second opinion"; they drew me in.

I don't know if I'm really qualified, I said, but I'm curious.

Who's not qualified, he said, his tone still suggesting some familiarity I didn't yet share. I ought to have felt suspicious, I guess, but either I'm not sufficiently guarded about things, or Gage's disarming demeanor had a way of preempting my defenses. You want to go get a pizza?

Sure, show me to the bathroom first, I want to splash some water on my face, I said; and, washing my hands, I looked at my face in the mirror, trying to take stock of where I was and what was going on, enjoying an odd feeling of being, by virtue of Gage's vague remarks and gesticulations, *implicated* in something.

5.

IT'S WEIRD, GAGE SAID, all these memories you have of Milpitas are specific to a time that's ten-plus years *before* most of the stuff I know about, the stuff that's my *field*, right, and here he laughed. The field of Where'd They Hide the Bodies, right? We were at a pizza place, the spot our friends usually picked for birthday parties when we were kids: it was largely unchanged.

But *your* memories are entirely firsthand, he said, firmly planted on actual ground, you know. My Milpitas is a combination of news footage, and stories in newspapers, magazines, secondary sources, right, and the time I ended up spending there gets sort of superimposed on top of all that, or maybe the previous time gets overlaid onto mine; but anyhow, it's a sort of stereoscopic image that never fully resolves: and then there's *you*, and there's no way you knew I was writing anything about any of this when you just sent me a postcard out the blue, right?

No, I said, as I say, I did read *The White Witch* several times, there are so many things in there that feel so ancient to me, I don't know if I can explain it—like, things I know are real but feel like they come from a different world, a world I can vouch for because I lived there, too, am I making sense?

Ah, that's great, he said, thanks, like what stuff specifically? Just San Luis Obispo stuff?

Sure, yes, I said, but for example the witchy stuff, the astrology booklet she buys at Jordano's: hand to God, my mom bought stuff like that at that same Jordano's, my mom wasn't especially witchy but it was sort of in the air back then; and so when I first read that, it was like I could hear the buzz of the lighting in the grocery store, the specific hum, it was wild.

Oh, for sure, he said, the lost age, the more books I write, the more I notice how almost everything takes place in the lost age, the window just shifts, it's sort of disturbing at first but then it's kind of liberating.

I'm not sure I follow you, I said.

Well, King Arthur, right, the king and his castle, *les chevaliers de la Table ronde*, the old magician training up the boy king, all the myth and legend, that all happens in some weird before-time, right? Which is both childhood and the Garden of Eden, do you follow me, lost ages, but over time either the lost age gets too found to persist, or the window shifts, some other age gets lost so that the unlost age can finally get a little room to breathe—

He must have seen my eyes clouding over, because his face assumed the gentle look of a teacher who knows his students won't ever be as bright as he was when he was their age, and he said:

But just King Arthur, OK, let's start there, we all know good King Arthur, right?

Sure.

Presumably a lot of kings before him, right?

Well, I said, this isn't really my area, but—

Grant me that Arthur isn't the first king.

Granted, I said.

Cool, he said. Now picture him on his throne, with his court, right, where does he live?

In the castle, I said.

In the castle, he said, which is a structure not imported into England until after the Norman conquest, which is, at the earliest, five hundred years after the death of the best candidate we have for the historical Arthur.

So, no castle, no king? I said.

No, no, that's not the point of the lost age, he said. The point is that the king is still in his castle, but to *you*, he doesn't look like what you mean by *king*, and his castle doesn't look like a castle.

So what does it look like? I said.

It looks, he said, like a dirt mound somebody piled up in a real hurry overnight to protect a very small group of people from attack.

Devil House

†††

SO ANYWAY, THE MONSTER, HE SAID, I was going to tell you about the monster. The first thing was my editor, he's got three names—here Gage shot me a conspiratorial look implying a shared Californian suspicion of old-money pretensions—he wrote and said he'd come across some news story. *Multiple Murders in Milpitas.*

Multiple Murders in Milpitas, I said.

Yeah, yeah, he said, fish in a barrel, right? and I remembered *you*, and that kind of fired my imagination a little, you know, the dreams of children or whatever, right? Lost age. So my editor sent me the story, and I read it, and he was absolutely right, it was directly up my alley, because it was tethered to a specific site, this shuttered porn store, and some kids had been in there, using it as a sort of clubhouse but also, like, as a house, some of them lived there, maybe. So it wasn't just the place where something happened, it had its own history on top of that. Something about places, they speak to me.

They have an energy, I said.

That's right, he said.

But this case, though, I said, this isn't *River's Edge*? I saw that movie.

No, no, he said, that's actually part of what makes this one interesting, because it wasn't all that long *after* the Conrad case, that was the *River's Edge* vic, Marcy Renee Conrad, 1981. Also Milpitas, but different case.

Wow, yeah, I said, "vic," that's victim, right, I feel like I'm out of my depth.

Ah, everybody finds their depth eventually, he said. Our pizza arrived, steam rising from the bubbling cheese on top.

But this other one, he said, the one I'm presently in hot water about. It's during the so-called Satanic Panic. What little coverage I could find was extremely lurid and sensational, the sort of thing you'd think everybody would have heard more about, especially the sort of thing *I'd* think *I* would have heard more about, being that whole field is my beat, right, but Ashton's pitch was, "Move into the house," so I—

You moved into the murder house? I said.

Yeah, that was the whole plan, he said, taking a huge bite, like a very hungry person, and so that's what I did, and then I did the thing I do, you know, getting as many primary sources as possible, I'm like a bloodhound, I need the scent of blood on a swatch of a shirt before I can get my barking up to its proper volume. And I got my hands on some crime scene photos, unpublished stuff, and hotline tapes, and then I fixed up the house so it would look just like it had looked on the night the crime, or crimes, took place. And all the while I'm writing the book, right, there's an element of mystery involved, because there are two dead bodies and no criminal charges as far as I can tell, and—

He pulled himself up short then. His face relaxed into a look of worry, or sadness, I wasn't sure—both, probably—and he said: Look, when I get going about this, I go pretty far down the rabbit hole, I've been neck-deep in all this stuff for several years now, are you sure you want to do all this? We could just, you know, eat some pizza.

I took a long sip from the translucent red plastic cup full of generic cola over ice that I can never help ordering whenever I'm at a pizza place, and I said: No, I'm good, this is good, in for a penny, in for a pound, right, let's hear it.

†††

IT WAS A WEIRD PITCH in the first place, he said, because when you do what I do, people are always telling you what you should write about next, and half the time it's the same thing, you know, some ancient story wakes up for whatever reason and everybody gets reminded about it at the same time, and then somebody who's read one of my books will say to themselves, Hey, that one guy who wrote that other book might be into this, and they write me letters, or emails, now, it's both ways, but they get in touch, and even when the idea's cool, I usually feel like I don't want to be running with something somebody else picked up, I do my own research. And then most of the time the idea doesn't really actually feel like something I'd do: like, maybe it'll be bloody enough, I do tend to lean in on the blood, but there won't be the complications, the knots in the thread, the parts that make you feel like everything was sort of doomed to happen the way it happened, that's kind of my zone.

Frankenstein's Revenge, I said.

He looked hard at me, like a jeweler inspecting an opal for imperfections, and then, as the memory awoke for him, said: Exactly. Exactly. Wow, yeah. The whole point of the game is that the monster gets free, right? There's no game if he doesn't break the chains, we should have called that game "Frankenstein's Chains." So, yeah, when people send me something, a lot of the time I'm just, like, Cool, wild stuff, and I don't ever think of it again, but Ashton is a smart guy, very little of my stuff would be half as good as it is without these little gentle prods he gives along the way, innocent questions about character or whatever that end up pushing me in the direction that leads to the good stuff—and, just here, there was a bubble in his monologue, a ripple in the current of the low-level mania that seemed to be animating him, and he took a bite of pizza

and mumbled, with his mouth full: Good stuff, his eyes searching for something somewhere in the grain of the table.

The good stuff, I said, just to fill up the empty space in the
conversation while he chewed his food.

Yeah, he said, wiping his mouth with the paper napkin—it
was printed in checkered red-and-white, the way all Italian
restaurants seemed to prefer their décor when I was a kid. The
stuff that gets me going, anyway. So I read the story he sends
me, and he's right, it feels like exactly my thing, I worry a little
that I've already done the kids-slaughtering-the-grown-ups
thing a little, but it's also just the one clipping, there has to be
more to it, and besides, it's in Milpitas, and I remembered you,
and our letters, and—listen, writers are terrible people, everything's just material to us, it's nothing personal but I'm still
sorry about it, but the point is, I was thirty-seven years old at the
time, and the second I saw the word *Milpitas* in the story I felt
a very deep resonance, an echo from childhood, and I remembered you, how you used to write me about the movies you
were watching on the TV your parents let you keep in your
room, it was always monster movies, and it just set my mind
going, there was something *in* there, you know?

I remembered my small black-and-white television, and the
feeling of security when I'd watch it late at night: everyone else
in the house asleep, and me watching cheap but terrifying
B-movies by myself; and I thought about Gage's lost ages and
that maybe I gleaned a little of them.

Well, now, I said, I'll read that when you're done with it, are
you almost done?

Oh, I'm done, he said. It's sort of going through some major
growth pains right now, there are several problems with it, I
think it might end up running aground before it sees daylight.

It's hard to explain. You can read the manuscript I sent Ashton if you want.

We finished the pizza and I said I should be getting some sleep, my flight left the next afternoon and I had to allow for drive time. I've got a couch you can crash on, he said, and I said I'd probably better try to split a little distance between here and the city, I saw several Super 8s from the highway, and he said he understood, he'd spent some time on the road himself.

As we were saying good night on his front porch, he said, Wait here, and went inside for a minute. When he returned, he was carrying a wooden box that looked like something you might pick up at an auction or a yard sale. It was dusty but sturdy. There were no distinguishing marks or labels on it, save for the dings and scratches old things tend to pick up over time. It looked big enough to hold several dictionaries, big ones. Good luck, he said, you can send this back to me whenever, we're into much, umm, later edits now, I don't need it.

I flew home from San Francisco the next day on a half-empty plane with my mysterious cargo in the overhead bin.

6.

MY WIFE LOOKED ACCUSINGLY at Gage's wooden box when I brought it home: in my travels, I rescue things like Gage's box from dusty shelves around the world. All over our house lurk its wide-ranging brethren: matryoshka dolls, monster model kits, manual typewriters, old radios; big rocks, knobby sticks, over-sized chunks of glass sanded smooth; off-brand comic books no one remembers, and trade publications that I will never read. It would be fair to characterize me as a collector of paperweights that haven't yet learned their function. No, no, I said, this wasn't me, you remember I told you about my friend Gage, the writer, the guy I knew in San Luis Obispo, he sent me home with a draft of his new book, the box holds it.

And to demonstrate good faith, I opened the box, which spoke rather more convincingly to her case than to mine. Even the title page was a mess; it presently read DEVIL HOUSE, but the same page had borne six other titles beforehand— OGRE HOUSE, TITAN HOUSE, SPECTER HOUSE, FIEND HOUSE, and BEAST'S LAIR—all of them struck through in turn with a ballpoint pen. I'd have thought you'd just make a new title page if you changed the name of your book, but reasoned that this might have been part of his procedure—tracking changes, keeping a record of the book as it grew from its beginnings to its final form. Maybe he'd typed them all out on one page to see how they looked, then scribbled through the ones that weren't as good?

But there was more to it than that. There were several yellow Post-its on the very same page, the handwriting on them tiny and obsessive, running from margin to margin like the work of an annotator with too much to say—one was a list of American cities (*from: Boston, Austin, Santa Fe, Taos, Dallas, Seattle, San Francisco*), another I couldn't figure out at all (*Archis, Ainesh, Rohak, Sarva, Surya, Sonny*). In addition, there were two semi-rectangular patches where it appeared something had once been affixed with clear tape and then removed.

There was something troubling about it. I felt like I had a decent enough read on Gage; I knew his work, and had spent a very pleasant evening with him. He seemed fairly together. But what did I know, really, I said to myself—maybe everybody's manuscript looks like this on its way to publication.

You're going to send that back to him after you've read it, right? asked my wife.

Oh, of course, I said, he said there's no hurry, but—

Naturally there's no hurry, she said, laughing, you don't want to be in a hurry when you've got a—

A big box, I said. When you've been married as long as we have, you understand each other even when your priorities diverge.

Then I turned over a couple of pages, and we both saw that all the pages were like that, more or less: annotations, decorations, circled words, notes in the margins, several different colors of ink, little drawings, punctuation marks.

I'll send it back to him when I get done, we don't have room for this, nobody has room for this, I said, laughing along with her.

†††

I FOUND A SPACE on the basement floor where the box could live comfortably for a few days; our basement serves chiefly as an oversized closet. I keep guitars down there, and boxful after boxful of old compact discs, and a Nintendo 64 hooked up to an old television that sits on the orange desk that served as my workstation for the better part of a decade. Tons of stuff. Over by a small freezer, there's a ratty tatami mat that used to be a pretty nice tatami mat; if I have anything that needs to be glued together or painted, that's where I set up to work, but I hardly ever have any work of that sort to do. Like many abandoned spaces, it's an indicator of where somebody once saw some possibilities.

I set the box down squarely in the middle of the mat, where it began acclimating to its new surroundings, it seemed to me, in a real hurry: the floor beneath the mat is concrete that some-body painted blue once, years ago, but the paint has long since worn down to a dingy grey patina. Old dinged-up box, ratty mat, worn-down floor. Everybody harbors unscientific ideas about the workings of the world, I'd bet—about causality, and sufficiency, about the relative weights of presence and absence, about every old thing—superstitions, habits of thought that we seldom, if ever, acknowledge, even to ourselves. I try to be aware of mine. I'll put something on the lip of a bookshelf, or in a dish or on a coffee table, and then I'll think, or perhaps *feel* more than think: There, that's where that thing belongs, it lives there now; and this feeling is invariably so satisfying that it re-sults in half a dozen things always gathering dust on window-sills or end tables around the house, just because, when I last set them down, they seemed to have reached the place where they belonged.

It doesn't quite aspire to the condition of a credo, this feel-ing, though I obey it as if it were law. It's a sort of organizational principle. And so, when, four days later, after I'd fully reentered the orbit of home life and could steal a little time for idle inves-tigations, I went down the basement stairs and pulled the string that turns on the light above the tatami-mat work space, the sight of Gage's box felt like an inevitable presence, something I'd always been meaning to attend to, something that already had something to do with me.

It was a weekday, I remember, and the kids were both in school, and my wife was at work; midmorning.

I heard everybody get home a little after three o'clock; only then did I understand that I'd spent all day in Gage's book, sorting through the pages, and the footnotes, and the diagrams, and all the attached materials: the maps, the police reports, the newspaper articles, and the photographs; this outpouring of marginalia, this vast constellation of data floating atop a story Gage had been trying, for some time, to tell, all seeming to invite the reader's attention now very forcefully in one direction, and now, just as insistently, in another.

†††

IF *THE WHITE WITCH OF MORRO BAY* HAD BEEN a sort of anchor, *Devil House* was a great net cast into largely unfamiliar waters. The Milpitas about which Gage wrote was unrecognizable to me: I'd transferred schools in the middle of first grade, spent my second grade year basking in the light of a kind, old teacher named Mrs. Wyatt, and then we were gone. My range within the city limits had been largely confined to the street I lived on. I didn't, I realized as I read, really know anything about the place.

In Gage's reconstruction of the Milpitas of 1986, it had been a satellite of San Jose: a place where people might live quietly and work nearby, or, in the case of Anthony Hawley, a place where somebody whose chances weren't panning out in the bigger town next door might try his luck. Satellites are sad bodies, ever beholden to the larger planets from whose shadows they spend half their existence emerging. Their solitude has its own gravity. This picture illuminated the oddly cloistered feeling I'd always associated with the three-block memory I had of the town: in a sense, my fragmented memory of Milpitas was accurate precisely because it was incomplete. It had been a place waiting to become something.

But his research had been meticulous, and his method was to increase the power of his microscope a little more each time he put a slide onto the stage. He loved to dwell on the details; I knew this from his other books. But the sources of these details were here physically attached to the manuscript by Scotch tape, jutting out past the edges of the page, sometimes obscuring the text to be read, sometimes interrupting the story for pages at a time: transcripts of interviews, whether conducted by Gage or by an investigating officer or somebody else entirely I couldn't know, sometimes sporting only initials from line to line (*D: So when was the last time you were in the store? S: You asked me that already*; page after page of this), sometimes just summaries (*Three former students, friends, phone only, character witnesses, great kid, just like everybody says, great kid*). Clippings from local papers, from tabloids after the story went national, prayer intentions for the victims in church bulletins. Crime scene photographs, the real thing: they made me feel sick, though they were also so worn by this time that they hardly felt real.

It was fairly massive, and hard to take in all at once, especially given how many dozens of pages there were with giant Xs through the entire text: but I did my best; the margins of each page, including the ones that were evidently being redacted, had been crammed to bursting with handwritten notes in tiny script, which I was able to read only with careful effort. These notes were often peppered with question marks, sprouting up like dandelions on either side of the page: *S family leaves immediately or later? D questioned and released? A directly involved? AG returns call or called back? Answering tapes in whose custody since '86? MH knows? EG body disposition? MG disposition? DH disposition? SH disposition? AW disposition? AR disposition?*

It all looked like somebody's personal project, the sort of thing that gets exhumed from someone's effects after they die and everybody's surprised: I didn't know he was working on anything, he never talked about anything of the sort, it must have been a private project or something. My errand, as I saw it, was to retrieve the story from the center of all this, which was, as far as I could see, either that a young person named Siraj had taken advantage of a disorganized situation to commit at least two murders, for which he had never been charged; or, just as possibly, that a group of teenagers squatting a former adult bookstore had conspired to murder the owner of the property and a developer trying to buy it, and had gotten away with it.

But the book seemed to be ducking the question entirely, which, to put it mildly, makes for odd reading in the field of true crime. Red herrings are common, of course—writers will milk a bad lead for fifty pages before it fizzles out. But this wasn't that. Of the two stories it seemed to be telling, the "Alex killed two people and left town" one felt truest to me, but Derrick seemed a likelier suspect: he had skin in the game, and would have been the one most personally insulted by the sale. The damage visited upon the victims' bodies felt like the mark of a person with a real grievance. I liked Derrick better than Alex for that. There was also Seth: I knew from my own past that kids like Seth were often placed on a pharmaceutical cocktail at an early age, and that they learned to tweak the recipe depending on the effects they preferred. I could believe, easily, in Seth defending his home away from home with extreme force. Castle doctrine. It appeals to unexamined but deeply held instincts.

The manuscript broke off abruptly, in the middle of a sentence; I searched to see if maybe there'd been pages out of order somewhere in the last chapter or two, but came up empty-handed, save for the stray documents that kept gumming up the works. Parking garage tickets, quarterly student evaluations, blurry printouts of police scanner transcripts.

Then I went upstairs and got on the Internet to see what other information was floating around out there about the case, reasoning that there had to be something; and of course there was more than something, and that's when I called Gage.

7.

WELL, HE SAID, naturally that's the thing, you can't just come right out and say what happened, you have to save it or else there's no book, there's no story, there's just some facts, and that's not what people are looking for in a crime book, writers have several ideas about why people want to read crime but it doesn't really matter why, is the thing, what matters is that people want to feel like they got, I don't know, a full helping, their money's worth, *enough*, you know, Wambaugh is great at this, or was, is he dead now, I can't remember. Anyway, he makes you wait, I have my own style and I try to get a few more cards on the table a little earlier, but still you have to hold a few things back, you have to work up to the payoff so that when you get there it feels like there was some purpose in the journey, a satisfying twang when you finally release the string, a general settling in to the moment they've been waiting for. Some people actually write their endings first, just so they can get it out of the way, I've told people in workshops to try that if endings are giving them trouble, but that's not me: I have to keep learning as I go, otherwise I'll lose interest, generally speaking this has been a winning ticket for me, except that the whole experience of the last however many, Jesus, *years*, that's obviously exposed some major weaknesses in the method, which I was pretty confident about before, I'm honestly in conflict about it now, because the whole situation is a little disastrous even if the near-term solution, "write a different book," right, is staring me right in the face.

Right, I said, I mean, that's my question, from what I've been able to dig up about the case I just, I'm not quite sure I get it, a lot of the details of the case in your manuscript I can't find, you know, at all, I can't find anybody else talking about them, I can't—

Corroborate, he said, the word you're looking for is "corroborate," that's what the copy editor asked me, we'd already agreed on the draft, my editor liked it well enough before it got to the copy editor's desk, but once it landed there she called me up, Tania her name is, she's incredibly bright, and she says, There's a lot here.

Then she asked for some historical sources, and I *had* those, newspaper clippings, stuff about the property, my documentation was super-good on that stuff, maps, deeds of transfer, receipts, it's great when you can find actual paper receipts, ledgers, I specialize in objects, they're the tools of my trade, and I sent those along and she called again a week later and she said, This is all great, you're the best; it feels good imagining she's got other writers who make her job harder, and here I am with all my stuff in order, I think I luxuriated in that feeling for an extra few seconds because I knew it couldn't last, and then she asked me whether anybody could corroborate the details about Siraj's family.

Because nobody wants to get sued, Gage said. You understand? And they'll come for the publishers before they come for the authors, because authors generally don't have any money, but again, while that would be the usual-case problem, it wasn't actually the problem at hand here, *that* problem was only just now about to break through the skin and start wriggling its little head around. That was really how it felt to me, you know, like a worm inside my book waiting to eat through the pages and leave me with nothing, you probably already know this, but that's what a bookworm actually is, a type of maggot that eats paper or possibly is only looking for the paste that binds the pages together, I ran across something about it researching something several years before all this, but now I was thinking, there's a third kind of bookworm, first there's the one who reads a lot of books, and then there's the one who eats through them, and then there's the kind you hatch yourself when you write one, did I tell you Jesse Jenkins's mother wrote to me while I was living at the place in Milpitas?

No, I said, you didn't. Well, he said, she did, giant long letter, I don't think I can really talk about it, pretty raw stuff, but it was weighing heavy on me, you can imagine, his mom, still alive after all that, still trying to push forward somehow, I mean all that was a long time ago for me, but then I started to wonder what actually constitutes a long time, I'm not sure a person's ever actually old enough to ask himself that question, but I'd been asking it anyway and wondering, it was Jana's letter that sort of opened up the amphora for me or something, do you follow me? No, I said, I don't think so.

Oh, he said, well, think about an archaeological dig, right, imagine yourself finding an old jar that used to store perfume thousands of years before you were born, and then opening it up, and sniffing at the rim, and then you—

Oh, OK, sure, I said, I get it.

Yeah, that's what it was like, I was in some kind of haze, there was this wet cloud that traveled with me, it had a very complex bouquet, he said, laughing a little. It was not a happy laugh. So when Tania called and asked me for corroboration, I don't really remember what my original plan had been if it came to that, but I kind of got sloppy with her, and I said, Oh,

I don't think we have to worry too much about Siraj's family, and she was like, Menlo Park, you said, wasn't it, and I said, Sure, if that's what I said, and that was kind of the butterfly on the branch with the snowflake that falls from it at the top of the mountain or whatever. The avalanche that crushes the village, you know, that kind of thing.

†††

I WAS STANDING IN MY BACKYARD with my cell phone to my ear, and the strangeness of the moment rose up for me, like an orchestral cue in a movie: there were pine trees overhead, volunteers, twenty feet tall without anybody ever having put any effort into cultivating them or tending to them. Extras. There's pine trees everywhere, of course, but back where we grew up, you don't see this kind of riotous self-propagation. Or maybe I just never knew where to look. The view you get of where you're from when you've been away is polyhedral; its lines appear to curve, and the overall shape shifts depending on where you're standing.

I was going to ask you about Siraj, I said, I recognized a lot of the stuff about his parents, I went through a whole thing with the Hare Krishnas myself, they actually catered my wedding.

No shit, Gage said, small world.

So, yeah, I said, Siraj, this was the guy I had the most questions about, it's hard to get a clear picture of him because he didn't seem to know any of the other kids, and—

The other kids, yeah, Gage said, and there was that laugh again, kind of bitter, I didn't get it.

You're right, he went on, you're a good reader, Siraj's on the outside. Derrick you know, he's any kid in California, Angela you know, she's got school spirit, right, Seth, we all knew a Seth or two growing up, Alexes too, God, do you remember Martin from Quintana? He was so normal when we were kids.

I don't remember Martin, I said, I only went to Quintana for summer school one year, the same summer you were just talking about, I think.

Oh, wow, you didn't know him, OK, that's good, whole different story, just one of those guys whose mind blew out early, by the time I was seventeen I remember Martin showing up at school needing a bath so bad, we were friendly and I'd get him to the showers in the gym when I could, it didn't do any good, what's a teenager going to be able to do about somebody who's genuinely sick and in crisis. He could barely talk, it seemed like, when he did talk you could barely hear him, he'd be mumbling without a lot of articulation, this was a friend of mine, still a teenager, imagine if you'd found me and I was like that, you know, imagine how that would feel.

Gage was quiet for a few seconds; I waited.

I wish you'd known him, he said when he picked up the thread. Very funny guy when we were kids. Ended up in the system. His parents knew we'd been friends, they called me to tell me about it, I was in college at the time, I could tell they'd assigned some particular weight to letting Martin's old friends know that he was being taken care of. It shook me up some, I mean, I was young, I didn't have a real understanding of what a big thing it is to land in a state hospital at nineteen, just a year out of high school; anyway, Alex's life wasn't like that, there are several ways in which Alex's life wasn't like Martin's but that's who I was thinking of the whole time, old Martin, funny as hell when we were kids, sometimes you could still see it in high school, that one time I got him to shower I turned around so I wouldn't be looking at him naked, and he stayed under the water for five or ten minutes and then I heard it shut off and he says: "Garçon, my spats," just a faint modulation in the monotone, even then I thought, He dug down, he found a little something of his old self, it must have been super-hard, I still think about it, Jesus Christ.

I heard him take a deep breath: in through his nose, big exhale through his mouth. So, yeah, Siraj didn't know Alex, and Siraj didn't really know Angela or Derrick or Seth or any of the other kids from school, and one reason for that is that he was a transfer student, it's hard to make friends at that age in the middle of the school year, everybody's little cliques are pretty well established by then, and the other reason, I'm still getting used to saying this out loud, give me a second; the other reason Siraj didn't know Alex or Derrick or Angela or Seth is that there's no such person as Siraj, he's a literary conceit, which as you might imagine is a pretty big no-no in true crime, very frowned-upon, and this was what Tania had to ask me point-blank the next time she called, I've never met her in person but I have to say I have a tremendous amount of respect for her, she just went straight for the artery: So my next question, she said, after two or three softballs about the original names of buildings or whatever, my next question is does Siraj actually exist, because, as I mentioned on our last call, I haven't been able to find any corroboration. And then she just let it *hang* there, I'd been wondering for a long time at that point how it would shake out if it actually came to that, and I know there's people who are great at lying and making shit up but that's never been me, I do nonfiction, true stories, it's what I'm good at, it's what they pay me for, I thought I'd done a pretty good job of making him real, pretty believable, right, weird kid, self-absorbed parents, no motive I guess but lots of things happen without real motive, motive's overrated as an aspect of the

crime, it's another thing I talk about when I do a talk, sometimes people just do things, you can't break your back bending
over to find a motive.

Well, OK, sure, I said, but I have to tell you, I thought the
same thing: All the other kids except maybe Angela have a
pretty clear motive to protect their home, right? Even if they
don't live there, they have a place, it's special, they don't have
a lot of other stuff going on in their lives, they're from pretty
much nowhere. I could see Alex losing it when people start
sniffing around while he's just trying to sleep, I can see Derrick
trying to protect Alex because he's got some idea about helping
his friends, I can see Seth getting himself into a bad situation
after staying up too many nights in a row. Any of those kids.

Those *kids*, yeah, Gage said, that's the other thing.

✝✝✝

TAKE SETH, FOR EXAMPLE, he said. You remember Seth, right?

Sure, of course, I said, owns a gym now, kinda closed himself off when he didn't like the way your interview was going.

OK, yes, he said. Seth is actually Joe. Joseph Caleb Clayton
when he was born, just Joe thirty-eight years later when he dies
inside the store where he'd been sleeping.

Wait, I said.

I know, he said. I have some leads on who his folks were but
there's only so much you can take. Several arrests for loitering,
public urination, the kind of charges mean cops use when they
just want to bother someone but also the kind nicer ones use
when they're trying to get somebody housed on a psych ward so
they'll at least have a place to sleep. From the write-ups alone
you get the sense that Joe mainly ran into the meaner type.
They use the term "non-compliant" to describe him, which is

their way of justifying use of force. Later down the line he notches several vandalism charges. Pay phones. Newspaper racks. From this I get a picture of a guy who's living on the street just trying to get by, and who is hungry, but doesn't want to hurt anybody, so he's knocking over newspaper machines for quarters. Maybe he found Devil House because he thought he'd be able to break into the machines back in the arcade, get a couple hundred dollars and stash it in a sock he keeps in a garbage bag. He was pretty burned out by the time he got there. Not everybody on the street is strung out but JC sure was.

There was a crack in Gage's voice as he spoke. He had been waiting to tell someone about Joseph Caleb Clayton. But Ashton sent you the news story, I said. It was teenagers.

No, he said, that's what Ashton thought when he sent it to me, too, because the way the place looked, it just felt like something a bunch of teenagers would do. And that was the sense of the case when it first broke. Some outlets jumped the gun a little. I found out the actual story early on, and then I had to make some decisions.

I reserved the several questions I had for the moment, hoping I'd still remember what they were when he got done.

Derrick Hall, OK, he continued. Darren Waters. Actually did live in Milpitas at one point. Held a job on the Ford line until his habits caught up with him. Like Joe, he bounced around a lot. San Francisco, Oakland. But because he'd held a job at one point his addresses were a little easier to trace if I put in the legwork, right up to when he falls off the map. Now, the only way his face ever turns up again anywhere is if some asshole puts his name out there and somebody prints a "How They Found the Porn Store Killer" piece. Not me. No way. He's Derrick Hall now. He's got a mom and dad who care about him, not the boys' homes where he actually grew up and didn't learn any applicable job skills and which graduated him to the street as soon he turned eighteen. He's got a future ahead of him where the good things that happen rise to higher stations than meeting Joe at a shelter and learning, over a cold can of Hormel chili, that they both used to be into monster movies on TV when they were kids. Like me. Like you, too, right? Like you.

So you found him and talked to him, I said.

No, he said. I found some guys who knew him when he died. Darren, anyway, he says, is in the line of fire right next to Joe when the police arrive, but they only get him in the leg. "Only," right? He had to pull the bullet out himself in the underpass that night. With his fingers. He was making a joke out of it within a year or two, which is how I know about it, from those guys. He would say, of any garbage he had to eat, that it was better than having to pull a bullet out of your own leg just to be able to sleep.

And Alex? I said.

Alex is possibly still in San Jose, he said.

San Jose? I said.

San Jose, Alex was actually from there, he said, or at least most recently from there, when you don't have a fixed address it gets hard to say where you're really from. Anyway. Once I started messing with the details it felt like it wouldn't matter if I moved a few of the principal players around. Nobody cares about the actual details of anything, they just want the feeling they get when the story punches their buttons. Ashton sent me an initial report he ran across. It felt exciting, it felt lurid. But once I started digging, I couldn't get the dirt off my hands. I'm the guy who found out what the actual story was, and the actual story was different from the one they pitched me.

Why didn't you just tell that story instead, I said.

Because I couldn't, he said. For a whole lot of reasons I couldn't. Some of them just easy technicalities, like not being able to chase down enough biographical details about people who've fallen off the map; only then, sometimes, even if you *can* track down their families, the last thing they want is to re-hash how someone they loved and cared for had to fall off the face of the earth and stay there because of their proximity to a murder scene. Think about it. And then there's the kinds of stories people *want* to read, I talked to you about that earlier, it's a very important question in the field: drug addicts, lost souls, they make great victims when your perp is some sociopath mowing them down in flophouses or whatever. But this isn't that. This is self-defense. You can try to break new ground with how a bunch of guys on drugs in a house they're squatting didn't deserve to get shot and APB'd just for defending their home, but—

Self-defense? I said. I pictured Marc Buckler, I pictured Evelyn Gates. It seems like a stretch.

Self-defense, he said, look it up, Christ, all over the country people shoot drunks who happen to have wandered into their back yards, on the Fourth of July, say, Memorial Day, whatever, castle doctrine it's called, you have a right to defend yourself within your domicile, it's a very old legal position. If I'm in your house without your say-so, then you have the right to consider me a threat. I thought about this long and hard and I know that's the applicable statute here, in recent years it's kind of been hijacked by gun nuts to justify opening fire on whoever they want, but I feel like there's something deeper in it, not property rights, none of that, more like something on the books to protect you when the emissaries of the king decide you've got something the king wants, you have to have something somewhere that says to the crown, this far and no farther, that's how I look at it, maybe I'm on my way to becoming some sad survivalist guy, plenty of stories there, those guys are pretty into dreaming about defending themselves with deadly force. I mean, don't get me wrong, nobody deserves to get killed, but what are these guys supposed to do, everybody's already thrown them away and they've got nothing, just nothing, and nobody was using that building for anything, they weren't hurting anybody, would it have killed these people to just leave those guys alone, just do something else instead of fucking with the one thing they had that belonged to them? Would it have been so bad to just write it off? They could have done that. They could have just turned the other way. All three of these guys were nomadic enough by nature that they were going to pull up stakes reflexively sooner or later. And instead they just take bullets in their legs, they're back out on the street with nowhere to live, strung out, desperate, scared, hurt. They drift, and they drown. No reason. And all the while I'm looking around, new construction going up, no room for anybody who doesn't already have money, all these people just invisible to the Evelyn Gateses and the Marc Bucklers, less than invisible, nonexistent. And I thought about it, and I thought about it, and I thought about it, and after a while I just couldn't stand it.

But Alex made it out, anyway, he said, and I tracked him down, he can be hard to understand but I got enough of the real story from him to turn it into what I got, a real enough story that people would maybe read it and care about it instead of just filing and forgetting it the way they do with every other story where some burnout gets kicked to death or set on fire or shot dead, at most a story like that gets half a day of social media outrage and then crickets, so I did what I did, I told Alex I was going to do it, he thought that was funny, he never laughs about anything but I got a little laugh out of him about that; he said, well, everybody was a teenager once, and then he zoned out again, he spends most of his time in the zone, who can blame him, people who live on the street see stuff every day that would crush your spirit but they just keep going, and then somebody writes an exposé for the *Times* or whatever every other year and people wring their hands, nothing does any good, but I got scared somebody would figure it out because the details of the scene were the same, all three of those guys really did dress up the store to look like a witches' coven, if you saw the crime scene photos you'd think they went on to become rich artists or something—

I did see them, I said, they're attached to your manuscript.

Right, yeah, he said

What about Angela? I said.

There is no Angela, he said. I wanted Alex to have another friend in the world. You know. His actual story is hard.

There was a silence in which I wondered why he hadn't told me Alex's real name, but I felt that in Alex we were somewhere near the center of something delicate, and I didn't want to break any membranes that weren't yet ready to break.

About the manuscript, though, he said as Angela West evaporated into the air. Can you send it back? I get paranoid about it. I don't know what I'm going to do next, but I know I need to be the only person who has a copy.

Sure, I said, there's a shipping place down the road.

Can you go there tomorrow? he said.

†††

GAGE, I SAID, I just found out about all this as you were telling me about it, hold your fire. I was laughing while I said it but I felt defensive: I'm a safe haven.

I know, he said, sorry, I get worked up, I mean I guess I know, but on the other hand I don't, the longer I do this stuff, the more enemies I see. If they never print this thing, maybe they're doing me a favor, maybe I'll end up looking at it that way, who knows. I don't think they're willing to print it with Siraj in it, but I kind of need to believe in Siraj, he's there to protect the others.

We were quiet for a minute. It was dark outside. Summer in the South. Cicadas. I didn't think anybody else would believe in Siraj, either. I thought Gage had spent too long trying to save people he couldn't save and that the effort had clouded his vision in one way but maybe clarified it in another.

I don't get how you can really protect anybody, I said after a while; I don't see who there is to protect.

I know, he said, with a tenderness I didn't expect: I know, that's how it is with everybody, the idea that people might need to be protected from the facts of a case, it runs counter to what we're taught, you know, but I had Jana Perez's letter right there in front of me, like an air raid siren sounding the alarm, it matters which story you tell, it matters whose story you tell, it matters what people think even if it doesn't matter to the people who needed it before the disaster hit. That's the thing, those of us on this side of the disaster, we get so dazzled by the fireworks, by the conflagration I want to say, that we don't see the gigantic expanse over there on the other side of the flames, but, you know. People have to *live* there.

Wow, I said.

Yeah, right, that's it, that's what's left, "wow," right, that's the pay line in my field, he said: "Wow," that's the triple bars lined up right there, ha, don't get me wrong, I made my bed on it and the sheets have a high enough thread count, but that's what I brought back from the castle, that's the loot, and what's that worth to any of those guys now, right, dead or vanished, chased out, exiled, right, that would be the word, "exiled"; "wow," maybe I can use that if I ever find a way out of the woods on this one, thanks, let me know if you're ever in the neighborhood again.

And I said good night, then, and good luck, and we sort of spun down the moment together until the energy dissipated a little; and then I stood there, thinking about my old neighborhood, and specifically about the Mean Man, looking out from behind his blinds, seeing everybody but never seen by anybody; and about the Frankenstein monster, tied to a garage door by invisible chains, waiting for his moment, ready when it comes. Getting loose enough to visit some great terror on his captors, wholly in the moment, lost in the play. I remembered, and I stayed with that vision for what seemed like quite a while out there, on the back porch, in the dark.

Acknowledgments

Two books were invaluable to me in building the mythical Devil House from bricks: Christopher Tyerman's *Who's Who in Early Medieval England* (Shepheard-Walwyn, 1996) and R. M. Wilson's *The Lost Literature of Medieval England* (Methuen, 1970), from which I nicked many of the sub-headers in part 3; world-building is tricky business, and no one knows this better than medievalists. I'm grateful for their work.

To my family and especially my wife, Lalitree, deepest thanks for the near daily forbearance of the mania that can accompany the making of a new book.

To Sean McDonald, whose editorial hand measures pressure in exactly the right proportions and who bears my love of obscurity patiently, protecting my book against its creator's love of lost and losable things, my deepest thanks.

To my band and crew—Peter Hughes, Jon Wurster, Matt Douglas, Brandon Eggleston, Trudy Feikert, Avel Sosa, and Ryan Matteson— nothing I do is possible without you. Thank you, forever.

Finally to Donna, a great friend, consultant, and confidant at almost every step of the way for this book, the particular gratitude that comes from knowing that this book attains whatever stature it has only from the twin graces of your ear and your good words along the way. May I repay your many kindnesses!